To Kill
a
Mocking Girl

Also available by Harper Kincaid

The Wonder of You

Bind Me Before You Go

You Do You (I Just Want to Pee Alone, #6)

To Kill

a

Mocking Girl

A BOOKBINDING
MYSTERY

Harper Kincaid

CROOKED
LANE

NEW YORK

Published in the United States by Crooked Lane Books, an imprint of The Quick Brown Fox & Company LLC.

Crooked Lane Books and its logo are trademarks of The Quick Brown Fox & Company LLC.

Library of Congress Catalog-in-Publication data available upon request.

ISBN (hardcover): 978-1-64385-304-8
ISBN (ebook): 978-1-64385-325-3

Cover illustration by Mary Ann Lasher

Printed in the United States.

www.crookedlanebooks.com

Crooked Lane Books
34 West 27th St., 10th Floor
New York, NY 10001

First Edition: May 2020

10 9 8 7 6 5 4 3 2 1

This book is a love letter to the town of
Vienna, Virginia,
a community that's become the home of
my heart, not just my stuff.
It is also dedicated to the staff of Bards
Alley bookstore, with deep affection
and gratitude.

Chapter One

"Curses, like chickens, come home to roost."
— Susanna Moodie, eighteenth-century Canadian author

Quinn Caine may have traveled all over the world, but she still thought nothing was more enchanting than spring-time in Vienna, Virginia, especially driving with the windows down on Church Street. That's where all the historic charm bloomed, with people she'd known since birth living close by. This was her hometown. Memories resided on each corner. As did oversized bags of dog food.

Quinn pulled up in front of the family business, Prose & Scones, Vienna's only independent bookstore. Mama Caine stopped sweeping the sidewalk of stray petals from the flowering dogwood trees, leaning her weight into her broom handle.

"Need any help?" she asked.

"Nah, I got it." Quinn hopped out of her truck and onto the curb, grabbing a sack under each arm before flinging them into the flatbed. Two pointy ears with a big smile and a wet nose poked out the passenger side window. Her German shepherd, RBG—Ruff Barker Ginsburg—always seemed to know when she was getting a treat. And sure enough, her mama's hand spelunked down her jacket pocket. Then, palm out, she offered a liverwurst yummy in the shape of a lil' cupcake, thanks to the new doggie "sweet" shop down the street.

"You spoil her, you know." Quinn shook her head, pretending to mind.

"Please. This here's just practice. Wait 'til I get my first grandbaby."

Quinn chuckled. "New rule: Every time you drop a grandbaby hint, I'm delaying marriage and conception by at least six months, even if I meet the right guy."

"*Fine*—eviscerate a mother's hopes and dreams." Adele Caine sighed, wiping the crumbs off her hand. Then, lightning fast, her expression clouded over. "In all seriousness, I'm glad you have RBG with you. Not just as company, but for protection."

Her daughter gave her an "are you kidding?" look.

"I'm *not* kidding, Quinn. It used to be the worst thing to happen was getting your bike stolen if you forgot to lock it up. Vienna's still lovely, but a lot has changed since you've been away."

She was right. The town was in the midst of some growing pains, having transformed more in the last few years than it had in the quarter century before. Mainstays such as the Freemason Store, the Vienna Town Inn, and Caffe Amour had remained intact, but many long-standing institutions had closed. To the residents of Vienna, those businesses were more than just places of commerce; they were extended members of the family.

"I know change is hard, but it's not all bad. I, for one, am doing a happy dance that we finally have some good tacos in town."

Quinn's attempt at levity was squashed by Adele's stern-mama look. Every mother had one, and Adele Caine could wither the plumpest of grapes into hard raisins with hers.

"I'm not talking about tacos, Quinn. Someone was murdered here not too long ago."

"Are you—oh, Mama, I'm sorry. I didn't know. Who was it?"

Her eyes went soft. "How could you have? You were living in the middle of nowhere on the other side of the world. Your father and I didn't bring it up because we didn't want you to worry. I wasn't going to waste one second of my time with you on Skype talking about such tragedies."

She had her there. "When did it happen?"

"Right before you came back. I don't know the details, but supposedly, it was a strange death. It hasn't been labeled 'murder' as such. But the police haven't ruled out foul play either." A strong breeze ruffled her blondish-gray hair all around, but Adele didn't seem to mind. "I'm sorry I don't know more."

Quinn reached for her mother's hand, giving it a reassuring squeeze.

Adele's cerulean-blue eyes lit up. "You know who would know?" She didn't wait for a response. "Aiden. He made lead detective last year. The youngest in history, I believe."

No surprise. Aiden Harrington was always going places. He had been her older brother's best friend and Quinn's secret crush since she'd been old enough to make pinky promises. He had movie-star good looks and a Superman physique, but those attributes—though a visually intoxicating bonus—weren't why her heart pulsed a secret beat just for him.

Aiden "got" her. He appreciated her vast—and sometimes pointless—encyclopedic array of knowledge. Growing up, some boys had mocked her for being the first to raise her hand in class or for outscoring them on tests. But Aiden would remind her, "Any guy who's intimidated by a smart girl will never grow up to be his own man. Keep those boys in your rearview,

3

Quinnie. They're well below your pay grade." Such high praise from a beautiful, older, more popular boy had been heady liquor for a young girl. Every smile he gave and any chance to share his air intoxicated Quinn, her heart a swelling hope. *Someday,* she would think to herself. It was her most private wish.

He had always been a natural protector, so she hadn't been surprised when he joined the police force after he graduated from the University of Virginia (double major in psychology and criminology with a minor in English literature—*swoon*). Her mom was right: Aiden was probably the perfect person to ask about what was happening in Vienna, but considering she regressed into an awkward, knobby-kneed tween every time she was in his presence, Quinn was going to pass on a one-on-one.

"Yeah, maybe I'll talk to him later," she lied.

"How many more pickups you got?"

Quinn glanced down the street. "Yours was the last one of the morning. We've been at it a while."

She caught her mama staring.

"You okay?" Quinn rested her hand on her shoulder, gently bringing her back.

Her mother smiled. "Oh, don't mind me. I know you've been home a little while now, but I swear, sometimes I look over at you and can't believe you're really here . . . that you're back for good."

"Well, believe it."

Even with the reassurance, Adele's hand still fiddled with a raven brooch on her jacket lapel. She collected intricate pins, getting the idea from former secretary of state Madeleine Albright. Years ago, Quinn had taken her to peruse the former secretary's brooches on exhibit at the Smithsonian Castle, each pin a tongue-in-cheek "tell" on her mood and sentiments throughout her tenure. Quinn's mama had been a collector ever since, encouraging her daughter to do the same. But Quinn wasn't into the same fussy finery. She opted for some quirky pop culture–inspired enamel pins instead, some of her favorites being "These feelings would go good with pie" and "You can't please everybody. You're not a taco."

Her mother rested her chin on top of the broom handle. "You ever miss the adventure?"

Quinn thought about it for a second. After graduating from The Catholic University of America, Quinn had spent the next three years teaching English all over the world, mostly in remote villages in Southeast Asia and Central America. For someone who hadn't previously left the East Coast, let alone the United States, it had been a heck of a learning curve, one she'd never forget.

"I miss the people—a lot—but that's about it. Don't get me wrong—it was a phenomenal experience. But this is home. Besides, after living in yurts and huts, indoor plumbing and heat rock."

Adele's eyes crinkled in the corners. "I bet they do."

Quinn went on, "Even more important, I promised my new bosses I was here for good."

That made her mama laugh, deep and throaty, since her parents *were* her "new" bosses. "You have no idea how happy we are to have you. You're not too overwhelmed now, with all the projects customers have brought in?"

"Not at all. You know I like being busy."

When Quinn had come back to the shop, she had been worried there wouldn't be enough work for her as a bookbinder. She had never been so wrong and was surprised by how many old books, journals, and even photo albums people had brought in for repair. She took the bounty as a sign her town was happy to have her home, enough for them to crawl into the creaking dark recesses of their attic spaces, confronting their forgotten, ancestral ghosts, all in order to dig up old family heirlooms for her to resurrect back to life.

Her dog gave a friendly yip.

"That's my cue to get going," Quinn said.

"Fair enough. Don't forget my morning sugar."

That was Caine family code for a hug and kiss goodbye. Quinn leaned in, taking in her mama's delicious scent of orange blossom honey and wildflowers. Quinn could always tell when she had spent time in her prized garden, with a cup of tea.

She waved goodbye as she drove slowly down the street in "Golda", her ochroid-colored, Ford F150, named after the first woman prime minister of Israel. Ever since buying her first car at sixteen, Quinn had been giving her vehicles nicknames—and she picked "Golda" for the same reason she'd chosen to buy a truck when she returned home from overseas. Both may not have been known for their conventional beauty, but they were tough, tenacious, and got the job done.

Quinn had it specially configured to play cassettes, along with outfitting Golda with the standard hookup for her iPhone. She pushed in her go-to driving mixtape, *Venture a Highway*—a word play on the classic hit by retro band America. Except this time Nick Drake's "Pink Moon" played, serenading her with the perfect song for driving down meandering roads. It wasn't until she was almost at her destination that Quinn realized her mama never had answered her question about who had been killed in their town.

I'll have to check on that later.

Quinn and RBG headed over to their next destination: Guinefort House—named after the only sainted canine in history—where Anglican nuns served the Almighty by breeding German shepherds and caring for rescues of all varieties. In fact, that's where Quinn had gotten her own canine baby. The dog food donations she coordinated through local businesses weren't much, but it was a small way for Quinn to give thanks and give back. The treats for RBG didn't hurt either.

Even with all the bookbinding work that had come in, Quinn still needed something outside the shop to help her start rebuilding her life. Most of the friends she'd had growing up had not returned to Vienna, and the handful that had were squatting in their parents' finished basements. She knew she was lucky, because the friends who had come back lived like retirees—complete with subsidized housing and working part-time in dead-end jobs. There was little more depressing for a young person than killing it through four years of college only to end up as a greeter at the local Walmart with your grandma's canasta buddies.

Originally a rural farm town on the border of American history, over time Vienna had evolved into a sleepy bedroom community and was now a hot spring for tony families to raise their broods. Being ranked by several national magazines and news outlets as one of the best places to live certainly contributed to Vienna's growing popularity and reputation. Blessings and curses often insisted on traveling in pairs.

When Quinn's pilgrim spirit had finally been ready to settle, she'd discovered that what once was home was now, in many ways, new country. The same was true for some of the people. When she had left to teach English overseas, her cousin had been Elizabeth Anne Caine. Firebrand redhead. Social justice warrior. A little lost. A big chip on her shoulder in the shape of a broken heart. Now, she was Sister Daria. Nun-in-training. A woman with purpose. Someone actually interested in following the rules for the first time in her life. Quinn couldn't help but wonder, *Who was this person disguised as her beloved cousin?*

Quinn understood a bit of the appeal: little compared to the beauty of Guinefort House, home of Sister's Daria's order. It was a Carpenter Gothic stunner, originally home to a family active in Northern Virginia's Reconstruction efforts before it became the spiritual center for Anglican nuns and novitiates. Christ Fellowship Church in Vienna may have only been planted in 2011, but the Anglican Church had deep roots in Virginia, dating back to before the American Revolution, with founding father George Washington attending services at The Falls Church during his tenure as the nation's first president.

Guinefort House's moniker made Quinn chuckle as well, as it had been named for the only canonized pooch in history. She always forgot to ask: Had the nuns decided to breed German shepherds because of the name of the house, or had they named the home once they decided to breed dogs to support their order and rescue mission?

Quinn avoided asking her canine version of the question "Which came first, the chicken or the egg?" because what she *really* wanted to ask her cousin and best friend was "Since when did monastic life become your go-to career option?" Quinn still remembered the shock she had felt over two and a half years ago after receiving Sister Daria's letter. Quinn was six months into her first overseas teaching gig at the time. Her cousin wrote that she wanted to dedicate her life to the service of others, and being a social worker wasn't enough. She was going to become a nun.

Out of nowhere, she had given away all her possessions and become a novice, taking her first vows two years later. Of course, Quinn had asked her why. So had the rest of the family. The only answer any of them received was that she felt called to serve in this way, through Guinefort House. In three more years, she'd take her final vows. Maybe by then Quinn would understand.

She texted her cousin to come out and help her lug in the bags of dog food, shoving the phone into her pocket while admiring the surrounding trees coming back to life. Vibrant purple crocuses peeked through the last of the winter white, warming her all over. Quinn adored the change of seasons. Maybe that's why she didn't sense the approach of Vienna's own ice queen.

"Wow, a whole flatbed filled with kibble. I knew you and that fleabag did everything together, but I didn't think you ate from the same trough."

Quinn sighed, not wanting to turn around to address Tricia Pemberley. Because she loved her town. She really and truly did. But she was over mean girls like Tricia, who thought winning a few shiny tiaras back in high school still gave her some imaginary keys to the kingdom.

RBG wasn't too thrilled either; her tan-and-black paws were on the gate of the truck, and she was grumbling low while staring straight at Tricia's blanching face. But then again, dogs were excellent judges of character. That was one of the reasons Quinn had named her pup after the famous Supreme Court jurist, Ruth Bader Ginsburg. Her girl was always able to assess people and situations. Quinn sometimes got it wrong, giving people the benefit of the doubt even when her instincts told her otherwise, but RBG? Never.

Tricia backed away. "Dear Lord, can't you keep that dog of yours calm?"

RBG gave one of her warning growls, then a couple of quick, low grunts.

Quinn frowned. "She can't help it. She's responding to *your* mood."

It was one thing for Tricia to pick on her, but no one—absolutely no one—was going to smack-talk her dog. "What are you doing here anyway? Don't you go to Saint Marks? Or did the priest's ears burn off after hearing your confession?"

Tricia narrowed her eyes. "Ha-ha. As if."

Just when Quinn thought she'd have to deal with Tricia's surliness alone, higher powers sent a reinforcement. At first, all she could see in her peripheral vision was flapping white and gray, like a wayward jaybird, hauling tail down the sidewalk. But it was Sister Daria. She wasn't going to come out swinging, but she sure looked like she was at least entertaining the idea.

She may have been a nun-in-training, but she was still Quinn's smart-mouthed, suffer-no-fools cousin and best friend. And one look at her expression told Quinn that Daria was in the mood to throw down some morning sass.

"Tricia, please tell me I didn't just hear you take the Lord's name in vain."

"Me? No! Um . . . well . . . good morning, Sister. We were just joking around." Tricia pinned Quinn with her gaze. "*Right*, Quinn?"

As if. "Well, actually—"

"Actually, I have some big news," Tricia interrupted, flipping the long bangs of her bob out of her face. She bared her teeth in something resembling a smile while thrusting her left hand forward. "Scott *proposed* last night! Isn't it beautiful?"

Sure enough, there was a big, round rock, set in platinum, glittering away in the morning sun. Quinn noticed how the diamond's fractal light shimmered like stars across Tricia's metallic nail polish. Between her smile and the ring's glimmer, she was her own constellation of happy.

Her cousin broke out in a wide grin. "Wow, that's wonderful!"

"Uh, congratulations, Tricia."

Better never break up with him. That is one man-boy who does not take rejection well.

Tricia was staring at Quinn. "Are you *sure* you're happy for us?"

She stilled. "What do you mean?"

"Your words say one thing, but your tone says something else." Tricia put her hand on her hip, elbow out.

"There's no tone, Tricia. Really and truly." She tried to reassure her.

She was being truthful too. Just because Quinn couldn't tolerate Scott for longer than a drive-by pleasantry didn't mean she'd begrudge Tricia Pemberley the joy she'd found in their impending nuptials. Although, the idea of those two as Vienna's new power-hungry couple was enough to make Quinn shudder. As Oscar Wilde once mused, "Some people create happiness wherever they go; others whenever they go."

Quinn summoned a kinder response. "I am very happy for you both."

Tricia's mouth pressed into a thin line. "Well then, that's good to hear. Glad there are no hard feelings."

Hard feelings over . . . what exactly?

Quinn gazed skyward, shaking her head.

Thankfully, her cousin threw her a Hail Mary. "That's an impressive haul you've got there. Seems like our 'pet' project has really taken off."

Ah, a change of subject. Quinn mouthed a thank-you. "Yeah, I was surprised too. It's twice the usual amount we get for donations. At this rate, y'all won't have to buy dog food for months. Speaking of which . . ." She dragged the words out. "I need to get these bags inside. Can I count on some help from the blushing bride?"

Tricia's smile melted off her face faster than lipstick on a pig in summer.

"Why, Quinn, that's a great idea," Sister Daria piped up. "What do you say?"

Tricia made an "eek" face. "Oh, well, y'all know I'm *all* about volunteering, but I've got to get a move on. You two have no idea how much goes into planning a wedding, especially since Scott wants to marry me as soon as possible."

Quinn pulled down the truck gate. "Why? Is he expecting?"

Her cousin stifled her snort, coughing to cover it up.

"You think you're *so* funny," Tricia huffed.

"Oh, c'mon now—I was just teasing. You are going to make a beautiful bride."

That was true. Quinn may not have thought much of Tricia as a human being, but she had been a gorgeous child, one who had grown into a stunning woman. There was a reason why she'd won all those pageants back in the day, even with her slightly tone-deaf rendition of "God Bless America."

Quinn grabbed one of the dog-food bags and handed it off to her, not really giving her a choice. "Making a nun do manual labor is, like, seven years of bad luck." She hoisted another bag toward Tricia. "That's no way to start off your married life."

The bride-to-be might pretend to be dainty, but that girl looked like she lived at the gym. She could handle the heavy bags.

Tricia grimaced. "I thought seven years of bad luck was for when you broke a mirror or something."

"Oh really? You want to risk it?" Quinn asked. "Nope, there's no way I can let you take that chance."

"Fine, but this load is it." She gave Quinn the stink eye before heading toward the kennel next to the abbey, with her arms full.

Sister Daria waited until the bridezilla-to-be cleared the doorway. "You know I am more than happy to help you bring this stuff in."

"Oh, I get that. And you will." She stretched herself across the flatbed for another bag. RBG head-butted the kibble in her direction, her adorable way of trying to help. Quinn cooed and gave her a scratch along her jaw and neck. Then she handed a couple of sacks over to her cousin.

"You know, using my being a nun as a way to mess with Trish only adds to my prayer load."

"Please, you know the only reason she was even over here this morning was to tell me they got engaged. Everyone knows I'm always here the first Friday of the month."

Her cousin's shoulders shook from her silent laughter. "Don't look at me to confirm your theory. I'm under contractual obligation with the big JC to assume the best in people— and you have no idea how much of a challenge that can be sometimes."

"Oh please, you're a softie."

"Maybe so, but don't forget: I can still pick a lock and hot-wire a car without getting caught."

"The Reverend Mother must be so proud."

"She *is*. Just because I've had a unique past doesn't mean I can't be your typical nun and be of service."

Quinn couldn't hold back the snort of laughter that time. "Being of service is one thing—being typical is something else."

"I'm not *that* unusual of a candidate."

"Oh please, what other novitiate chose their name after their favorite MTV animated character?"

Even with her arms full, her cousin waved the comment away like an annoying bug. "That's just a coincidence. Saint Daria was *real*. After she helped convert a bunch of Romans, Daria was sent to a brothel as punishment, where a lion defended her honor."

"Aaand?" Quinn dragged out.

Daria rolled her eyes. "Okay, *fine*. The pontiff still ordered her execution. She was first stoned and then buried alive, but hey, how many saints end up with Disney-inspired happy endings?"

"Fair point, but face it: you're the order's first novice with a master's degree *and* a rap sheet. Don't get me wrong: you know I think you're the coolest, but how you passed whatever test it took to get in there in the first place is a frickin' miracle."

Her cousin gave an impish look. "Be nice now. Who else is going to say extra prayers for a smart-mouth like you?"

She dropped the haul just inside the door of the kennel next to Guinefort House, noting Tricia had done the same. She glanced left and right—no signs of Vienna's mocking girl anywhere.

"Where did she go?"

One side of Sister Daria's lip quirked up. "She took off as soon as our backs were turned."

"Figures." Quinn walked to her truck, RBG's cue to crawl through the cab's open rear window and wait for her in the passenger seat. Quinn hoisted herself through the window to clip RBG's seat belt. "I can drop her off and come back and pick you up you for breakfast, if you want. Or you can squeeze in. There's room."

"Don't worry about it," Daria said. "I'll meet you over there. I want to change out of the penguin outfit first."

"Why are you wearing it anyway?"

Sister Daria fanned her arms out. "We like to dust off the old wimple-habit combos when we have to confront owners of puppy mills, which I had to do at the crack of dawn this morning, along with some animal control officers. We've found some of these mill owners respond to old-school authority better than police uniforms sometimes."

"Man, it's a good thing you've never succumbed to the dark side."

Sister Daria winked. "May the force be with you, nerd-girl."

Quinn waved as she maneuvered herself into the driver side, closing the door. "See ya in a few!" she said, pulling away.

Minutes later, she rolled her truck toward one of the town's more impressive historic estates, right on the curve of Walnut Lane. But this was not her house.

Once the home to Harmon Salsbury, a Union captain in the Twenty-Sixth Regiment of the Colored Infantry during the Civil War, the Salsbury House had belonged to Quinn's Auntie Johanna and Uncle Jerome "Jerry" Caine for more years than she'd been alive. "Belonged to" was Quinn's phrasing, not theirs, for she knew they regarded themselves as the house's caretakers, not owners. An apt ideology for a town steeped in often-told American stories, albeit with a surprising twist of agency for its black citizenry.

Ever since her return from overseas, Quinn had lived behind her aunt and uncle's residence, in a renovated, farmhouse-chic gem. Painted in traditional red with white trim, the once dilapidated barn was where they used to play hide-and-seek behind haystacks as kids. When Jerry and Johanna remodeled the barn, they admitted that they intended for their daughter—Quinn's cousin—to have it. But when Elizabeth, now Sister Daria, took the veil, shunning all worldly comforts, she convinced them to work out a sweet rent-to-own deal for Quinn.

"At least it stays in the family," Aunt Johanna had said with a sigh. "Plus, I know you'll love it right. You're a details girl, the same as me."

Quinn had been grateful for the chance to be a homeowner at such a young age, especially in a coveted and increasingly expensive area. Otherwise, there was no way she could afford to live in Vienna on a bookbinder's salary.

Quinn knew the arrangement had been bittersweet for them. Her aunt and uncle had wanted a traditional path for their daughter: to get married and have children. She had thought her cousin was halfway there when she met Raj back in grad school, the only man Quinn thought worthy of such a gem of a girl. Until something changed, and then he wasn't anything anymore.

In addition to her rent, Quinn demonstrated her thanks to her aunt and uncle by feeding and caring for the chickens on the property and maintaining Aunt Johanna's herb and vegetable garden. Sometimes, Quinn would catch Aunt Johanna watching her doing chores from the kitchen window, a sweet, sad smile on her ageless face. She'd give an enthusiastic wave, but Quinn knew: her presence was a consolation prize.

As soon as she and RBG walked through the front door that day, her dog baby went straight for her water bowl in the galley kitchen, slurping up the cold refreshment. When Quinn had adopted RBG, she had gotten into the habit of slipping a couple of ice cubes into the dog's bowl, wanting her to have fresh, cold water at the ready. In no time she realized RBG liked munching on the ice cubes just as much as she enjoyed the drink, and every time she heard that crunching sound, Quinn couldn't help grinning to herself. Along with the chickens clucking in the yard, the sound of crushing ice made her feel at home.

"All right, I've gotta go, girl. See ya soon!"

RBG looked up from her bowl, tail wagging while she licked her nose. She gave a short "ruff" as if to say goodbye. Quinn smiled to herself as she locked the door: *I swear she understands most everything I tell her. I don't care if everyone thinks I'm a crazy doggy mama.*

Once buckled up in Golda and back on Church Street, Quinn got lucky with a parking space right in front of her favorite eatery. Three tiny bells rang over her head as soon as she walked in the door.

"Oh good! Quinn's here. You get a good haul today?"

Even after having one heck of a morning, Quinn never got sick of walking into Church Street Eats and having her people check in with her. That included Ms. Eun Hutton, who owned the place, with her husband, Greg. He did the cooking, and she did what she called "the managing of all the things," which some thought was code for waiting on customers and keeping up on the town gossip.

"Best one yet." Quinn slid onto a stool at the counter. Ms. Eun handed her a laminated menu and a glass of seltzer, her usual.

Greg flipped a couple of sausage patties. "Hey, so where's Mother Teresa?"

"She's on her way. She just needed to change first." Quinn and Daria usually had breakfast together after she unloaded the monthly donations.

Ms. Eun pretended to glare over her shoulder at her husband. "Now why do you do that?"

"What did I do?" he asked, a wicked grin curling under his mustache.

He totally knows what he did.

Ms. Eun thrummed her short fingernails on the counter. "*You* know . . . calling her everything except by her saint's name."

He shrugged his shoulders. "To me, she'll always be little Lizzy Caine. Not Sister Maria, Donna, Conchita, or whatever it is now." Greg eyed Quinn. "Hey, give an old man a break. I used to coach her softball games and break up her fights."

Quinn grinned. "Ah right—I forgot about those."

As a teenager, her cousin had taken it as her personal mission to pummel anyone who bullied another kid. Quinn despised bullies just as much but preferred less physical, more clandestine methods of retaliation.

Ms. Eun leaned her forearms on the counter in front of Quinn. "So, did you hear the news?"

She didn't even wait for Quinn to respond.

"Tricia Pemberley and Scott Hauser got engaged last night."

"I heard," Quinn told her. "Tricia came by the abbey this morning."

Ms. Eun rolled her eyes. "Well, *of course* she did. She's always been bothered that you two dated."

Quinn let out an exasperated sigh. "I don't see why. It was barely a blip on the radar."

"Maybe not to *you*, but it was to him. You'll always be the girl who got away." Ms. Eun wasn't done. "And some people think you might still be harboring a secret crush of your own because you haven't been seen with anyone since being back in town."

"You can't be serious." Quinn stared, pausing mid-sip. "I've only been back a couple of months. Who works that fast?"

"Good point, but no one could fault you if you had your eye on someone. Anyone in particular?"

And there it was . . . Quinn had walked right into that trap. Rookie move.

"Not these days, no." She took another sip of her seltzer. "And for the record, I'm good with that."

The little bells over the door rang.

Ms. Eun appeared unconvinced. "Really? Because there are some really nice boys at my church that I am more than happy to set you up with, especially since you're—"

"Leave her alone." Daria walked in and parked herself at the counter. Now she looked more like the cousin Quinn had grown up with, wearing jeans, sneakers, and a worn Young Life T-shirt. "Trust me, Quinn. I've seen the boys at her church. You aren't missing a thing."

Ms. Eun gave her the stink eye. "Hey, just because they're not Anglican doesn't mean the boys at my church aren't good enough for Quinn."

"Hey, I'm not saying they're not good enough because they're Presbyterians," Daria said. "I'm saying they're not good enough because they're *boys*. In case y'all haven't noticed, Quinn is all grown up now. She needs a *man*."

Greg called out from behind the grill. "Eunnie, you gonna find out what the girls want, or you gonna keep yapping about boys like you're at a sleepover?"

"All right, all right . . . I'm getting to it." She leaned a slender hip against the counter, taking a pencil out of her pixie-cut black hair. "What'll it be?"

Her cousin didn't need to see the menu. "I'll have the Gooey Grilled Cheese and a ginger ale."

The tiny bells above the door rang again.

Ms. Eun wet the tip of her pencil on the tip of her tongue. "And you?"

Quinn handed back the menu. "I'll have the Shredded Herbed Chick Omelet."

Ms. Eun nodded, jotting her order down. "Side of almost-burnt home fries?"

Quinn smiled. They knew she adored the crispy potato edges. "Always."

Someone spoke behind her. "You know, Mom still considers that *her* chicken recipe. If she catches you eating any version of her creation outside the house, she'll go nuts and burn a bunch of sage in your old bedroom to cleanse your chakras or something."

She knew that voice.

Quinn spun her stool around. "Only *our* mother throws parsley, sage, rosemary, and thyme onto a chicken and proclaims Simon and Garfunkel taught her to cook." She jumped into her older brother's arms. "I can't believe you're back!"

There he was, her handsome, brilliant, and irreverent brother—Sebastian "Bash" Caine. She hadn't seen him since her welcome-home party.

"Of course I am. Where else would I be?" Bash gave her a long squeeze before smiling at their cousin. "Hey, dork."

Sister Daria laughed. "Hey, stink face." She gave him a tight hug. "Look at you! Still in one piece."

"So far, so good. Must be all those extra candles you're lighting for me."

Her cousin scoffed through a laugh. "The Catholics do that, not us, genius."

"Then do that thing where you toss my sins on bread crumbs into the river instead."

Daria's eyes darted between Bash and Quinn. "Is he trying to be annoying? Because I know *you* know that's the Jewish atonement tradition of *tashlikh*."

Bash knew exactly how to push people's buttons. It was a miracle he was as well liked as he was. "It used to be harder to rile you up," Bash said. "You're getting soft-headed in your old age, cousin."

Greg opened one of the ovens and retrieved a succulent roast chicken. "By the way, Adele Caine is a kick in the pants, but for the last time, this is *not* her recipe."

"It's not yours either, Mr. Hutton," Daria piped in. "It's from a song."

Quinn ignored the religion and chicken debates. "I thought you weren't coming back for another week or two."

Bash shrugged. "That was the plan, but rainstorms rolled in. So, I was able to get back earlier than expected."

Just then, her cousin received a text and frowned.

"Everything okay?" Quinn asked.

"Yeah, it's fine, but I've got to head back." Her eyes darted from her phone to the Huttons. "Can I get that to go?" Her expression said everything was definitely *not* fine.

"Sure thing, Sister D." Mr. Hutton placed a grill press onto her cheese sandwich. The husband and wife team worked lightning fast, getting everything together.

Ms. Eun brought her the food in a bag, along with a ginger ale that had a paper straw already in place. Her cousin handed over payment, but Ms. Eun brushed it away. "Your money's no good here, honey."

Daria's expression softened. "Thanks, Mrs. Hutton."

Ms. Eun gave Daria a hug. "Try and stay out of trouble now."

Her cousin's brows went up. "Me? I never get into trouble."

That comment earned Quinn's "you don't fool me" gaze. "You mean you learned how not to get caught anymore."

Bash chimed in. "She's right, you know."

Daria grumbled while grabbing her bagged lunch. "Oh, hush already."

"Bye, Sister! Be careful!" Ms. Eun called out, waving.

Quinn watched her cousin walk out the door and hurry down the street. She'd have to call her later and find out what was up.

Meanwhile, her brother combed his fingers through his sandy-brown hair as he twisted side to side on his stool.

"Hey, Bash. Taking a break from saving the world?"

He gave Ms. Eun a playful wink. "Something like that. How's my girl doing?"

And sure enough, that's all it took to make a grown woman blush. "Don't give an old woman hope. Now what can I get ya?"

It didn't matter that Eun Hutton was twice his age and happily married. Bash was a natural flirt, a particular gift he shared—often. Everyone knew he was just playing.

He grabbed the menu off the counter, giving it a compulsory glance, although Quinn didn't know why: Bash had been ordering the same thing since he was a kid. In fact, he loved their burger so much, Ms. Eun had it named after him.

"I'll have my usual. Make sure that boyfriend of yours makes the fries extra crispy."

"I heard that," Greg called out over his shoulder. "It's technically still breakfast, but since you save lives, I'm going to let that go."

"Appreciated."

Greg wasn't done. "And stop flirting with my wife. Go get one your own age."

Bash's teasing eyes glimmered. "But you got the last good one."

Greg let out a *womp womp*. "Yep. Sucks for you."

Bash chuckled, then sat up straighter when a curvy woman in a short skirt walked by. Of course, he noticed.

Quinn eyed the exchange. "I'm guessing this means you're no longer seeing the emergency operator in Colorado?"

Bash might be a flirt, but when he was seeing someone, he was loyal. So, for him to be even glancing at someone else told his sister all she needed to know: he wasn't dating Ms. 9-1-1 anymore.

"We're going there already? I haven't even gotten my food yet."

"Consider this the beginning of your meal." Ms. Eun plopped down a glass of Coke in front of him. "Now, spill."

He stalled, taking a big gulp. "Thanks, but I'm going to be a stickler and wait 'til I get my burger before I start the sharing circle." His phone started ringing, cutting him off. He checked the screen, and his eyes widened. "Oh crap, didn't expect this call so soon. Sorry, Quinn, I have to take this."

"Oh, it's okay. You weren't even supposed to be back for another two weeks. This whole moment is like an extra gift on Christmas, except it's April."

His expression warmed.

She patted her messenger bag. "Besides, I brought a book with me."

"Of course you did. Be right back."

He ruffled her hair like he'd been doing since they were little. He sauntered to the back of the restaurant, heading for the bathroom.

Quinn opened her cross-body messenger bag and took out her latest book. She was going through a cozy mystery phase. This new series had a feisty amateur sleuth marooned, right on the beach, in a Pinterest-worthy retro-chic Airstream. Too bad it looked like the murderer might have just moved in next door.

The tiny bells over the door jingled yet again.

A woman's shrill voice filled the space. "Are you sure you want to eat brunch *here*? I can call over to Bazin's and have my regular table ready."

"Don't make a big deal, okay? You can live without your prosecco for one meal."

The woman talking didn't seem to care that everyone at the eatery could hear her. Quinn knew who both of them were without turning around, and started praying she wouldn't be noticed.

It was her ex-boyfriend, Scott, otherwise known as Tricia's current fiancé. He had just walked in with his mother, a woman who considered herself the epicenter of high society, if Vienna had such a thing. Although the town certainly had its share of well-heeled residents, few regarded having money as a status to hold over others' heads. It was no wonder when people described Millicent "Milly" Hauser, they usually said, "Her house may be in Vienna, but she still lives in McLean," a not-so-subtle dig at her *and* the haughty neighboring town inside the Beltway.

Ms. Eun interrupted. "Actually, we *do* have prosecco. They come in these cute lil' bottles. Oh, and feel free to grab any available table."

"Why don't we park over at the counter?" Scott asked.

Please don't sit by me. Please don't sit by me.

There was silence for several seconds.

Scott's mother spoke up. "We'll take a table over there . . . such as it is."

Quinn kept her head in her book, hoping that if she ignored them, they'd go away-her version of *Field of Dreams*, but, well, the opposite. Her book was on the counter, so she propped both elbows on either side of it and gazed down, letting her hair fall forward in an autumnal wave, her lame attempt at hiding in plain sight.

Even with her head down, she could feel Scott standing behind her.

"I know you believe books are magic, but please tell me you don't actually think you're wearing some sort of invisibility cloak to hide yourself."

She let out a breath she hadn't realized she'd been holding. Closing the book, Quinn met Scott's gaze. "You get points for throwing in a Harry Potter reference. What's up?"

He smoothed his hand down the front of his mint-green, Vineyard Vines button-down shirt, every blond hair on his head laquered in place. He gave a toothy grin. "Nothing. Just came by to say hi."

"Okay, well . . . hi."

He gave a quick nod. "I heard Tricia came by Guinefort House this morning, saying you really needed her help."

Oh did she now?

Quinn feigned a smile. "Yes, she really was such an asset, I couldn't have managed without her. Will you let her know I said it was okay to come back and volunteer again with the heavy lifting next month?"

See? Clandestine methodology. She had learned that maneuver from reading Mother Teresa's biography. True story.

Scott beamed. "I'll do that. Wow, I had no idea she was even interested in helping out on a regular basis. Isn't she great?"

Tricia was a queen-bee train wreck who talked through her nose, but no way was Quinn going there. "I don't know her very well," she lied. "But congratulations. I heard this morning you two got engaged."

"Did you see the ring I put on her finger?" He actually puffed his chest out like a ready-to-mate peacock. "Over three carats."

"I'm happy for you both." She waited to see if he was going to tell her what he wanted.

He just stared, looking a bit put out.

"I'm sorry—is there something you needed?"

He huffed. "Geez, Quinn. I thought me getting engaged to another woman would get *some* sort of reaction out of you. You and I have history."

Oh wow. Cue the awkward. "Scott, we dated for, like, a minute and a half, three years ago before I left town. By all means, have a happy life. Live long and prosper. May the force be with you, and all that good stuff."

Her words seemed to help him relax. His shoulders dropped as he let out a long breath. "Thanks, I appreciate that."

25

Something was still working behind his eyes. "I'd still like to talk to you about another matter. Another time, that is."

She felt the lines furrow between her brows. "About what exactly?"

"Scott Alexander!"

His mother must've been in a state, because she was using both his first and middle names, which everyone knew moms said in lieu of doing what they really wanted, which was to slap the spit out of their children's heads. Didn't matter that her son was twenty-seven years old.

"What?" He did not bother to hide his annoyance.

Kitten heels together, arms straight at her sides, she resembled a coiffed mannequin in a Bergdorf's window. "You are being rude, that's what," his mother bit back.

Quinn tried to diffuse the tension. "Hello, Mrs. Hauser. It's been a while since I've seen you and Scott."

Vienna's version of Cersei Lannister revealed the barest hint of a curled mouth. "Hello, dear. You're looking well."

"Thank you. Congratulations on the happy news, by the way."

The cords along Mrs. Hauser's sinewy neck tensed before her features smoothed over. "Yes, well, Patricia comes from a lovely family, although I'll never understand why she and her sister chose a career in *sales* of all things. No advanced degree of any kind." She huffed, shaking her head. "But I suppose we can't make our children's choices for them now, can we?"

Quinn had no idea how to respond to such a hostile remark. She didn't even like Tricia, and she still felt the need to defend her.

"You know, Mrs. Hauser, Tricia is a highly successful realtor, one of the best in the area."

"Yes, I've spotted those billboards as well. So ghastly! They must've cost a fortune." Mrs. Hauser's gaze scanned Quinn up and down, like the Terminator's, but without the warmth. "I suppose every mother thinks no one is good enough for her son."

And with that petrified turd of a comment, his mother walked to the booth on the other side of the restaurant.

Just then, Bash waltzed out of the bathroom, pegging Scott in Quinn's personal space and barreling straight for them. "Everything okay here?"

Ms. Eun placed their food down with a thud. "Chow's up!"

Scott startled. Of course, Bash was six feet three and her ex was only five eight, so she understood why he was getting jumpy.

"Nope. No problem." He gave her a quick, pained smile. "See you later, Quinn."

Her brother did that staring down "I'm not gonna *blink* until you're gone" thing, waiting until Scott was across the room and seated with his mom before he slid back onto the stool.

"Is that numb-nut bothering you?"

She stole one of his fries. "Not really. Until today, that is."

He grabbed the ketchup. "Why, what's so special about today?" He opened the top and slammed the heel of his palm on the side of the bottle.

"He got engaged to Tricia Pemberley. She even made a special trip over to Guinefort House to let me know."

He barked out a laugh. "That's awesome. They'll both be miserable for the rest of their lives."

Quinn kept her voice low. "I don't understand why he's here with his mom. They never come here."

"No kidding." Ms. Eun butted in. "The only time that boy ever came in was when the two of you were dating. And now he's back." She gave Quinn a pointed look.

Quinn groused. "Oh, c'mon now. He's *engaged*."

Ms. Eun remained unfazed—and unconvinced. "He's never gotten over you. Everyone knows that."

"Please, he just never got over someone breaking up with *him*. '*No one breaks up with Scott Hauser*'—I still can't believe I went out with someone who talks about himself in the third person."

"He was—and will always be—a self-centered bro-hole." Bash took a whopper bite of his burger.

"He says he wants to talk."

Bash swallowed. "Well, *that's* not happening."

She shoved a bite of her omelet into her mouth. "Um, I tink dass *my* dwecision to make," Quinn said through a mouthful of herbed chicken goodness.

Greg yelled out, "Hey, beautiful bride of mine, we've got other customers!"

Ms. Eun shrugged her shoulders. "That's my cue."

As soon as she was out of earshot, Bash leaned in. "Want some good news?"

She swallowed another bite. "Of course, I do—*spill*."

"Guess who was just hired as the new assistant fire chief for Fairfax County?"

She dropped her fork on the plate. "No way."

Another happy smile. "I just got off the phone with the chief. That means no more traveling the country, living out of crappy motels. I'm moving back for good, and I start Monday."

Quinn waved both hands like they were on fire, something she did when she was over-the-moon excited. "Holy shi—are you serious?" She didn't wait for his response. "I can't believe it! This is huge!" She threw her arms around him, rocking him side to side.

"But wait—there's more."

She released him. "What? If I order now, I get the Ginsu knives too?

Eun came back to refill his Coke. "What's going on?"

"You know what? Let me tell you on the way." He retrieved his wallet and placed a couple of twenties on the counter.

Quinn scrunched her nose. "You know, I can buy for us, Bash."

He brushed his sandy-brown hair out of his eyes. "I know, I know . . . you are woman, hear you roar. All for it, except you forget, when you're out with your big brother, I've got you, the least of it meaning me paying for breakfast."

She really did have the best brother ever created.

"Not necessary, but always appreciated." She hopped off her stool and adjusted the strap of her messenger bag.

"Thanks, guys." She waved to the Huttons.

"Stay out of trouble!" Ms. Eun called out. Her husband moved away from the grill, draping an arm over his wife's shoulder.

Bash leaned close to her ear. "I need you to come with me on an errand, by the way."

"Sure. Where we going?"

He held the door open for her. "To face the enemy."

Chapter Two

"She believed sarcasm and rude remarks kept the monsters at
bay. They didn't."
—Louise Penny, *A Rule Against Murder*

If Quinn had known her brother's errand involved meeting up
with the Pemberley sisters, she would have opted for a root
canal instead. Or a pap smear. Maybe even a series of bee stings,
the next more painful than the last.

And she was allergic to bees.

They pulled up in front of the old tomato canning factory,
dormant and abandoned for as long as Quinn could remember.
Now, the once-rusted behemoth to industrialization gleamed
like a shiny new penny in the sun.

"Can you believe it?" Her brother maneuvered into the
parking space. "They finally did something with this heap and
converted it into loft condos. I heard about the property from a
buddy of mine."

Quinn knew all about the defunct factory because she'd
written a paper on it in the eighth grade. "This place has quite
a history—did you know that?"

"Not really, but I have a feeling you're going to tell me."

"This is true. I am, but I'll give you the SparkNotes version." she said. "During World War Two, this canning factory was Vienna's answer to a nationwide call for us to plant 'victory gardens.' It was a way to feed ourselves and send canned food overseas to soldiers. Pretty cool, huh?"

Bash put his truck into park with one hand, the other draped over the steering wheel. "It is, which is why we're going to put up with them."

She blustered. "Yeah, but I thought you were kidding when you said we were going to face the enemy."

He took the key out of the ignition. "Listen, the TnT twins aren't my idea of a fun hang either, but they are top-notch realtors."

"Yeah, but do they have any ethics? They'd sell their grandmother for parts if they could." Quinn glanced at her brother's profile. "Why not go with Ms. Jennifer over at Plum Street Properties? I used to babysit her kids. Plus, I can guarantee she has a soul."

He exhaled. "I hear you, but those two have got the exclusive on this building. Trina has promised to take two percentage points off her commission."

"That's not a big deal. She's representing both sides of the potential sale."

"This is true."

"And—an extra bonus for her—she's always had a thing for you. Big time."

He responded with a wicked smile. "They all do. It's a curse I live with."

Quinn pretended to gag.

Suddenly, there was a loud knock on Bash's driver-side window. Sitting in her seat, Quinn almost jumped out of her skin. He rolled down his window, but just an inch.

"Hey, Bash!" Trina's pearly white smile gleamed—until she spotted Quinn. "Oh, I didn't know you'd be here too, Quincy."

"Yeah, I'm here," she answered, not bothering to correct her.

"Just give us a sec." Bash rolled the window back up in her face before turning his attention to his sister. "What's up?"

"That girl's been saying my name wrong on purpose since Girl Scouts." Quinn whipped off her seat belt. "Let's just get this over with."

"Hey, wait a minute." He tugged her sleeve as she started to exit his truck. "Just say the word and we'll get out of here. Nothing's worth you being made to feel bad."

She opened the truck door. "Ugh, don't be nice to me. It makes it harder to stoke my hate fire."

He laughed as they both hopped out of his truck.

And there stood Trina Pemberley, Tricia's twin, identical in almost every way. Both had medium-length, bobbed ash-blonde hair and the same wide-set hazel eyes. They favored pastel-palette Chanel suits and long nails painted rose-gold. Quinn once overheard someone say the two coordinated every aspect of their look so as to remain "on brand" for their business. But Quinn remembered them from third grade, when they moved into town, before they became Northern Virginia's wonder twin–powered real estate team, and they always matched, even then: same clothes, same hairstyle, same hella-awful attitudes.

Even so, Quinn could always tell them apart. Most who grew up with them could because, although neither was exactly known for being particularly pleasant, Trina was the one with more edge. She was in charge, the sister whose smile never reached her eyes—because something darker already resided there.

"I'm telling you right now, you're going to love this place—I just know it!" Trina touched Bash's arm as they walked inside the building. "By the way, no need to thank me, but FYI? You're getting the first look-see, except for the other realtors of course. As of right now, you have your choice of units, but I'm telling you, they won't last. I expect we'll be sold out in a few weeks."

"Appreciate your time." He gave her his tight, polite smile, the one he reserved for judgy church ladies.

Well, glad Mom and Dad didn't raise stupid. Bash may be a flirt, but at least he's not courting crazy.

They walked into the elevator, and Trina leaned over to press the button for the top floor, making sure to brush up against Bash in spite of there being plenty of room in the lift. Quinn summoned all her willpower so as not to roll her eyes into the back of their sockets.

"There are only eighteen units in the whole building, and because of the factory's structure, most have awesome views of the whole town. You can't build this high in Vienna anymore—the town council won't allow it—but back in the forties, they made an exception, for the war effort. It's a shame because unless the building's this high up, you can't get views like this. Personally, I like the top the best. Don't you agree, Bash?"

Quinn coughed into her hand. Her brother pretended not to catch Trina's tacky innuendo.

The elevators doors opened, and Tricia was waiting for them—same outfit as Trina, only a different color.

"Hey, Bash!" Her eyes twinkled like a crazed cheerleader's—until she spotted his sister. "Oh, Quinn. I didn't know you'd be here."

At least this one got my name right. "Yep, same here. But my brother asked me to come."

Her face brightened. "That means you're serious, if you're bringing family along. Am I right?"

Bash opened his mouth to answer, but the other sister got there first.

"Well, *of course* he's serious. Otherwise, he wouldn't have called *me* for a tour,"

Trina butted in, threading her arm through Bash's. He went along, being a gentleman.

"Bash, why don't I show you around. Let's start here." She waved toward the kitchen like a double-jointed Vanna White. "You're going to *love* this smart fridge. I swear, it does everything except make you dinner."

There were only two apartments on the top floor, which meant the loft space they were touring was mammoth, much bigger than Quinn's cozy farmhouse. She was about to take a look around, but Tricia placed herself in Quinn's path.

"So, we're all kumbaya-happy over here?"

Quinn's head jerked. "Uh yeah—why wouldn't I be?"

"You know, you're not always going to have your big brother around to protect you."

Wow. Some people won't let their high school days—or attitude—die the quiet death they deserve.

"Are you serious right now? Protect me from *what* exactly?"

Tricia breezed by her questions. "Just don't get any ideas about Scott, and you and I will be fine."

Quinn choked on her laugh, whacking her chest with her fist.

Tricia's face soured. "I mean it. Leave him alone."

Blowing out an exasperated breath, Quinn tried to think how to answer in a way that would finally get through the woman's thick skull. "Tricia, have I done or said *anything* to indicate I would go after him . . . *ever*?"

Tricia crossed her arms in front of her, doubt coloring her delicate features. "No, but sometimes an ex becomes a lot more appealing once he's off the market."

"I promise you, that is never, *ever* going to happen." *Because those were the longest three weeks of my life.*

Tricia didn't seem appeased. "I don't know. Something's up with him."

"What do you mean?"

She stared at Quinn without seeing her. "Maybe you're not the one I should be worried about."

True story. Your future mother-in-law uses your picture as a personal dartboard.

Tricia kept talking. "It's just . . . Scott is trying to be his own man, and I'm trying to help him with that."

Quinn couldn't believe Tricia was confiding in her. "That's good, isn't it?"

"I guess that depends on who you ask."

What the heck does that mean?

Trina cleared her throat from the kitchen, glaring daggers at her sister.

"Forget I said anything." Tricia grabbed Quinn's wrist, panic-stricken. "I mean it. We never had this conversation."

Quinn placed her hand on top of Tricia's. "I promise. I won't say a word. I hope everything works out. Really."

Any hardness residing in Tricia's features melted away, transforming an aesthetic beauty into an actualized vision. "Thank you, Quinn. And I'm . . ." Tricia gave a quick glance over at her twin across the room, an air of resolve settling in. She met Quinn's gaze. "I am sorry about before. There's no reason to drag you into my drama, and I appreciate you not saying anything."

Quinn was too stunned to respond, and before she had a chance, Tricia was already halfway to the kitchen. She followed.

From there, Trina took the lead, weaving together the building's storied history and the preservation efforts while making sure to highlight all the latest technology the builders had included. She was impressive—Quinn had to give her that. She also noticed Tricia didn't utter a word the rest of the time, either simply nodding along with what her sister said or staring out the floor-to-ceiling windows. Either way, she was no longer in the room with them.

Eventually, Trina was done with her pitch. She did a little twirl in the middle of the room, her chartreuse print skirt flaring out. "So, what do you think? Is this your new home, Sebastian?"

Her brother's eyes scanned the loft, his feet moving the rest of him wherever his gaze landed. "It's worth considering." He stopped, focusing on the twins. "Give us a minute . . . alone?"

Trina's micro-bladed brows arched. "Uh, sure thing." She eyed her sister. "Come along."

Tricia nodded. "Let us know if you have any questions. We'll meet you and Quinn downstairs."

Bash waited until the Pemberleys were in the elevator. "So, what do you think?"

Quinn walked over to the windows, taking in the expanse of their town. "Well, Trina was right: you can see everything from up here . . . there's Church Street Eats . . . and there's Sarita's Ice Cream Shoppe." She sighed. "I miss Nielsen's."

Nielsen's used to be on the corner of Church Street and Lawyer's Road, and they'd made the best ice cream—or, as they called it, "custard"—in the mid-Atlantic. The shop had closed a few years back, tired of paying Vienna's escalating taxes and rent, and everyone in town missed them like a phantom limb, especially in summer.

"Where's Prose and Scones?"

Bash scanned the view. With his chin, he motioned toward the left. "Right over there. See the red roof? That's our bookstore."

Quinn pressed her nose against the window, watching her breath fog the glass. Bash copied his sister, writing "Well?" with the tip of his finger into the condensation.

She let out a soft laugh and bumped her shoulder with his. "You know, this place is amazing. It's just a shame those two will get the commission. Feels like we're supporting the White Walkers in their quest for dominion over the Seven Kingdoms."

His eyes gleamed with amusement. "I'm thinking someone may be bingeing too much *Game of Thrones*."

Quinn summoned her best fake-British accent. "There is no such thing as too much *Game of Thrones*, and I will cut out your tongue and feed it to my hounds if you utter such blasphemy again."

Then she cocked her left brow, like a super villain, for extra effect. He stared for half a second before they both dissolved laughing.

He wiped his eyes with the back of his hand. "Damn, Sis, I forgot how funny you can be."

She offered a curtsy.

"I think I'm going to take it," he said.

"Do you have that kind of money?"

He gave her a look. "Yeah, I have it."

"Well, la dee dah. I guess they pay firefighters more than I realized."

"Quinn, I was a wildlife firefighter on the federal level. I made decent money, plus most everything I own I can fit into the back of my truck. You do the math."

"Fair enough." She felt her pocket vibrate. She took her phone out. It was her alarm. "Listen, I gotta get back and walk RBG."

"And how is Ruff Barker Ginsburg these days?"

She shoved her phone into her back pocket. "As long as she gets in her exercise and favorite treats, that's all she needs."

"If only people were as easy."

"'Girl, you know it's true,'" she teased, quoting vintage Milli Vanilli. They'd played a lot of the ill-fated duo when she lived overseas in Cambodia—early Madonna hits and George Michael too. Now she couldn't hear most bubblegum pop songs without thinking of her life back in Phnom Penh. Each place where she'd lived and worked had its own soundtrack.

He fished his keys out of his front pocket. "Ready to go?"

"No, you stay here. Work out your deal with the blonde Kardashian twins downstairs. I feel like walking anyway."

His brows knitted. "You sure?"

She took a hair tie off her wrist, threading her reddish-brown hair into a ponytail. "Yeah, I need the walk."

"All right then." He opened his arms. "Bring it in for the real thing."

She gave him a hug, and he rested his chin on the top of her head. "So happy you're home for good," Quinn said.

He held her for an extra beat. "You being back here meant it was time for me to come home too."

She craned her head up. "I don't want to be the reason you stopped doing something you love."

He let go. "I like putting out fires. And I can do that anywhere. Besides, you're not the only one who got their wanderlust out of their system."

Quinn found that hard to believe. Growing up, Bash had always been the one who could never sit still. Their father used to joke he was like a wound-up husky, needing to be exercised several times a day in order to keep him out of mischief.

"You're going to be bored silly here."

He stared out the window before meeting her gaze. "Please, besides the job, what do you think my life's been like outside of work?"

He didn't wait for her to answer. "I'll tell you what it was. Two choices: either going to bars in nowhere towns with a bunch of kids in my unit or staying behind in dumpy motels, watching bad TV. It's nearly impossible to have a real relationship. I'm over it, Quinnie. I want roots and I want family, maybe even one of my own."

Bash was all determination and resolve. She could feel the energy coming off him in waves, charging the molecules around them. Quinn could appreciate her brother missing home, longing for family, but no way was either the mitigating factor for his return. She knew him too well.

"You came back for Rachel."

Bash swallowed. "Yeah . . . it's her. It's always been her."

Well, it's about time. She had known Rach was the one for her brother since he first brought her home to meet the family back when they were in high school. Maybe that's why Quinn had taken it almost as hard as Rachel when he broke off the relationship later on.

"Winning her back is going to be . . ." She wanted to choose her words carefully. "A challenge."

He frowned. "Yeah, don't I know it."

She looked around the loft. "And this place, while completely awesome, screams bachelor pad, not 'man who's ready to settle down.'"

"You think?" He turned around, looking with new eyes. "I hadn't thought . . . she likes to cook. In college, she was the only girl I knew who'd rather host a dinner for our friends than hang at a party. She'd spend days planning the menus around these crazy themes."

Quinn remembered. "My favorite was her 'Lip Sync Mashup Meets Lip-Smacking Mexican.'"

He smiled. "Yeah, that was cool, but a lot of pressure to come up with a rap on the spot. If that had been a drinking game, I would've gotten myself sick."

"What about her ode to all things Freddie Mercury and Queen—'Bohemian Rhapsody Round Table.' That was awesome."

Bash smiled wide. "Yeah, the whole menu was served on those lazy susan spinning serving trays. The woman actually tracked down edible gold to give the desserts 'Freddie flair.'" He rubbed a hand up and down his face, letting out a groan. "I don't know. Maybe this place is all wrong. I just . . . I walked in and I could see her here, see *us* here."

"I get it," she told him. "But maybe you should put your energies into learning who she is now. Let me tell you from experience, there's no place like home, but that doesn't mean home and the people here don't change."

"Since when did you get to be so smart?"

She shooed away the compliment. "It's always easier to give advice than to follow it." She checked the time on her phone— she was running late. "I've got to get going. Text me later and tell me how it all went." She waved before walking to the elevator.

"Hey," he called out. She turned around to see him glancing up at the sky.

"Yeah?"

He motioned out the window. "Storm's coming," he warned. "You need to be ready for it."

Chapter Three

"By the pricking of my thumbs, something wicked this way comes."
—William Shakespeare, *MacBeth*

RBG growled, the kind starting low and in the back of her throat. Then came the whining. The combo always meant something had tweaked her.

"It's a squirrel, you silly dog. It's always just a squirrel. In a tree. When I'm *trying* to *sleep*."

Her girl huffed before giving her a look. People say humans make a bad habit of anthromorphizing their pets, but Quinn swore her dog had about a hundred different emotions and opinions, including the attitude she had just thrown down.

Then RBG started grumbling again, her eyes laser focused out the open window.

Quinn squinted at her phone: it was a little after one in the morning. She grabbed a pillow and smooshed it over her head.

It didn't help. RBG's guttural noises turned into barks, and now it was Quinn who was in a tizzy.

"Fine, fine. I'm *awake* now." She threw down the pillow and sat up. RBG didn't even flinch. Every muscle was rock solid, her whole body at attention.

She shuffled out of bed. "You know, there's nothing back there," Quinn said through a yawn, as she wiggled on a pair of jeans, putting on her sweater. "You're going to feel so silly when you find out you got all worked up over a lil' bitty squirrel. Just sayin'."

Quinn shoved her feet into her sneakers and patted the side of her thigh, her signal for RBG to follow. Her dog baby bolted off the bed and trotted to the door, nudging the leash with her nose.

Quinn clipped it on her and grabbed her keys and phone.

After leaving her home, RBG pulled Quinn down Windover Avenue. She still didn't know what RBG had sensed, but every time Quinn tried to haul the dog back, she'd strain at the leash until she almost choked herself. And so they continued walking, Quinn thinking the whole time that RBG was leading them on a fool's errand.

Until she veered right on Knoll Street. Quinn heard the sound of someone grunting, and then a thud, like something heavy had been dropped. She followed the noise, walking at a faster clip. She turned on her phone's flashlight feature in order to avoid tripping on the uneven road with gnarled roots busting through the crumbling asphalt.

"C'mon, where are you?" She swept the range of light left and right. Tree. Branches. An owl. Nothing unusual. Nothing that could have made that sound. Was she hearing things?

That's when Quinn noticed something: it had gotten quiet. She slowed her pace, scanning the area with the light. They were in the trees now, on the edge of the manicured section of Sarah Walker Mercer Park, but it was pitch-black. She thought streetlights usually shone around there, but maybe she was wrong. She knew up ahead was a paved area, but she couldn't see it from where she stood. Quinn peeped down at RBG, and her girl looked up at her. "Huh, maybe it was the wind?"

That's when she caught it—the sound of a door slamming shut, followed by a car peeling away, screeching like a banshee through the night. And it couldn't have been that far away because Quinn could smell burnt rubber on the breeze. She ran toward the sound, hoping to catch a glimpse. The car left a trail of billowy white smoke all the way down Nutley Street. It went so fast, Quinn couldn't even be sure of the car's color.

"Damn it."

RBG started to whine.

"It's okay, girl." Quinn fumbled with her phone—her hands were shaking—trying to steady herself in order to shine the light. She was going to find a seat on one of the park benches and catch her breath before heading back home.

But then her light caught on some pink fabric and something that resembled . . . hay?

She moved at a snail's pace, just a little bit closer.

"Wait, that's not . . . oh no . . ."

It wasn't hay. It was hair. Human hair. And it was blonde . . . ash blonde.

Quinn's gaze darted up and down the body, her brain trying to catch up to where her eyes and gut had already arrived.

That's because the body wasn't just *any*body.

Face up, with empty eyes and mouth hanging open, lay the last person she'd ever expect to find: Tricia Pemberley.

RBG strained the leash, itching to investigate, but there was something wholly unnatural about the way Tricia was lying there.

"No, girl. Stay." Quinn's voice came out hoarse because she was finding it hard to breathe. She was no medical expert, but it didn't take one to know for certain: Tricia was dead. With her hands shaking even more badly now, Quinn slid the bar on her phone and called the police.

* * *

The cop tapped his pen on his notepad. "Did you get a look at the license plate?"

Her mind going blank, Quinn shook her head.

"What about the make or model of the car?"

"No, I just heard it. It took off so fast, I couldn't even tell you what kind of car it was. There was all this . . . this white smoke coming from the tailpipe."

She thought she knew almost everyone in Vienna, but this guy was new-ish. There was something familiar about him, the way someone would be if you'd met him once at a party or if he was a customer who had come into the store more than once, but not enough to be a regular.

"You say you knew the victim?"

It was weird to hear him say that, to think of Tricia Pemberley as a victim of anything. *I can't believe she's really dead.*

Quinn snapped out of her fog. "Yes, I've known her almost all my life."

"Would you say you two were close?"

"No, not at all."

Now it was the officer's turn to express surprise. "Oh? Were you two enemies?"

"What? No! We may not have been friends, but . . ."

Something in his expression hardened, grew cold even, before he smoothed it over. But she hadn't missed it.

"Tricia was gorgeous, successful, and engaged to a guy with big bucks. I'd understand if you were envious, wanting what she had."

Oh great. Another one who thinks every woman's sole purpose is to find a husband.

"Listen, Officer"—she glanced at his nametag—"Wyatt Reynolds, I don't know where you came from before being assigned to the Vienna PD, but trust me when I tell you, I wasn't

44

jealous in the slightest. And there's no way I'd ever hurt her—or anybody for that matter. Especially like that. No one deserves that."

The sirens' blare cut through the atmosphere, with blinding lights flashing by; it was a squad car, followed by an ambulance and an SUV. Officers Shae Johnson and Ned Carter emerged from a black-and-white. Shae had graduated five years ahead of Quinn, and Ned was one of the few people who had been born and raised in town, part of the local Carter family, all descendants of Keziah Carter, a freed woman of color who, in 1842, purchased fifty acres of land from what had been the original Wolf Trap plantation, almost unheard of in the Antebellum era. If someone encountered a Carter around these days, chances are he or she was one of Ms. Keziah's descendants, but Quinn—just like everyone else in town—rarely thought about the Carters' history. For her, Ned was just one of her father's good friends, two grown men who had bonded over their mutual interest in mushroom hunting, of all things—particularly morels—enough to form a mycological club. They even had T-shirts saying "I'm not weird—I'm a fungi."

Of course, emerging from the SUV was none other than Detective Aiden Harrington. He might have been the same age as Bash and just as tall, but he was the physical opposite in every other way. While Bash had a slender build, a mop of light brown hair, and boyish good looks, Aiden was all thick, ink-black hair and stormy gray eyes, and he was built like a Mack truck.

In other words, he was all man—admittedly too much man for Quinn, growing up. After all, there was a six-year age difference between them. When she'd been twelve and he'd been seventeen, that had been a big deal, an impossibility. Not that this had stopped her from writing "Ms. Quinn Caine-Harrington" all over her notebooks back in school.

But now, she was twenty-five and he was thirty-one. When she had come home from her latest—and last— overseas teaching gig, her family had thrown her a welcome-home party at The Maple Avenue Restaurant—part of the trend in town to have a place with the most unimaginative, prosaic name, all while serving truly inventive food. She knew he'd be there—she was counting on it. She'd even had her hair and makeup done, finally allowing her longtime hair stylist, JoDene, free reign to bibbity-bobbity-boo on some highlights, give her hair more than a typical trim. Quinn had even sanctioned use of that torture device-slash-curling iron of hers, which JoDene wielded like a *Lord of the Rings* con-jurer, transforming her rod-straight mop into these loose, beachy, sun-kissed waves.

And when she spotted him enter the restaurant, Aiden made a beeline her way, like the detective/rock star he was, if there ever was such a thing.

They locked eyes.

He smiled—no, scratch that—he *beamed*.

And when they were finally toe to toe, her head craning up—even in those ridiculous heels, to take in those eyes warm and soft only for her, she knew, down to the marrow of her bones, this was their beginning.

Quinn and Aiden. Aiden and Quinn.

She had the fantasy tattooed in her mind: her friends would tease and call them "Q&A," and they'd share a look between them before laughing long and deep the whole time.

That *had been* the fantasy, until he'd reached out . . . to ruffle her hair.

Just like her brother did.

"Good to have you home, Quinnie," he said, before saunter-ing over to chat up the new redheaded server.

Quinnie. He had called her *Quinnie*. Only her family still used that childish nickname—oh, and apparently, Aiden Broadwater Harrington.

That's when it had hit her—he would only *ever* see her as Bash's little sister, the tag-along-kid who made sure to blend in well enough so they'd not mind her presence much. It didn't matter that she was a young woman now, one with an Instagram-worthy dress and strappy, grown-up shoes, magic hair, and dewy-fresh makeup. She would always just be lil' Quinnie Caine.

She had plastered on a smile for the rest of the evening, making sure to visit with each and every person who had come by to welcome her home. But under the surface and out of sight, the tiny, long-nurtured hope of there ever being a Quinn and Aiden went out, the same way Tinkerbell's light died when children dared say they didn't believe in fairies. Flutterless wings lay dormant, her long-held dream dying under twinkle lights.

That had been five weeks ago. She had seen him since, but not often and never for long. Now, while the other officers were securing the scene and the EMTs ran over to Tricia, attempting to revive her, Aiden stalked over to where she was standing, along with Officer Reynolds and, now, Officer Carter.

"Tell me you've got a good reason for being out here, Quinn." Aiden stopped in front of her, hands on his hips, exposing his sidearm.

Officer Reynolds's face blanched. "You know each other?"

"Yeah, you could say that. Now answer me, Quinn."

At least he's not calling me Quinnie.

He was wearing an olive-colored corduroy blazer with a pressed, button-down shirt and black jeans. He was also clean-shaven and smelled like sexy-musky-man. He always looked good for work, but considering it was almost two in the morning,

Quinn was guessing he had been involved in another kind of activity before being called to the scene.

"Sorry if I interrupted your hot date." *Hashtag sorry, not sorry.*

A vein in his left temple pulsed. "Are you kidding me right now?"

"Hey, I wasn't looking to cause any trouble. I promise," she said. "RBG got spooked is all, and once we were out here, we heard a thump. By the time we found her, someone had taken off in their car. I called nine-one-one first thing."

"Can you explain to me, then, why you were out here alone in the first place? Vienna's safe, but it's never a good idea for a woman to walk alone at night."

"Aiden, I told you. RBG got spooked, barking and growling until I took her out to take a look. And P.S.: She's a German shepherd. I was safe with her."

He frowned in response.

"Hey, I wasn't even sure what I heard out here," Quinn went on. "It could have been the wind for all I knew. I wasn't going to call nine-one-one until there was something to see."

"Or until you were sure your accomplice got away," Officer Reynolds muttered.

Officer Carter flashed a warning glare. "Reynolds."

Aiden pinched the skin on the bridge of his nose. "Please tell me you didn't touch the body? Or contaminate my crime scene any further?"

"No, of course not. I just . . . I just can't believe Tricia's dead."

RBG let out a short woof. Guess not everyone was broken up about her passing.

Quinn couldn't stop staring at Tricia's lifeless face, numbly watching as one of the EMTs performed CPR through a protective barrier. With gloves on, the other tech held her wrist, feeling for a pulse. For ten minutes, nobody else dared move except the EMTs. It was as if they were all collectively holding their breaths until Tricia could regain hers.

"I'm sorry, folks, but I'm going to have to call it," one of them said. "Her lungs have collapsed, and there's evidence of paralysis, not just on the left side of her face but also in her throat and upper extremities."

Quinn couldn't believe what she was hearing. "But aren't you going to take her to the hospital? Don't give up yet!"

"She's gone, miss," the other EMT said, his expression somber. "Detective, I'm going to call the ME."

Aiden gave a nod.

"And now it's time you come down to the station with me." Officer Reynolds grabbed Quinn's upper arm in a vise grip.

RBG went nuts, barking and snarling. If Quinn hadn't been holding her leash, RBG would've tackled the officer to the ground. She tried dislodging her arm. "Hey, let go!"

Aiden got right in his face. "You will take your hands off her right now. Are. We. Clear. Sergeant?"

Officer Reynolds released her arm, which Quinn immediately started massaging. RBG rubbed her head against her leg, licking her hand. "It's okay, girl—I'm fine." She stroked the dog's head and scratched along her jaw.

"She still needs to come in for questioning, make a statement," the officer bit out, beads of sweat peppering his upper lip.

Aiden grimaced. "I don't know how they conduct themselves at the Baltimore PD, but in Vienna, we respect the chain of command, which means *I* give the order, not the other way around. Understood?"

Officer Reynolds gave one last glare toward Quinn before answering, "Yes, Detective. Understood."

Just then, the medical examiners arrived. Unfortunately, they were followed by a TV news van.

"That's just great," Aiden muttered. "Reynolds, make yourself useful and get the others to finish securing the scene. I don't want to see any of those vultures near here."

With those parting words, Aiden stormed off toward the medical examiners; all the while Reynolds leaned into her air space, a fiery gleam in his eyes.

"Don't even *think* about going anywhere. You may have them fooled, but I'm onto you. And there's no way I'm letting you get away with it."

Chapter Four

"If all the world hated you, while your own conscience approved you and absolved you from guilt, you would not be without friends."
—Charlotte Bronte, *Jane Eyre*

"Off the record, having a lawyer *and* a person of the cloth meet you at the station makes you look even guiltier."

If Quinn thought she had misjudged Officer Wyatt Reynolds's surly behavior before, his words now were a reminder that she'd been spot on: he was convinced she had killed Tricia and was hell-bent on proving his theory correct.

She had called her parents while still at the crime scene, asking her mom to bring over something for her to wear. And that's because—in the backseat of a police cruiser, with Shae Johnson on guard—she was made to peel off her clothes and surrender her shoes for forensic testing, to rule her out as a suspect. *And that was my favorite sweater too. Might as well toss it right in the giveaway pile because no way in Hades will I ever wear it again.* Disposable booties donned her feet, along with a Vienna PD sweatshirt with matching sweatpants—all about three sizes too big for her.

Her dad and Sister Daria were already waiting for her at the police station when they arrived. She ran into their waiting arms, bathed in relief to be with family. She broke off mid-hug. "How did you know I was here?"

Her cousin let go. "Would you believe it if I told you our bond is so strong I felt your distress, even in the middle of the night?"

Her eyes rounded. "Really?"

"Wow, still gullible." She shook her head. "Your parents called me. The Reverend Mother insisted I come, so Uncle Finn picked me up."

One glance at their drawn, weary expressions wracked her with guilt; she hated that she'd woken them up in the middle of the night. Without a word, though, her cousin took her hand and gave it a firm squeeze, a simple gesture that meant everything, reminding her she wasn't alone and hadn't done anything wrong.

She offered a grateful smile, then eyed over their shoulders. "Where's Mom?"

"On her way," Daria told her.

"Your mother went over to your house to fetch you your own clothes and let in RBG," her dad finished. "Officer Shae Johnson dropped her off."

Well, that's good. One less thing to worry about.

Then Finn Caine peered over his glasses toward Wyatt. "By the way, Officer, we're her *family*, and it is wholly appropriate that we are here for Quinn. The fact that my niece is a novitiate and I'm a retired attorney should have no bearing on the efficacy of my daughter's statement for your investigation, nor her presumed innocence. And frankly, your remarks are unbecoming of an officer of the Vienna PD. I know most of the fine men and women who serve with you, and none of them would condone such behavior or act in such a manner."

Quinn's gaze widened. "Wow—go, Dad."

"Yeah, Uncle Finn. Go *you*," her cousin added. "You've been getting your geek on at the bookstore for so long, I forgot that you used to kick butt in the courtroom." She eyeballed the officer. "Rarely lost a case in thirty-one years as a litigator. Not that Quinn needs him for that, but good to know, wouldn't you agree?"

For the first time since Quinn had met him, Officer Reynolds seemed unsure of himself in the presence of the Caine clan. Quinn had forgotten how intimidating her father could be when he was in "lawyer mode." A lifelong rower, her father still had broad shoulders and a full head of salt-and-pepper hair, although there was way more salt these days. When in a loving, playful mood, her mama called him "Clark," as in Clark Kent, because he could be both dashing and nerdy, having a habit of hiding behind his glasses when uncomfortable. Watching him staring Officer Reynolds down like a guard dog, Quinn knew it was the other guy's turn to fidget.

Sister Daria had also inherited the fierce Caine spirit. Since returning home, Quinn had learned something vital: that habits often serve as superhero capes.

Just then, the double doors of the police station swung open as Bash and her mom hurried in.

"We're here! We're here!" Adele Caine called out as she performed a combo power walk/jog into the station. She had her hair in a loose bun, tendrils flying, with one hand grasping the ends of her lavender shawl to her bosom. Quinn noticed she had her Lady Justice pin on, which made the corner of Quinn's mouth curl up. Bash had a canvas bag tucked under his arm.

Adele was out of breath when they reached her. "Sorry we're late, honey."

Quinn's gaze darted back and forth between them. "Everything okay?"

"It's all good," Bash interjected. He handed over the canvas bag, but just as she was about to take it, Officer Reynolds swiped it out of his hands.

"Hey! That's for me!"

Bash scoffed. "Dude, really? It's not like any of that stuff's going to fit you."

"Ha-ha, very funny, and I don't need you to tell me my job. I'm entitled to take a look." He stuck his hand in the bag, rummaging through, practically sticking his face inside.

Her father rolled his eyes, and her mama looked as if she was ready to smack him into next Tuesday. "Jesus be my fence," she said under her breath. "Don't you think you're going just a *tad* overboard? There's no contraband in there, Officer. Just my daughter's shorts, a blouse, and sandals, along with a fresh pair of panties."

Officer Reynolds's face reddened at the mention of her unmentionables. He thrust the bag at Quinn. "Fine. All clear. You can change after you give your statement."

Sister Daria tsked under her breath. "It's not like they were going to sneak in a file for Quinn to shave down metal bars or something." She turned her focus to her aunt and Bash. "What took y'all so long to get here? You live less than five minutes away."

Bash shoved his hands in his pockets. "The streets around the house have already been blocked off for the morning's festivities. It slipped my mind that this weekend is Walk on the Hill."

Walk on the Hill was one of many beloved traditions in her town. Held each spring since 1974, the event offered self-guided tours for fifty-odd participating gardens in Vienna's historic Windover Heights neighborhood.

In Quinn's opinion, her parents' home wasn't just a lovely addition to the tour: it was a highlight. Mama's flowers were some of the prettiest around, but she made it extra special by offering folks homemade ginger-mint iced tea, along with sachets of fresh lavender and seed packets so they could start their own award-winning gardens. It was also common for Mama Caine to don a pair of fairy wings, made with the same iridescent fabric as her "magic" wand. "For the wee ones," she'd explain to the people who thought she might be a bit touched in the head. She'd lead them through her gardens, where it wasn't unusual for a child to find hidden treasures like Chinese yo-yos or rainbow-haired troll dolls. Quinn and Bash used to debate whether it was the kids or their mama who had more fun with the town tradition.

"Mom, you really don't have to be here. You've got the walk starting in a few hours." Everyone knew she spoke the truth. The official time might say two o'clock, but it wasn't unheard of for people to start first thing in the morning.

Adele brushed Quinn's words away. "Nonsense. I'll take a lil' ol' disco nap and be ready to go in no time."

"Mama, c'mon—"

Her mother interrupted, "Someday, you'll have children of your own, and you'll understand there is no choice."

Officer Reynolds cleared his throat. "If you follow me, I can take your statement in our interrogation room."

The whole Caine brood started walking behind him, until he stopped and turned around. "You do realize you all can't be in there with her, right?"

Bash's mouth pressed into a hard, thin line. "And why the hell not?"

"It's fine," Quinn interjected, not wanting a scene in the middle of the police department. "Y'all wait here."

"I'm coming in with you—as counsel," her father insisted.

"But why? I didn't do anything wrong. I don't need a lawyer."

"Well, of course *I* know that," he said, giving the officer some side-eye. "But I'll come anyway, to make sure *he* knows that."

One glance at her father's face and Quinn knew better than to argue with him. "Fine. Suit yourself."

The two of them followed Officer Reynolds through the station. She spotted Shae Johnson leaning on Ned Carter's desk. She also recognized a couple of people who had attended Madison High School in her year. The receptionist was getting herself a cup of coffee at the Keurig station in the back. Quinn recognized her as a frequent Prose & Scones customer and one of her mama's book club friends.

They didn't sneer, but none of them smiled either. Every one of them was assessing her with what her father called "cop eyes," wondering if she could have done such a heinous thing.

Officer Reynolds opened the door. "Have a seat. We'll be in in a minute."

Taking the middle seats, they sat down in a nondescript room, with gray plastic chairs not quite molded right for the human form. Below her feet was the kind of wiry, industrial carpet found in school trailers. After scanning the room, Quinn was surprised there wasn't one of those two-way mirrors.

Her father adjusted himself in his chair. "Listen, kiddo, you've done nothing wrong."

"I know." She craned her head, still taking it all in. "I just feel like I've been summoned to the principal's office or something."

He gave her a pointed look. "Just tell the truth. Leave nothing out."

Quinn opened her mouth to answer just as the door to the interrogation room swung open. This time, it wasn't just Officer Reynolds; Shae Johnson and Aiden came in as well.

"Hello, Caine crew." Aiden gave a reassuring smile while glancing her over. "Rough night?"

I guess that's polite guy code for looking like racoon dung. "You could say that."

Shae dropped a legal pad and pen in front of her. "We're going to have you write a formal statement, but first we'd like to ask you some questions." Her gaze volleyed back and forth between Quinn and her father. "Are you being represented by counsel?"

"Not real—"

"Yes, she is," her dad interrupted. "I'm retired, but I've maintained my legal license."

Shae seemed to study Finn Caine for a couple of beats. "You do realize she's not under arrest, that we're just here to find out what happened? We're not pointing any fingers."

Finn Caine nodded. "I understand, Shae. Still, I'd like to be present—especially since there are some on your team who have demonstrated a rather hostile attitude toward my daughter."

The mood changed in the room, most of the charge coming off Officer Reynolds. "I would think, *counselor*, as a longtime Vienna resident, you'd be just as upset as I am over what's happening here." A thick, purple vein down the middle of Officer Reynold's forehead thumped, sending out its own kind of distress signal. "Over thirty years without a murder and now, two in less than six months. Strange, dontcha think?"

Her father's face turned scarlet. "She wasn't even in the country when the good doctor died."

This is going nowhere fast. "Let's get this over with, okay?" Quinn pulled her chair closer to the table.

Aiden and the other two officers sat across from her. Quinn noticed that Wyatt was the only one of the three who had not brought in a notepad and pen, which she could interpret in one of two ways: either he had an outstanding, eidetic memory, or he wasn't much interested in the details, which was a scary trait for a cop to possess.

Officer Reynolds's beady eyes bore into hers. "Isn't it true, Miss Caine, you and the victim had an altercation earlier in the day, before you found her murdered?"

She stilled. "How on earth do you know about *that*?"

He smirked. "I have my sources."

It should be a crime for someone to come off this arrogant. Quinn wanted to smack the smug right out of him.

Shae Johnson glanced up from her note-taking. "So, you did have it out with Tricia just prior to her murder?"

Quinn grimaced. "Sort of, but we cleared things up later." She studied Officer Reynolds. "I'd still like to hear how *you* knew we'd had words."

He scoffed. "I don't have to tell *you* anything."

"Enough, Reynolds." Aiden eyed the sergeant before turning his attention back to her. "Why don't you start from the beginning and just tell us what happened when you saw Tricia earlier."

"Okay, well, I was dropping off the dog food donations I had collected for Guinefort House's kennels. Everyone knows I'm over there the first Friday of the month. The next thing I know, I see Tricia. She came by to let me and my cousin know she got engaged to Scott Hauser the night before."

The tips of Officer Reynolds's finger did a staccato tap on the table, which was as annoying as it sounded. "I thought you stated that the two of you weren't exactly friends."

"We aren't—I mean, we weren't."

Both of Officer Reynolds's dark, bushy brows shot up. "Hmm . . . well now, I'm a guy, and I know nothing about typical wedding brouhaha, but it seems to me that coming over to where she knew you'd be is something good friends would do."

Quinn tsked, shaking her head. "Well *that* right there is proof you're not from around here. Because if you knew Tricia

Pemberley—God rest her soul—you'd realize there's nothing she enjoyed more than flaunting what she perceived as her good fortune, in someone else's face."

Aiden's nostrils flared. "But why you, Quinn?"

She exhaled loudly, tossing up her hands before they landed in her lap. "I don't know. For some reason, she had it in her head that I might want her fiancé back, which, I can promise you on a stack of Bibles, could not be further from the truth. By the way, when I saw her later, over at the old tomato factory lofts with her sister and Bash—my brother is looking for a place to live—it was Tricia who ended up apologizing to me. We were fine."

Aiden's jaw hardened. "Wait a second, what do you mean by wanting him 'back'? Does that mean you actually *dated* Scott Hauser?"

It's like he didn't hear anything I just said! And why should he care who I dated? I'm just "lil' Quinnie Caine," remember?

"Scott and I dated for, like, a few weeks before I left for my first assignment teaching abroad, which, by the way, was *over three years* ago."

Aiden was unappeased. "How did I not know about this? And what were you thinking, dating that guy of all people?"

Wow, if I didn't know better, I'd think he was jealous.

"Well, Aiden, not that it's any of your business, but back then he had worked hard to prove he wasn't the same frat-boy Neanderthal he was back in high school and college, so I gave him a chance."

The detective grumbled something incoherent under his breath, all the while jotting something down on his legal pad.

She went on, "When I realized he was still pretty much the same, though, I broke it off. Needless to say, he didn't take it well, which, may I add, was due to his huge ego—*not* because I really meant anything to him. That was it. End of story as far as I was concerned."

"But not for Tricia." Officer Reynolds leaned forward, staring her down. "It bothered her enough to wake up early to meet you at Guinefort House."

Her father let out some kind of grumble/growl. "Are you suggesting my daughter was having an illicit affair with that idio—pardon me—that man?"

"I'm not suggesting anything," he spat back.

Shae Johnson cleared her throat. "We're veering off track here," she said, directing her remark to the other two. When she glanced back at Quinn, her expression softened. "So, she came by the kennels to torment you, then she left. Later that same day, you and your brother met up with Tricia and her sister to look at a unit at the lofts. While there, any hard feelings on either side were appeased. Am I getting the gist of what happened?"

"Yes, we left that loft on good terms. In fact, she apologized for trying to involve me with—in her words—'her drama.'"

Aiden stopped writing, meeting her eyes. "Did she elaborate on what she meant by 'her drama'?"

Quinn nodded. "Tricia said something along the lines of Scott wanting to be his own man, something she was trying to help him with—how, specifically, I have no idea." She shrugged her shoulders. "Sorry—I don't have any more info."

Officer Johnson nodded. "Okay, it's been a long night. Why don't we skip forward to later in the evening."

Quinn was grateful for the redirect. "I was sound asleep, when RBG—that's my dog—started growling and barking. I had the bedroom windows open, and she was spooked by something she heard or smelled outside. Usually, it's just a squirrel or a bird, and I pet her until she settles. But tonight, nothing I did or said was working, so I got dressed and decided to let her sniff it out for herself."

Shae Johnson stopped writing. "Do you remember what time this happened?"

"Yes, I remember because I glanced at my phone and got very annoyed. It was 1:07 AM."

Her father pinned her with a steely glare. "Did you ever *think*, Quinn Victoria, to just close the window instead of going out in the dead of night?"

Detective Harrington leaned forward, a brief touch on the table, near her father's forearm. "Finn, you've got plenty of time to give her a proper dad scolding later, but for now, we really need to get this statement down."

Finn frowned but also acknowledged Aiden's sound advice with a nod. Meanwhile, Quinn wondered when those two had gotten to be on a first-name basis. Wasn't it just yesterday that Aiden had been hanging with Bash, rough-housing in the front yard, her dad chastising them to stay away from his wife's prized peonies?

"Anyway, as I told y'all before, we were walking down Knoll Street when I heard a thud, like something being dropped. Then a car door slammed and took off—fast. RBG and I bolted over but were too late to see the car because there was a lot of white smoke from where it sped off. Plus, the lights were out around the park. We found her right after that."

Officer Reynolds scratched the back of his neck, sporting a confused look. "And you mean to tell me, you and Tricia had no other contact besides the run-ins earlier that day, first at the abbey and then at the lofts?"

She nodded again. "Yes, that's what I'm saying."

"And you hadn't had any contact with that Hauser guy for years either?"

"Well, I did run into him earlier at Church Street Eats while grabbing breakfast with my cousin, but other than that, no."

He scoffed, crossing his arms. "Well, I find that highly unusual—and suspect—that these two just magically appeared in your life on the same day Tricia Pemberley was murdered."

Quinn dug into her messenger bag until she felt what she was searching for and then tossed it across the table toward them. "If you think I'm hiding some secret relationship with Scott, or hiding anything for that matter, then take my phone and see for yourself. You won't find any texts or emails from either of them."

He eyed her phone. "What's your password?"

"I have the same password for everything, which I know isn't smart, but it's easier that way. It's written in the notes section. Oh, and the code to get into the phone is 1993."

Aiden pressed both fingertips into his temples. "You use the year you were born as your code? You *do* realize how unsafe that is, right?"

Quinn sighed. Whatever adrenalin spike she'd experienced beforehand had long worn off. "I'll change it when you give me the phone back."

Shae Johnson took the phone. "Commentary aside, let me confirm: except for the incidents you shared, you haven't had any other contact with Tricia or Scott recently?"

"Up until yesterday, I hadn't seen or spoken to either one of them in years, which was why I was surprised Scott asked to talk to me."

Aiden wrote some more on his pad, not looking up. "What was that about?"

She eyed her father, who gave her a brief nod. "You'll have to ask Scott because I have no idea what he wanted except to tell me he got engaged. Then, his mother made a mean crack about

Tricia and then yelled at him to sit with her. Frankly, I thought the whole exchange was unnecessary and a little weird. We have nothing to do with each other except for living in the same town."

Aiden stopped writing and peered at her. "What crack did Milly Hauser make?"

"She complained that Tricia was—in her words, not mine— "only in sales." Then, my brother showed up and Scott left us alone."

All three officers' phones beeped, almost in unison. Officer Johnson and Aiden stopped taking notes, both checking their messages.

Aiden shared a look with the other two, then stood up. "All right, I think we have what we need for now. Make sure to include everything you know in your written statement." Aiden checked his phone again. "One more thing: Can anyone else verify you were home all evening until you went for a walk with RBG?"

Quinn hunched her shoulder toward her ears. "Um, I don't know. You're free to talk to my dog."

Shae smiled. Her father chortled to himself. But Aiden's grim expression indicated that he did not find her funny. "But there wasn't anyone else over?"

"What—you mean like a boyfriend?"

He blew out a frustrated breath. "*Yes*, Quinn, like a boy-friend. Stop stalling and answer the question."

She glanced over at her dad, thinking, *What the heck is that about?*, only to find him biting the side of his lip, fighting a smile.

Quinn refocused on the surly detective. "No, I didn't have a boyfriend over."

"Okay then," Officer Johnson chimed in, "why don't you write down everything you told us. Sign it too. In the meantime"—she picked up Quinn's phone—"I'll get this over to our IT specialists. They'll search your texts and emails to verify your statement in terms of lack of recent contact with Tricia or Scott. Assuming there's nothing incriminating in it and that the Huttons can verify your account of events at Church Street Eats, you should have it back in a day or so. We'd also like to interview your brother, to verify your story."

"Fine. Do what you have to do."

Her dad dragged his chair back along the carpet, then stood up. "Aiden, a moment?"

He gave one of those chin lifts men give to each other, and they filed out of the room. She took hold of the pen and started writing. She wished they had given her a laptop, or even a type-writer, because writing longhand took quite awhile. She had to stop several times to rub out the cramps in her hand.

As soon as she was done, she left the room, holding onto her bag of clothes. Daria was waiting for her.

"You okay?"

Quinn blew out an exhausted breath. "Yeah, I know they're just doing their jobs, but that was annoying."

Sister Daria cracked her knuckles. "That's true for Aiden and Shae. But what's the other one's deal?"

"You mean Officer Reynolds?"

Her cousin watched him stalking away from the other officers, the dark cloud above his head almost visible to the naked eye. "Yeah, there's something really off about him."

Quinn was relieved her cousin felt the same vibe. "Totally. You missed it, but during the interview, he kept calling Tricia by her first name, like he knew her. I've watched enough cop shows to know they say phrases like 'the victim' or 'the body.' They don't personalize like that."

Daria kept her voice low. "Do you *really* think she was murdered?"

"None of us can be sure until there's an autopsy, but I'm telling you, Daria, no twenty-five-year-old dies of natural causes looking the way she did."

"You never told me. How bad was it?"

Quinn would never forget the sight of Tricia, lying there on the paved section of the park, her limbs in unnatural, distorted angles; a sharp contrast to the fluid symmetry of the compass rose. "That's because I don't want you having the same picture in your head as I do in mine. Part of her face looked paralyzed. Her body jack-knifed like a twisted pretzel . . . Trust me, it'll take me forever to get over that sight."

Her cousin's brows scrunched together. "That sounds like she had a stroke of some kind."

Quinn readjusted the strap of her messenger bag across her chest. "I don't know—do healthy twenty-five-year-olds have strokes?"

"We need to find out."

"We?"

Daria nodded. "Absolutely. Listen, no one who knows you thinks you did this terrible thing. But for some reason, that cop has it in for you. We need to find out the truth before he tries to pin this on you."

"C'mon," Quinn tsked. "He may be a tool, but do you really think he'd exclude evidence that would prove I'm innocent?"

"I don't know, Ms. Hufflepuff, but you're my family, so we're not going to take that chance by assuming he has the best of intentions."

Daria meant business. Growing up more like sisters than cousins, they'd had countless nicknames for each other. When she used "Ms. Hufflepuff," it was her cue that Quinn was being too trusting and naive. Those Harry Potter house monikers worked both ways.

"Someone's being extra cynical today—and that means *you*, Ms. Slytherin."

"I make no apologies. I'd rather be cynical then caught off guard and have you suffer the consequences."

"I read this study the other day—this team of experts estimated that at least four percent of people on death row right now were unjustly convicted. So that means if we had a hundred of those inmates standing here, four would be innocent."

"You're such a nerd." Daria fidgeted with her cross necklace. "But stop reading that stuff. You're not going to jail. Not on my watch."

"I'm not worried about going to jail. I'm ticked off there's a murderer in our town. Maybe even more than one if that doctor didn't die from natural causes. I didn't like Tricia all that much, but it doesn't matter anymore. Vienna should have been her safe place. We need to find out what's going on. We need to take our town back."

Chapter Five

"You may be as different as the sun and the moon, but the
same blood flows through both your hearts.
You need her as she needs you."
—George R. R. Martin, *A Game of Thrones*

"There's crime scene tape all over this place. Everything's
blocked off. What do you think we're going to find that
the police didn't?"

It was a fair question, one Quinn didn't have an answer for,
at least not yet. Since both had only grabbed a few hours of
sleep after being at the police station, their combined mental
clarity was running half-speed, at best. That's what she got for
spending most of the night trying to clear her name.

Quinn still insisted on returning to Sarah Walker Mercer
Park, the place where she had found Tricia's body. Only three-
quarters of an acre, the park sat catty-corner between the elementary and high schools. Her mama had told her the area
used to be, of all things, a public works property yard, but the
town had decided to clean it up in an effort to attract more
families by building more green space. After Tricia's death,
Quinn wondered if anyone would ever come back.

"Remember how you used to find me here, cutting classes?"

Quinn chuckled. "Actually, I'd forgotten about that. I'd always find you making out with what's-his-name."

"Spencer. Spencer Something-Something," Daria answered.

"Right. Whatever happened to him?"

Daria gave a crooked smile. "Last I heard, he came out of the closet and was living with his boyfriend in Richmond. They own a construction company together. I guess being with me confirmed for him he wasn't into women."

Quinn took her hand. "Please tell me you don't believe that." She studied Daria's face for clues. "I may not have remembered his name, but I *do* recall he was over the moon for you. And rightfully so because you are a crazy-beautiful, scary-smart girl that any man would be lucky to call his."

Meanwhile, throughout Quinn's little speech, Daria looked like she was holding back a cackle.

Quinn's brows came to a "V." "What?"

Daria pulled her cousin close and gave her a tight hug. "I was kidding about what I said." She let go of Quinn. "Spencer was probably just trying to figure himself out back then, which was fine with me because I wasn't looking for anything serious anyway. He sure was beautiful, but he wasn't joining Mensa anytime soon. Besides, you know I don't believe being gay is a choice. We're born the way God made us, and He doesn't make mistakes. Love is love and all that."

Quinn had to admit she was relieved by her cousin's declaration. When Daria had written to her about her intentions of becoming a nun, Quinn knew full well the Anglican Church's conservative position on gay rights. She'd wondered if Daria had changed her stance but had been afraid to ask. Now that she'd received her answer, Quinn had other questions waiting in the queue.

"Hmm, can't imagine the sisters of your order are clamoring to march at the next pride parade with you anytime soon."

That comment made Daria squint in her direction. "No, probably not."

"So, how do you deal with that, then?"

Daria shrugged. "We agreed to disagree. That's all."

She wanted to do a deep dive into that whole "agree to disagree" landmine, but thought it best to keep the conversation light, especially since they weren't enjoying a casual springtime stroll in the park. They were searching for clues left by a killer.

RBG was pulling her, so Quinn let out the retractable leash some, walking through the parts of the park they still had access to. "So, wait a second—did you know Spencer was gay back then? And why didn't you take him back to your house to fool around? Both your parents were always at work, so you'd have had the place to yourselves. Why go to a public park?"

Daria gave her a look like Spencer wasn't the only one who was thick. "Because I didn't want him to think he had free rein, that's why. I might have been rebellious, but there was no way I was going to sleep with him." She let out a soft laugh, shaking her head. "Of course, in hindsight, Spencer never exactly pushed to go home with me—and he always kept the action very PG. I'm thinking there may have been a sign or two I missed. Oops."

Daria went back to dragging her flip-flopped feet, her toes combing through the Kentucky bluegrass like rake tines. Quinn was doing the same, even though RBG kept trying to pull her to the other side of the road.

"Hold on, girl. Let's look around here first."

It really was a shame someone thought this cozy little park was the place to bring such ugliness. It had a rain garden and walking paths, all surrounding the paved inset compass rose marking the true north of Vienna, or at least where they memorialized those they loved and missed. There was a seating area honoring the late Sarah Walker Mercer. She'd died when Quinn was only two years old, so Quinn didn't remember her, but she had heard, more times than she could recall, Ms. Sarah called "the mama of the neighborhood." She had been the custodian for Louise Archer Elementary School for years, and living next door to the school allowed her the opportunity to care for anyone in need. There was also a memorial tree planted to honor Maxine Shelley Turner, "Max" to her friends. She was an honors student from their town and a victim in the Virginia Tech shooting of April 2007. Neither Quinn nor Daria had known her, but everyone had been stricken by Max's loss. Somehow, this small patch of manicured green was able to hold the pain of a whole town without being weighted down by it. A miracle, the more Quinn pondered on it. Next time they came to this park, there would probably be a memorial tree or bench in Tricia's memory.

The sinewy arms of neon tape blocked a proper exploration, so Sister Daria and Quinn walked along the edges of the grass, scanning for anything even resembling a clue.

Her cousin batted gnats away from her eyes. "I don't even know what I'm looking for."

Quinn sighed, the heaviness not leaving room for her hopeful heart. "I know. Me too."

In spite of Quinn's best efforts to stay near the garden, RBG kept insisting they explore across the street. "All right, fine. Have it your way," she relented. She crossed Nutley Street, where the car had screeched away into the night. Quinn spotted the tire treads, seared onto the asphalt like a newly inked tattoo. She stopped and took a bunch of photos of them on her phone. Not like she'd know what to do with them, but she wasn't going to ignore any markings the potential killer might have left behind.

There were several houses on the street, each with their own personalities: colonials next to split-levels alongside modern Craftsman. Her section of town, northwest Vienna, wasn't a cookie-cutter suburb, and Quinn appreciated the small slice of heterogeneity in an otherwise homogenous area.

The sun peeked from behind a chorus of clouds, casting much-needed light and warmth down on them. Something shiny glittered by a fence a few yards away. RBG got there first, sniffing until Quinn was able to bend down and examine what had caught the sunlight.

It was an iPhone with a Kelly-green silicone cover, enough of a match with the grass that it was able to hide in plain sight.

"Daria! Come here quick!"

She dug into her messenger bag for a pencil and a plastic bag, the kind used to pick up dog mess. Using the end of her pencil, she turned the phone over.

"What's up? What'd ya find?" She hovered over Quinn's bent frame.

"You're blocking the light. Move over." Quinn noticed the iPhone was the latest model, so there wasn't the old "home" button like in previous incarnations.

Daria positioned herself in front of Quinn and out of the sun, crouching down and balancing on the balls of her feet. "We shouldn't touch it."

Quinn eyed her. "We aren't," she said, putting her hand inside the clean plastic bag. "See? An instant glove. Of sorts."

With care, she used her wrapped hand to press the side button. The screen flashed on, making both of them rear their heads back in surprise.

"Look, cave girl. Fire."

Quinn laughed hard enough to cough.

Daria peered closer. "It's actually kind of cool, the phone still having power. It's like a modern-day Chanukah miracle. Except, of course, it's April. And instead of keeping a menorah lit for eight nights on little oil, the phone battery survives for over twenty-four hours on just five percent power."

"Way to keep things Old Testament," Quinn answered. "Look at the home screen."

Sure enough, there was a photo of Tricia with Scott. He was on bended knee, ring in hand, while she cupped her face, crying happy tears.

"He must've arranged for someone to take their picture right at the big moment," Quinn said, her voice soft. "Look how happy they are."

"Were," Daria corrected.

"I really was happy for them," she said. "As happy as I could be for two people so utterly self-involved."

Daria's expression softened. "I know, sweetie."

The screen shut off. Quinn was about to pick it up with her bagged hand, but Daria stopped her. "Better not. You don't need any more heat than you're already getting. We need to call the fuzz."

Quinn bit her bottom lip to keep from laughing. "Ten-four, good buddy. Is there a reason why you're talking like a rerun of *Starsky and Hutch*?"

Daria didn't return the humor. "The sooner we get this phone to the police, the quicker you get off that crazy cop's hit list of suspects."

"Fine." Quinn stood in place while reaching for her phone-well, not exactly her phone, but an old one her parents gave her to use in the interim. She paused.

Daria also stood up. "What is it?"

"I don't know. Feels weird calling Aiden."

"You're not calling him for a date; you're letting him know that Vienna's own *Rizzoli and Isles* found evidence his entire department missed."

Quinn whacked her chest with her fist, trying to clear her lungs. "Oh, *that* should go over well."

Sister Daria studied her. "You still like him, even after all these years?"

"It doesn't matter. He has always and will always see me as a little kid."

"Even after your welcome-home party? You looked uh-mazing that night."

Quinn picked at the hangnail on her thumb. As close as they were, she hadn't shared with her cousin the buildup and letdown of that night. Not because she didn't trust Daria to handle her with care; more like she was too humiliated to admit her delusions out loud.

"He patted my head and called me 'Quinnie.'"

Daria winced. "Ouch."

Quinn gave her a look.

"Well then, he's obviously not as smart as everyone thinks he is."

Quinn shrugged. "People like what they like. I'm not going to hold a grudge because I'm not what he wants."

Sister Daria offered a conciliatory smile. "I'm thinking maybe you're the one who should've been the nun, not me. Your response is much kinder than mine would have been."

She didn't want to talk about Aiden anymore. The unrealized fantasy was still too depressing. "All right, let's get this over with." She slid the bar on her phone and called the elusive detective/rock star, Aiden Broadwater Harrington.

He answered on the first ring.

Chapter Six

"It is our choices, Harry, that show what we truly are,
far more than our abilities."
—J. K. Rowling, *Harry Potter and the Chamber of Secrets*

"Why am I not surprised to find you two skulking around my crime scene and getting into more trouble?"

Quinn couldn't believe her ears. "Getting into trouble? Did you hit your head on the way over here? Because from where I'm standing, I'm quite the helper."

Sister Daria pretended to scowl. "Ahem." She gestured back and forth between them with her forefinger. "*We* are quite the helpers."

Quinn gave a brisk nod. "Apologies, cousin . . . we would appreciate a little, well . . . appreciation."

Aiden towered over her, arms crossed. "And I'm trying to catch a killer, something I can't do if you're tampering with evidence."

"But she didn't!" Daria said, elbowing her. "Show him."

Quinn reached into her messenger bag. "Yes, let me show you, my doubting detective, oh ye of little faith." She pulled out the clean plastic doggie bag and pencil. "See? I used these as a makeshift glove and stylus. Clever, eh?"

Sister Daria tossed her fiery-red hair over her shoulder, raising her chin. "We're ready for that mea culpa–slash–thank-you anytime now."

Aiden gazed up to the heavens, muttering, "Deliver me" under his breath.

Quinn leaned into her cousin. "I don't think that's an apology."

Daria gave him the stink eye. "No, I don't think it is. Rude, by the way."

Aiden opened his mouth to respond, but then a squad car pulled up to the curb—flashing lights and all—where the three of them were standing. RBG pressed her body into Quinn's legs, something she did when she was in protective mode. Officer Reynolds and Shae Johnson unfolded themselves from the car. Quinn stroked RBG's head and down her back, letting her know everything was okay.

Sister Daria's whole face scrunched, like something reeked. "Oh don't look now, but the *other* one without manners is here too." She straightened her spine as they approached. "Just so you know, I'm this close"—she held up her thumb and forefinger, an inch apart—"to reporting your conduct to your superior."

"Good afternoon to you too, Sister." Officer Reynolds adjusted the holster on his belt. He looked to be around their age, with sable-colored hair and brown eyes. He would've been more handsome if his face wasn't set in a permanent scowl. But it was, so he wasn't.

As Quinn watched Officers Johnson and Reynolds standing side by side, something hit her. "Wait a second—aren't you usually partnered with Officer Carter?"

Now it was Shae's turn to frown. "The captain thought it'd be good for me to partner with Officer Reynolds for a little while."

Sister Daria barked out a laugh. "You mean he's hoping you'll teach him how to *behave*, since everyone witnessed how awful he's been to Quinn." She met Wyatt's gaze. "Who, by the way, is innocent of any crime you may think she's committed in that head of yours."

That vein in the middle of his forehead was beating like a drum again, but Shae gave him a "don't go there" glare, so he didn't take her cousin's bait. "We heard over the radio, you found evidence relating to Trish's murder?"

Quinn and Daria locked eyes, both thinking the same thing: for a new cop in town, he sure sounded familiar with Tricia Pemberley. Only those closest to her were allowed to call her "Trish."

Her cousin pointed toward the fence line. "Yes, it's right there, exactly where we found it."

That's when Quinn noticed Shae Johnson was holding a couple of evidence bags and latex gloves.

Aiden reached out. "Here, let me," he instructed.

She gave them over. He slid on the gloves and opened the evidence bag, bending down to the grass, in a fluid motion, to retrieve Tricia's phone, then sealing it right away. She couldn't help but marvel at the grace of his movements, at how someone so built could move with such ease.

Wyatt Reynolds stepped forward. "I'm happy to take those in for you, sir."

Sister Daria huffed. "Oh, so you can try and frame my cousin for murder? I don't think so."

His face turned beet-red. "You know, just 'cause you sometimes wear that penguin getup doesn't mean I won't cite you for interfering with this investigation."

Sister Daria stepped forward, getting right in his face. "Calling you out on your offensive and biased conduct isn't a crime,

Officer Reynolds. But harassing innocent citizens of this town *is*, the last time I checked."

Spittle gathered in the corners of his mouth. "You know what else is a crime? Planting evidence and pretending it's something you found."

She reared back.

Quinn piped in. "She would never—*I* would never do such a thing!"

His eyes squinted. "Pretty convenient if you ask me, finding her phone."

Officer Johnson tugged at his sleeve. "You need to back up, Reynolds," she told him. "Besides, hate to break it to you, but it's plausible we missed this one, with the phone case blending in with the grass and it being just outside our search radius." Shae Johnson kept going. "And think about it: Why would Quinn have called us—*twice*—if she were guilty?"

Officer Reynolds scowled. "Because she wants to appear innocent." He tapped his head. "Reverse psychology."

It was now Quinn's turn to look up to the heavens and mutter, "Deliver me."

Aiden approached him. He was a good four to five inches taller than Wyatt, and Quinn noticed how Officer Reynolds thrust his chin out and squared his shoulders back—a shorter man's habit, one she remembered Scott doing often. Quinn felt like Jane Goodall with an ape in the wild, seeing the runt attempting some sort of dominance in spite of being out-alphaed.

"I'm going to have Shae submit the evidence, Reynolds. That way there's no chance of anyone being accused of impropriety. And I suggest you rein in that attitude. If I have to warn you again, I will not hesitate to write you up. Do we understand each other?"

Reynolds's cheeks puffed out like a blowfish. Quinn could almost taste the bitter in his mouth.

"Yes, sir," he muttered.

"I'll check these into evidence straightaway," Officer Johnson said, her gaze settling on the cousins. "Our tech guys will comb through her data. This is an important find. Thanks."

Daria threw her hands up. "See? Now *that's* how you say thank-you."

Quinn ignored her cousin's outburst. "I read a study by the United Nations that stated while most men are murdered by a stranger, the majority of women—I think it was fifty-eight percent—are murdered by a partner or family member."

Three pairs of eyes stared back at her.

"What? It means her phone will, most likely, have pertinent personal info to lead you to her killer. That's a good thing."

Officer Reynolds's mouth was hanging open. "Now how and why do you have that kind of information?"

Aiden and Sister Daria said in unison. "That's just Quinn."

She ignored both of them. "Anyway, it's going to help loads." She shoved her hands deep into her pockets. "Especially if she's like most people our age. We live on our phones."

"Right, well, I'll meet you two back at the station in a bit," Aiden said to the officers.

"All right." Shae took the filled evidence bags from him. "You two? Maybe leave the rest of the police work to us from now on."

She might have made it sound like a question, but there was no mistaking that it was a command. Shae wrapped her hand around the bend of Officer Reynolds's elbow, almost dragging him back to the squad car like a stubborn mule.

As soon as they were inside the car and headed in the opposite direction, Quinn let out a sigh of relief. "Well, glad that's done."

"Indeed." Daria glanced at the time on her phone. "I need to get back to the abbey."

"Yeah, I need to get to the bookstore. I have a ton of projects to work on."

Aiden's gray eyes darkened, something she noticed they did whenever he had a lot on his mind, as if he had his own rain clouds following him around. "Listen, you two finding that phone . . . it's appreciated, but Reynolds made a point others can make just as easily."

Her eyes widened. "What—that we planted that phone there? That's ridiculous."

He blew out an exasperated breath. "*You* know that and *I* know that. But others don't. The more time I have to spend proving you're innocent, the less time goes into finding out who's guilty."

He had a point there.

"But your cousin is right," he added, taking a couple of steps into Quinn's space, close enough for her to catch a hint of his soap-and-cotton scent. "You two found something my entire team missed."

Her gaze focused on the tops of his shoes, suddenly too shy to meet his eye. "Oh, well, it's understandable, with that green cover and the tall grass not being mowed by the fence. Anyone could've missed it."

"Everyone else did miss it, but not you," he said, his stare so strong she felt it warm her skin. "I'd try recruiting you for the police force, but Adele and Finn would tan my hide for even thinking it."

She looked up, to determine if he was teasing her or not, but all she could see was him beaming down at her like the sun framed around his head. Her mouth went bone dry.

"C'mon, let me give you both a ride."

* * *

Quinn should've known something was up as soon as she walked into the bookstore. Instead of being at her garden, hosting the Walk on the Hill, her mom was behind the register. That was her first clue. Being greeted by her pained expression? That was clue number two.

"Oh, honey, I didn't know you were planning on coming in today. I would've told you to take the day off, especially after that ghastly scene at the police station."

Usually Mama Caine welcomed her with a warm smile or chilled tea. Her dad would glance up from his book, his round spectacles perched on his forehead like a hood ornament, and give a short nod before returning to his reading. And then, if it was busy, Quinn would pitch in behind the counter, serving drip coffee, wine, or a variety of easily assembled nibbles. If it was quiet, she'd retreat to her office in the back.

It was late Saturday afternoon, and besides her parents, there wasn't another soul in the entire store. She double-checked the time on her watch: it was just shy of five o'clock, exactly when the place should've been abuzz with people enjoying glasses of sauvignon blanc or a cold pale ale. Usually, there would already be customers assembled on the white leather cushion stools in a row by the counter while others would be seated outside on the front patio.

They were more than customers, really. They were her neighbors and friends, people she'd known all her life, as well as new faces of those who had just moved to Vienna. Because Prose & Scones was more than a bookstore: it was the town's unofficial welcome center.

One of the ways the Caines made everyone feel at home was by planting annuals and tending to the perennials in the patio's surrounding flower boxes. Virginia bluebells, three-petaled purple spiderworts, and orange daylilies as bright and brilliant as summer decorated the outside of their shop. Even though the town did a splendid job of landscaping, mother and daughter took it upon themselves to do some extra gardening along the green patch that divided the street from the sidewalk. Not too much—just a little something-something, to make their slice of Vienna more colorful and fabulous.

There was also a lovely bench nearby, painted with classic book titles under stars, parked right before the patio entrance. That was Quinn's preferred seat when they weren't hard at work, not only because the bench artist had depicted copies of her favorite books but also because of its ideal placement in the sun.

Quinn froze by the register, the perfect vantage point to survey everything around her: the store, the patio, and the bench—all vacant. If it weren't for the Spotify playlist strumming in the background, there wouldn't have been a sound.

That is, until the toilet flushed.

Her father emerged from the bathroom, surprise coloring his features as soon as he spotted Quinn. "Oh, we should have called." He plastered on a smile. "Go home and rest. You've had a day of it already."

"Wow, you two really suck at this whole distracting thing." She whizzed past her mama at the register and then her dad by the lavatory. "Excuse me, I have work to do."

Before either could stop her, Quinn had made her way to the back of the store and opened the door to her office.

As usual, there was her desk, felt-lined, with many of her bookbinding tools laid out like a surgeon's instruments: her awl, different-sized bone folders, and her favorite English backing hammer. On the shelves she had stocked a variety of adhesives, small rolls of linen tape, stacks of book boards, and a ream of white woven bound paper.

The adjoining bookcase housed all her current bookbinding projects. Not long ago, the well-maintained piece had been teeming with old books and photo albums, aged yearbooks and rare diaries—assignments that would take her months to refurbish. On last count, she was working on three simultaneously, with over forty in the queue.

It only took her five seconds to ascertain that she was now down to twenty-three.

Hot tears stung her eyes as Quinn tried to swallow the sorrow lodged in her throat. A large, warm hand rested on her shoulder. A chin nestled on top of her head.

"They'll come back around. You'll see," her dad said into her hair.

"These are supposed to be my people. They've known me forever." Quinn willed her voice steady. "How could they think I would do such a thing?"

He turned her around to face him. "They don't know *what* to think, with the shock of it all. What you're witnessing is a knee-jerk reaction. Not many may have liked Tricia Pemberley, but that doesn't mean they aren't feeling this loss in a profound way."

Her mother hurried over. "Listen to him, honey. What you're seeing is a small sample size, not the majority."

"Not by a long shot," her father added.

Quinn couldn't help but balk. "How can you say that when there's not one customer in here, and with half the projects gone!"

"Because I'm older than you and, hence, can take the long view." Her father pushed his glasses up the bridge of his nose. "Give them time. Soon they'll remember who *they* are, and then they'll remember who *you* are."

Adele stroked her daughter's hair, cupping her chin in her hand. "The people who took back their books were people who

83

don't know you—or our family—well at all. You stay strong, you hear me? This here's just a tiny glitch on the radar. It'll pass, no matter how big a mouth Milly Hauser has."

The blood drained from her face. "Is Scott's mom telling everyone I killed Tricia?"

"Adele," her father warned.

She gave him her "oh hush" look. "It's better she hears it from us than from some other busybody out there." Adele let go of Quinn's face. "She's carrying on, saying you must've been more devastated by his engagement than you let on and that you convinced yourself that if Tricia was out of the way, Scott would find his way back to you."

Quinn pressed the backs of her fingers to her lips, trying not to vomit.

"If it's any consolation, you're not the only one Milly's indicting. She also castigated Trina, right in front of King and Cole."

King & Cole was the local funeral home. Founded in 1881, it was also the oldest business in town.

"What did she say?"

Her mother brushed wisps of hair out of her way. "I don't know. I wasn't there. I only heard what happened secondhand, on our way into the store today. Supposedly everything started off fine enough. The Hausers accompanied the Pemberleys to make all the arrangements. But as they were leaving the funeral home, Milly Hauser started carrying on, right there on the street, in front of everyone, how she wouldn't be surprised if Trina turned out to be the killer because she was raving mad with jealousy over her twin marrying first, especially to such a prize as her son."

Quinn blinked. "Wow, she's even more delusional than I thought."

"Milly Hauser may not be my favorite individual, but she's a mother who loves her children. Seeing your child in pain is an extraordinary hell I don't wish on anyone."

Her father stretched up to turn off the light in the back office. "Indeed, but let's not lose sight of the fact that William and Abigail Pemberley are the grieving parents—not Millicent Hauser."

"Dad, why are you shutting off the light? I was about to go in there and get some work done."

He peered down, his spectacles slipping down to the tip of his aquiline nose. "I'm calling time of death on the workday."

Quinn groaned. "Dad jokes? Really?"

Her mother glanced at the watch on her wrist. "But we don't close until eight."

Finn Caine cleared his throat. "I am very well aware, love of my life, but after selling only two coffees and a tacky greeting card so far, I say we pack it in."

Adele's hands went to her hips. "Excuse me, but we don't sell 'tacky' greeting cards."

His brows perked up. "The card said, 'Everyone wants your opinion. Signed, Alcohol.'"

Quinn laughed, snorting a little. Adele let out a titter.

"Fine, let's close early. We now have ourselves a free Saturday night. Any suggestions?" her mother asked him.

His impish glint faded away. "As much as I'd prefer to take my bride out, we need to go to Whole Foods and stock up."

"For what?" Quinn asked.

Awareness set into her mother's features. "He's right. We need to make a meal for the Pemberleys. Offer our condolences, even if the funeral's delayed because they're waiting on the autopsy."

The idea of Tricia being the subject of such an invasive examination was almost too much for Quinn to bear. She turned her head away, willing herself not to lose it.

Finn Caine brought her in for a hug. "Listen, kiddo, deep down the Hauser's and the Pemberley's know you didn't do this heinous thing. But you're a walking, breathing reminder of what was taken from them. Milly may be letting her ire out on you, but that won't last. Carlson has always known how to calm his wife. He'll get her to reason. Then, soon enough, the real culprit will be found and brought to justice."

Her mother joined their hug. "Until then, hold onto us. Because until they catch who did this, you might be the town scapegoat."

Chapter Seven

"Resist much, obey little."
—Walt Whitman, *Caution*

Quinn must have walked through those metal and glass double doors thousands of times. Even before she attended James Madison High School as a freshman, she had often visited on Bash's behalf. Football games. End-of-year awards ceremonies. She knew her way around the halls well before her own first day there. Another reason for her familiarity: her family's church rented the high school's auditorium for their Sunday services. Maybe someday the Anglican congregation would build their own edifice, but for now, they preferred that the money raised go to help people in need instead of to a building fund.

Quinn really wished Bash was with her now, but he had been called into the fire station unexpectedly and couldn't join the Caine clan for church that Sunday morning. At least her parents could make it, as well as her Aunt Johanna and Uncle Jerry. She spied Daria on the dais, tuning her acoustic guitar with the other church musicians in preparation for the service.

It wasn't like she was alone—not even close—but she kept thinking about what Tricia had said about her leaning on her brother for protection. Had she been right? Did she use Bash as a shield when she felt unsure of herself? And if so, did the habit stem from just having an older sibling, or was she relying on his being a guy—a good-looking, popular one at that—as a way to avoid uncomfortable confrontations?

She suspected there was a grain of truth in Tricia's words because they stung. Even with her delayed reaction, she still experienced a physical sensation, right under her ribs. The Pemberley sisters might have resembled twin Barbie dolls, but to assume that their *Real Housewives* appearance foretold all they were would be a tremendous disservice to them both. They had earned high marks throughout school, not an easy get in the nationally ranked Fairfax County school district. They were the tops in their field, another hard-earned accomplishment in the competitive Northern Virginia real estate market. And they had deserved their mean-girl reputations not just by being aloof and callous, but through their ability to assess other people's frailties fast enough to spew back the perfect zinger. A bull's-eye every time. Quinn always thought it a shame they used their powers in such a twisted way. Because even Darth Vader eventually came back from the dark side. She had hoped, someday, they would too.

Plenty of people offered Quinn a tentative smile, a brief wave, but they kept their distance. She wasn't sure if it was because they thought being near her might be bad luck, like finding a body was somehow contagious. Or perhaps they were giving her space out of respect for her privacy even while in public. She really wanted to assume the latter but was afraid it was the former.

Truth was, she didn't know what to think anymore. Quinn was numb and exhausted. She followed her family, without thought, through the aisle. Quinn was always last because she preferred the end seat. It was less claustrophobic for her.

"You've got a lot of nerve, showing your face, especially in a house of God."

She swirled around. It was Trina Pemberley, standing behind her. Seeing Tricia's twin made her gasp, like seeing a ghost in the flesh. Same ash-blonde bob and wide-set hazel eyes. Same rose-gold nail polish. Even though her glare contorted her face, Trina was still beautiful, although she wasn't wearing her usual classic designer suit. She had opted for simple black jeans and a cream-colored, button-down Ralph Lauren shirt with a Kelly-green cardigan.

"Um, oh wow, Trina," she sputtered. "What are you doing here? This isn't your church." Quinn realized how awful that sounded. "I'm sorry. I didn't mean for it to come out that way. It's just . . . I can't even imagine what you're going through."

Trina ignored Quinn's condolences, her anger so strong it was like a living thing between them. With teeth. "I came here to see you. I need to hear you say it . . . admit what you did."

She was gob-smacked. "I—I swear, I didn't do anything, Trina."

"You're lying!" she screeched, silencing everyone around them, but Trina didn't notice. She grabbed Quinn's wrist. "Just tell me why . . . why would you kill my sister?"

Her throat closed up. "I—I didn't. I didn't do anything but take my dog for a walk and find her."

It was like Trina hadn't heard her. "While you were traipsing around the world, avoiding any real, adult responsibilities, my sister was building a multimillion-dollar business with me, fighting off the most eligible bachelors around, including *your* ex. Did it stick in your craw, witnessing all she had, seeing her take chances you'd never have the guts to even consider?"

"You know that's not true," Quinn hoarse-whispered.

"We understand you've been through a lot," her mother chimed in. "We would like to be here for you, if you'll let us."

A chorus of voices piped in, agreeing with Adele Caine.

"You all can believe Quinn's little saint act, but trust me when I tell you it's all a bunch of crap. She's jealous. She's so consumed by it that she lashed out and hurt the most important person to me." Her fury sliced through Quinn. "It had to be you—just admit it. You killed her. You killed my sister!"

"I'll get you, my pretty, and your little dog too."

Quinn pushed the sarcastic thought aside, trying to imagine how she'd react if someone she couldn't stand had found her brother dead in the middle of a park. She swallowed, the thought too horrible to let sink in. She glanced around, noticing Trina's parents weren't with her. "Listen, are you here on your own? Would you like to sit with us?" she asked. "You don't have to go through this by yourself. I want to find her killer as much as you do."

"Uh *no*, I will *never* sit near you, Quinn. The only place I want to see you sit is in jail for the rest of your life, and I'm not going to rest until that happens." She glanced around before her gaze locked over Quinn's shoulder, and she muttered, "That figures." Then she met Quinn's eye and said, "This isn't over. Not by a long shot."

Trina sidestepped out of her aisle, looking like she was ready to burst out crying, almost breaking into a run out of the high school auditorium/church. Quinn started to go after her, but someone from behind wove his arm around her waist and pulled her back to a hard-muscled front.

"Let her go. Give her time to cool off," the deep voice said. "Just know you did everything right just now."

She turned around, her gaze traveling north: inky black hair. Pale gray eyes. Broad frame in a blue chambray button-down shirt. No tie. It took her brain a minute to catch up with what her eyes were taking in.

"Aiden?"

He was holding her in his arms. "That's me."

"But what are you doing here? You never come to church."

It was true. The last time he had set foot in any house of God was when he and Bash had attended their friend's wedding at Temple Rodef Shalom, a reform synagogue in Falls Church. His mother was a lapsed Catholic, and his father was an atheist.

"I wouldn't say 'never'—just not in the last thirty-one years," he said, giving her a wink and, unfortunately, letting her go. "Move over already. I'm blocking the way for everyone."

Quinn spun her head around, only to see her entire family leaning forward, watching the two of them. Smiling bright and wide, looking like the Muppets.

"You heard the man: *Scoot*," she said, imploring them with her gaze to keep cool.

The Caines moved down a seat and, to their credit, kept their yappers shut.

Guess miracles do happen every day.

Pastor Johnny checked his microphone. "Everyone please take a seat. And let's pray for Trina and the Pemberley family."

Sister Daria and the other church musicians started playing "Awake, My Soul and With the Sun." It was one of Quinn's favorites.

She whispered. "Okay, for real now: Why are you here?"

Aiden's mouth was close to her ear, tickling the tiny hairs. "I have something for you." He reached into his back pocket, handing her a small, wrapped package.

"What is it?"

He let out a soft chuckle. "Open it and find out."

She took it from him, her heart beating into her throat as she ripped the newspaper wrapping. Quinn smiled because he had inadvertently used the Modern Love essay section of *The New York Times.*

"Not the usual gift wrap," he whispered.

"Oh please, you didn't need to get me anything at all."

As she peeled back the paper, she gasped: it was her phone! Also inside was a tiny, ivory square card that read:

You're in the clear. I never had a doubt. Love, Aiden

"I wish I had showed a couple of minutes before I did. Maybe I could've said something to Trina, helped calm her down."

She nodded. She heard him—technically. But all she kept thinking was: *Love, Aiden. He wrote "Love, Aiden."*

Quinn wanted to allow the glorious, silken liquid of those words to seep in and feed the seeds of hope that lay dormant, but she resisted. She wouldn't be a fool for far-fetched optimism again.

"So, I'm no longer a suspect?"

"You were never a suspect," he corrected.

"Then I'm no longer a person of interest?" she asked, keeping her voice low.

"Regarding the murder investigation? Not really. I mean, we're still waiting for the forensics on your clothes and shoes, but that's just a formality. Consider yourself in the clear."

"Will everybody please rise," the pastor instructed. Everyone stood up, but the two of them stayed put while the parishioners sang.

Aiden went on. "I can't share details of the investigation, but I could at least share this piece of news with you straightaway."

She turned the phone on its side, making sure the sound was off. "You could have easily dropped this off. You didn't have to come over here, in front of everyone."

His eyes gentled. "That's exactly why I *had* to come. Time to put all the gossip to rest."

Pastor Johnny motioned for the congregation to sit. Quinn glanced around, noticing even more smiles amid furtive glances.

"Anyone who knows you already knew the truth," he said, as if reading her mind. "Sometimes people just don't know what to say."

Quinn knew the feeling, because she didn't know what to say either. Between Trina confronting her and having her detective crush hand-deliver the good news, all the events had set off a deluge of emotions within her.

She somehow made it through the rest of the service, long enough to hear the pastor's sermon on the importance of avoiding idle gossip, quoting Ephesians 4:29 and James 1:26. At one point their eyes locked, and she felt as if he was speaking right to her, saying he had her back. It felt almost as good as having Aiden come down to church just to give her the good news. His presence was proof of her innocence, as everyone's gazes told her.

After Holy Communion, he concluded the service. Everyone around them buzzed with well wishes and heartfelt hugs. Perhaps because she was no longer a person of interest to the police, she could now see everyone and everything clearly. Her mental filter had taken her many convoluted thoughts and sifted through the emotional sediment until a clean feeling had finally washed her soul to say, "These *are* your people, and they believe in you."

Her father shook Aiden's hand. "Good to see you, Detective."

"Likewise. I had to give Quinn the good news in person."

Her dad nodded, patting him on the shoulder. "You being here, sitting next to my daughter, made a big statement, one I won't forget."

"Here, here," her auntie said. "I think such chivalrous acts call for one of my fresh baskets. You like tomatoes and buffalo mozzarella with basil?"

Aiden's eyes darted to Quinn before answering. "Who doesn't?"

Aunt Johanna clapped. "That's what I say too! I grow the basil and tomatoes in my garden. I'll throw in some cukes and okra too, but you're going to need to fry the okra. Only way they taste decent."

Her aunt Johanna had been born and raised one hundred ninety miles south, in Suffolk, Virginia. And she was a southern gal through and through, including having a killer recipe for fried okra. Although she'd say it was her homemade fried chicken and biscuits that besotted Uncle Jerry. They'd met at a dance while he was stationed at Langley Air Force Base in Hampton. He always liked to say her beauty and wit caught his attention, but it was her cooking that sealed the deal.

"It's true, son," her uncle said, adjusting his spectacles the same way her dad often did. Quinn never could decide if those kind of shared trait was a product of nature or nurture. "Best damn fried okra in all of Virginia, if you ask me. Her secret is putting beer in the—"

She swatted his upper arm with the back of her hand. "Jerome Reginald Caine! You will not share my culinary secrets with the free world! My mama and meemaw would roll in their graves if those leaked outside the family."

"Such family treasures would be lost on me anyhow, Doc," Aiden piped in. "I cook just well enough to stay alive and somewhat healthy."

Her mama and auntie's faces brightened. "Well then, Quinn should come over to your house sometimes and make you a batch," her auntie went on, the gleam in her eyes hard to miss.

"As a treat, of course. She also makes some tasty fried pickle chips."

Quinn could feel the blood rush to her cheeks. "They'll throw in a couple of camels and some goats to sweeten the dowry price if you act now," she mumbled. Fortunately, no one seemed to hear her.

Uncle Jerry had lost patience. "Let's get a move on now. The Nats game starts in thirty minutes, and I plan on eating an array of food not recommended by the CDC, the FDA, or my own personal physician. And I'll be doing all of this from my chair. At *home*."

"Quite right," her father chimed in. "Quinn, I know you were planning on accompanying us when we took all the food we made over to the Pemberleys', but considering what happened earlier, I think it's best just your mother and I go."

She couldn't argue with that logic. She wanted to offer her condolences to the family, but not at the price of upsetting Trina more. She might be a piece of work, but she was a piece of work who had just lost her other half—literally.

"Yes, go home, honey." Her mom stroked her daughter's hair. "Take RBG for a walk. Get some fresh air in your lungs."

"I can drive her," Aiden offered, his hands in his pockets as he rocked onto the heels of his shoes.

"That would be lovely." Adele gave Quinn a knowing smile. Quinn closed her eyes for a moment, only wishing the earth would crumble fast and swallow her whole. Could her mama be any more obvious?

"Hey, family!" Sister Daria headed their way, still holding onto her acoustic guitar. "Aiden, it's good to see you. When I saw you sitting with Quinn, I thought I was hallucinating for a second."

He chuckled. "Don't get too excited. My attendance today isn't the start of a new faith streak. I just came over to give your cousin back her phone."

"Well, that's nice of you." She kept her expression free of the same nonsense the rest of her family was sporting.

Thank you, cousin, for not prolonging the awkward.

But Sister Daria wasn't done. "You know, Quinn and I usually grab brunch after services, but I can't today. Maybe you two could go instead?"

Annnnd scratch that last thought about her being the "cool" one of the family.

"Oh, don't feel obligated to say yes," Quinn rushed to say. "I know how swamped you are with the investigation and all."

"Normally, I'd be happy to, but I'm due back at the station before noon. But as I said, I'll drive you home."

Even though Quinn was wiped, the idea of going home just then sounded depressing. "You know what? Just drop me off at the bookstore. I want to get to work."

Her dad's brows furrowed. "Are you sure? I've got Sarah covering for us today."

Sarah Katz was a longtime Prose & Scones staffer, having worked at the store before the Caines bought it from the original owner, Jen Morrow. She was the one who had held the Caines' hands when they first took over, because while Finn Caine was a fine lawyer and Adele had been a stellar landscape architect, they hadn't known diddly-squat about the book business when they'd started. If it hadn't been for Sarah, they'd have gone under before they had begun. In fact, it was with Sarah's encouragement that Quinn had become the only bookbinder in Vienna. Now that she was basically cleared of any wrongdoing, Quinn wanted to get back to it. It was her quiet way of saying thank-you to the people who had stuck by her.

"Nope, I've made up my mind." Quinn felt an unexpected boost of energy. It was time to *go*. She moved with the crowd out and down the aisle. She motioned for Aiden to follow. "See everybody later. Get a move on, Detective!"

He laughed and sauntered behind. Of course, she ended up being the one waiting because he took his sweet time getting to his SUV.

She shielded her eyes from the sun with her cupped hand. "Proud of yourself? Could you walk *any* slower?"

He squinted and smiled. "It was quite the show. At first, it was just a brisk walk, but then you broke into a half gallop and finally skipped the rest of the way. I forgot that about you."

"Forgot what about me?" Butterflies flapped their wings inside her stomach.

He dug into his pocket for his car keys but didn't press the remote button until he was close enough to open the car door for her himself.

"Thank you." She folded into the passenger seat and tucked both legs in.

He rested his forearm on top of the passenger door, dipping his head low enough to be able to make eye contact. "I'd forgotten how you entertain yourself even doing nothing."

"I do?"

His eyes held a playful glint. "Oh yeah, ever since we were kids. Skipping to the car, working out the song order for one of your playlists, then humming the songs to make sure they've got the right flow. You used to practice old school break-dance moves in your parents' kitchen when you thought no one was around." He glanced back down at her. "I've never met anyone who could make even the most prosaic activities their own little party."

Her mouth gaped.

"Watch your hands and feet," he instructed before shutting the door.

What just happened?

He got in on the other side and closed his door. "Ready to go?" he asked before pushing the button for the ignition.

She nodded, made mute by his soliloquy.

Quinn knew she was being ridiculous, but her body was also reacting to being in an enclosed space with Aiden. Her palms got sweaty. Her mouth became sandpaper.

"Hello? Earth to Quinnie?"

Ugh, that nickname again.

"Do me a favor, Aiden. Don't call me Quinnie."

Silence.

Wow, did I say that out loud?

Yes—yes, you did.

Aiden put the car in drive. "My bad. I thought you liked the nickname."

From my family? Sure. From you, not so much.

She gazed out the window without really seeing anything. Tree. Bird. Bike. Mailbox. "It's the name of a little kid. I know to you I'll always be little Quinnie Caine, but I'm all grown up now." She let out a sigh. "Since you haven't noticed."

Aiden brought the car to a stop. "We're here."

She turned her head. Yep. There was Prose & Scones. She was both disheartened and relieved the store was so close by.

"Okay, cool. No problem. Thanks for the ride." She grabbed the door handle, ready to push herself out to the curb if needed.

Except his hand held onto the sleeve of her cardigan.

"Quinn, look at me."

"No thank you," she told the car floor mat.

That made him laugh. "Eyes over here . . . *Quinn.*"

Taking a deep breath, she finally looked his way.

His expression gentled. "I see you."

Everything inside her stopped and whirled all at once.

"I see you, Quinn Caine. That's a promise."

He wasn't done.

"I'm proud of you too." Then he reached out and rumpled her hair. "Now, go get 'em."

She couldn't believe it. He'd rumpled her hair—*again*. Just when she thought she was getting through to him, he pulled out that lame maneuver.

Why do I even bother?

She got out of the car, on autopilot, slamming the door and refusing to look back.

Speed-walking through the store, Quinn stopped just long enough to hug Sarah because she was the best hugger—her gesture to let her know her current sour mood had nothing to do with her. It wasn't Sarah's fault Quinn wanted what she couldn't have: Aiden would never really see her as a full-grown, actualized romantic possibility.

She got to her office, flicking on the lights, then shoving her latest favorite mixtape, titled *That's How the Light Gets In*—the classic title a borrowed line either from Ernest Hemingway's A Farewell to Arms or from Leonard Cohen's song "Anthem," she couldn't remember—into the retro tape player and plopping into her cushioned chair. She tried to breathe deep, to get the air working in her lungs, anything to try and ride out the humiliation she had felt in that car, all while listening to the rhythmic cadence of "Under the Same Sun" by Ben Howard. To the left side of her workspace, she had hung a corkboard with pinned comic clippings from *The New Yorker* and random poems from *The Sun* magazine. And in between the clippings, she had a series of her enamel pins at the ready so she could choose the appropriate pin to coincide with her current emotion.

"What pin pairs well with being patronized by a man you can't get out of your head or heart?" she muttered to herself. "'Smelly Cat from Friends?' Oscar the Grouch saying, 'I Love Trash'?" Nope—she needed a giggle as well as a reminder:

1-800-HIS-LOSS

She took it off the corkboard, grabbed a pin backing from the miniature clay pinch pot on her desk, the one she'd made in fourth grade, and fastened it right above her heart.

Strangely enough, the tiny act of proclamation made her feel better.

Then her phone rang. It was Daria. Quinn touched the speaker button.

"Hey."

"Hey, yourself," Daria answered. "What's wrong?"

Only one word had come out of her mouth, and of course that's all it had taken for her best friend to know something was up.

"Don't ask." She twisted around in her chair, grabbing a series of three thick books tied together. "I'm still surfing the shame wave, and I'm not up for the replay and feedback loop just yet."

"Ahhh," Daria dragged out. "Must be something with Aiden."

Damn it. "Stop with the whole perspective thingy. It's annoying."

"Copy that. Whatcha doin'?"

She let out a long sigh. "I'm at the store, about to work on projects. You?"

"Oh, nothing much," Daria said. "I have the rest of today off."

"Wait—aren't Sundays like your busiest day of the week? That's like giving an accountant April fifteenth off."

"Funny," Daria deadpanned.

She then proceeded to talk about her latest attempt at expanding Guinefort House's dog program into training emotional support dogs. "The others want me to wait awhile, to focus on my own spiritual process before I suggest changes. But I think it's a good tie-in with my master's in social work, don't you?"

"Absolutely," Quinn agreed, even though she wasn't really listening. That's because the three yearbooks in hand, one from Louise Archer Elementary, one from Thoreau Middle School, and the last from James Madison High School—all had her same year of graduation. They were really banged up except for one, even ripped in some places. On top of the stack was a folded note.

"Hold on a sec," she told Daria. "Something interesting came in."

"I'm about five minutes away. Want me to pick up a chai tea latte for you?"

She knew her so well: Her bookstore served delicious drip coffee, but sometimes Quinn needed the high-octane sugar rush only an overpriced, fancy latte could provide.

"When have I ever said no to that offer?"

Daria chuckled. "Exactly. See you in a bit."

"Okay, bye."

Quinn hung up the phone and unfolded the note:

Hey Quincy,

> *Sorry I missed talking to you in person about the project. Please keep it quiet, as I want it to be a surprise for Tricia. These are her yearbooks from sixth grade, eighth grade, and senior year. I looked through them the other day and noticed her boyfriend (soon to be fiancé) had written something awesome for her each time, even before they were a couple. Unfortunately, the books aren't in great shape. Any chance you can fix them up for her? I'd love to give them as a present, as*

part of her hope chest. Expense is not an issue. Call me with a quote, and let me know when you can have them complete.

Thanks, Trina P.

She checked the date on the letter: it had been written two days before Tricia's murder. Perhaps Scott had given Trina the heads-up about his impending proposal, maybe had her take the photo that was on her sister's phone. And in her excitement, she had perused all their old stuff and found these.

Thumbing through the high school yearbook first, she found the inscription Trina had mentioned. Scott went on and on about how smart and beautiful Tricia was, how lucky he was to know her. It was obvious he was smitten. It wasn't Shakespeare, but it had its charm. Of course, there were plenty of other inscriptions from other male admirers, although many were written more in acronyms than prose, like S.W.A.K. and 2Good2B4Got10.

Gag.

She perused their middle school yearbook, also finding another note of admiration from Scott. As she skimmed through the others, most with names she'd known forever, there was one in the corner of a back page, in thick black marker, that caught her eye.

I will never forget you. Don't forget about me. Baltimore is not far away. You are the prettiest girl in the whole school. Text me at 703.555.9294.

Love, Wyatt

Holy shitake, could it be?

A knock on the door scared her bad enough to make her jump in her seat and cry out.

The door opened. "Gee-Zeus, what's the matter with you?" Daria came into the small space, putting her latte down on her desk. "You look like you saw *Poltergeist, the Live Show*."

"Hold on, I need to see if I'm right about something." She flipped through the yearbook, scanning through the faces of the eighth-grade class.

Daria took a sip of her coffee before placing it besides Quinn's on her desk, then grabbing the elementary school yearbook. "Oh, this is from your year. I'm not in it, then." She skimmed through the annual. "Wow, this is wild. Look how young everyone was . . . I wonder if Mrs. Kass still works there. She was my favorite."

"Me too, but she left years ago. She's the author of a bestselling picture book series now. The name escapes me . . ." she said, her voice drifting off as she scanned through the names and faces. "Quentin . . . Ranier . . . Reginald . . . ah, there it is— Reynolds. Wyatt Reynolds."

Daria bent over to see. "You mean the officer with the stick up his—"

"Yes, the same one—look!"

Sure enough, there was Officer Wyatt Reynolds in early teen form.

"Wow, he was actually a really cute kid," she said. "How come I don't remember him?"

"See if he's in the yearbook you've got," Quinn instructed.

Daria leafed through it. "Nope, he didn't attend Louise Archer Elementary."

Quinn did the same with the high school yearbook before answering, "Nope. He didn't graduate with my class. It seems as if he was only here for middle school before he moved to Baltimore."

She couldn't get over the photo of him either: sable-colored hair in a mop, big brown eyes, and a huge smile—complete with a full set of braces.

Quinn thumbed through the rest of the yearbook. She perused the club photos toward the back, noticing the only activity Tricia had participated in that overlapped with Wyatt was Safety Patrol.

"Figures," Daria snorted. "I never could stand those guys. Power hungry, even then."

"Indeed." When she got to the end of the yearbook, she saw there was a pouch filled with papers. "Should I?" she asked.

Daria gave her a look.

"I know. Dumb question." Quinn dumped the contents of the insert out onto the desk. They were all handwritten notes, like the kind kids pass in class. "There must be dozens in here."

"Divide them up so we can both read them."

They divvied the pile, realizing quickly that most were from the same person: Wyatt Reynolds.

Daria let out a low whistle. "Whoa, this kid had it bad for her."

"I'll say . . .

"There will never be anyone as pretty as you, Tricia. You are also nicer than your sister, and I don't think you get enough credit for that. I will always be here to make you feel better."

"You don't think he still has a thing for her, do you?" Quinn asked.

"Probably. It sure explains why he was so jacked up about her death and talking as if he knew her. Because he did."

They both got quiet, because they were thinking the same thing, but each was waiting for the other to say it first.

"Okay, fine, I'll say it," Quinn started. "You don't think he'd . . ."

Daria scratched the back of her neck and shrugged. "That's a big leap, Quinn—from schoolboy crush to stalker-killer."

"I heard Aiden say Reynolds transferred from Baltimore not too long ago. Do you think he came here for her?"

Daria shuddered. "Can you imagine? Holding a torch that long for someone, with little to no encouragement for years?"

Quinn scanned all of the unfolded pages. "Why would you assume that? Look at all these notes. What do they have in common besides most being from Wyatt?"

Daria drew a blank. "I don't know. They're all written on notebook paper?"

She held a bunch in her hand. "Tricia *saved* them. A girl doesn't keep notes from someone she doesn't at least care about in some way."

"Good point."

Quinn sighed. "Of course, these notes don't prove anything."

"They're proof he had some sort of relationship with Tricia. What else is he hiding?"

Quinn cracked her knuckles. "Okay, let's just say, for argument's sake, that Wyatt Reynolds returned to Vienna because he was obsessed with Tricia. Wouldn't you think, then, he'd kill Scott, and not the object of his affection?"

"True, true," Daria said, leaning her shoulder against the edge of the bookcase by the door. "Although, it depends on how far down the rabbit hole he went in terms of his fixation. If he's truly been obsessed with her all this time, he may see Tricia's engagement as a betrayal, one needing to be punished. Maybe it went too far."

"I wish I had looked through her phone before handing it over to the police, to see if Wyatt's been in contact with her."

"Well, that ship has sailed," Daria chewed on the corner of her thumb. "We're probably way off here, by the way."

"Why do you say that?"

Daria shrugged. "Because don't police officers have to take a boatload of psychological tests before graduating from the academy? I'd think obsessive tendencies would have shown up."

"They have to take the Minnesota Multiphasic Personality Inventory." It's a multiple-choice personality assessment exam. Candidates also have to sit down for an in-person interview with a psychologist," she added, noticing the expression on her cousin's face. "What?"

Daria tsked. "Yeah, I *know* what an MMPI is. I'm a licensed clinical social worker, remember? The question is, how do *you* know all of that?"

"I remember Aiden telling me and my family over dinner, years ago, when he was going through all the testing himself."

"So, then Wyatt had to pass those tests too." Daria checked to make sure the office door was all the way closed and locked. "Listen, I don't know if I'm breaking the rules or anything, but there's something you should know."

"Breaking what rules?"

Daria paused before blurting out, "Okay, this is between us. You promise?"

Quinn tsked. "As if you even have to ask."

She nodded. "Right. Well, remember the other day when we were having breakfast, but I had to leave early?"

"I *do* remember. In fact, I meant to ask you later if everything was all right, but, in typical 'me' fashion, I forgot."

"No biggie. Sister Lucy called, saying some policeman had come to the abbey wigging out. She needed me to come back right away."

Quinn put her cup down. "What happened?"

"Well, I got there, and it was Wyatt."

Quinn looked aghast. "Talk about an order of humble pie with extra awkward sauce."

Her cousin slapped her thigh. "I know, right? Anyway, I tried to talk to him, but he wouldn't share why he was upset, even after I told him I was a licensed social worker. He insisted on speaking to—and I quote—'a real priest.' When I explained to him that we were an Anglican order—of *nuns*—he got all flustered and left in a tizzy."

Quinn let that one sink in.

"Do you think I broke any rules telling you that?" she asked.

"Oh yeah, you screwed the pooch on this one."

"Great." Daria slumped in her chair.

"Since when did my cousin, the former detention mainstay and misdemeanor queen, suddenly give a flip about rules?"

Daria responded by nibbling on the edge of her thumb again.

"Hey, it's me." Quinn placed her hand over Daria's favorite chew toy. "Consider me your walking secret repository. We've always shared stuff we couldn't—and shouldn't—say to anyone else. I'm your vault and you're mine. Okay?"

Daria seemed to relax. "You're right. I'm being ridiculous. You're my family," she sighed. "Of all the vows, it's the one asking for obedience . . ."

She didn't need to finish the sentence; they both understood that the struggle was real. Quinn loved her cousin. She respected her too. However, even after two years, her becoming a novitiate was still something of a mystery Quinn was trying to solve.

"Even if he didn't kill her, there's something fishy going on with Officer Reynolds," Daria finally said.

"Agreed."

Her cousin eyed the mess on Quinn's desk. "Should we take the yearbook and notes to Aiden?"

Quinn shot her a look. "In the words of the late, great Whitney Houston, that's a 'hell to the no.'"

She picked up her coffee. "Wait—why?"

"Because I'd like to avoid yet another head pat from the man, followed by a 'Go get 'em, tiger.'"

Daria almost did a spit-take. "He did what now?"

"Yep. Ruffled my hair like I was five."

Her cousin swallowed. "Oy. That's no *bueno*."

Yeah, no kidding. "So, we're on our own here. If we find something linking Wyatt and Tricia in the present day, even if it was just in his paranoid imagination, then we'll loop Aiden in. If it's nothing, then no harm done and no patronizing, paternalistic shade. Are you with me?"

A once-buried, mischievous spirit sparked behind Daria's eyes, glittering with a fire Quinn hadn't seen since she'd been back home. "Oh, I'm with you, cuz. You and me. We've *got* this thing."

They did their special handshake, one they hadn't done in years. Forget Bat-Signals. The Cousin Secret Handshake heralded the beginning of a new era: the end to either of them residing in their comfort zones. The last time they'd enacted "the shake," they had both landed in jail for a night, but Quinn brushed that thought aside. That was high school. They were grown women now. How much trouble could they possibly get into?

Chapter Eight

"Very few of us are what we seem."
—Agatha Christie, British mystery author

Quinn opened the first volume. It had taken her longer to restore Tricia's yearbooks than she'd thought it would-over a week-but once they were done, she had insisted Sister Daria come over.

"You wouldn't believe how much work this one from our elementary school days needed." She breathed in deep through her nose, floating in the delicious aroma of aged schoolbook. Forget the beach; Calvin Klein needed to bottle various book scents for its next fragrance line: library book smell, brand-new book smell, aged book smell—not to be confused with old book smell, which, FYI, was just mildew.

Even though she didn't receive a response, Quinn kept going. "I had to glue the bindings on the folio, then I had to rebuild the spine. It was like someone had flapped the book like a spastic bird, breaking the thing right down the middle."

Daria glanced up from her book. "Uh-huh."

"The one from high school just needed the gold lettering filled in and a few stitches. Easy-peasy. The middle school one was in the best shape."

"Okay cool," Daria said in a rush. "Can we go now?"

She knew Daria had no interest in her bookbinding prowess, but something about the condition discrepancies between the yearbooks kept niggling at her.

"It's weird." Quinn kept turning around and examining the middle school yearbook again. "Most people keep them all together, in the same place, so the condition of each remains fairly uniform."

Her cousin let out a loud sigh, which Quinn ignored.

"It's like she had made sure to put this volume away on the shelf. She took care of this one, Daria, like it contained something precious. The others might as well have been left lying around in the back of her closet or something."

"And?"

Quinn put the book down. "Annnnd . . . my theory is, those notes—or something else about middle school—meant something to Tricia. Enough to care for this book better than the others."

"Or she put it somewhere and forgot about it," Daria countered.

"That could also be true."

Quinn checked on the books one last time. She wanted each scholastic tome to be perfect, not only because her work reflected on her and her family, but because she was putting a great deal of weight onto mere paper: willing books to serve as olive branches.

She placed the three yearbooks inside a reusable bag. It had taken time to repair Tricia's yearbooks, mostly because she'd needed to special-order a particular brand of gold leaf to redo the monogram on the front of the senior year annals. The company was still in business, but the shade of gold had been more yellow back then. All the current metallic tones skewed toward rose gold or silver, avoiding anything brassy or classic gold.

"Okay, enough theorizing for now. We're never going to get answers sitting around here. Let's go."

The cousins walked out of the bookstore and down the brick-laid path along Church Street. Plenty of people were sitting outside on painted benches, leaning against lampposts while licking ice cream cones and sipping chilled coffee drinks. As usual, residents of Vienna only had the pleasure of a few traditional spring days before sliding right into the heat of summer. It was early May and already almost ninety degrees.

"I have to admit, I'm nervous."

Daria cackled. "Well, of course you are. The last time you saw her, she was spewing venom all over you like a spitting cobra. I'm surprised your stomach's holding up. It used to be, someone would look at you funny, and you'd be running for the bathroom."

Quinn gave her cousin some side-eye. "Wow, way to score low on the comforting scale, Ms. Social Worker–slash–Woman of God."

"Please, you have no idea how lucky you are. I'm so much nicer than the older nuns."

"Setting the bar high, I see."

Her cousin gave her a playful shove with her shoulder as they walked. "C'mon, I'm here *with* you and *for* you. Besides, it'll be good to see if you two can clear things up before the funeral. The last thing anyone needs is a scene at Tricia's gravesite. No one wants to upset their mom and dad more than they already are."

"I can't even imagine what they're going through." Quinn noticed no line at the coffeehouse as they were getting closer. She grabbed her cousin's arm. "Wait. We need to bring Trina sustenance in the form of caffeine, foam, and sugar."

Daria stopped walking, shaking her head. "You're stalling again."

"No, I'm not. That girl always had a coffee with her through school. It's one of her favorite things. Trust me, a chilled coffee drink will break the ice."

"Very punny." Daria rolled her eyes. "Come on—you're buying."

They walked through doors, the intoxicating aroma of java surrounding them like a siren's spell. Caffe Amour was the real deal, roasting beans on site from growers all over the world. Quinn got a kick out of the pile of burlap sacks in the corner, imagining little kids would love to jump all over them, like on those cool bean bag chairs from the seventies. Mr. Amour's state-of-the-art roaster sat almost smack dab in the middle of his shop, gleaming brilliant, a circular, silver cauldron. Customers would often catch him hovering over his beans, whispering incantations soft and low to them.

Her cousin pointed up in the air as they walked in. "They're playing one of my favorites." Daria waved to the people they knew inside—which was most everybody. If a Vienna neighbor wanted the latest "tea"—gossip, not Lipton—this was the place. If you actually wanted somewhere quiet to get work done, buy some Bose noise-canceling headphones or park at the library, because it wasn't going to happen over here.

Quinn listened. "Who's playing?"

Daria's mouth sprang open. "Wow, are you telling me that *you*, former college DJ and forever vinyl record hoarder, aka queen of the mixtape *and* playlist, can't name that tune?"

Two lines creased between Quinn's brows. "If you're trying to irk me, you're succeeding."

"Doesn't take much, does it?"

"It's times like this when I wish we were still little because I could get away with flicking your head really, really hard."

Maxie, one of the baristas, leaned over. "Don't feel bad. None of us knew who it was either." She tightened the ribbon on one of her blue-dyed braids. "The band's called Rainbow Kitten Surprise. One of the new guys brought it in."

Daria sported a wicked grin. "My seemingly sweet cousin is actually a closet music snob, and her not knowing some new hip band is killing her inside—the same as if I forgot evening vespers."

Maxie laughed aloud, mouth wide enough to spot her tongue piercing. "We all got our thing. What can I get ya?"

Quinn ignored her cousin's glee. "I actually want to order a drink for someone else."

"Coolio, what can I getcha?"

"It's for Trina Pemberley. She must come in here a lot. Her office is a block away?"

All humor left the barista's face. "Yes, she's a regular."

Guess someone's either not a fun customer or not a generous tipper. Probably both.

Quinn went on. "You wouldn't happen to know her coffee order offhand, would you? I need to stop over there and am looking for any help I can get."

Someone behind them spoke up. "Oh please. Everyone knows you didn't kill her sister, so there's no need for you to kiss the butt of the Wicked Witch of Vienna Northwest. Didn't you see the *Vienna Patch* this morning?"

Quinn and Sister Daria turned around. It was Withers Hammock, a third-generation Vienna native, like the Caines, and one of Finn and Adele's neighbors. It was appropriate they would run into her at Caffe Amour because everyone knew Ms. Withers was the unofficial town crier. Folks around said she knew what happened to people before they knew it themselves.

Daria bit first. "No, we didn't see it. What does it say?"

"Hold on." Her blunt-cut, straight black hair, with a lone blonde streak down the side, fell forward as she scrolled through her phone. Quinn had always admired her style, eschewing the typical suburban mom uniform for her own take on Gen X-chic. Today she was wearing faded black skinny jeans with a well-worn Sufjan Stevens concert T-shirt and high-heeled, gladiator sandals. Quinn bet she had a whole closet filled with vintage tees from the coolest bands over the years.

"Here it is." She squinted, trying to read the print on her phone. "It says the autopsy results indicated she died of liver and kidney failure. 'While foul play hasn't been ruled out, the results are inconclusive.' The article also states that 'this is the second suspicious death in Vienna in under six months, the last being Dr. Chaim Levine, who also died of liver and kidney failure.'"

Maxie rang up their coffee order. "Whoa—doesn't sound like either went gently into that good night."

Quinn appreciated the barista's apropos use of Dylan Thomas in the moment. *Fellow English literature majors unite!* "Indeed not. Having the liver and kidneys shut down like that . . . it sounds painful."

Withers put her phone away. "You think they're linked?"

"It seems the reporter who wrote that article does." Quinn paid for the coffee while Daria took it from one of the other baristas down the line. "We've got to get moving. Give my best to your parents."

"Sure thing. You're coming to my mom's show, right?"

"What show?"

Withers reached into her bag and pulled out a glossy five-by-seven card, handing it over. "I'm sure we sent one to your folks. I should get both of your addresses for the next time."

Daria tittered. "No need to send one over to the abbey. It's not like we can afford any of it. Didn't I hear some of her work was purchased for the Smithsonian's permanent collection? That's awesome, by the way."

Her mom, Mei Hammock, was a reowned pottery artist, a master of the Kintsugi technique that she learned in her native Japan before moving to the United States years ago.

Withers waved away the excitement. "It's great—don't get me wrong—but this show's not some high-falutin' shindig. Think of it as part art show, part fundraiser for The Women's Center."

Withers Hammock had followed in her father's footsteps and earned her PhD in psychology, except once she was part of The Women's Center's team, her love for systems and finance made her a natural to take over as executive director. Quinn hearing Mei Hammock was availing her art to benefit the counseling nonprofit didn't surprise her in the least. It was hard to say no to Withers.

"Listen, whatever happens when you go over to the Wicked Witch's office, come to the funeral, regardless, okay?" Withers asked.

The service was being held at Vienna Presbyterian, the Pemberleys' home church. Then her family would head over to Flint Hill Cemetery.

Quinn gave a nod. "All right, I'll be there."

"Good. You come too, Daria."

"Will do. Give my best to your family."

They both waved, getting out of the coffee shop and on their way. Quinn held the large, iced ten-ingredients-in-one-coffee drink in hand. "Well, that was an interesting development."

Daria made an inaudible sound. "I have a bad feeling. These murders are definitely linked. Do you think we have a serial killer in our town?"

Quinn peered over. "And I thought I was the designated over-reactor in this sleuthing duo." She switched the drink to the other hand, wiping it down her shirt. "Don't jump to conclusions. Remember what we learned in science class: correlation isn't causation."

Daria snorted. "If it looks like a duck and sounds like a duck . . ."

Before too long they had arrived at Trina's office.

Quinn took in a deep breath. "Okay, here goes nothing."

She swung open the door, stepping into the lobby. Soothing notes of bossa nova floated through the office's surround sound speakers. Quinn whiffed a couple of times, detecting hints of coconut and citrus in the air. It was like walking into a synthe-sized vacation, and she'd bet money the twins had paid for one of those scent-designer companies to pump fragrance into their air. Everything was in its designated spot, exactly where it was supposed to be—except for the people. There wasn't a recep-tionist at the front desk, nor other realtors circling around. It was as if they had walked into an alternate universe—and just as creepy. She checked the time on her phone.

"It's not lunch hour or anything." Quinn peeked behind one of the dividing low walls for signs of life. "Wonder where everyone is?"

Daria pointed toward the back, at a closed door. "Well, only one way to find out. I can hear her talking. Sounds like she's on the phone."

"All right, let's do this." Quinn straightened her shoulders and walked across the office, her gusto wasted on a bunch of empty Eames chairs. Her stomach growled.

"Ignore that, please," she told Daria.

"Couldn't eat beforehand, huh?"

"Yeah," she confirmed.

"Because you get all gassy when you're nervous?"

Quinn huffed. "I know what you're doing—trying to make me laugh so I can relax. It's. Not. Working."

Daria shrugged. "Fine. Resist my helpful intervention." She gestured toward the door with her chin. "Knock already, then."

Quinn did as she was told, hearing Trina stop talking for a second before calling out, "Come in! The door's open."

She turned the knob and stepped inside. Trina's office looked like something out of *Elle Décor*—at least Quinn thought so. She'd never actually read that magazine, but if she ever had, this office would definitely be exactly the type of "workspace" featured. Lots of white with dove-gray chevron patterns. A bright kelly-green velvet couch with matching chaise lounge. White fur throw pillows. There was a wet bar off to the side, mirrored, with a gunmetal-gray bar glass set. It was more like a chic nightclub than a place of business, except for the wall filled top to bottom with real estate awards and plaques. It was the quintessential Trina Pemberley alpha woman cave.

Quinn had expected to find Tricia's twin a wreck, or at least as much as she'd allow. Maybe her eye makeup would be smeared from crying. Perhaps she would have given up her signature suits for a mopey T-shirt and sweats. At the least, Quinn expected her to be in the same state of mind she was in when yelling at her at church two Sundays ago.

But none of those assumptions proved to be true. Trina Pemberley was flawless. Every hair in place. Not a smudge fettered her complexion. Her eyes were clear and bright, like those of someone who had gotten plenty of rest.

Quinn didn't want to judge someone else's grief process, but Trina didn't appear to be struggling anymore over the loss of her sister, or if she was, Trina had completed the five stages of grief in record time.

"What are you doing here?" she snapped.

Well, there's that.

Daria ignored her comment. "Where's your staff?"

Trina's gaze turned from hot pokers to ice. "They had to go, not that it's any of your business."

This wasn't going the way Quinn needed it to.

"I'm sorry we didn't call first. I wanted to bring you your favorite coffee," Quinn put the drink on her desk, then held up the book bag. "I also brought you Tricia's yearbooks."

Trina let out a sardonic laugh. "If you think I'm drinking *that*, you're crazy."

Daria groused. "Don't be ridiculous. My cousin wouldn't poison you."

Quinn forced a polite smile. "Well, at least take the yearbooks."

Trina stood up. "Ugh, I forgot about those. That was when I thought . . . never mind. Give them to me." She held out her hand while tapping one of her pointy, high-heeled toes against the marble floors.

Quinn held out the bag, and Trina grabbed the handles, immediately diving inside to retrieve the yearbooks. Once the first book was in her hands, she stopped dead, studying the repairs. She did the same with the next two, examining them before placing them with care on her desk.

"These look brand new."

Quinn smiled. "Thank you. I wanted to get them just right."

Trina looked confused. "But you never called me to confirm a quote. I'm not paying you for these."

If there's a special prayer for patience, Jesus, put it in the front of my prayer book-now.

"I didn't call because I'm not charging you."

"So . . . what . . . you think fixing a few old yearbooks makes up for what you did?"

"Get off it, Trina," Daria snapped. "Everyone knows Quinn's been cleared of any suspicious involvement. I'm sure you've heard the results of the autopsy, just like the rest of us."

Those words only made Trina purse her lips even tighter. It was *not* a flattering look.

"Fine. Whatever. I'm still not paying for it."

Quinn gazed upward, taking a deep breath. "Again, there's no charge."

Trina gazed back down at the yearbooks. "These actually don't look horrid."

Daria sat down in one of the chairs opposite the desk. "Listen, we also came by to ask you something."

Trina blew out an exasperated breath. "Well, make yourselves at home, why don't you?"

Quinn sat down in the chair next to Daria. "I noticed, going through the yearbooks, particularly the one from eighth grade, that she had saved a lot of handwritten notes from Wyatt Reynolds."

Trina's face contorted like she had eaten a lemon. "Ugh, that freak. He is so lame. Always has been."

Interesting. "You remember him from middle school? Because I didn't."

Trina rolled her eyes while plopping back down in her chair. "Well, of course you wouldn't remember the turd. He wasn't in honors classes with us. Tricia met him through one of the clubs or something. Of course, I wouldn't have given him the time of day, but she always had a soft spot for the lost puppies who followed her around."

Of course, Tricia didn't like actual dogs, but whatever.

Trina started tapping her long fingernails on her glass desktop. Just talking about Officer Reynolds worked her up. Quinn and Daria shared a look.

"You guys don't even know," she went on. "Even after he moved away, he was still trying to get with her. For years even. As if he'd ever have a chance. When he learned to drive, he came all the way down from Baltimore just to take her out for a coffee after school before turning around and heading home again. I think it died down for a while in college, mostly because we moved across the country. But he stayed in touch with her, one way or the other. I told her over and over to blow him off, and now . . . she's gone."

Daria seemed to be taking in what Trina had shared. "And how did Tricia feel about him?"

Trina scoffed. "My sister didn't 'feel' anything for him, at least not romantically. They were friends. Of course, she knew he was in love with her, but that was part of her game—to make as many men fall in love with her as possible—at least before that idiot, Scott, came into the picture."

Quinn couldn't help but think it wasn't looking good for Officer Reynolds. "Did you see the two of them together in the days leading to her death?"

The front door to the main office buzzed and opened. "Hello, anyone here?" someone called out.

"Excuse me, that's one of my clients. I trust you can show yourselves out?"

"Sure thing," Quinn said. "Thanks for talking to us."

Trina breezed by but stopped short before opening the door. "Hey, listen . . . um, thanks for redoing her yearbooks. And the coffee." She looked over at Quinn, as if seeing her for the first time. "It took guts walking in here, especially after I bulldozed you at your church."

If Quinn wasn't witnessing the moment in real time, she wouldn't have believed it. "Don't worry about last Sunday. It's already forgotten. Call if you need anything."

Trina nodded and then walked out, her red-bottomed Christian Louboutin shoes clicking against the marble, echoing through the space.

Daria stood up. "All right, well, *that* was informative. Let's get out of here."

"Hold on. I need to use the bathroom."

Quinn walked toward the private en suite inside Trina's office. The bathroom was just as stylish as the rest of her office, with lush, deep emerald-green ferns alongside sparkly silver fixtures. Hanging on the inside of the door was a framed poster—one of the twins' first ads as a real estate duo. Arms folded and back-to-back, they looked like they could conquer anything as long as they were together.

Quinn finished up, washing her hands with the lavender-scented French soap, realizing too late that Trina was out of towels. Turning off the water, she flicked the droplets into the sink, looking around for something to dry her hands on. There was nothing.

"Great," she muttered, noticing the closet on the other side of the bathroom facilities. She opened the folding doors. Inside were tons of bathroom supplies as well as extra business "swag." She reached for some paper towels, only to notice some signage propped up in the back.

But these weren't the typical posters—at least not for their business.

A knock on the bathroom door made her jump.

"Hey, are you feeling okay?" Daria called out from the other side of the door.

Quinn rushed over, turning the handle to let her cousin in. "Hurry up!" she whispered loudly. "And close the door!"

Daria did as she was told, her head rearing back when Quinn locked the door behind her. "What's going on?"

"Let me show you." She went back over to the closet, being careful when she took out the posters and laid them on the floor. "Notice anything?"

Daria's eyes darted back and forth, recognition dawning on her. "Oh wow, these only have Trina in them."

"Right. What else?"

"Well, instead of saying 'The Pemberley Sisters: Northern Virginia's Real Estate Duo,' these read 'The Pemberley Group: Featuring the #1 Realtor in the DC Metro Area' . . . wow, she didn't waste any time."

Quinn gave her a look. "C'mon—there's no way she could've had these done so fast."

"Well, let's see." Daria bent down. She leafed through the posters. Each one had Trina in a different pose with another outfit.

"These were well thought-out. She had to have time to plan her outfits, choreograph how she wanted each photo posed." Quinn studied the posters, crouching down to the floor, getting closer. "She even changed her makeup for each look. That takes a lot of time, Daria."

Clipped to the last one was a receipt. "Ah, here we go." Daria scanned the paperwork, frowning. "Right, this says someone from Donnell Printing took this order March twenty-fourth, completed it by March twenty-sixth, and it was picked up the first week of April. If I had to guess, I'd estimate the actual photo shoot was way before the print date."

Quinn counted back on her fingers. "These were printed three weeks before Tricia died."

The cousins locked eyes. She could see Daria visibly swallowing.

"She was making a move to go solo. But why? They were an off-the-charts successful real estate duo. Why would she risk that, along with having to change the branding—"

"And the staff," Quinn reminded her. "Something was going on between the twins. And it wasn't good." She took out her camera phone.

"What are you doing?" Daria eyed the bathroom door.

"Getting photos of the evidence. Trina would certainly like the law to sniff around Officer Wyatt, but this here proves she may have motive for pointing the finger at him—"

"And far away from her," Daria finished Quinn's sentence.

"Exactly."

Quinn took photos of the posters and the receipt, then Daria helped tuck them back in the closet, closing the folding doors. By the time they exited the bathroom and the office, they saw Trina escorting her client into her car. She even offered a quick head nod before getting in herself.

Daria gave a perfunctory wave back before leaning over to whisper, "She's never been nicer to us, and I can't help wondering: Is it because losing someone close to her has softened her heart—"

Quinn finished her sentence. "Or because she's a mastermind, working us so we point the finger at Officer Reynolds for her murder."

Chapter Nine

"I didn't attend the funeral, but I sent a letter saying I
approved of it."
—Mark Twain, American author and humorist

B lack might have been Quinn's favorite color, but it lost much
of its stylish appeal when it was mandatory attire for a funeral.
She had on a midi-length dress, with one of her many book purses
tucked under her arm. It was a creative find she had procured
thanks to the awesomeness that was Etsy. This particular clutch
was made from the memoir *Love is a Mix Tape* by Rob Sheffield;
a modern-day ode to the author's wife, who died in her twenties.

It was subtle. No one would probably make the connection,
but Quinn gained comfort holding the repurposed tome to love
and loss close to her. Despite their contentious history, Tricia's
death had shaken her; for although not a happy relationship,
theirs was an entanglement nonetheless.

As the Caine family walked into the church, Quinn secured
her dog baby to one of the posts, pouring the contents of her
water bottle into a portable dog dish.

Quinn scratched behind her ear. "I won't be too long, sweet
girl."

RBG woofed, her tongue hanging out the side of her mouth.

Bash came up next to them, offering his arm for Quinn to hold. She accepted, giving him a small, grateful smile.

"Good thing we got here on the early side," he said. "The girl actually packed quite the crowd. Who would've thought?"

Their mother, holding onto their father's arm in front of them, twisted her head around to shush him. "Sebastian Monroe, please keep your voice down. We're in a house of God."

Uncle Jerry chortled. "Oh please, Adele. Everyone else is thinking the same thing."

Aunt Johanna pulled at his arm. "Maybe so, Jer, but she's right. Keep your yapper quiet."

Bash leaned close to Quinn's ear. "I bet there are maybe six people in this whole place who will truly miss her. She was beautiful and smart, but not in the way that counted. Otherwise, the woman was vindictive and petty, and she and her sister seemed to take great joy in other people's misery."

Everything he said was true.

He also wasn't done. "So, why do I feel so awful?"

Quinn understood it was a rhetorical question. Most of the people in the chapel were folks she knew weren't close to Tricia, but they came anyway. To pay their respects. To offer comfort to the family. Vienna was a loyal town—tribalistic even, in the sense that they stuck by their own no matter what. Vienna Presbyterian was a mammoth congregation, able to seat hundreds of parishioners. One glance was all it took for Quinn to realize it would be standing room only soon enough.

Bash gave a quick wave. "Hey, there's Aiden. Looks like he and his family saved us seats."

Oh, that's just great. Better make sure my hair's ready for another rumple.

"Hey, man." Aiden did that one-arm man hug all guys seemed to do. He locked eyes with her. "Hey, Quinn."

Don't get sucked into his hot-guy vortex. Remember, he sees you as just a kid.

"Hey, Aiden," she said, being polite but turning her focus to his folks. "Hello, Mr. Harrington, Mrs. Harrington. Are the girls here?"

Aiden's mama smiled, making the same gray eyes as her son's crinkle in the corners. "Thanks, sweetie—no, they couldn't come. They just had spring break a couple of weeks ago and are deep into midterms."

Grace and Jessica were Aiden's younger sisters. Grace was a senior at Virginia Tech, and Jessica was a sophomore at James Madison University. Quinn's dad used to lament for their parents, who had an overlap of college tuitions.

Mrs. Harrington's manicured hand rested on Quinn's shoulder. "How are you holding up? Aiden says you've been an absolute rock through everything going on."

"I'm all right, Mrs. Harrington. I think we'll all feel better once Aiden catches whoever did this wretched thing."

"No truer words said," Mr. Harrington interjected, draping his arm over his wife's shoulder. Like Aiden, his father was also a mountain of a man, which was why it was all the sweeter when he kissed the top of Mrs. Harrington's head while giving her shoulder a cuddle. She beamed up at him—a private moment between two people married for thirty-two years. Growing up around families like the Harringtons was part of what made Quinn a self-professed, old-fashioned girl. Forget swiping right and guys sliding suggestive remarks into a woman's direct messages on Instagram. Couples like her parents and the Harrington's were the real "#relationshipgoals."

"So, Bash? How's the new job at Fairfax Fire working out?"

A good question, one Quinn hadn't even gotten a chance to ask her brother. In fact, today was the first day she'd spent any kind of time with him since he had accepted the job offer.

He did his typical "aw shucks" expression. "It's good. Busy. And not in the way I expected."

"What do you mean?" Quinn and her mama asked at the same time. They glanced at each other.

"Jinx. You owe me a soda," Quinn teased.

Her mama waved her off. "Little girl, I gave you *life*. We're square." She turned her attention to her oldest. "Come on now. Explain."

Bash shrugged. "Don't get me wrong. It's cool. It's just that the chief has spent more time introducing me to political big-wigs than having me get to know and bond with the other men and women of the unit, or even on learning their procedurals."

The rest of them shared knowing looks with one another.

Their father cleared his throat, adjusting his glasses. "And what do you take that to mean, son?"

Bash didn't hesitate. "I think it means the chief may not want to be chief much longer. I just wish he had told me as much during the interviewing process. This is going to be a much different job than I'd anticipated," he said, seeming to let that knowledge sink in more now that he'd said it aloud.

Quinn let that one marinate too, for all of five seconds, before saying, "Wow, if that's right, that would make you the youngest fire chief in Fairfax County history."

Everyone was now focused on her. "Now how would you know that?" her brother asked, shaking his head.

"C'mon are you new here? That's just how Quinn rolls." Aiden gave her a quick wink. "If I was a betting man, my guess would be that as soon as your sister found out you were going to be working for Fairfax Fire, she jumped online and started researching everything she could about the department, including its current chief. Am I right?"

Bull's-eye. Wow, he really does know me.

She blushed. "I have no idea what you're talking about," she lied, trying to avoid his gray-eyed gaze.

"Hello, Sebastian."

Quinn knew that voice. Even if she had been unable to recognize its delicate cadence, no one else on the planet called her brother by his full name, not even their parents. She and the rest of their little group turned around.

It was Rachel Slingbaum, her brother's ex.

But Rachel wasn't just an ex-girlfriend. She was the one who got away, something Quinn took no pleasure in knowing he'd regret one day. Quinn might have been the younger sister, but even she knew Bash had made a terrible mistake when he broke up with Rachel in college. He had been at UVA with Aiden, and she had opted for Brandeis University in Massachusetts. They had made it work, up through their sophomore year, but the distance had gotten to him, and frankly so had the need to experience college life in all its debaucheries. Quinn even remembered Aiden giving him a hard time about what he called his "bonehead" decision.

"Hi, Rach, it's really good to see you." One second in Rachel's presence and Bash got a dopey look on his face. "Although I'll admit, I'd rather it be under better circumstances."

"I know. It's terrible what happened. It seems I keep coming to funerals."

"Wait, what do you mean? Who else?" Bash stepped closer, as if he could serve as a human shield between her and all the world's hurts.

Rachel threaded her long, caramel-colored hair behind her ear, awareness tingeing her cheeks as two families watched this exchange.

"Hello, Mrs. Caine, Mr. Caine," she said, leaning over to give each of them a hug before offering the same to Quinn. "So good to see you, by the way. We need to have coffee soon. Catch up and all."

"I'd like that." Quinn meant it too. Rachel was the best, almost like another sister. Speaking of other sisters, where was Daria? She should've been there by now.

"Hi, Rachel. It's been too long," Adele Caine said, her husband echoing her words.

Bash was losing patience. "Honey, are you going to tell me what you meant?"

She sucked in a lungful of air. "Please, don't call me that." Her voice came out in a hoarse whisper. He had embarrassed her, but if Quinn had to guess, it wasn't because she didn't like him calling her something affectionate. It was because she *did* like it, too much for her comfort level.

Rachel went on to explain. "My uncle Chaim died a few months ago. It was awful. We convinced him to move here last year, after his divorce. Everything was going so well, until . . ."

Quinn knew it was rude, but she couldn't help barging into the conversation. "Until what?"

Rachel let out a heavy sigh. "That's it. We're not sure. He was healthy—maybe not in the best of shape, but otherwise fine. Never missed work. Always busy. He had a bad stomach flu and then that was it. He died. Out of nowhere. My family and I are still reeling from what happened." She stared off, the pain still fresh. "You'd think, being a doctor, he would've known his whole body was shutting down."

Over thirty years without a murder and now two in less than six months. Strange, dontcha think?

Quinn would prefer not to give Officer Reynolds any credit, but he had a point. "Did you have them do an autopsy to find out why his organs shut down so fast?"

The local paper was quick to draw parallels between the doctor's death and Tricia's. Were they right?

Rachel shook her head. "My uncle was modern Orthodox."

Quinn drew a blank. "What does that mean?"

Bash's ex explained, "There's different levels of religious observance and interpretation. Him being Modern Orthodox meant he followed Jewish law, but in a way that allowed him to live in secular society. And the Modern Orthodox don't believe in conducting autopsies unless there's strong cause."

Bash nodded. "It's a way of demonstrating respect for the dead."

Rachel eyes shone with unshed tears, as she gazed at Bash. "That's exactly it."

A sense of dread enveloped Quinn. Both she and Aiden locked eyes for a second before she asked. "Your uncle was Dr. Chaim Levine?"

Rachel's eyes widened. "Yes! Did you know him?"

Quinn reached out to squeeze her hand. "No, but I heard about his death when I got back. I am so sorry for your loss."

Rachel squeezed back. "Thanks, I appreciate that. He really was such a wonderful man. If you'd known him, you would have liked him."

The reverend tapped the head of the microphone, making sure it was on. "Everyone please take their seats. Our service to honor the life of Tricia Pemberley is about to begin."

Rachel took a quick glance over her shoulder. "I better get back to my seat. Lyle is waiting for me."

The color drained from Bash's face. "Lyle? You're here with a guy name *Lyle*?"

"Hey, be nice. He's a guy I've been seeing," she said before leaning close to Bash's ear, an attempt at privacy, but Quinn overheard 'can't see you' and 'it's too hard.'"

They watched her walk away to join the guy she'd mentioned, who was waiting for her down the aisle on the other side of the sanctuary. He was the same height as Rachel—five feet nine—with dark brown hair, thick black glasses, and an olive skin tone. Besides being slender, there wasn't one physical similarity between him and her brother.

"Well, at least she doesn't have a type," Quinn offered, a paltry condolence.

"How serious do you think she is about him?"

She studied Rachel and Lyle standing together. No lingering gazes between them. No clandestine touches. People kept approaching her: a former classmate, the wife of a family friend. Every time she introduced Lyle, he gave one of those tight-lipped, constipated smiles. Obligatory, with no heart behind it.

He is sooo totally wrong for Rachel.

He kept glancing over at the cross hanging over the dais, a mixture of apprehension and unease settling on his shoulders. Quinn couldn't help but think that if the cross at a Protestant church spooked him, it was his good fortune they weren't over at one of the Catholic sanctuaries. Those usually depicted Christ in the throes of crucifixion, bloodied wounds and all.

Bash was losing patience. "Well?"

"Not that serious. Rachel said he was a guy she was seeing. Not her boyfriend."

"There's a difference?"

"Uh, yeah, definitely, a big difference," Aiden interjected into their conversation, sandwiching himself between them. "Move down, Bash. I need to talk to Quinn."

Usually the maneuver would've been enough for her brother to raise an eyebrow, but he was too consumed with all things Rachel to notice. Like a mindless lemming, he moved down a seat.

"The service is starting. We'll talk another time." Quinn stared straight ahead, pretending to be absorbed in the service. She noticed funeral programs for Tricia's service had been wedged in front of the prayer books in each of the pews. She slid one out to take a closer look. There was Tricia in full color on the cover, with a curlicue font reading: "Tricia Pemberley: A Celebration of Life."

But Quinn's efforts at distraction proved futile. Aiden got close enough for his lips to touch the shell of her ear, sending a shiver of goose bumps through her. *Damn him.*

"If you think you're going to continue blowing me off, you are sorely mistaken," he whispered, moving her hair off her shoulder. "Are you going to the gravesite after the service?"

"I wasn't planning to, and I'm not blowing you off," she said, still not looking at him and also working really hard not to think how electrifying it felt, his hand touching her hair.

"You won't even look me in the eye, Quinn—ever since I dropped you off at the store the other day."

He had her there, but no way was she agreeing out loud.

Aiden had more to say. "Also, don't think I missed that look on your face."

Her brows came to a "V," and she finally met his gaze. "What look?"

"The one you made when you heard about Rachel's uncle."

"I don't know what you mean," she fibbed. "She's suffered a loss. Of course I'm going to feel badly for her."

"You suspect a connection."

She froze—until she realized he meant a connection between Tricia's death and Rachel's uncle's—not between him and her.

Quinn used her program to shield her face so no one could see her whispering. "It's hard to know since the family's not permitting an autopsy."

132

He scratched under his chin, his nails dragging through the stubble. "Yeah, I had no idea Rachel's family was so religious."

"Her uncle was—they're not. They're probably just respecting his wishes."

She glanced over. Wheels were turning behind his eyes, making him see without seeing. "Aiden?"

He came back. "You and me . . . after the service. We're going to have a little chat."

"But what if I—"

"Cancel them," he insisted. "And don't even think about trying to sneak out of here. I know you better than you think, Quinn. I'll find you—and I'll arrest you if I have to.

Chapter Ten

"True courage is in facing danger when you are afraid."
—L. Frank Baum, *The Wonderful Wizard of Oz*

Inside almost every grown adult resided a little, snack-sized Veruca Salt who wanted—and expected—to get her way. Quinn Caine's twelve-year-old self was the same, still coveting the attention of her brother's best friend. Preteen "Quinnie" couldn't fathom why her twenty-five-year-old self would purposefully avoid spending time with Aiden Broadwater Harrington.

In fact, she was having a fit inside her head, but the grown-up version was doing her darndest to ignore her inner child. Instead, she sought out everyone else in the sanctuary. The memorial service was over. Some had already left, making their way to the gravesite, but plenty of others lingered. Those were her people now. Sooner or later, Aiden was going to get called away. She could wait him out.

Quinn shuffled in line to pay her respects with the other tongue-tied mourners. What do you say to parents burying their child? Nothing other than "I'm sorry." There's nothing to ease their pain. They had aged ten years overnight, although, somehow, Trina appeared the same.

They were a curiosity, Abigail and William Pemberley. Quinn had always wondered how two amiable people had spawned such mean-girl twins. Her aunt Johanna was good friends with their mother, who often said it'd be a task finding a sweeter soul than Abigail Pemberley. Her husband, William, was well liked—maybe a bit of an overgrown frat boy, calling other men "dudes" and "bros," but otherwise inoffensive.

Now a fourth of their family was gone. Quinn couldn't imagine what she would do if anything happened to Bash. It would be a chasm without end, like Alice falling down the rabbit hole, but never reaching the bottom. An absurdist existence where nothing made sense, where something as fundamental as the laws of gravity could no longer be counted on.

"Mr. and Mrs. Pemberley, Trina, I am so sorry for your loss. I wish I could say something to take the pain away."

"I know, dear," Mrs. Pemberley said, nodding and reaching out to grasp Quinn's hand. "I should've come by the store to see if you were okay after finding our baby the way you did."

Mr. Pemberley leaned in. "You should know, we never believed the nonsense that was circulating," he said. "Other than going to the funeral home, this is the first time we've left the house. Abby is right—we should've come by the store. Maybe that would've help dispel the rumors sooner."

Quinn placed her hand on top of the one they were holding. "Please don't worry about me. Truth always has a way of coming out—at least that's what my nana used to always say."

They smiled. Trina had her back turned already, talking to someone else. Quinn glanced down at the handkerchief she held. A tiny smear of mascara, but otherwise dry as a bone.

Meanwhile, the Pemberleys stared at Quinn, as if waiting for her to say something else.

"I don't know if this offers any solace, but just so you know, I watched the EMTs work on Tricia. They did everything they could to try and bring her back."

"I know. They told us," he said. "I'll never understand it—a perfectly healthy young woman suffering from liver and kidney failure. And the partial paralysis. It doesn't make sense."

"I hate to ask this, but do you know of anyone who would want to hurt her? Or did they find anything suspicious? I'm just trying to make sense of it."

Tears welled in Mrs. Pemberley's eyes.

Smooth, Quinn. Why don't you just ask if you can peek in the coffin before they haul her into the ground?

"No one poisoned my sister—at least nothing showed up in the toxicology report," Trina chimed in. "Why don't you tell that detective you're so friendly with to arrest Wyatt Reynolds already?"

Her mother looked stricken. "Trina! How could you say such a thing? We don't know if he had anything to do with it."

"Who else could it be? Did you notice he's not even here?" she snapped. "Listen, Quinn, we're not dumb. Tricia and I knew not everyone liked us. We're very alpha, and we make no apologies. But no one had enough issues with Trish to hurt her. Except for Officer Reynolds, who was obsessed with her for years and was losing his mind that she was going to marry another man, even though the two of them had never had so much as a real date."

Trina had a point: those she knew in Vienna might not have cared for Tricia, but high school was years ago, and most just regarded the twins as an immature nuisance. Did someone from around here really harbor enough ire to murder her? And where was Officer Reynolds anyway?

At least Trina was finally calling her by her correct name. Progress.

Quinn couldn't help but notice that Trina vacillated between the present and past tense when discussing Tricia, saying "we" instead of "I" as well. Understandable, considering they were twins who did almost everything together. Quinn knew some would give way to speculation regarding Trina's use of the present tense when talking about Tricia, but she wasn't so quick to do so. It was junk science, and she understood if she was going to catch Tricia's killer, harping on her usage of "is" versus "was" wasn't going to cut it.

But she couldn't shake the image of what she and Daria had found in the back of Trina's office. Each poster with shining white teeth. She'd had plans to carry on solo for a while now, before Tricia's murder, but why fix what wasn't broken?

Unless, of course, something had ruptured, maybe beyond repair. Maybe that's why Trina had reached out to Quinn to fix Tricia's old yearbooks as part of an engagement present.

Mr. Pemberley's color turned ashen. "Trin, the medical examiners *and* the police have been very careful not to classify Tricia's death a homicide. They really don't want us going around saying otherwise."

"Ugh! As if I care what the police want. Wake *up*, Dad! What's it going to take for you and Mom to realize Trish was murdered!"

The now half-empty church carried her voice, loud and strong.

Abigail Pemberley closed her eyes and swayed, grasping her husband's arm. Trina reached for her. "Oh, Mom, hey, I'm sorry. I just can't—"

Mrs. Pemberley opened her eyes and cradled her daughter's cheek. "Shh, I know, baby. We're all upset. But I think I really need some air."

Mr. Pemberley held his wife up. "If you'll excuse us, Quinn, we need to go."

"Yes, of course." She moved back, trying not to step on anyone's toes.

A wave of people split and undulated, like the Red Sea. Thinking of the biblical reference reminded her of Daria. She texted her: *The funeral is over. Are you okay? What happened?*

No response.

Quinn hoped taking her time had discouraged Aiden from sticking around, but as she perused the sanctuary, sure enough, he was waiting by the exit sign. He must have felt her gaze because he turned his head, caught her staring, and gave one of those self-satisfied, Cheshire cat grins.

She rolled her eyes and turned away. She wasn't going to offer him a scintilla more of satisfaction.

As more funeral attendants filed out of the church, Quinn spotted Scott standing with his parents. His mother had a vise grip on his arm. The three of them were off to the side, talking in hushed tones with the reverend, who seemed to be trying to console Scott.

Even from across the room, Quinn could tell he was devastated. His tanned complexion had gone chalk white, his eyes glittery with tears. His shoulders slumped, and his slow breath seemed labored. She noticed his mother, who whispered something in his ear. He straightened his posture.

The guy had just lost the woman he was going to marry, and she's worried about him standing up straight? Quinn's feet walked toward them before her brain realized she was on the move.

"Excuse me, Reverend, Doctor and Mrs. Hauser, Scott," she said, nodding at each of them. "I just came over to offer my condolences."

The knuckles of Milly Hauser's hand, holding her son's forearm, turned white with her grip. His dad offered a sad smile.

"Thanks, Quinn." Scott smoothed his palm down the front of his tie. "It was nice of you and your family to come."

"Yes, well, at least you were raised right, demonstrating some rudimentary manners. Everyone around here is acting as if Abigail and William are the only ones who lost someone. That girl was like a daughter to me. And my poor boy! What's he supposed to do now?"

"Mom, *enough*," Scott muttered back, his cheeks flushed.

Quinn didn't know what to say. But then again, she had never known how to talk to Milly Hauser, even when a tragedy hadn't occurred.

"You'll have to excuse my wife." Embarrassment colored Dr. Hauser's complexion. "She's overwrought, as we all are. You understand."

"Pardon me, Carlson, but I do not need you to apologize on my behalf."

The reverend cleared his throat. "Grief is a circuitous process, and there's not any one way to go through the path that the Lord has paved for us."

Mrs. Hauser pressed her lips into a thin line. "With all due respect, Reverend, that sounds like a bucket of bull crap they teach you in the seminary to placate the grief-stricken."

Scott twisted his arm out of his mother's grasp. "If you'll excuse me, I'm going to walk Quinn out."

Mouth dropped open, eyes blazing, Mrs. Hauser looked ready to spit nails. "She is more than capable of walking herself out. You will stand here with your family and—"

His father lost patience. "Enough, Milly! Let the boy breathe for once."

Staring straight ahead, as if the church exit was his last hope, Scott grabbed Quinn's hand and pulled her out of the sanctuary. She wanted to rip herself out of his grasp but didn't want to upset him—while also not wanting people to get the wrong impression about the two of them either.

Her eyes searched, scanning the area, but Aiden was no longer standing by the exit. *Great. Just when I actually need him, he splits.*

Once they were outside the church, she gently pulled her hand away and walked over to where she had secured RBG. Shoving her clutch under her arm, she took the water bowl she had left for her in one hand and the leash in the other, walking across the street so her dog baby could relieve herself. Scott followed.

"Hey, um, sorry about my mom back there," he said, gazing off nowhere in particular. "She's taken Tricia's death hard, which is ironic considering she didn't seem to like her very much when she was alive."

Figures. Quinn placed the water bowl down while RBG sniffed around in the grass. "Oh, it's okay. She didn't like me very much when we were hanging out either."

She couldn't tell if he was processing anything she said.

"Scott? Do you need to sit down? Maybe I can get you some water from the church?"

RBG woofed.

Quinn couldn't help but smile. Tail wagging, brown eyes dancing, her dog was working the cute. "You had your water already," she told her.

She whined and Quinn knew why—the water hadn't been cold enough for her liking. She had spoiled her dog baby by putting ice cubes in her bowl back home.

Meanwhile, Scott didn't answer.

She placed her hand on his upper arm. "Scott? You okay?"

He snapped out of whatever trance he was in, nodding. "Remember, before all this happened, when we bumped into each other at Church Street Eats, I asked if we could talk?"

"Sure I do."

He rubbed the back of his neck. "Yeah, well, what I had wanted to ask . . . I don't know if you know any of this, but Tricia was planning on leaving real estate."

Quinn stilled. "Really? Why?"

"She was sick of it, to be honest. It was good money, but she wanted a challenge. We both did. One of the things that brought us together was our desire to do something different for ourselves. Bonus if it had nothing to do with our families."

"That's great, Scott," Quinn said. She meant it too. "What did she want to do instead? Did she have any idea?"

"She did, actually. We both did." For the first time in a long while, he had a genuine smile. "We had this dream of opening up a law practice together."

"Really?" As soon as she said it, Quinn realized how she sounded. "I'm sorry—I just had no idea either of you had that kind of interest."

If he was bothered by her surprise, he didn't show it. "That's okay. No one did. Long story short, we studied our asses off for the LSAT and applied. A few months ago, we both got our acceptance letters from our top choice law school."

"Wow, that's impressive. Congratulations!"

"Yeah, our plan was to marry in the summer, then leave everything behind and enroll this fall."

So that's why Tricia said he wanted to get married as soon as possible. And I had made wisecracks.

Quinn felt like an ass, especially because Scott's excitement over their plans was palpable and infectious. Still, something wasn't adding up.

"Not to be rude, but why ask to talk to me? It sounds like you have—or had—a solid plan in place."

The smile faded away. "Well, when Tricia told Trina what we planned to do . . . let's say, she wasn't taking it well. I knew my mom would flip out just as badly.

"Anyway, I remembered you and your brother pursuing paths your parents were originally less than thrilled about. I wanted to ask you how you got them to come around. That's why I wanted to talk to you."

And I thought he was going to hit on me that day. Someone call Tina Fey and let her know I've got Mean Girls, the Sequel, *all covered. Yeesh.*

Scott had been right too. After Bash blew off a spot at University of Virginia's law school in order to earn a master's in emergency fire service administration, he later joined a national emergency firefighter relief agency. For years, he traveled all over the country, either making department assessments or jumping into the action himself. His mother had been beside herself with grief over his decision; his father offered reluctant respect.

Quinn hadn't offered much reprieve for her parents either. After she graduated college, she had forgone a bookbinding apprenticeship in Washington, D.C., in order to teach English all over the world. First stop: Phnom Penh, Cambodia. Her mom had had nightmares of her stepping on some long-forgotten land mine, and cried for a solid month.

Quinn wished she could offer some sage advice. "Honestly, there was nothing we could say to abate their fears. In the end, I think they just had to have faith in us to not take unnecessary risks. The rest, well, was time." Something he said niggled her. "What do you mean when you said Trina wasn't taking it well?"

"Oh, it was bad. Fights all the time, then calling Trish at home after arguing all day. She even came by my office, offering me money to break up with her sister and walk away forever. Can you believe that? Personally, I was ready to write her off, but it was her sister, and Trish really wanted Trina to come around and support her. It never happened. This past month they only talked if they absolutely had to."

Sounds like motive to me.

"Hey, thanks for listening," he said.

"Anytime."

"I better get going." Scott looked around the almost-empty parking lot. "We still have the whole graveside thing to do."

She nodded. "Okay. Drive safe." She picked up the water bowl and emptied the remaining liquid into the grass while giving the leash a gentle tug. "Scott?"

"Yeah?"

"Whatever happens, finish what you and Tricia started. Go to law school."

He gave a noncommittal shrug. "We'll see. Thanks."

Just then, a car came barreling right for them, honking several times in a row.

It was Aiden in his SUV.

Guess he hasn't given up on our talk. Great.

She could see him through the windshield: he was definitely agitated, and not in the normal Aiden way. Something was wrong.

She opened the car door, letting RBG hop up and into the backseat, before getting in.

"Is everything okay?" Quinn folded herself in. She hadn't even shut the door yet when he was already putting the vehicle into drive.

Aiden's hands clenched the wheel. "Have you checked your phone?"

She buckled her seat belt, although he pressed his foot on the gas—hard—before the click, reeling her back and making RBG slip.

"You're driving like we're in a getaway car! Slow down!"

"Asked you a question, Quinn."

"No, Aiden, I didn't check my phone during the *funeral*. My bad. Why? What's going on?"

He rubbed a hand down his face before switching on the emergency lights. "I was in the middle of checking emails while you were conversing with that tool, when I got a call for a ten-seventy-one."

Aiden was cutting through traffic, weaving in and out, using the service road to pass slower vehicles. Quinn grabbed onto the handle hanging by the passenger door—her brother called it the "oh crap" grip.

"In English, please. What's a 'ten-seventy-one'?"

He didn't take his eyes off the road. "A ten-seventy-one is police code for a shooting in progress. Quinn, the call came from Guinefort House."

Chapter Eleven

"This wasn't just plain terrible; this was fancy terrible. This
was terrible with raisins in it."
—Dorothy Parker, *Women Know Everything!*

"**I** think I'm going to be sick."
It was a toss-up what made Quinn more nauseated: Aiden's
maniacal driving or the thought of her cousin in mortal danger.
Every time she peeked out the car window, familiar scenery
morphed into a long blur—tree-lined roads becoming streaks
of green and brown, stretched out like pulled taffy.

It was a blessing her parents couldn't see her now. The
irony wasn't lost on her—three years in places considered
unsafe by the U.S. Department of State travel advisory, only
to finally be at home—and headed straight for a suburban
combat zone.

She gazed over at Aiden, whose jaw was locked, his tight-
fisted grip on the steering wheel. Quinn knew him well enough
to know he was already going through about a hundred different scenarios on how the scene at the abbey was going to go
down. If only she had a clue.

"Please, Aiden, talk to me." She swallowed, willing her voice to remain steady. If she sounded like she was going to crack, no way was he going to share anything with her.

He gave her a stern look. "You are here as a courtesy. Do you understand? Once we arrive at the scene, you are not to get out of the vehicle. You are not to call your family or anyone else. If there's press on the grounds, you will not talk to them."

"I get it, absolutely." She tried reminding her lungs how to breathe.

"All right, before the funeral, at zero nine hundred hours, a Caucasian male came into the abbey's receiving area, demanding to speak with Daria, threatening to hurt himself. Thank Christ, before she went down to talk to him, she called the station and alerted our desk captain, saying it could be a ten-fifty-six-a—"

"Again," she interrupted, "English, please."

"That's a suicide attempt," he told her. "Anyway, she talked to him for quite a while, trying to calm him down. His behavior presented as erratic—screaming one minute, crying the next. He was perseverating, repeating on a loop about how he lost the love of his life to some rich guy."

They were in front of Guinefort House. Aiden stopped and parked the car, both of them taking off their seat belts. Quinn hit the button on the passenger-side door to roll down the window. After the drive through the seven circles of hell, Quinn needed some fresh air to stabilize her stomach.

Even before Aiden had his door all the way open, a couple of his police officers, along with a flurry of press, surrounded the car, pulling on the door so hard Quinn was amazed it didn't rip off its hinges. Unfortunately, another swarm of press was headed for her too.

"Excuse me, miss. Who are you?"

"Detective Harrington! Is it true the shooter's one of your own?"

"Is he holding hostages? Has he given a list of demands?"

"Miss, are you connected to the shooter or hostages inside?"

She had to push them out of her window with one hand while hitting the automatic button with the other. As soon as Aiden exited the vehicle and closed the door behind him, she locked the doors.

Like a swarm of moths following a light, the press trailed Aiden's footsteps as he approached Guinefort House. When he was far enough away, Quinn didn't hesitate to turn off the SUV and grab his keys.

She glanced over at RBG, who gave her a head tilt.

"I know what I said, but it's Daria. I can't just sit by and do nothing."

She got out of the vehicle, and RBG bolted out after her.

"What are you doing? You could get hurt!"

RBG stopped, giving a quick shake of her head.

Quinn slammed the door. "Okay, *fine*. But be quiet. And stick by me."

She wasn't going to get too close because, in spite of her current actions, she actually didn't have a death wish. But her cousin was in there. And if she was right, she had a pretty good idea who the shooter was. One of the journalists had asked Aiden if the culprit was "one of his own." Could it be Officer Wyatt Reynolds?

Please, who else *could it be?*

Vienna and Fairfax County police officers had surrounded the perimeter of Guinefort House. There was a fire truck parked, and Quinn could hear the blare of an ambulance coming closer.

She might have promised, but if Officer Wyatt Reynolds was the shooter, Aiden needed to be informed of what she knew:

the yearbook with notes from eighth grade, the vigilance he'd taken to keep in touch with Tricia through the years. Quinn could kick herself for not disclosing the information sooner, all because she hadn't wanted to hear another patronizing speech.

She was thinking she still had some growing up to do after all.

Even surrounded by other cops in a tight huddle, Aiden wasn't difficult to approach. He must've sensed movement nearby because he stopped mid-sentence when he realized she was there.

"What did I say?" His temples were visibly throbbing, even from a distance.

Both hands went up in surrender. "I know, I know! But if that's Officer Reynolds in there with my cousin, I might have information about why he got so worked up in the first place."

He blinked a couple of times.

"Do you know this bystander, Detective?" one of the other cops asked.

"Yeah, get into position. I'll be right back."

Aiden stomped off, making sure to grab Quinn by the hand, dragging her away from the scene. As soon as they were out of earshot of the others, he let go. RBG whined, pressing her body against Quinn's.

"Tell me why I shouldn't get one of my guys to throw you in the back of a squad car right now and take you home."

Quinn took in a deep breath. "You have every right to be upset with me, but listen first."

She then proceeded to tell him everything she had learned so far—about the yearbooks and the notes, and Trina saying Reynolds had been into her sister for years. She also told him about finding the posters and the receipt in Trina's office. She showed him the photos she'd taken and shared the details of her conversation with Scott earlier.

Aiden rubbed two fingers across his forehead like he was trying to press his brain back into his skull. "You and I are going to have a long talk when this is over."

She had expected that response.

"If your parents knew what you and your cousin have been up to, they'd lock you away for good."

"*If* they find out."

His nostrils flared. "Excuse me?"

"Nothing. Never mind."

He gazed skyward, mumbling "Deliver me" under his breath.

"You seem to say that a lot around me."

His face ticked. "Is it any wonder?"

Her head dropped, staring down at her feet as she balanced on a protruding root of a nearby tree.

She heard him blow out an exasperated breath. "Anything else I need to know?"

Quinn met his eye. "Nope, that's it." She pantomimed an "X." "Cross my heart."

Hands resting on his hip, he nodded. "All right, wait here. I'll update you when I can." With those parting words, he jogged back over to his squad, who were still in a huddle.

While she felt better having told Aiden all she knew about the case, she realized the police on the scene barely knew the fine women of Guinefort House. They certainly didn't know her cousin, which meant none of them had as much skin in the game as she did. They also didn't have a clue about the house's layout or the grounds-and some of its secrets.

But Quinn knew the area well. They could blindfold her and she would be able to find her way out.

At least this time, I didn't promise.

Quinn made a *shh* sound to her dog baby, her forefinger to her lips, as she skirted around the gravel path to the soft grass along the edges. She wanted to—no, she *had* to—get close enough to hear their plan. Daria was too important. Since the day Quinn was born, her cousin had always been there. Maybe with a different name, but the same smart-mouthed, not-as-tough-as-she-seemed cousin. They were more than first cousins. They were even more than best friends. They were sisters.

The officers were in a tight circle, but Quinn knew this land because Daria had shown her. She shared the mysteries hidden in its soil and among the cherry blossoms and dogwoods. And one of those secrets was, if she stood on the eastern curve of the slope on a windy day, any conversation from the abbey's lawn followed a natural drift and could be heard as clear as if she were standing right next to it. It had something to do with the density of the tree cover above, flanking the property left and right, forming a domed arch with its foliage and branches, so thick sound bounced off and around.

Once Quinn moved into position, she could hear everything they were saying. And, sure enough, it was Wyatt Reynolds inside with her cousin—and he was armed. The police were proceeding with caution so as not to escalate the situation.

Quinn crouched down next to her baby, petting her fur. "I hate thinking of Daria in there. There's nothing worse than an idiot with a little power, in this case, power being a gun."

She eyed the huddle below. Those guys were still talking. The Fairfax County officers wanted to wait for the hostage negotiator to arrive. Aiden and some of his colleagues wanted to proceed without them. Since Wyatt had been one of their own, they thought they could coax him to surrender his weapon without force.

"This is ridiculous," she heard Aiden say. He broke away from the group, heading right for the abbey entrance. Just like that. No announcements on the bullhorn. No final call to either his or the Fairfax County squads.

What's he doing?

Her heart was beating hard inside her chest. What if she lost them both?

In an instant, impatience turned to fear. She wanted to call her mom. She longed to crawl back into her sumptuous queen-sized bed with RBG and have a do-over on this day. She wished she could pull her cousin out of that abbey and never look back.

None of the other officers were following. They were calling out to Aiden, yelling back and forth, but nothing else. That's when she decided she couldn't let him go in alone.

She took off her heels, unclipped RBG's leash, and proceeded around the property to the adjourning kennels. As she approached, the dogs inside were going crazy, feeling the tension in the air, most likely smelling whiffs of fear. For sure she thought her dog baby would join in, egged on by the other dogs, but RBG just gazed up at Quinn, her chocolate-brown eyes locked with hers, waiting for her signal.

"You are soooo getting a liverwurst cupcake when this is all done."

In a loud whisper she heard, "What are you doing here?"

Quinn glanced over. It was the Reverend Mother, and she did not seem pleased.

"We need to cover the detective. He went in there by himself!"

The Reverend Mother's gray eyebrows furrowed. "Young lady, that's not your job. Let the police handle this!"

Her eyes homed in on the back doors to the abbey. "I don't have time to argue. Let me have Rueger."

Quinn had come to the kennel enough times to know many of their canine charges. Most became companion dogs; others were sent for further training for the blind or for police units.

Then there was Rueger. He had been one of those chosen for police training, but he was sent back—not because he wasn't smart enough or didn't know the commands. He mastered those in no time.

No, Rueger had a mind of his own. If the dog thought he had an opportunity at taking out a criminal, he took it, without regard for his own safety. He'd been shot at more times than any other rookie—human or canine.

And that's why he was ultimately rejected by the Fairfax County Department's K9 unit—and exactly why he was perfect for what Quinn needed him to do. Besides, he was her cousin's favorite.

Sister Daria hadn't even tried to fake being upset by the police department returning him. She loved that dog, calling him her "spirit animal." Quinn still remembered what Daria had said: "I know what it's like to not be able to handle authority figures. He and I will be just fine together."

The Reverend Mother must've had a hunch of what Quinn was up to and, without another word, went back into the kennels and retrieved Rueger.

"Be careful with him," she said. "Otherwise, you won't have to answer to me. You'll have to answer to that stubborn mule of a cousin of yours."

Quinn nodded, not wasting any more time, gesturing for the dogs to follow her.

Without shoes on, it was much easier for Quinn to creep along the back way, through the grass and the nuns' vegetable garden, to the sliding doors. Usually, they were unlocked. Peeking through them, Quinn could see Aiden talking with Officer Reynolds, who had her cousin in a headlock, with his gun out.

The situation had escalated to a hostage negotiation.
This is bad.

The problem was, if she slid the door, the sound might startle the idiot and make him accidentally shoot Daria—or Aiden—or one of the other sisters. Quinn had a direct line to him. She'd have to move fast to get her cousin clear, but Quinn knew she didn't have the kind of training to make that work. She peered inside again, trying to figure out what to do.

Meanwhile, both dogs were pacing back and forth, Rueger growing more agitated, a rumbling growl vibrating through his strong body.

"I know, I know," Quinn whispered. "I want to save her too."

That's when something else caught her eye—the back window in the kitchen. Wide open. No glass. No locks. No screen.

Rueger and Quinn locked eyes as something was communicated between them. She pointed over to the open window.

"Do you think you can make it?"

He woofed. RBG licked the side of his face, and Quinn swore Rueger smiled big for her.

Quinn scratched his head, then nodded. "Okay then . . . go get her!"

That's all it took. Rueger ran back and around in a wide circle, gaining speed and momentum—and holy shitake, he jumped right through the window in one graceful leap! She heard dishes crash. Then some yelping and yelling. Quinn peeked through the glass doors just in time to witness Rueger barreling from the kitchen, right for Wyatt, who had twisted his body to see what was happening. Recognizing an opportunity, Aiden lunged forward and wrenched her cousin out of Wyatt's grip, shoving her behind his body, a human shield. Meanwhile, Rueger leapt into the air and tackled Wyatt to the ground, his mouth wrapped around his throat.

"Omigosh, he did it!"

Quinn was still whispering.

She pulled at the door handle, but for the first time ever, the latch was locked, and she couldn't get in. *Good thing I didn't try Plan A. I would've caused a ruckus and still wouldn't have been able to get to Daria.*

Without thinking, she and RBG ran around the abbey, back the way they had come, just in time to see the commotion carrying on in the front.

"All clear! All clear!"

Sure enough, there was Wyatt Reynolds, walking out of the building, head down, hands cuffed behind his back. He was wearing his uniform, but Quinn noticed he no longer carried his badge or his gun.

Out of the corner of his eye, he spied her watching, and then his eyes locked with hers. She half-expected him to lunge her way, yell at full volume that he was going to make her pay. But instead, his eyes pleaded, looking wild and desperate. He skidded to a stop.

"I didn't do it, Quinn. You've got to believe me." He panted, unable to catch his breath, sweat rolling down the sides of his face. "Oh God, what have I done? What have I done!"

Aiden held him firm by the forearm. "Keep moving, Reynolds. Don't make this any more difficult than it already is."

Reynolds held her eyes as Aiden guided him down the steps. Aiden could've gotten rough with Wyatt, yanked his arm clear out of the socket to get him where he needed him to be. No one would've uttered a peep, especially after one of Aiden's own had threatened a bunch of nuns. But Aiden kept his emotions in check, remaining professional as he guided Wyatt straight into the back of one of the awaiting cop cars, still keeping him in handcuffs.

As soon as her brain registered what had happened, she didn't even think: her legs bolted forward.

A bunch of people yelled at her.

"Hey!"

"Where ya goin'?"

"You can't go in there!"

She went right inside, her eyes scanning the vestibule. If not for a small stack of Bibles on the console and the modest cross nailed to the wall, it would be the same as any other home in the area. But when she spotted a couple of bullet holes along the wall by the powder room, everything started feeling all too real.

To the right was the well-worn sitting area, filled with aging, donated furniture—including a couch from her parents—where several of the sisters sat together, holding hands and praying. She rushed past them into the kitchen, scanning for the face she knew almost as well as her own.

"Quinn! I'm here!" she heard from the other side of a small crowd. An EMT was treating a bad scrape across Daria's neck, dabbing the wound with a soaked cotton swab.

Rueger was panting, smiling—if dogs actually did such things—and glued to the other side of her.

Grinning at Quinn, Daria patted his head, scratching the back of his neck. "My hero!"

Quinn sat in the empty chair next to her, clasping her cousin's hands.

They gazed at each other, and she felt the tears pooling.

Her cousin patted the back of her hand. "I'm *fine*. I promise. It looks worse than it is."

She had a long, angry, serrated scrape along the diagonal of her throat, still beading small drops of crimson. "How did that happen?"

The lady EMT reached for a sterilized bandage. "When Detective Harrington secured the hostage, Reynolds's gun must've scraped her."

"It's not a bullet graze," Daria told her.

Quinn gave her a look. "I wasn't thinking it was a bullet graze."

Daria let out a barking laugh. "You're *totally* lying. I can tell by the way you're studying the direction and texture of the wound, that's exactly what you're thinking."

She wasn't wrong. "*Fine*, I was. Happy now?"

The wearing on her from what had happened showed as Daria sighed heavily. "I'll be happier after they finish this up and I can get my statement out of the way."

The sound of footsteps came from behind them.

"It seems most of my time these days is spent escorting Caine women to and from my police station."

Quinn sucked her top lip between her teeth. She definitely knew that voice.

Sister Daria gave a half wave. "Hey, Aiden, I'm almost done here."

"Take your time," he told her with a gentle smile. Quinn noticed all the women—and a couple of the men—swooned in their work boots. One of them might have even been another novitiate in Daria's cohort. If Aiden noticed their reactions, he didn't let on.

"I'll wait for you outside and then drive you over to the station," he told her.

Daria stared at Aiden, her eyes watering. "You saved my life. I owe you big time."

"That's my job," he said, as if it were nothing, as if he had picked up a gallon of milk on the way home. "Besides, I had help."

As if on cue, Rueger let out a happy bark, but then he must have spotted RBG and took off for her. They padded their way out the front door, as though they walked together every day.

Daria chortled. "I think we've made a match."

Everyone around them joined in. Quinn did too, but that wasn't her only reaction. Her hands were shaking, so she stuffed them in her pockets. *Must be the adrenalin.*

"Meantime, *you*"—Aiden pointed over to Quinn with his chin—"come with me."

Everyone in the kitchen went *ooohhh* out loud, like they were back in grade school. She wanted to crawl under the stairs and make herself a Harry Potter home.

She followed Aiden out of the residence, with all eyes on them.

"Where are we going?"

Aiden grunted as he stomped. "Somewhere I can speak loud enough to get through that skull of yours."

She stopped. "I don't need another lecture or for you to pat my head or rumple my hair."

He whirled around and got very close to her face. "Is it possible you can wait until we get into the SUV to talk?" She didn't budge and he noticed. "Please." he added.

She could do that. "Yes, I can grant you that courtesy, seeing as you saved my cousin's life and all. You were like a superhero back there."

His gaze heated, moving from her eyes to her mouth and back again.

In her nervousness, she babbled on. "Although I'm betting what you did violated ten different rules of police protocol. If I had to guess. I need to remind myself to look that one up when I get home."

He took a deep breath. "In. The. Car."

"Fine."

They walked along the narrow gravel driveway. Spotting her heels, she scooped them up before hopping into his SUV, and even though it was obvious he was beyond ticked off, he still opened the car door for her.

He closed it the normal way, not in the passive-aggressive slamming-hard fashion she was half-expecting. He folded himself in on his side and shut the door.

He raised his hand. "Let me speak first."

She closed her mouth.

"If you share what I'm about to say outside this car, not only will I deny it, but I will charge you with interfering with a felony investigation. Do we understand each other?"

With eyes as round as saucers, she nodded.

"You could've gotten yourself killed back there."

"I know. But I didn't."

His gray eyes darkened. "You could've gotten your cousin hurt or killed."

She shut her mouth.

"That scenario could have gone down a million and one ways, most of them bad enough I don't even want to picture them."

Quinn looked down at her hands.

"What you did was reckless and dangerous, and it scared the sh—" He stopped himself, running his hand up and down his face a bunch of times. "Just tell me you understand that?"

Quinn knew he was right, which was why she kept staring at her hands.

He wasn't done. "It may also have been the bravest thing I've seen in my life. The dog wasn't bad either."

Wait. What?

She looked up. "Really?"

"You were magnificent."

She sucked in some air, not realizing she had been holding her breath, something she did when she was nervous.

He had more to share. "Now, this bizarre situation aside, I could say over and over again for you not to continue investigating and asking questions, but I know you well enough to understand you won't stop until we catch whoever did this. You may not have liked Tricia, but on some level you feel it's on you to make this right. You're wrong, by the way, but I understand the instinct. Are you with me so far?"

She tried to wet her lips, but her mouth had gone dry, so she nodded instead.

"Okay, well, after you found Tricia's phone, we did a scan and found texts and emails from Wyatt. A lot of them. Trina was correct that he's been obsessing over her for years. However, it wasn't a stalking case because Tricia answered him—often—and not to blow him off. It's obvious to anyone from the outside that she was leading him on, but I'm guessing Reynolds never got that memo.

"But it was worse than even her sister knew. He fixed her speeding tickets. He gave her tips on future zoning ordinances discussed inside the department—anything that could possibly help her business. As far as I was concerned, he was as good as fired, but we kept him on, thinking maybe he'd lead us to the killer."

"You don't think it was him?"

"We can't rule anyone out, but he was on duty the night she died. I don't know—maybe he slipped her something before then. Not all substances are caught by a tox screen. But it had to be something because someone doesn't go from perfectly healthy to dying of liver and kidney failure, partially paralyzed, without something to help that along. We're investigating that now. We had hoped Wyatt would lead us to the answer, but obviously the plan has changed with this whole mess." He stopped to grab a water bottle from the center console, cracking open the cap seal and taking a long drink. Quinn couldn't help but watch his throat work, his Adam's apple bobbing up and down. Everything about him was utterly masculine.

Note to self: You really need to get out of the house more.

"Why are you telling me all of this?"

Aiden scanned the scene out the window before answering. "Because, while I knew much of what you've already shared, you got pieces of evidence and some informal statements no one on my team could get—and that's impressive."

"Thank you."

"I'm not finished." He put the water bottle back in the console, wiping his mouth with the back of his hand. "Obviously Wyatt's off the force and remains a person of interest in the case. Trina is also a person of interest. And as torn up as Scott is, we can't rule him out because, unfortunately, most female murder victims knew their killer intimately. But the first two's motives are sketchy. It's speculation. We still don't know what killed her."

Quinn piped in. "Two healthy individuals dying of sudden-onset organ failure featuring partial paralysis. That can't be a coincidence."

"What? The Levine case?"

"Absolutely."

His jaw shimmied back and forth. "You're right, it's odd, but there's nothing tying them together. I can't request a court order to exhume a body without something linking Doctor Levine to Tricia in some way. It's a specious connection, at best."

Out of the corner of her eye, Quinn spotted her cousin leaving the abbey, a bandage on her neck, heading toward Aiden's SUV. Rueger was trotting next to her and along with RBG.

Aiden noticed her cousin's approach as well. "Hey, not a word about what we just talked about, even to your partner in crime over there."

Quinn didn't like the idea of keeping a secret from Daria. But then again, wasn't her cousin keeping a few of her own? Like, what had really happened between her and Raj, and why the sudden interest in religious life as soon as Quinn left the country?

One has nothing to do with the other. You know better.

"Honestly, Daria's been the one urging me to talk to you from the beginning, so maybe you don't want to be so fast to leave her out of the loop."

A shadow of disappointment flashed across his face. "May I ask why you didn't?"

"Talk to you in the first place?"

"Yeah."

She sighed, staring out the window. "Because I didn't want you to mess up my hair yet *again* and tell me to go back to playing with dolls."

He let out a laugh. "Quinn, every time someone gave you a doll, you chopped the hair off and threw it away."

"You know what I mean. Don't play dumb."

His brows went north. "Play dumb? With you? Never."

"Whatever," she said retrieving her purse from the car floor and getting out a piece of gum. She had a sour taste in her mouth.

He eyed the book purse. "Nice choice by the way—the story of a man who loses his wife at the prime of her life. Fitting for the funeral today."

That surprised her. She gazed down at her *Love is a Mix Tape* book purse. "You've read it?"

He gave a lopsided smile. "Yeah, Quinn, I've read it. Cops read, you know."

161

Of course, he'd read this book, and of course he understood her silent tribute.

"Stop being so cool, Aiden. It's hard to stay annoyed at you when you do that."

"You're wrong about one thing, though, smarty-pants," he went on.

"What's that?"

He brushed some stray hairs off her cheek. "I don't see you as a kid. Not anymore."

Holy—did he just say what I think he said?

Just as Quinn and Aiden were finally getting somewhere, Daria came barreling to the car and opened the door, letting Rueger and RBG hop in first.

"Make room for me, lovebirds," Daria said.

She froze, ready to die all over again, until she realized her cousin was talking to the dogs. Quinn's eyes scanned Aiden's face, but he was back in cop mode.

The moment was gone.

As soon as Quinn buckled herself in, Daria shut the door, scooted over to the middle, and leaned over, her forearms resting on the backs of their seats.

"All right now—tell me what I missed."

Chapter Twelve

"I feel like someone after a deluge being asked to describe the way it was before the flood while I'm still plucking seaweed out of my hair."

—Norman Rush, *Mating*

"Wow, two Caine women tangled with the law in under a month. I believe that's a new record."

Uncle Jerry was what her mama called "a real pot stirrer." Quinn and Daria's latest brushes with Vienna PD's finest served as fodder for his favorite pastime: teasing with love. This had been his third joke in the last couple of days, but every time, his exaggerations grew more outrageous, even as his gaze lingered on Daria's neck bandage.

Quinn watched father and daughter taking turns needling the other. Bad dad puns. Inside jokes. Father and daughter spoke each other's language of twisted humor. Her cousin was close with both her parents, but someone would have to be blind not to notice her special bond with her father.

Everyone was at the store that day—not just family, but half of Vienna too. Quinn's dad was ringing up a bunch of books on current events at the front register. Her mother was serving coffee and Mary Lee's famous crackle treats—which everyone coined "crack" brownies because they were that good and addictive. Aunt Johanna and Uncle Jerry were sitting at the counter, chatting with Adele and the other customers as if they had all the time in the world. Daria had come in for a brief visit—mostly to get away from the press parked at the abbey. The attention was driving her batty, but having Rueger by her side seemed to make her feel better.

These were the days Quinn reveled in. They had propped the back door of the shop open, enjoying the rare treat of a fresh cool breeze. Whatever heat of summer they'd suffered under a few days ago had now been replaced by cooler temperatures and the promise of rain. They knew the breezes and low humidity wouldn't last, so they had to soak in the outside goodness while they could. Quinn also had her office door wedged open so she could work and still feel a part of the store's happenings, although considering the books for elementary school kids were situated right by her office, her work was becoming more show-and-tell than productive work session.

She didn't mind. Quinn got a kick out of demonstrating how a book was put together and letting the children's little fingers pull the linen thread to make the stitches. They found the process almost as thrilling as discovering a new favorite picture book.

Daria came over to help. "Who wants a story?"

"Me! Me!" the little ones exclaimed, some jumping up and down in place, their tiny arms shooting straight up while waving their hands.

"Thank you," Quinn mouthed to her cousin, who smiled and settled into the green leather chair in the corner, the one with the white canvas pillow saying "Just One More Chapter."

Daria perused the teeming bookshelf and chose one of her go-to standards, *Dragons Love Tacos*, and started reading. She was one of the most animated, versatile storytellers around, using her background in drama to conjure funny voices, especially her dead ringer of a British accent. The kids adored her.

Quinn was about to go back into her office to work on a journal with a juicy tale. It was delicate work, the leather worn, the boards partially rotted. It had belonged to Rachel's maternal great-grandmother, and she felt honored Bash's ex trusted the family heirloom to her care.

Before getting started on the project, Quinn happened to glance up, a quick peek out the back window, only to spot Rachel Brooke Slingbaum in the parking lot with her brother. Even with the door open, she couldn't hear what they were saying, but she could tell by their body language they were having one heck of an impassioned discussion. They were almost nose to nose, her hands clasped together, with his cupping hers. He leaned his forehead against hers, closing his eyes as she shook her head. But she wasn't moving away either.

Quinn couldn't remember the last time she'd seen two people so much in love. She wanted to be happy for them, but one glance at their expressions foretold they weren't getting back together anytime soon. Quinn knew her well enough to understand Rachel was a stubborn woman. She was loving and generous, funny and brilliant, but she had her pride. And she could hold one mean grudge.

The spontaneous story time ended, and the children dispersed back to their parents. Daria curtsied, with a round of applause from the grateful parents, appreciative of the small break.

"I'm here all week. Don't forget to tip your waitresses on the way out."

Everyone laughed, including Quinn. But that didn't mean Daria hadn't caught her staring out the window toward the drama in the back lot.

"Think those two will work it out?" she asked.

Quinn exhaled loudly. "Who knows? It's going to take a lot more than some texts and a couple of conversations for him to win her back."

Daria scratched her chin. "When it comes to women, Bash hasn't ever had to work too hard. Think he has it in him?"

Quinn blew on some wet glue on one of the book boards. "That is an excellent question."

Just then, Rachel backed away and headed straight for her car. Bash didn't move, standing off to the side, hands fisting his hair, watching her drive off. Quinn hoped he was going to walk back to the store so she could ask him what happened.

But he didn't. He left his car in the lot and took off in the other direction. She had no idea where he was headed, but she could tell he was all worked up: head bowed, shoulders tense and hunched up to his ears, his pace fast.

She wanted to run after him.

"Don't," Daria said, reading her mind. "Let him have some time, get himself sorted out."

"But I could help him. Tell him what he needs to do to win her back. She needs a big gesture, something to prove he's going to stick around this time."

Daria gave a slight headshake. "Stay out of it, at least for a little while."

"But why?"

"Because he's over thirty and it's time he figured some of this out for himself. His moving home and wanting some roots is a good start. Now, let's see how far he gets on his own before we need to throw a life raft over."

The phone rang in the store. "Hold that thought—I have to get this." She picked up the phone. "Good afternoon. Prose and Scones. Quinn speaking."

"Oh good! Just the person I was hoping to talk to," the elderly voice said on the other end.

"Well, you've got me. Who, may I ask, is calling?"

"This is Reverend Mother Eugenia from Guinefort House."

Oh wow. Why do I feel like I'm in trouble?

"Good afternoon. Are you looking for Daria?"

"No, I am calling for *you*, my dear," she clarified. "I'd like you to join us for dinner this evening."

Phone to her ear, Quinn's eyes darted toward her cousin, who mouthed, "Who is it'?"

Still maintaining eye contact, Quinn answered, "Sure, I'd love to come to dinner, Reverend Mother."

Daria's face fell.

Uh-oh. Something was going on.

"May I bring something?"

"No, just yourself," the Reverend Mother said. "Dinner is served promptly at five thirty."

Five thirty? Was the abbey now offering an early-bird special or something?

"Sure thing. Thank you for the invitation."

"Until then." She hung up.

Quinn returned the phone to its charging cradle.

"Did the Reverend Mother of my order just invite you to dinner tonight?"

"I guess so. Have any idea why?"

Daria started chewing on the corner of her thumb. "I haven't the first clue. Whatever it is, it can't be good. Forget those clouds hovering over your brother; we need to get ready for the real storm coming."

Chapter Thirteen

"Hearing nuns' confessions is like being stoned
to death with popcorn."
—Fulton J. Sheen, Catholic bishop, author, and television host

The upshot to having a weakness for retro fashion was that Quinn already had the perfect outfit for dining with a superfluity of Anglican nuns. It was another midi dress, this one in celadon blue, with a most charming Peter Pan collar. There were tiny fleurs-de-lis embroidered along the trim of the cream-colored fabric, which only served to complement her gold cross stud earrings.

When Quinn knocked on their door, one of the nuns answered, conducting a slow perusal, a hint of a smirk curling at the corner of her mouth.

"Nice touch with the cross earrings. The purse is even better, although Maria von Trapp was Catholic, but that's just being petty now, isn't it?"

She was talking about the book purse Quinn had in hand, another in her growing collection: an upcycled copy of *The Sound of Music*. Artist Melissa Mason—Etsy shop owner extraordinaire of Viva Las Vixens—had turned the hardcover book into a purse, this time with a short, carved bamboo handle.

Quinn was standing on the stoop where, just a few days before, Detective Harrington had carted away former police officer Wyatt Reynolds in cuffs. The difference in circumstances was jarring.

The nun's small, dark eyes and sharp bone structure only added to the severity of the first impression she gave. "I am Sister Theresa."

Quinn opened her mouth to introduce herself, but she was cut off.

"Oh, no need. I already know who *you* are." She stepped back, holding the doorknob in hand. "This way, girl."

As Sister Theresa allowed her to step into the foyer, Quinn marveled at how everything was in order, as if nothing had happened. The only remnants were the two bullets holes in the wall plaster.

"Follow me," the nun said, closing the front door and proceeding down the hall. "I see you have a gift under your arm. If it's not something all of us can enjoy, the Reverend Mother will give it back. She takes her vow of poverty quite seriously, as do we all."

Chill, sister, I've got this. That's what she wanted to say, but Quinn didn't have the cojones to execute her usual sass. Daria had been telling her for the last couple of years that the nuns of her order didn't suffer fools—or sarcasm—but it was still something else, witnessing it for herself.

"The gift is something to share," Quinn told her, wondering where the sister was taking her. They had already passed the dining room. "Is Sister Daria around?"

Sister Theresa half-glanced over her shoulder, stopping at a closed door at the end of the hall. She knocked.

"It is open," a voice called.

The sister placed her hand on the knob before turning to face Quinn. "The Reverend Mother will see you now." Sister Theresa opened the door but stepped aside so Quinn could enter. As soon as she did, the door closed.

And there she was—a kind, weathered visage and warm, hazel eyes with bushy eyebrows that had gone gray before the rest of the hair on her head. With her rounded belly and drooping earlobes hanging low, she reminded Quinn more of the Buddha than the head of a Catholic order.

She waved Quinn into the room. "Come in! Come in! So good of you to come on such short notice." She gestured toward the chair. "Please, sit down."

The Reverend Mother was already seated in one of those old recliners that looked like it had been swiped right off the set of the TV show *All in the Family*. She had a small, cherry-wood side table next to her, covered with well-worn books, next to which was red wine in a simple glass. The room had wall-to-wall shelves, teeming with old books, the kind found in archive collections and libraries. Even though Quinn was well aware that the smell of old books emanated from lignin, a chemical utilized in cheaply produced paper since the 1840s, Quinn didn't care: she still thought the smell was divine—and she helped herself to inhaling deeply.

"You're like me," the Reverend Mother said, chuckling.

"Really? In what way?"

"You are madly and deeply in love with books. I can't get enough of them. I imagine it's the same for you?"

"It is." Quinn wanted to read each and every title, badly, but perusing books wasn't why she had been invited, or perhaps *summoned*.

The Reverend Mother sported an impish grin, her eyes twinkling with amusement. She motioned again to the chair opposite her. "Sit. Please. I promise, I won't bite."

Quinn took the gift from under her arm and handed it over. "This is for you—and the order. You can share it is what I mean." She sat down, smoothing her skirt down with the palms of her hands.

"Thank you."

She wasn't a delicate woman: meaty hands, a wide face, broad shoulders. But she had intelligent eyes and brisk, deliberate movements. Quinn had the impression nothing about the Reverend Mother was frivolous or haphazard.

As Quinn watched her, a small smile formed. "I like how you rip through the paper. Not being fussy about it, I mean."

The Reverend Mother nodded, stopping mid-rip. "I quite agree. It's more fun this way. Of course, when I was growing up, in a blighted town in the middle of nowhere that I've never missed, someone would've slapped my hands for being so wasteful." She pushed the memory aside with a shake of her head. "I was so poor when I joined the order, I thought I was already in heaven: three squares a day, clothes and shoes replaced as soon as they wore out, clean water . . ." She sighed. "Pure heaven."

Quinn stilled. "I can't imagine. Where did you grow up?"

"Bill Clinton grew up in a place called Hope, Arkansas. I grew up twenty miles away in a town called Despair."

She righted in her chair, mouth agape. "Really?"

Her eyes glittered. "Yes to Arkansas, but no, my town wasn't called Despair. Old joke. Might as well have been, though."

Quinn relaxed. "Oh, you almost had me there."

"I know," she chortled. "Now, let's see what we have here. I need my reading glasses." She reached into an inside chair pocket and retrieved them.

Quinn didn't wait for the Reverend Mother to fully open the gift before explaining. "It's a rare American first edition of Dorothy Sayer's *The Mind of the Maker*. It's not worth as much as, let's say, a British first edition, but that's not the point really. Her publisher, Bloomsbury Press, issued a handful of these. It's a fine-condition, calf-skinned leather with marbled end papers, blind-stamped decorations, and gildings. I hope you enjoy it."

The Reverend Mother had put on her reading glasses and was leafing through the book, letting the gold edges of the pages fan through her fingers. "What a delightful gift. Unnecessary, but appreciated."

Quinn's shoulders dropped. "You're welcome. It's my pleasure."

She picked up her glass of red wine. "Please, help yourself. There's one for you right there."

Sure enough, Quinn gazed to her left, and there was a full glass waiting for her on a matching side table. She picked it up, holding it between her hands. The room was a bit warm, and she wondered if they had the air-conditioning on. The glass felt cool on her skin.

"Should we have a toast?"

Quinn hunched her shoulders up. "You lead the way."

The Reverend Mother raised her glass. *"Dignitas amicorum pie zeses vivas!"* She leaned forward to clink.

Quinn held back her glass. "Wait—what does that mean?"

Her lips quirked. "I like that. Demonstrates you have your own mind and you're not just toasting to appease an old woman." She gave a little wink. "It means 'Worthy among your friends. Drink so you may live, and may you live on.'"

"Well, that's quite lovely." She clinked her glass with the Reverend Mother's, then had a tiny taste, surprised by a burst of berries, vanilla, and lavender flooding her senses. "Whoa, this is really good."

"It's a 2016 Chateau des Annibals."

Quinn blushed. "I don't know anything about wine except it's probably not good to drink it from a box."

"Don't knock the box. A bad enough day sometimes requires a big box of wine."

Quinn let out a soft laugh. "That's true."

"Over Christmas, people want to share in the joy of the holiday spirit—and want to ensure that we do too. In other words, we are gifted copious amounts of wine." She took another sip. "I encourage it, of course. When you've given up money, sex, bearing children, and free will, it is important to savor the few allotted comforts."

"I'll drink to that." Quinn allowed herself another couple of mouthfuls before putting her glass down. "I want to thank you for the invitation to join you tonight, but I have to admit, I'm curious as to why I'm here."

Someone knocked on the door.

"Hold that thought." The Reverend Mother put down her glass. "Come in!"

It was Sister Theresa again. "Everything's ready. Dinner is served."

The Mother clapped. "Wonderful!" After a couple of tries, she hoisted herself out of her chair, shooing Quinn away when she reached over, trying to help. "No, thank you, my dear. I'm only seventy-eight. My predecessor, Sister Angelina, lived to be one hundred and three, most of it with her wits intact and her joints as spry as an eighty-year-old's. I plan on meeting that challenge." She wove her arm through Quinn's, leading her toward the dining room. "Before she died, I asked her the secret to such longevity. Can you guess what she answered?"

"I'm thinking a deal with the devil would be the wrong thing to say here."

The Reverend Mother threw her head back and laughed. "That's a good one. I'll have to remember that one for the next retreat." She patted Quinn's hand. "Sister Daria did mention you shared her wicked sense of humor."

Even though the dining room wasn't far, the Reverend Mother moved at a snail's pace. "Sister Angelina credited two hours spent daily in prayer and meditation, an hour walk each day—rain or shine—and thirty minutes, at a minimum, playing with the newborn puppies. Quite a delightful prescription, if you ask me."

When they arrived in the dining room, the nuns were already standing by their chairs, including Daria, who was positioned next to the head of the table, which had been held for the Reverend Mother. There was a vacant seat on the other side of the Mother's chair.

A woman of God flanked by Caine women. She imagined her uncle would have a field day over such an occasion.

Uncle Jerry would also get a kick out of her cousin being a quiet, anxious wreck. Quinn offered an encouraging smile, but she could tell it didn't penetrate.

They all sat down at the same time, and then the Reverend Mother led grace.

"This is quite a feast." Quinn dolloped a serving of morel mushrooms on top of a heaping pile of mashed potatoes. That was before the roast chicken made its way onto her plate. It smelled decadent— not as good as her mama's, but tasty-delish nonetheless.

"Do y'all always eat like this every night? If so, you need to get the word out—hashtag grace *and* grub, on the house."

"As if we want to court *that* kind of aggravation," Sister Theresa muttered.

The Reverend Mother swallowed the bite in her mouth. "Oh, I almost forgot! Do you know everyone here?"

Quinn scanned the table. "Mostly."

"Ah, well, everyone introduce yourselves."

A tiny lady next to Daria offered an enthusiastic wave and a toothy smile. "Okay, I'll start . . . Oh! Reverend Mother, *may* I start?"

The Mother waved a hand in the nun's direction. "Yes, yes, of course . . ."

The sister answered with a series of seal-like claps. "Oh good! Well, hi, I'm Sister Cecilia, but everyone calls me Sister Ceci. I run the adoption program, and I'm a novitiate, just like your cousin. In fact, we're roomies! Isn't that great? Of course, she asked me not to speak before five AM, which is fair when you think about it—"

The Reverend Mother cleared her throat. "Remember, brevity is the soul of wit and, may I add, courtesy."

Sister Ceci's large, rounded brown eyes widened. "Oh! Yes!" She looked apologetic. "Sorry."

The nun next to her offered a shy smile. "Hello, I'm Sister Lucy. I'm finishing veterinary school, and when I'm not in school, I help with all the dogs' medical needs. I help choose which dogs make the best candidates for either the police K9 units or for the assisted disabled program." Sister Lucy smiled but had trouble meeting Quinn's eyes. "I'm, um, much more of an animal than a people person."

This nun couldn't be more different from the last.

"I loathe small talk too," Quinn offered.

Sister Theresa flapped her hand to get her attention. "We've met already, girl. No need for a whole conversation. I do all the cooking and shopping and laundry. I'm like the wife around here. Next."

"I can see what Daria was talking about. You *are* 'the charming one.'"

Oh nooo, did I just say that out loud?

The room went dead silent, and her cousin's face grew even paler, if that were possible. Quinn dared not move, not breathe . . . until Sister Theresa burst out laughing.

"That's good. 'The charming one'! I like that." With her elbow leaning on the table, she pointed at Quinn with her fork in hand. "I think I may actually like you."

Quinn offered a weak grin. "Um . . . thanks?"

A cherubic brunette was next. "I'm Sister Agnes Elizabeth. I run the kennels. Thanks for the dog food. It's a big help."

"You're welcome."

The only sister left was the one sitting to Quinn's right. She had warm olive skin and startling pale green eyes.

"And last, but never least, I am Sister Margarita. I do whatever needs to be done. We welcome you here."

"We also want to thank you," the Reverend Mother chimed in, cutting into her chicken. "God bless you and Rueger. Without your quick thinking, our Sister Daria might not be here with us now, with barely a scratch."

"Praise God!"

"Cheers to Quinn!"

It was her turn to shake off the compliments. "No need to thank me. Rueger did all the hard work."

"That's true," Sister Theresa threw in. "But he doesn't have your table manners, so he can't be here tonight." The others chuckled and she laughed at her own joke. "See? Charming!"

Most everyone commenced eating, and so did Quinn until she realized the Reverend Mother had stopped. She seemed to be assessing, the wheels turning behind her eyes.

Quinn swallowed her food, placing her fork and knife down. "Is everything all right, Reverend Mother?"

She gave a slight nod, her gaze volleying between Quinn and the others at the table. "As you can tell from everyone's description of what they do, each of us plays a vital role in the running of this order. No one is more important than another, which means every individual is crucial to the whole."

"I think Karl Marx said the same thing about Mother Russia."

Crap. I really shouldn't drink wine on an empty stomach.

Daria kicked her under the table. Hard.

"Ow! That was unnecessary." Quinn rubbed her shin.

Her cousin glared and pleaded in one look. "Quinn, I'd hardly compare our order to the Communist Party."

Reverend Mother wasn't bothered in the slightest. "Actually, your cousin makes an apt comparison. There's a compelling argument to be made. Both require officiants to consider the needs of the collective over their own, to eschew a life of luxury and privilege, to surrender their own will in service to others. Your cousin is a thinker. I appreciate such qualities, especially in young people."

Quinn gave a tight smile. It was affirming that the Reverend Mother thought her wine-soaked brain was, at the very least, entertaining, but it was obvious she had upset her cousin, and that was the last thing she wanted to do.

"I appreciate your kind words, but Daria is right: I was out of line. I use humor as a coping mechanism. Really inappropriate humor."

Sister Daria's shoulders dropped, her demeanor relaxed.

But the Reverend Mother had a different reaction. With elbows resting on the arms of her chair and the fingertips of both hands meeting in an inverted "V," she seemed to be turning something around in her mind.

"Your cousin is more like a sister to you, from what I'm told. We are also her sisters. Different, but the same. As her family, we want what is best for her. Agreed?"

Quinn nodded. "Of course."

With a soft touch, she tapped both forefingers together in a steady rhythm. "Sister Daria is trying to balance her new life with her old one, admittedly a challenge I myself didn't have to face. You see, back in my day, we didn't have such an option. When a novitiate took her vows, she left her family of origin behind, only granted permission to visit maybe once a year. Less often if she lived far away. Letters were allowed, of course, but phone calls were a luxury."

Quinn couldn't even begin to imagine the hardship of being cut off from her family. Even when she was across the world, assigned to towns with only the most basic of necessities, they wrote letters, sent emails, even Skyped once a week. And even with the conveniences modern technology afforded her, she still remembered many, many times going to bed aching for home.

The Reverend Mother wasn't done. "When I regard Sister Daria, I see a life on the edge of a precipice. Sway too much one way or the other, and each side suffers. The balance is lost, and so is the novitiate."

The tension in the air thickened. The few who were still eating stopped. Quinn felt a droplet of sweat roll heavily down the back of her neck.

"When Sister Daria first came to us, my inclination was to refuse her. So many red flags signaling to me: a broken heart unable to heal, her cousin far away, a youth spent rebelling for the sake of rebellion, unfocused in her professional life. But I took a chance, and not because our numbers are diminishing, which they are. I decided to put my faith in her the way the Father bestows His Grace upon us: unproven, unearned, yet so needed. Like Him, I saw a young woman"—she turned to Daria—"I saw *you*, Sister, a brilliant, compassionate, angry, lonely soul, thirsting to share exactly who she is with this world.

I wanted to give that to you, and that's what we've tried to do here at Guinefort House."

Her cousin's hand covered the Reverend Mother's. "You did—you *have*! I'm so grateful to be here."

The Reverend Mother patted Daria's hand in reassurance. "I know, dear. But your cousin and your family are *not* happy you're here. That is understandable. Many dreams they had for you are dying, just as many you have for yourself are blooming."

Everyone turned to stare at Quinn.

What the heck was she supposed to do now?

There were two ways to handle the situation at hand. Either she could play dumb, or at least innocent, saying what they all wanted to hear, that whatever made her cousin happy would be enough for her. Or she could tell the truth, finally share all the questions and doubts she'd harbored ever since she'd received that first letter while in Cambodia.

She locked eyes with her cousin. "It *did* seem to come out of nowhere. I mean, before I left, I could probably count on two hands the number of times you went to church."

Daria's cheeks reddened. "All right. That's fair. What other questions have you been holding onto?"

Quinn glanced around. All eyes were on her.

"Well, since you asked . . . whatever happened with you and Raj?"

Her cousin bristled. "You *know* what happened."

"Actually, no, I don't," Quinn countered. "You two were together for, what, three years? He was practically a member of the family. And then you show up solo, two hours late to my going-away party, talking about how the two of you decided it 'just wasn't working out.' That was it. No more discussion. No deeper explanation. And every time anyone tried to bring it up, you'd walk out of the room."

Her cousin folded her arms tightly across her chest. "Actually, that sounds like a really good idea right about now."

"See?" Quinn tossed her hands up in exasperation. "You keep running away. It's like you don't trust me or something, which, I've got to say, hurts."

The veins in Daria's neck pulsed. "What? Like you tell me everything going on with you?"

Quinn's head jerked. "What do I have going on that you don't know about? It's not like I have a life!"

Whoa, that felt strange to say that out loud.

But Daria wasn't hearing her. Not really. "How about your decision to go teach across the world? We were supposed to get an apartment in the city that summer, but you bailed. Why? To teach English? If you wanted to truly help disenfranchised children you could have accomplished that in Southeast D.C., South Arlington—you didn't need to leave everything behind and go to the other side of the globe!"

Holy cow, she'd had no idea her cousin was this angry.

"You're right, I could have, but I wanted an adventure. Can't you understand that?"

Daria's eyes gentled from anger to sorrow. "Of course, I understand, and this, here, is my adventure. More than that, it's my calling."

She didn't believe her. "If that's true, how come I hardly hear you talk about the work you do here? I think you spend more time with *me* than you do at the abbey."

Daria huffed. "Because you came back! I've wanted to enjoy my cousin and best friend finally being home!"

Quinn had gotten so caught up in their "discussion," she had forgotten they had an audience. She shrank back. "Reverend Mother, Sisters, I apologize for airing all this ugliness at your table. I've been a horrible dinner guest."

Daria grumbled. "That's for sure."

The Reverend Mother raised a hand. "We are her family, and you are her family. We broke bread together, and we share the contents of our hearts and minds together. Like Sister Theresa, I too abhor 'small talk.'"

"As usual, you are being too kind, Reverend Mother." Daria laid her palms flat on the table, taking a deep breath. "Quinn, I know you think you're looking out for me, but you have disrespected me and this house. I think it's best you leave."

Quinn's mouth gaped. "You're kicking me out?"

"If you want to phrase it that way, then so be it." Daria stood, clearing her plate and utensils. "Maybe this relationship isn't as healthy as I thought it was."

Her ears started ringing and her throat tightened. Quinn felt like someone was breaking up with her. Actually, it was worse.

"Y-you can't mean that."

"I do." Daria's eyes blazed anger, pain, determination. "Go, Quinn. And don't come back unless you can support my decision."

Chapter Fourteen

"If you cannot get rid of the family skeleton, you may
as well make it dance."
—George Bernard Shaw, Irish playwright and theater critic

"You've been moping around the store for five days now.
Don't you think it's enough already?"

Quinn had her face buried in a book but eyed her father
over the pages. "Feel free to continue work on your social skills,
Dad."

If he was bothered by her attitude, he didn't let on. "I know
you're going through a hard time over the falling out with
Elizab—I mean, Daria."

"I'm fine," Quinn lied, not bothering to look up from her
book, although with the mention of her cousin, the words
blurred on the page. Tearing eyes aren't conducive to reading.

He swiped the book out of her hands. "You need a change
of scenery, kiddo."

"Hey! What are you doing?"

"Doing you a favor." He placed the book inside the cubby
under the register. "Dress for hiking and meet me at the house.
We're going foraging today."

"But what about the store?"

Sarah stopped mid-task, shelving a title in her beloved poetry section. "We've got it covered. I'm here and your mom's coming in an hour." She placed the rest of the stack she had on the nearby table. "Isn't this your day off anyway?"

Quinn could feel her face turn crimson. Sarah was right. She rested her head in her hands. "Ugh, I have no life."

Sarah offered her a patient smile, brushing wisps of her dark hair behind her ear. Quinn thought it was cool that Sarah wasn't self-conscious about her hearing aids, being born partially deaf. Quinn's own mother was prescribed a hearing aid set a fraction of the size, but she refused to wear them half the time, feeling uncomfortable and citing, 'Most people have nothing interesting to say anyway.' Adele Caine was only ever rude when something or someone questioned her vanity.

Sarah gave her a look. "That's not what I meant and you know it. I'm just saying, it's a beautiful day."

Quinn met her gaze. "It is, but it doesn't mean, I don't know . . . mushroom picking?"

Her father peered over the rim of his glasses, pretending to grumble. "Excuse me, young lady. You don't know what you've been missing. Out in nature? Close to the earth?" Finn Caine let out a slow, happy sigh. "Nothing like it. It'll clear your head, give you a different perspective. Now, go and get ready. As I said, we are leaving in less than an hour."

He had a point: she'd been a Gloomy Gus all week, mostly because she kept replaying what had happened between her and Daria, on an endless loop. She still couldn't believe her cousin had kicked her out. In the history of Quinn and Daria, neither had ever done something so heartless. Of course, Quinn wasn't blameless, and she knew it. Sometimes she wished she had just shut her mouth. Kept the peace. But underneath that impulse resided a sadness she couldn't shake. When had their relationship become conditional on being silent? They'd always been able to speak truth to each other.

Well, almost always.

Back at her beloved farmhouse, she donned a three-quarter-sleeved T-shirt and long khakis, tucking the pant legs into her hiking boots. She wished she could bring her dog baby along, but her dad had vetoed the suggestion.

"Too dangerous, honey. Most of the mushrooms are harmless, but not all of them."

As Quinn folded herself into her dad's Volvo station wagon, she could tell by the goofy smile on his face that he was jazzed she had agreed to come along. *Not that I had much choice.* With his eyes fixed on the road, he beamed an ear-to-ear grin, and her usually taciturn father jabbered the whole way.

"I know you and your brother think foraging a strange hobby, but I tell you, Quinn, it's like going through a secret portal into another world. Not quite as magical as C. S. Lewis's wardrobe to Narnia, mind you. Speaking of which, remember when you were younger, every time we visited a house with an armoire, how you'd insist on going inside, needing to check if any of them was the long, lost portal of your book dreams?"

Quinn's body shook with her silent laughter. "Oh yes, I remember. Found my share of unmentionables in many of those. If only I'd found the spell for forgetting embarrassing stuff I learned about people. Made it hard to share a meal with them afterward."

"Well, maybe today will be the day we find something magical, like a fairy glen or a gnome's hidden hideaway on our expedition."

She rolled her eyes. "Forest fairies? Clandestine gnomes? C'mon, Dad."

He adjusted the air vent away from him. If Finn Caine had his way, he'd never have the air-conditioning on. "All right, I may have overstated the finds of the forest." He coughed into his hand. "I suppose the window for magical thinking has closed for good?"

Quinn glanced over. He had worked relentless hours when she and Bash were little, a necessity to support the family, considering her mom's landscaping business was seasonal. But she knew he regretted missing so much of her childhood.

"Afraid so, Dad. I'm all grown up." *Supposedly.* "But I can open another kind of magical portal." She pressed her finger onto the window button, the glass squeaking loudly as it slid between the rubber casing inside the door. She turned off the air-conditioning.

"Better?"

He followed suit, then closed his eyes for a couple of seconds as the wind blew onto his face and through his hair. She marveled at the change in him. "You're like a happy puppy with his head out the window."

Any tension stuck inside his corporeal being melted away. "Nothing like the real thing, as I always say."

She rested her cheek on the curve of her arm, bent and leaning against the passenger-side door. Eyes open, she stuck her head out. The wind against her face. Hair surfing the breeze like waves in the ocean. Her father was right. There really was something to being outdoors.

Before too long, they arrived at one of the mycological group's surreptitious foraging spots. As she got out of the car, the rest of her father's friends were already waiting.

"Good to see you, Quinn."

She smiled. "Thanks, Officer Carter."

"Out here in the green, you can call me Ned."

Quinn eyed her dad, shrugging. "No offense, Officer Carter, but it'd feel weird. My parents have always insisted on their children not calling adults by their Christian names."

He chuckled, along with the rest of the group. "That's fine, but even from the cheap seats, it's easy to see you're grown."

"Don't remind me." Her father retrieved some empty bags from the trunk before slamming it shut. "You know everyone else here?"

She knew Officer Carter, of course. She was also acquainted with her parents' neighbor, Mr. Esfahani, owner of what she liked to call "the big fat Greek wedding house" because it had a long driveway lined with eight goddess statues from Greek mythology, even though he was Persian. There was also Dr. Barbara Franklin, the local allergist who kept Quinn stocked with EpiPens in case she was stung by a bee. But the last person was a surprise.

"Sister Theresa, I didn't know you were a member of Vienna's Mycological Society."

The nun was nonplussed. "How else do you think I procured those tasty morels we ate the other night? Those beauties can go for eight dollars a pound at Whole Paycheck."

"Whole Paycheck?"

Dr. Franklin laughed. "She means Whole Foods. Sister Theresa has a wry sense of humor."

"Quinn knows all about it," Sister Theresa interrupted. "She calls me 'the charming one.' No truer words said, in my opinion. Now, are we going to chat like a bunch of kids at recess, or are we going hunting?"

Officer Carter grinned, gesturing forward. "Lead the way, Sister."

Mr. Esfahani pointed. "Nice shirt, by the way."

Quinn gazed down, almost having forgotten what she was wearing. It was a T-shirt her dad had stuffed at the bottom of her Christmas stocking years ago saying "I dig fungi."

They started walking into the forest. "Thanks, Mr. Esfahani. As you can tell, Sister Theresa isn't the only one with a rapier wit."

He just nodded and veered off. Dr. Franklin leaned in. "He's not much of a talker. Nice man—don't get me wrong. Some are part of this group for the exercise and camaraderie, others strictly for the 'shrooms. Mr. Esfahani falls into the latter category."

"As do I," the sister interjected. "So, do you know what you're doing out here?"

"What do you mean?"

She let out a frustrated sigh, scratching at the mole by her ear, something Quinn hadn't seen at dinner the other night, what with her wearing her wimple.

"I mean, do you know what to look for, girl? You can't just pick up *any* mushroom. Some are edible, some aren't—and by inedible, I don't mean they don't taste good. I mean, they can make you sick—even kill you!"

Her father placed his hand on Quinn's shoulder. "Don't worry. We're going to work as a team. I'll show her the ins and outs."

She groused. "Very well then, carry on."

The rest of the group fanned out, gazes on the ground, walking with care through the grass and trees. Her father handed Quinn a printed burlap bag that read "I didn't like the fungus at first, but then he grew on me."

"Wow, that one might rank in the top five corny dad jokes of all time."

He broke into a huge grin. "Oh, that's just one of them. Your mother had a bunch made for me. Perfect, right?"

Quinn shook her head. "Enabler," she teased.

He aired out his bag, waving it to and fro a couple of times. "Okay, so we're looking for edible mushrooms, so think morels, chanterelles, oyster mushrooms, champignons, and also 'hen of the woods,' which, confusingly, is entirely different from 'chicken of the woods.'"

"Is that similar to 'chicken of the sea'?"

Her father's shoulder bobbed with his chuckle. "Not your best, but still amusing." He walked a bit farther, until he arrived at the base of a tree with some old growth. "Ah, this is a perfect *laetiporus sulphureus* specimen." He bent his knees and grabbed a bunch with a gloved hand. "Your mother's going to love these. They're meaty." He fished deep in one of his pants pockets, retrieving a pair of small leather gloves. "These are for you."

She put them on, a perfect fit. "Mom's?"

He nodded. "Same hands."

Quinn followed his lead, gazing at the ground, focusing around mature trees. "Any truffles to be found?"

"Ha! I wish!" Officer Carter saddled over. "I could've paid for some of my boy's college with some good truffle green."

Quinn smiled. "All drama aside, you must be happy to be getting your usual partner back now."

He took out a cotton bandana, wiping his bald head in a circular motion. "You've got that right. I never liked the idea of Shae being partnered with that boy. Something off in his eyes, you know? But the chief had his reasons at the time."

"Do you think he was 'off' enough to be the killer?" Quinn asked.

He blew out a raspberry. "Who knows. The evidence will out the truth in time. I'm just glad Wyatt Reynolds is behind bars."

"Unless he makes bail." Dr. Franklin butted in.

Quinn froze. "Is it possible some judge can let him out?" Just the thought of Reynolds free to roam around made the ground shift under her feet.

Her dad gave them all a withering glare. "Some of us came out here to get away from the town's troubles, not to bring them into this natural sanctuary." He pointed at Quinn's bag with his chin. "Less talking, more digging."

Dr. Franklin sighed, wiping her brow with her cotton-gloved hand. "You're right, Finn. My bad. We need to enjoy this unseasonably long spring while we can. These mild, wet conditions are perfect for mushroom growth."

With that, they both went back to what they were doing, and her father continued his lesson. "All right, I want you to find some on your own. I'll give you some simple rules to follow."

"Okay, hit me with the knowledge, Dad."

His eyes crinkled at the corners, and there was another grin as he pushed his glasses up the bridge of his nose. "All right, sometimes it's easier learning what to avoid than what to look for. So, avoid mushrooms with white gills, a ring on the stem, or a bulbous sack at the base. Avoid the red ones too."

"Oh, so take the blue pill instead of the red one this time?"

He looked blankly at her.

She shook her head. "Guess you didn't see *The Matrix*?"

"You know I'm not much of a cinophile. You have to rely on Bash to understand those references."

That was true. Bash had always been the one to take her to the movies growing up—he adored them as much as she did. Although she was watching more documentaries these days. The fallout with Daria had given Quinn more time on her hands, and she found Netflix helped fill the void. Or so she tried telling herself.

As she continued foraging, Quinn had quiet time to think, and she found her mind whizzing with a million different thoughts at once: how to patch things up with her cousin without ripping her integrity apart. She harbored mixed feelings about the Reverend Mother, who, though she might have been a delightful hostess, Quinn couldn't help but feel had instigated the argument between them. Quinn didn't care for small talk either, but she also regarded the woman's actions as provocative, needling a confrontation between the cousins.

There was also the lingering problem of who'd killed Tricia.

They had arrested Wyatt Reynolds—that she knew. He had been fired from his position at the Vienna Police Department. Another fact. The other day, over coffee, Bash had shared that when Aiden and his team combed Wyatt's apartment, they found his whole second bedroom had been built as a shrine to Tricia. "Aiden said the scene gave him the creeps. Something right out of a true crime podcast."

Quinn always thought it ironic when people cried that the sky was falling out of fear of immigrants sneaking over the border to "terrorize citizens," when the most dangerous criminals were seemingly innocuous white guys right from the good ol' U.S. of A.

After hearing what the police had found in Reynolds's apartment, Quinn would've sworn on a stack of Bibles he was the killer. But Wyatt had been on duty the night Tricia had been found murdered. Still, that didn't mean he hadn't slipped her something before his shift, something easy to do if they were social. Unfortunately, the results of the autopsy weren't public record, but if they had found some kind of inorganic poison in her system, Quinn had to imagine they'd inform the public. Wouldn't they?

It doesn't make sense. Wyatt wanted Tricia for himself. Surely he'd try to "off" her fiancé before hurting her—at least that's what Quinn's logic dictated.

A little voice in the back of her mind spoke up: *But you're not dealing with logic. You're dealing with rage and an anger stoked hot enough to murder.*

Maybe someone didn't like the idea of Tricia hanging out with a man who wasn't her future husband. Wyatt wasn't the only man in Tricia's life who got jealous. There was another: huge ego, crazy-possessive, always something to prove, and someone who drove one of those ridiculous sports cars that emitted a ton of white smoke—if memory served.

Scott Hauser.

The idea of him killing Tricia made the bile rise up in her throat, but Quinn couldn't deny it: her fledgling theory had legs. What if it had been Scott driving the getaway vehicle? He might have been on the short side for a guy, but Scott was strong. He worked out daily, so he could've been the person who had unceremoniously dumped Tricia's body in the middle of the park. She needed to find out where he was the night his fiancé died, but it wasn't like she could just walk up to him and ask. That was more cojones than even Quinn possessed.

Crap on a cracker . . . she wished she had been able to identify the car. The only evidence left had been the tire treads.

Wait a second. Hadn't she taken photos of the marks left on Nutley Street? She dropped her mushroom bag, with only a few inside, and whipped out her phone, scrolling through her pictures: her dog, a plate of food, Mom, books, dog, dog, another dog photo . . .

"Bingo." She *had* taken them.

She ran over to Officer Carter, who had his head halfway inside his foraging bag, sniffing his fungi finds. He peeked up when he sensed he had an audience.

"Rosalie is going to love these cooked up in some garlic and butter! Mmm!" He must have noticed Quinn's agitation because he straightened up, peering down at her. "You alright there? Something's got you more wound up than an eight-day clock."

He's got that right. "Let me ask you something. Did you ever see the movie *My Cousin Vinny?*"

Two lines formed between his brows. "Of course I did. I'm a cop. I watch all the cop movies."

Awesome. At least her dad's friends were up on pop cultural references. "Okay, so the part in the movie when Marissa Tomei testifies as an automotive expert, being able to tell what kind of car the real culprits were driving based on the tire marks. Was that part real?"

"Oh, that's real all right." He shooed some gnats away from his face, probably drawn to his perspiration. "Although her testimony wasn't totally accurate."

"How do you mean?"

He scratched the underside of his jaw. "There were actually three cars—not two—made in America with a similar body type to the Buick Skylark that had positraction and independent rear suspension and enough power to make those marks."

Mr. Esfahani stared. "Now how would you know that, Ned? I own a car dealership, and I wouldn't have known that."

Officer Carter cracked his neck with a swift twist. "Oh, I didn't know it either until I had Lucas over for a movie and barbeque night at my house last summer." He turned to Quinn. "Lucas is a master mechanic. He owns Frankie's Garage. When that part of the movie played, he had to walk out of the room, he got so aggravated with the mistake."

Now her wheels were spinning.

"I see that crazy look in your eye. You're not planning on doing anything outside your jurisdiction as a private citizen. Right?"

Dr. Franklin scoffed. "Ned, never tell a woman with determination and gumption she's crazy."

Ned's expression transformed right in front of them, from affable forager to steely-eyed cop. "She got lucky last time, Barbara—that maneuver with the dog and the nuns. Next time, Quinn might not come out the other side."

"Agreed." Her dad walked over, his fungi bag filled to the brim. "I thought we were foraging, not talking about something that can get you hurt."

Two against one. That's never good.

"Dad, bad mushrooms aren't the only things in Vienna that can hurt someone. There's a killer out there."

"I am well aware, Quinn Victoria, but last I checked, you fixed books, not criminal wrongdoings."

She sighed, her hands on her hips. "You're right. And the last thing I want to do is worry you."

A wave of relief washed over him. "So, we're done with all this?"

"You won't hear another word."

He pinned her with his gaze—his equivalent of making her chug a bottle of truth serum—before letting out a long breath, like a bird trapped inside a house that suddenly finds an open window. "Good. Now, let's see what kind of haul you managed."

She nodded, opening her bag and directing her focus down on the paltry fungal treasures inside. That way, her dad and Cop-Eyes-Carter wouldn't catch the look of guilt written all over her face. Quinn had told the truth—and lied—all in the same breath:

Finn Caine would not hear one more word about his daughter meddling in the Pemberley case. And that's because she was keeping her mouth shut.

No way was Quinn quitting her investigation.

She was finally gaining some momentum—her first real lead—as well as earning some begrudging respect from Aiden. But in the process of trying to catch a killer, had she laid the groundwork for losing her father's trust?

Chapter Fifteen

"It's easy to be friends when everyone's eighteen. It gets harder, the older you get, as you make different life choices."
—Zadie Smith, British novelist

Foraging mushrooms in nature might have been a Pinterest-worthy, albeit strange, way to spend an afternoon, but it wasn't the place to find a cell signal. As soon as Quinn got back to civilization, she tried phoning Aiden. Her call went right to voicemail.

The same happened the next day too. When she texted him her latest theory, he replied with "Got it. Thanks." And that was it. No follow-up. No 'How are you, by the way?" Nothing.

Guess we're not "partners in crime" after all.

"Working solo is better anyway," she lied to herself. Quinn checked her lip gloss in her car visor mirror before exiting the truck. "Here goes nothing."

Quinn wasn't meeting a date, although she was starting to think maybe she should be more open to the idea. Because being hung up on a guy who was letting her down was beyond a drag. Anyway, Quinn had decided to head straight for the source for all things happening—and in the town of Vienna, that meant meeting with the "Clink-n-Drink" ladies.

Rumor had it one of their daughters had coined the nickname as a tribute to the moms who enjoyed their weekly "wine o'clock" soirees. The Clink-n-Drink gals not only knew what was happening in Vienna's business community, they knew everyone's business *in* the community.

Withers Hammock was one of them. No surprise. So was Sarah Jovanovich, owner of the most adorable dog "barkery" in town, a business she readily admitted to opening just to have the excuse to take her mini Australian shepherd, Skipper, to work with her every day. If Withers was the town crier, then Jennifer Ranier was its mayor, at least in spirit. A former Texas sorority girl, Ms. Jennifer knew everybody's life stories, because she was uber-friendly and extroverted. It also didn't hurt that she was a realtor, which meant she'd been in almost everyone's home at one time or another. The last one was Carina Adelman—definitely the odd duck of the group: first, because she was from San Francisco and not from below the Mason-Dixon line like the rest of them, but more so because she was an introverted author who preferred books to people. On paper, they sounded like the start of one of those tacky jokes: "A Catholic, a WASP, a Jew, and an Anglican walked into a bar . . ." And yet somehow their friendship worked.

Quinn might not have walked into a bar, but she did arrange to meet up with them at Maple Avenue Restaurant during happy hour. To call them gossips would have rendered them a tremendous disservice. Rather, they were the town's civic memory, its pendulum marker, and its caretakers. It just so happened they knew exactly the kind of dirt under everyone's fingernails.

So now the Clink-n-Drink gals were seated in a semicircle around her. The owner of the restaurant herself was waiting to take their order.

Quinn wanted to start off on the right foot. "Ladies, drinks are on me. Order whatever you want."

They shared glances with one another and tittered.

"Ah, honey, you're sweet, but that is totally unnecessary." Ms. Jennifer leaned toward the the owner. "You are not to take one cent of this young lady's money. You hear me?"

She laughed, offering a pretend salute. "Yes, ma'am."

Ms. Jennifer nodded. "Now Amy, why are you the one waiting on us? Aren't you in rehearsal for *The Pirates of Penzance* or something?"

It was a good question. Amy Lyons not only owned the restaurant; she was one of the most sought-after local thespians in the DC Metro area—not a small feat considering the innovative theater scene. If she wasn't at Maple Avenue, she was in rehearsal for another new production.

Amy blew wisps of hair from her deep-set hazel eyes. "Petra's having the baby."

"Omigosh, how exciting!" Ms. Jennifer turned to Quinn. "Petra helps run the place with Amy. This marks baby number three for her. I don't know how she does it."

"Nice."

Ms. Withers muttered. "You'd think she never heard of a baby being born before."

Ms. Jennifer opened her mouth, but her friend raised a palm to her face. "I know you want to ask another ten questions, but some of us are starving and need sustenance." She shrugged Amy's way. "I'm sorry if I'm being rude."

Amy chuckled. "No problem, Mrs. Hammock. What can I get you?"

"We want a bottle of prosecco, right?" She checked in with the group. Everyone but Quinn nodded. "Do you not like prosecco? That can't be possible. It's the house wine of Vienna!"

"I'll just have a bottle of Pellegrino, a glass with ice, and a wedge of lime."

Carina tilted her head. "Are you in the program or something?"

Quinn's eyes widened. "Excuse me?"

She wiped the corners of her mouth with a cocktail napkin. "The program. AA."

Sarah's mouth dropped. "Car, I can't believe you just asked her that!"

"Why? There's nothing to be ashamed of. I, myself, come from a long line of addicts and alcoholics."

Quinn wished she could've recorded what was happening. The Clink'n'Drink ladies were hilarious. "Not in AA. I'm just not much of a wine drinker."

"Carina, leave her alone." Sarah elbowed her friend. "Can we get an order of truffle fries and some of that Brie toast too? She gets 'hangry' this time of day."

Quinn smiled to herself. They sounded like one of those old television sitcoms—like *Golden Girls*, but younger. She could sit there and listen to them all day.

The rest gave their orders.

Quinn cleared her throat to get their attention. "Okay, now for the uncomfortable portion of our scheduled program. Do you have any theories about who could've wanted Tricia dead?"

Sarah took a big swig of water. "First that doctor what's-his-name and now this. It's awful."

Ms. Withers swirled the ice around in her glass. "I can't believe it. Everyone's wondering what's happening around here."

"I showed a condo to the loveliest young man the other day. He's an officer at Vienna PD," Ms. Jennifer said while cutting into her Brie toast. "He said that before all this ugliness, there hadn't been a murder in town for over thirty years."

Ms. Withers eyed her plate. "Who eats a Brie bite like that? It's finger food. You're like Costanza on Seinfeld, eating a candy bar with a knife and fork."

Ms. Jennifer put down her utensils and scrunched her nose like a bunny rabbit. "Hey, I actually *like* that episode and thought it was a good idea."

"It's a fancy-pants, fussy idea is what it is," Ms. Withers answered. The other two friends shared a glance.

"The twins and Scott graduated your year, right?" Ms. Carina picked up a couple of fries. "You and your friends must know more about Tricia than any of us."

Quinn hunched her shoulders. "I don't know about that. We weren't exactly close, and not too many of my former classmates still live around here."

"Yeah, but there's got to be a few." Sarah speared a Brie bite with her fork.

Ms. Withers stopped mid-sip. "Now you too?"

"What? Jen had a good idea. This way, I don't get cheese grease all over my fingers."

"That's a fair and valid point." Ms. Carina waved Amy over. "Can we get another order of those Brie bites?" She handed her the empty plate. "They went fast, as you can see."

Quinn grabbed some more fries. They were ridiculously addictive. "Was there anything going on with her family?"

"Tricia's? Oh please, her parents are the nicest people." Jen took the bottle and refilled her glass as well as the other ladies'.

Ms. Withers leaned in and said in a low voice. "Can't say the same for her fiancé's family. Scott's all right and Carlson's a sweetheart, but Milly . . . yeesh. Can you imagine having *that* woman as your mother-in-law?"

"What about Maxie? She graduated with you, right? Maybe she knows something."

Quinn hadn't thought about Maxie. "Hmm. Maybe."

Ms. Carina rummaged through her purse. "Hey, does anyone have an extra hair tie? I'm feeling all schvitzy up in here."

Quinn had never heard that word before. "Uh, is that like psoriasis?"

The usually taciturn author stifled a laugh. "No, honey. It's not a disease. *Schvitzy* is Yiddish for 'sweaty.'"

Ms. Jennifer took a hair tie off her wrist and handed it over. "I brought an extra one just for you."

Ms. Carina fanned her pretend tears. "See? This is why I love you!" She took the tie and threaded her hair through before refocusing on Quinn. "By the way, I still think talking with people Tricia had regular contact with is the best way to go."

She had a point. Maxie worked the morning shift at Caffe Amour, only a block away from the twins' real estate office. She knew Trina's coffee order without having to blink. When Quinn had mentioned Trina, all the joy had drained away. Perhaps she knew something about Trina that others didn't? Maybe she'd observed something critical between Tricia and her killer?

"That's a really good idea. Thank you."

Ms. Carina beamed, giving her a wink. "If you end up solving the case, you know I'm writing a book about you, right?"

Quinn snort laughed. "Oh please, who would ever want to read a book about me?"

Chapter Sixteen

"Sometimes being a brother is even
better than being a superhero."
—Marc Brown, American children's book author

"How are things going between you and Daria?"
Quinn eyed her brother over her auntie's beanstalks, as
he leaned his shoulder against the tool shed.

"I don't know. How are things going between you and
Rachel?"

He frowned. "That bad?"

She didn't answer. Instead, she picked up an extra gardening tool and handed it over. "You know Aunt Johanna's motto:
'If you have time to lean, you have time to clean.' Weed with me."

Even though he was in what appeared to be a new pair of
jeans, he didn't hesitate to come on over, take the weeder, and
get right to work. Being a Caine meant two things: keeping
one's nose in a book and being knee-deep in the dirt. Family
lore told tales of how all Caine children kept seedlings in their
tiny hands so they could till soil while tottering at the same
time.

"You know you and Daria are going to be fine, right?"

Quinn blew out an exasperated breath as she wrenched at a strong weed root. It was stubborn and barely moving. "Yeah, I know. I need to go over there and apologize. But, I don't know . . . How do I say I'm sorry for hurting her while at the same time standing by the questions I brought up?"

Bash stopped what he was doing, glanced over at the hand tools Quinn had laid out on a nearby blanket, and handed her a small shovel. "Dig deeper."

She gave him the "are you kidding?" look. "If you are trying to turn this moment into some lame life lesson metaphor, I'm going to brain you next time your head turns."

He tossed the shovel into the dirt in front of her. "See? Now you're making it weird." He pulled out a chunk of weeds, throwing them on a pile Quinn had started.

"So, what about you and Rachel? Where does that stand?"

He chuckled under his breath. "I know you've been dying to ask. Surprise you held out this long."

"Ha! I would be offended if it weren't true, but you're right— I have been waiting with bated breath. And I believe I deserve a gold star, if you must know."

His usual humor evaporated.

Oh crap, did I overstep? First Daria, now Bash. "What's wrong?"

He pushed the weeder in deep, almost like he was trying to excise something out of himself. "She says she still loves me."

Spring bloomed inside her chest. "That's great, Bash! So then why are you—"

"Because she doesn't want a thing to do with me, that's why."

Quinn jolted like she'd been slapped. "Elaborate, please."

He brushed the dirt off his hands, resting his weight on his haunches. "Can we take a walk or something? I need to get some energy out."

203

"Sure, let me just wash up and get RBG and my purse."

"You don't need your purse. If you need anything on the way, you know I'll just buy it for you."

She was going to fight him on that one but decided against egging him on. He might have been keeping his ire to himself, but Quinn could tell: he was in a state over Rachel. They both washed their hands at the outdoor garden sink, and then they were off.

They left Salsbury House's gardens and walked down Lawyers Road, keeping quiet, both lost in their own thoughts. Until she remembered she had wanted to bring her tire marks photos over to the garage.

"Hey, do you mind coming on an errand with me? It shouldn't take long, and it's kind of important."

He shrugged, staring straight ahead. "Yeah, sure."

She waited for a block. Then another. Bash gave a chin lift to someone he knew. He smiled when appropriate, but he wasn't himself. And it tore her up.

"Okay, I can't stand it anymore. Tell me what happened."

He grumbled. "She said she wants a solid relationship, someone she can count on."

"Well, great! Because last I checked, you're back home for good and next in line for fire chief. How much more reliable and solid can a man get?"

He gave her a look like she wasn't getting it. "Not professionally. She thinks I suffer from FOMO when it comes to women."

"You? Fear of missing out? But you're totally loyal when you're going out with someone."

He sighed. "She doesn't see it that way."

"I don't understand. She's acting like you cheated on her." A wave of dread iced her insides. "Please tell me you didn't cheat on her, Bash."

"No, of course not. I would never do that." He blew out a frustrated breath, an invisible weight settling on his shoulders. "But she knew I broke things off between us in college so I could sow some wild oats. She learned I got around some." His head drooped, and his eyes fixated on one foot in front of the other. "She says she doesn't want to spend the rest of her life looking over her shoulder, wondering when I'm going to go off on another wild hair."

"But that's not fair!" Quinn realized she sounded like a petulant child, but she didn't care. The idea of Rachel blaming her brother for his adolescent idiocy was too much for her to bear. "How many people are ready to settle down at nineteen, twenty years old?"

"Apparently, she would have married me then, if I had asked. That's how in love with me she was. I—I broke her heart."

Think, Quinn. You know Bash. You know Rachel. You can help him figure out what to do. First, though, the obstacles . . .

"What about the other guy, the one we saw her with at the funeral? Is that serious?"

Bash looked like he was ready to spit nails just hearing about the guy.

"His name is Lyle Sapowitz. They met at some fundraiser a few months ago. He's a lawyer, already a junior partner. He's a Jewish parents' dream and my basic nightmare."

"Why?"

"Because she says it's important to her family that she marry someone Jewish."

Quinn was flummoxed. "But I thought her parents loved you."

"They did, until . . ." He didn't finish the sentence. There was no need.

205

Instead of going to Church Street, Quinn led them down Ayr Hill Road and then took a left on Mill Street.

"You know, Rachel gave me her great-grandmother's old diary to rebuild."

Bash was only half-listening. "She did? That was nice of her."

"She told me she wants me to repair it so she can give it to her parents as an anniversary gift. She and her brothers are throwing a big party for them."

"Her brothers are good guys, but useless when it comes to anything practical, which means she'll be planning the party all by herself."

She nudged her shoulder with his. "You should come by the store and read this journal with me."

He blustered. "Yeah, that's not happening."

Just because she was the younger sister, did that mean she couldn't slap the stupid out of his head? "Ugh! You can be so obtuse sometimes! Daria was right."

He stopped walking. "Wait, what did Daria say?"

It was her turn to blow out an exasperated breath. "She thinks you're awesome, of course, but that you've never had to work at anything when it comes to women. They always make relationships easy for you. Too easy, apparently."

Bash studied her face. "Is that what you think too?"

"At this precise moment? Kind of."

"Nice," he said, his voice sharp.

"Bash, instead of getting defensive, *listen*."

"Fine—*what*?"

Quinn sought to find the right words, how to explain the heart of every woman to her loving, smart, popular, and totally clueless brother.

"Every woman is like a rare first-edition book. Some have all the bells and whistles—I'm talking fine Morocco spine labels, gilt titles and tooling to the spine, raised bands, fleuron cornerpiece designs, and inner dentelles—"

"Quinn, I love you. But what the heck are you saying?"

"I'm saying a woman wants to be read like she's your favorite book, to be studied as if she were a classic novel. If she gives you an opening to know her in any way—a story, a paragraph even—she wants you to cherish her enough to take a shot, hold onto every word. Whatever it takes to know her better, to be with her, even if it's not in the way you want. Do you understand?"

"Yeah. But she gave the journal to you, not me."

She cocked an eyebrow. "All is fair in love and war. Take whatever of her you can get."

"I don't know, Quinnie . . . Rachel is still really pissed off at me, even after all these years. How do I get in there?"

"The same way you deal with any out-of-control blaze. What are you always telling me? Find the entry points, the weak spots. If she's still that mad at you, it means she's still in love with you. If she wasn't, she wouldn't care anymore."

"You think so?"

Quinn wasn't used to seeing her brother this unsure of himself. "I know so. In the meantime, respect her boundaries and wait for an opening. Be patient. It'll come."

He offered his fist, which she bumped in return. "All right, I'll wait—and read the diary while I'm parked in purgatory. Happy now?"

"No, but I *will* be when you win Rachel back. By the way, when you do finally have an opening, just remember it's going to take more than you reading some old woman's journal to win back her trust. You *do* realize that, right?"

Bash gave her his "I get it—now back off" look. "Yes, wise one. I understand."

They were now in front of Frankie's Garage, *the* place in Vienna for auto repair. If rumor was right, the owner knew everything about cars, and since Marisa Tomei's *My Cousin Vinny*'s character wasn't available, this guy would have to do.

"Good, now I need to talk to this guy."

Bash's brows furrowed. "Wait a second. You need to talk to Lucas? Why? Is something wrong with your truck?"

"No, I need his expertise about the tire marks left on Nutley Street the night Tricia died. They may belong to the car owned by Tricia's killer. If not that, then the car belongs to the ass who dumped her body in the middle of the night in a little park, and he or she knows the murderer."

His face brightened for the first time that day. "Hey, that's just like from *My Cousin Vinny*."

There's hope for him yet.

Chapter Seventeen

"There are no strangers here; only friends you haven't yet met."
—William Butler Yeats, twentieth-century Irish poet

"You know, I usually charge a lot of cake for this kind of analysis, but since you're Bash's sister, it's on me."

To say Lucas Diaz was a unique character was an understatement. He was beyond handsome, in spite of the scar running along the side of his face from his temple down to his strong jawline. Maybe even because of it. He was about ten years older than her—four more than her brother, but Bash and Lucas had known each other for years, in spite of not traveling in the same social circles.

Her gaze volleyed back and forth between them. "It seems like you're well acquainted. How did you two meet?"

The men locked eyes before Lucas barked out a laugh. With the back of his hand, he gave a playful slap to Bash's upper arm. "C'mon, man. Don't look so freaked. If I still had a beef with you, you wouldn't have made it ten steps onto my property."

Bash tsked under his breath. "Oh, *sure*. You're probably mapping out where to dump my body as we speak."

His paranoia made Lucas bend over, laughing even harder. "Man, that look on your face! That's payment enough." He wiped under his eyes, shaking his head, still smiling. "Nah, no worries. For real. She set me straight. We're cool."

Quinn made a noise to get their attention. "Anyone want to clue me in on what you're talking about?"

They both answered at the same time. "No."

Ugh, boys are so annoying, even when they grow up. "Fine, have it your way."

As the two caught up, Quinn couldn't help but stare at Lucas. Her interest wasn't romantic; he wasn't her type. She'd just never seem someone as outwardly unique as him in lil' ol' Vienna. The town had plenty of characters, but most wore their eccentricities hidden well under their turtleneck sweaters and L.L. Bean vests. Lucas, on the other hand, was wearing a well-worn Black Flag concert T-shirt, broken-in Levis, and Doc Martin boots. Quinn marveled at his tattoo sleeves, arms inked from up past his short sleeves down to his wrists, and he wore his thick black hair styled in a stiff mohawk. She couldn't imagine how much Aqua Net a 'do like his took to hold up. He was a throwback to DC's early eighties hardcore punk scene in real time; a Latin Henry Rollins surrounded by mostly white people with easy-wear haircuts and really ugly, comfortable shoes.

"It's a shame you didn't come to me right after this happened. I could've done the photos myself." He studied the tire mark pictures on her phone. "Nah, I can't see a thing on your screen. I need my system."

Quinn had no idea what "his system" entailed, but if Bash trusted Lucas, so did she. They followed him to the back of his garage, up the stairs, and to his home on the second floor.

If the downstairs was a typical garage with rows of tools, cans of motor oil, and cars hoisted up on hydraulic lifts, the upstairs was its polar opposite, with hand-scraped zebra hardwood floors covered with South American throw rugs. He had silver gelatin prints hanging on his walls, some from photographers she recognized. And sketchbooks. Teems and teems of sketchbooks in various styles and levels of completion. There were also a few in-progress metal projects lying around, upcycled parts of engines transformed into hanging clocks and nightstand bases.

"Whoa. This place is amazing."

Bash nodded. "Oh, I know. He's a creative genius. You should see his art studio down the street."

That was surprising. "I didn't know they had art studios in this part of town."

"They don't," Lucas interjected. "I own the block. My studio's the only one." He opened a door on the other side of his living room. "This way."

They walked in, and compared to the rest of the house, his office was sparse, void of personality. There were three computer setups and a real 3D printer. Like a surgeon, he held his hand out to her, saying, "Phone," like he was asking for a scalpel, then proceeded to hook it up to his computer, uploading her photos of the tire marks.

"Quick question: How long-after this bro-hole took off did you get these photos?"

"The following morning. Why?"

He grimaced. "That's too bad."

Bash bent close to the computer screen, studying the photographs. "Why? What's the problem? They look good to me."

Lucas moved the rolling office chair, sat down, and grabbed onto the end of the desk, pulling himself forward. "It's decent, but if other vehicles drove on it, it's not a reliable sample."

"Oh, you don't need to worry about that," Quinn told him. "That part of the street was blockaded by the police straightaway."

He banged his hand on the desk, a brilliant grin beaming her way. "Fan-frickin'-tastic." Then his face fell, his gaze darting back and forth between Quinn and her brother. *"Donde están mis modales?* Mi madre would kill me for being such a bad host."

He bolted out of the room, like a toddler on a sugar high, swiping two chairs from the other room and carrying them in. He plopped them down. "Sit," he commanded. "Are you thirsty? Hungry? Eva just dropped off some of her paella last night. Best you'll ever have."

"Eva?"

Bash squirmed in his seat. "Eva's his sister. She's a chef, has her own restaurant in Falls Church."

Quinn really needed to get out more. "That's cool."

Lucas threw a wicked grin at her brother. "Worth it just to see your reaction."

Bash grunted. "You are such a—"

"Hey, *tu hermanita* is here. Watch your language."

Her brother avoided eye contact with her. *Pfft. I've seen that before,* she thought. Bash only got that way when confronted with his exes—or their disgruntled family members. She didn't know the details, but she didn't need them: it was obvious he had dated Eva at one point and, as with every other woman, it hadn't worked out.

Guess that's what they were talking about earlier. Lucas had remained true to his word: he was over it and was now more interested in the evidence in front of him. It was like Quinn could see his brain working as his eyes darted over the images.

Still staring at the photos, he began explaining: "Tire tread marks like these are classified as pattern evidence because each tire pattern leaves behind a unique impression."

Quinn leaned forward, elbows on her knees, chin in hand. "Makes sense. Go on."

"Yeah, it's amazing what we can learn; patterns like these can help police narrow down the brand, style, and size of the tires. There's actually searchable databases law enforcement uses to narrow down the info."

Bash cradled the back of his head with both hands. "Damn shame we can't get our hands on a database."

Lucas muttered something unintelligible under his breath. "Man, you think I'd have this whole setup and not have access to one of those databases along with a ton of others?"

The last thing Quinn wanted to do was get him into trouble. "Is this legal?"

"One hundred percent. I don't mess with that. Not worth the risk." He rubbed his chin in an absent-minded way as he continued studying her pictures. He then grabbed the computer mouse, using it to copy and paste different sections of the tire patterns into a separate document, then through another browser.

"Okay, so now I've sent marked sections of the tire patterns through. The system will analyze them and come back with what brand of tire left the impression. After we get that info, it'll help me narrow down what type of vehicle the tires would be used on. What would be even better, if you have a suspect, we could match the tires of their vehicle to these markings, see if we have a match."

Bash frowned. "There is no suspect. Not yet anyway."

She kept her Scott Hauser theory to herself for now.

Lucas shrugged, the palm of his hand fanning back and forth along the edges of his mohawk. "That's today. Something may come up soon. And when it does, we'll really have something."

"I need to write all this down." Quinn grabbed her messenger bag, retrieved a little notebook and pen, and started writing. "There's gotta be, like, thousands of tires, especially if it's a popular model car. How does that help us?"

"Good question. Let me show you." He enlarged the photos on the screen. "It's nearly impossible for two vehicles to leave the same tire mark. As someone drives a car, the wear and tear on the tires changes the impression patterns. See over here?" He pointed, making an imaginary circle with the tip of his finger. "The outer edge of this tire is worn down. That means the alignment of the vehicle you're looking for is off. Way off. And see these veins running through? That's probably from twigs or thin branches stuck in the tire treads.

"Since we just have these photos, the only kind of prints we can use are visible prints. They're visible to the naked eye and can be collected by photography without the use of any special equipment or powders. Hopefully, Vienna PD also got some plastic prints."

Quinn kept writing, trying to keep up. "What's that?"

He eyed her taking notes and smiled. "It's a three-dimensional print, taking a cast by using a powdered stone material to make an impression. It's a good way to render exactly what kind of debris and stuff got wedged into the treads. You'd be surprised at how much gets lodged in there. If criminalists really wanted to get their geek on, they would go for some latent prints, the kind not visible to the naked eye. They're used all the time for flat surface samples, using an electrostatic and a gelatin lifter dust print lifting."

The computer beeped with another pop-up screen.

Lucas rubbed his hands together like an evil genius. "Okay, now we're cooking . . ." He scanned the database document. "The vehicle you're looking for, besides being out of alignment, has a nine-rib tire—ribs are the traction elements of the tread— which means there is a good chance you're looking for a vehicle with Parnelli Jones Firestone brand tires. Also, I'd eliminate the car's two front tires as the source of the tracks because the design is so different. The two rear tires are of the same size and design as wheels on the road in 2013."

Bash and Quinn glanced at each other, then back to Lucas. He wasn't done.

"Based on the limited information I have, you're looking for someone who drives either a 2013 Nissan Altima or a Honda Accord sedan—same year—who lives in a wooded area. My bet is they keep the car parked among the trees, not in a garage or driveway, since there's a fair share of twigs in the treads. Also, see these thin lines with these attached globs, near the twig impressions?" He didn't wait for an answer. "Those are made by pine needles, but not just any pines. Those globs are sap—and there's a lot of it. I don't know what kind of pine trees produce that much this time of year, but find someone who does. It might help you narrow it down to certain parts of Vienna. And then look for where cars are parked under a cluster of the same pine trees. Maybe then you'll find your Honda or Nissan, and hence your body schlepper."

"Wow, this is like a visit to science-nerd heaven."

That made him laugh. "Bash always said you were the smart one of the family."

"Yeah, and he also says he's the looks and I'm the brains."

Lucas stood up while hitting "Print." "I know that game. He says that because he doesn't want you to know how beautiful you are; otherwise, you'd really drive all the boys in town crazy, and he and your father would never sleep." He looked over at her, giving a playful wink. "It's a classic older brother trick. I should know."

"Hey, stop flirting with my sister."

Lucas sauntered over to the printer, gathered the pages, and stapled them in the corner before handing them over to Quinn. "It's too easy to torture your brother. Hope this helps."

Bash rubbed his face with both hands. "Listen, man, we appreciate your help, but do you realize how many Nissan Altimas and Honda Accords are out there?"

Plus, there's no way Scott would drive either of those cars. He's too much of a snob.

Lucas nodded. "That's fair. Hold on a sec."

He went over to one of the other computer setups and remained standing as he bent over the keyboard, typing at a furious pace. A couple of tabs opened on the screen.

"Assuming the car is registered to a Vienna address—and who knows if that's the case, but whatever—then you would have six hundred and sixty-seven vehicles to cull through."

Quinn perked up. "Any chance you have the names of those car owners?"

His eye twinkled. "As a matter of fact, I do." He hit a couple more keys, went back to the printer, and removed those pages, stapling them together as well. He handed them over.

She took them, folding them in half. "Thank you for this and the impromptu forensics lesson. How did you ever learn all this?"

He shrugged, leading them out of the office. "Here and there."

Well, that was forthcoming.

They descended the stairs and entered the garage again. As they cleared the docking bay, a familiar figure was tapping her foot while standing by the latest model Lexus SUV.

It was Milly Hauser.

"Young man, I've been waiting out here for ten minutes!"

Lucas muttered under his breath, *"El diablo ha venido a castigarme."*

Bash suppressed a cackle.

"What does that mean?" Quinn asked.

Bash whispered in her ear. "'The devil has come to punish me.'"

Lucas approached Mrs. Hauser. "Do you have an appointment?"

Her expression soured. "Well, no, but it's making this weird sound, like nails being dragged down a chalkboard. I can't take it!"

Now she had his attention. "Any idea where inside the car the noise came from?"

"How am I supposed to know that? I have a masters from Smith College—that's one of the original Seven Sisters schools—*not* a mechanic's certificate."

Wow. What an elitist.

Scott's mother may have been rude, but Quinn was raised to be polite, regardless. "Hello, Mrs. Hauser."

"Hello, Quinn, Sebastian. It seems you two keep a wide array of company."

"Yeah, we're lucky that way," her brother answered.

Lucas walked over to her car, popped the hood, scanning it for all of five seconds. "That looks okay." Then he sauntered over to the driver's side and crouched down, balancing on the balls of his feet as he bent his head to peek under. He reached through the wheel well, feeling around. Then he pulled out, of all things, a handful of pine twigs.

And they were covered in sap. White sap.

Her hand fluttered to her cheek. "Well, will you look at that!"

His brows raised. "Yeah, look at that." He gave a pointed gaze over his shoulder, back to Bash and Quinn. "You find any more clues, come on by. I'm happy to help."

Mrs. Hauser fidgeted with her pearls by her throat. "Clues? What kind of clues? Please tell me you're not trying to investigate Tricia's death on your own." She forced a smile. "We'd all be devastated if something happened to you, dear."

Sure you would.

Quinn was about to argue the merits of her efforts, but the woman's face paled, and she started swaying like she was going to be ill at any moment.

"Are you feeling all right, Mrs. Hauser?"

"Yes, of course I am. It's just hot in here."

Quinn didn't want to pry, but something was definitely wrong. Scott's mother was always impeccable, from her hair and makeup to her outfits and coordinated accessories. But her coloring was off, with a sickly sheen coating her skin. She had applied her cosmetics with her usual precision, but the colors of her lipstick and eyeshadow were about five hues off from being the correct shades. Not the norm for her. She also pressed a hand into her stomach as if she were holding herself up through sheer force of will.

"Well, thank you, Mr. Diaz, for helping me. How much do I owe you?"

"No charge."

Quinn could tell that surprised her, but then again, she was still reeling from whatever was upsetting her stomach.

"I appreciate your kindness. I'll be sure to return the next time I have engine trouble."

She tried to maintain her composure, but there was no hiding her rush to get back inside her SUV. She hopped in like her heels were on fire, slammed her vehicle door, and skidded out of the garage, driving like a woman with a bounty on her head.

"I'd bet twenty bucks she hurls in her car," Lucas said.

Quinn shot him a look. "Okay, am I the only one who got freaked when you pulled those branches from her wheel well?"

"No, it weirded me out too."

Bash leaned his weight against one of the garage poles. "Well, unless a genie came by and granted someone's wish to turn an Altima into a Lexus, I'm thinking it's just a coincidence."

Quinn shoved her notebook and pen away. "Or she parks that car in the same location as our Accord or Altima."

All three let that thought sink in.

"She seemed fine until she heard you talking about gathering clues."

Quinn shook her head. "I don't know about that. Mrs. Hauser looked genuinely ill, like she was hit with a stomach bug."

Lucas shrugged. "They do have that kind of onset sometimes."

Her brother crossed his arms, nibbling at the corner of his bottom lip. "I don't know if I buy that."

"Bash, what are you saying?"

He shook his head, staring off at the same point where Milly Hauser had just stood. "It's one of two possibilities. One"—he held up his thumb—"she really *is* ill and needs to puke."

"And two?" Quinn asked.

"Milly Hauser heard what we were talking about, and it's a guilty conscience, not a stomach bug, that's got her insides in a twist."

Lucas wrapped the tree branches with a clean cloth and handed them to Quinn. "Well, take these to someone who knows about trees. Maybe they'll be able to tell you what pine trees produce tons of white sap in the spring. When you do, you're that much closer to the killer's getaway car."

Chapter Eighteen

"The trouble with having an open mind, of course,
is that people will insist on coming along and trying to put
things in it."
—Terry Pratchett, *Diggers*

Quinn's head was still spinning from what had happened at the garage. She needed to speak with her mother straightaway. She was a landscape architect and Quinn would bet a month's salary she'd be able to tell her where to find this particular stratum of pine trees. She was also dying to sit somewhere quiet and comb through the names Lucas had given her. And she was itching to walk on over to the coffeehouse and talk to Maxie, like the Clink-n-Drink ladies had suggested, but she had other places to go. She had promised to cover the store for her parents so they could have some much-needed time to themselves.

Guilt needled her: she hadn't been much of an employee these last few weeks. She really needed to make it up to them. Quinn arrived at Prose & Scones, said her hellos to everyone, and then headed straight for her office.

There was no way she was going to be able to wait until she got home that night to scan through Lucas's lists. She was dying to take a peek, to see if anyone in the Hauser family owned a 2013 Nissan Altima or a 2013 Honda Accord sedan. Doubtful, but she still had to double-check. Quinn fired up her computer so she could track down where Scott's parents lived. She had been over to his place a long time ago, a swank—and personality free—condo in Tyson's Corner. But never to the Hauser's home.

Opening her bag, she grabbed all the pages; then a hard knock made her jump.

The door swung open. And it was the last person she'd expected to come by.

It was Daria. No habit, no wimple, just a simple peasant-style dress and flip-flops.

Daria stood in front of her, hands on her hips, face beet red. "I figured I'd grow old and feeble-minded and *die* before you came by the abbey to apologize. So I'm here, saving you a trip and me anymore aggravation."

No "Hello." No "How are you?" No small talk.

Pure Daria Caine.

She may have barged in on a boat christened *Attitude*, but this was her best friend in front of her, and with one look, she knew Daria had been experiencing just as much anguish as she had been over the last week.

And just like that, whatever anger Quinn had been holding onto evaporated as soon as her brain caught up to what her eyes were taking in.

Quinn slumped in her chair. "I know, I know . . . I'm sorry."

"Well, I'm sorry too." Daria fidgeted with her cross neck-lace. "I can't even remember the last time we had a fight like that."

"That's because we've *never* had a fight like that."

Tears welled in Daria's eyes. "I really am sorry for kicking you out of dinner."

Quinn swallowed the knot in her throat. "Yeah?"

She nodded. "Oh course I am. You missed a really delicious dessert."

That did it. The tension broke, and the cousins laughed and hugged it out.

"I missed you, Hufflepuff."

"You too, Slytherin."

Quinn felt eyes on her, and sure enough, standing front row center over her cousin's shoulder, right outside her office door, was, well, most of the family.

Quinn rolled her eyes. "Take a picture. It'll last longer."

Aunt Johanna laughed. "Then close the door! The whole town can hear you."

"Good idea." Quinn walked over and shut the door.

Once inside, Quinn pulled out a tucked-away stool for her cousin to sit on.

"Listen, I didn't mean for you to have to be the one to come over. I've just been trying to comb through the mess and figure out what I wanted to say."

Daria tossed her hands up, an exasperated expression coloring her features. "Quinn, this is you and me. When have we ever needed to filter what we say?"

"Honestly? Ever since you decided to become a nun."

Instead of defensiveness, Daria just offered a sad smile. "Can you help me understand why my decision upsets you so much?"

That was a reasonable question.

"I don't know if I have an answer to that. I guess if I had been around to see your evolution in this direction, I'd understand better. It just seemed out of nowhere to me."

"I get that."

"You don't talk to me about that kind of thing. At least not anymore."

Daria wasn't so quick to respond now either.

Quinn went on. "Listen, I don't want to push you to talk or anything. It's just—"

Daria closed her eyes.

Ah crap, did I blow it again?

Quinn kept rambling. "Nothing you could ever say or do would make me love you less. I hope you know that. I'm talking big love, like way up here." She reached up high, flopping her hand back and forth. "You know what? I'm doubling down. I'm like Father, Son, and Holy Spirit love levels over up in—"

"Stop! Stop talking. I know you love me."

"So then what's the prob—"

"Raj broke up with me because I wasn't Indian," Daria blurted out.

Quinn wasn't sure she'd heard right. "I don't understand."

Daria sighed, slumping in her seat. "Honestly? Neither do I."

"But you were tight with his family! They *adored* you. You went on holiday to India with them—twice!"

"They were fine with me as the girlfriend. They preferred that if he was going to "sow his oats," it was with one white woman instead of dozens. They basically kept me close so they could keep an eye on him."

She couldn't believe what she was hearing. How could anyone think her cousin wasn't good enough?

Of course, she understood the arguments against cultural assimilation on an intellectual level, but Daria was brilliant—and hilarious. Compassionate and original. And she was beautiful. Even though she had always despised any kind of popularity contest back when she was Elizabeth, her cousin had won the Homecoming Queen title two years in a row. And those silly high school titles were the least interesting facts about her.

"Why didn't you say anything?"

Daria picked at her fingernails. "There's more."

Quinn held her breath.

"He said he loved me, but he could never have a 'jailbird' as the mother of his children."

Oh no he didn't.

"He said *what* to you now?"

Daria let out a shaky sigh. Quinn could tell she was shoring up everything she had so as not to cry.

Watching Daria trying to hold it together sparked a deep, almost primal anger. Quinn could feel her cheeks and neck getting hot. "Tell me." Her voice cracked. "Please tell me he didn't have the nerve to say that to you."

"Yes, those were his exact words."

"Wait a second—you have an expunged juvenile record, which means you don't have *any* kind of record anymore. Besides, it was for taking a couple of joy rides and hanging out on school property. You never got caught for anything else. Big deal!"

Daria met her gaze, her hurt scoring through her. "Evidently it was to him."

Quinn grabbed her messenger bag, stuffing the papers back in and taking out the keys to her truck, holding them between her fingers like a weapon. "I am going to *kill* him. I have a big brother, a dad for a lawyer, and a shovel. No one will miss him."

Daria put her hand out like a stop sign. "You will do no such thing. Sit down." She leaned closer. "Please."

Quinn plopped her bum on the hard seat. "How can you be so calm? Don't you want to gouge his eyes out?"

"Oh, trust me, I did," she said with a half-hearted laugh. "When he left—and then you left—I spiraled. But this time, instead of drinking too much and acting like an idiot, like I would have in college, I started going to church. A lot. At first, I'll admit, it was an escape. But then, I don't know . . . something clicked for me. It was like a peace I've searched for had been waiting for me this whole time.

"I'm sorry I didn't share this with you. It's just that . . . have you ever experienced something so painful that it took all your energy just to survive it, never mind having to retell it to someone else?"

Yes, every time Aiden Harrington pats my head, I keep each cringe-worthy moment all to myself.

Quinn knew it wasn't the same thing—not even close. But she had nothing else from her own life to compare it to. At that moment, she felt like an overprotected, sheltered baby.

Daria wasn't done. "Besides, if I didn't tell anyone, I didn't have to live my humiliation outside my own head."

Quinn grasped her hand. "I understand, but you have no reason to feel humiliated. He's the one who should be embarrassed for being such a poor excuse of a human being. He basically led you on for three years."

Daria squeezed it back. "I just . . ."

"What?"

She met Quinn's eye. "I just never knew someone could be so callous. And I have to admit I've been wondering . . . what's wrong with me that I never picked up on that side of him before? I prided myself on being shrewd, a good judge of character. But looking back, I had some real blind spots when it came to him. No wonder pride's a sin . . . it's like believing I could read into someone's heart, like I had some unique gift or something. What a crock that turned out to be."

It was a special kind of agony, seeing someone she loved suffering so. Now that Daria had abandoned the tough-girl facade, Quinn was bearing witness to her pain: raw and exposed, the kind that hurt to watch.

"Listen, if the church gives you comfort, if you've developed this rad relationship with the big JC, then you have my full support."

Daria wiped tears away. "I appreciate that. But, you know, I'm not one hundred percent sure this is the life I want either. I have doubts, just like everybody else. That's why the process takes years. It's why I'm a novitiate."

Quinn let her words sink in. "Makes sense."

Both of them got quiet.

Daria took a cleansing breath. "I'm sorry I got so defensive the other night."

"And I'm sorry I picked a nice dinner to bring up my issues with you."

"Well, that's not *all* on you. The Reverend Mother played a hand in that."

Quinn grimaced. "Yeah, I know, and I am not happy with her right now."

"Don't be mad. It's her job to gauge my readiness, and she's all about complete transparency. I knew she'd poke the bear. That's why I was so nervous that night."

Quinn still wasn't thrilled, but what Daria said made sense. "I guess I get it."

"So, I'm waiting."

Quinn tilted her head. "Waiting for what? I already said I was sorry."

She laughed. "That's not what I meant. I'm waiting to hear an update on your progress with finding Tricia's killer. I know there's no way you just sat on your hands this past week."

Quinn's face brightened. "You know me so well. I have *a lot* to tell you." She got the pages out of her bag again and handed them over, explaining everything that had happened thus far.

"So, unfortunately, they're not in alphabetical order. Do you mind going through them and seeing if you can find a Hauser or any other name we'd recognize?"

She held out both hands, pretending to grab air. "Gimme . . . the highlighter too." Daria opened the cap, putting the highlighter tip right under her nose. "Is it weird that I love the smell of markers?"

"Yes. But I like the smell of gasoline. So, there ya go."

Quinn got on her computer to look up the Hauser home. *It's scary how easy it is to find where people live.*

"Looks like they're all the way over by Wolftrap."

"What street?"

Quinn squinted at the screen. "Foxstone Drive. Know it?"

"Yeah, it's near Foxstone Park."

She stared at her cousin. "How is it I've lived here all my life and I've never even heard of that park?"

Daria gazed up from the pages. "I don't know. It's definitely a woodsier section of Vienna. Lots of pine trees, but that's hardly enough to even be a correlation. We have pine trees everywhere."

Quinn eyed the couple of branches she had tucked away, wrapped in one of Lucas's rags from the garage. Was it also weird she was walking around with branches in her messenger bag? She needed to get these to her mother to examine.

Let your mom and dad have their day off. Everyone needs time as a couple, even people who have been married forever.

Ensuring marital bliss for the parental unit wasn't Quinn's only motivation for delay. Truth was, she had a ton of work to do. The deadline to finish Rachel's project was coming up fast, and she still had a quarter of the job left to complete.

"Do you mind if I work on Granny Nora's journal while you comb through the names?"

Daria glanced up for a split second, eyed the diary on Quinn's desk, and shrugged. "Why are you even asking? We're in your office. Of course you have to work." She went right back to scanning the pages. "All right, so it appears the Hausers do not own an Altima or an Accord sedan. These are only the 2013 models registered?"

"Yep."

"There's a lot."

Quinn chuckled. "No kidding. It hurt my eyes just looking at it." She opened the journal and checked the new spine she had glued in. "Looks good," she mumbled to herself, reaching for the linen thread and needle. She laid the thread next to the journal's original stitching. "That looks like a match to me. What do you think?"

Daria craned her neck for a peek. "Yeah, it's ivory. It's fine."

"Not a real details girl, are ya?"

"Not those kinds of details. Better you than me."

Quinn threaded the needle, perusing the pages as she stitched the binding. She started laughing.

"What's so funny?" Daria asked.

"I'm just reading some of the diary as I fix it—and even though young Nora was madly in love with this man named David, Rachel's great-grandparents kept inviting different single men from the congregation over to dinner. Every Shabbat, a new face. Guess they didn't like David too much."

Daria giggled, snorting a little. "That's right out of *My Big Fat Greek Wedding*!"

Quinn clucked her tongue. "Poor Toula."

"Poor Ian."

Quinn cut the end of the thread with her scissors, shaped like bunny ears. "Well, it worked out for them. I love that movie."

"Me too."

Quinn eyed the pages in Daria's hands, noting she was on the last one. "Any luck?"

Daria made a stink face. "Nope, that would've been too easy." She handed them back, and Quinn shoved them in her messenger bag. "What time is it?"

Quinn glanced at her computer screen and gawked. "Gee Zeus, we need to go."

"Yeah, I gotta motor." Daria tucked the stool back under the desk.

"Hey, so what made you finally come over here today?"

She chewed her bottom lip. "Um . . . Bash called."

Quinn stopped packing up. "What?"

She swore under her breath. "Crud, I wasn't supposed to say anything."

Quinn's brows shot north.

"He came by after your little field trip to that mechanic—whatever his name—and said he was over us fighting and, besides, it was obvious you and I were a much better crime duo than you and him."

"He just can't help himself. He has to try and fix everything for everybody."

Daria suppressed a grin. "He's not the only one."

Quinn ignored that comment. "I'm surprised that's all it took for you to come over."

"Well, the Reverend Mother did say I need to work on not being so prideful."

"You're stubborn is what you are."

Daria gave her a pretend glare. "Don't push it. I only allot myself so many acts of contrition a week, and I'm fresh out."

"Fair enough. Now let's get out of here. It's been a day." She turned off her computer.

"Oh, and he wanted to thank me too."

"For what?"

"For the great advice he was never supposed to hear—about putting real effort in with Rachel for a change."

Now it was Quinn's turn to chew on her lip or a hangnail—anything to not have to respond.

"You are sooo busted!"

Quinn let out a squeak. "I know! But you weren't there. Trust me, he needed to hear it. I was moved by the Holy Spirit to speak."

"Really? You're going there?"

Quinn didn't bat an eye, pretending to take a card out of an imaginary deck and slapping it down. "Consider it in play!"

They stared at each other before dissolving into snorts, laughs, and giggles.

Daria wiped her eyes. "I really missed you."

"I missed you too. C'mon—the Gooey Grilled Cheese is on me this time."

Chapter Nineteen

"You think those dogs will not be in heaven. I tell you they
will be there long before any of us."
—Robert Louis Stevenson,
nineteenth-century Scottish novelist

"Well, I, for one, am tickled hot pink you and Daria
made up."

"Me too, Mama. Me too."

After her first good night's sleep in days, Quinn stopped
by the store—twigs in hand—dying to ask her mother about
them. She had caught her at the perfect time: hours before
they opened, with Adele sweeping the sidewalk and no one
around.

Her mama stopped what she was doing, snatched her glasses
off the top of her head, and examined the branches.

"They're just ordinary pine branches, honey. No special
variety, if that's what you're asking." She peered over the rim of
her spectacles, something her husband did often. "Do I want to
know why I'm looking at these for you?"

Quinn pressed her lips together in case anything tried to
spill out.

Adele Caine mumbled an "mm-hmm" before having more to say. "Whoever those trees belong to should know, though, they need an arborist—and fast."

Quinn's ears perked up. "Really? Tell me why."

Adele pointed toward them. "There's copious amounts of white sap. Imagine a tree like you would a human body. A tree's normal excretions run clear to golden when healthy. But when sick, white indicates disease—the way pus forms in a human wound when fighting infection."

Quinn tried not to gag. "Well, that's a lovely image."

Adele ignored her. "Those trees are gravely ill. That's all I'm saying."

Quinn wrapped them back up in the rag Lucas had given her, and shoved them in her bag. "You wouldn't know exactly what would cause these particular kinds of symptoms in pine trees, would you?"

Holding her broom with both hands, chin resting on top, Adele shrugged. "Oh, I don't know for sure . . . sometimes it's a reaction to storm damage, but usually it's from bacterial cankers."

"What? Like canker sores?"

"No, smart-mouth. A human canker sore is from a virus. The ones I'm talking about emanate from dead spots on trees, usually caused by fungi growing under the bark."

"I'm assuming it's not the good kind of fungi, like the mushrooms Dad likes so much."

Her mom tittered. "No, they're not the same." She propped the broom against the store's doors, then bent over to fill up the large water bowl for the neighborhood dogs, from the hose off to the side. From over her shoulder, she added, "Those trees can be saved if the owners prune them back and cut away the sickness. I'm no arborist, but I'm guessing time is running out."

Quinn sighed, realizing that her trying to find a cluster of sickly pine trees in town might not be the most solid lead. But perhaps she'd have some better clues after visiting Caffe Amour.

She had made arrangements to meet Maxie at the coffee shop before her shift began. Quinn knew it was a reach, but after the car registrations ended up leading nowhere, she was open to anything. Sister Daria had perused the list of car owners the night before, and not one had jumped out. It amazed Quinn how Vienna felt to her like such a small town, but in reality, there were sixteen thousand five hundred residents. Truth was, she didn't leave her Northwest neighborhood often. Her slice of Vienna was a fraction of the rest of the area, her own portion of the 'small town'.

"Do you mind if I leave RBG with you?"

Her mama rested a hand on her hip. "Of course not. Just tie her up on the patio under the shade. I need to pinch some heads."

She meant buds in the flower beds. Unfortunately, her dog baby was in a "not having it" mood as Quinn tied her leash at her mama's request—almost as if she knew Quinn was going out on a quest without her.

"I'll be back soon. Be good."

In no time, she was down the street, with Maxie already waiting for her. This time, her hair was dyed purple. "Whoa, a new color. What's the occasion?"

Maxie fiddled with the end of her braid. "I think I may have OD'd on Prince."

"I don't think that's possible. Prince was awesome."

Maxie grinned widely. "Totally. *Purple Rain* was on TV last weekend, and my mom, my sister, and I decided to make it the theme for the weekend. We're talking cupcakes made with purple icing, popcorn popped from purple corn kernels. I think I drank my body weight in purple Kool-Aid. Purple hair was inevitable after that."

Quinn had always liked Maxie. They had never hung out in high school, but they'd always gotten along. Maxie played saxophone and had been in the marching band back in the day, so their paths had rarely crossed. Probably because Madison High School's marching band was mafia-family close.

Maxie handed her a glossy flyer. "I'm playing at this big fundraiser for The Women's Center at the end of May— Memorial Day weekend, actually. It'd be cool if you could come, maybe bring some friends."

"Oh right, I heard about this already. I'm definitely going. Weird they're having it the same weekend as Viva Vienna."

Viva Vienna was a big deal and an event that rarely shared billing with anything else. Sponsored by The Rotary Club every year, it was a three-day smorgasbord of rides, craft booths, carnival games, live music, and crazy-delicious amusement park food. Turkey legs the size of an arm, shaved ices as big as a human head, along with fried Oreos, soft-serve ice cream, and rainbow-flavored cotton candy. Outsiders might think it was only for children, but Vienna residents of all ages made it a destination. Although, considering over fifty thousand people came every year, Quinn guessed the secret was out that the weekend was quite a time for everyone.

Maxie blew off her concern. "The event is at seven. Plenty of time for people to go to Viva, then clean up for the fundraiser."

"True. Remember how we'd get those wrist bands from Doctor Garan's office when we were kids?"

Dr. Arnold Garan was one of the local orthodontists, and every year, to demonstrate his appreciation for all the crooked teeth he wired into submission, he gave out free admission wristbands to his patients. Those bracelets weren't cheap either. They granted the wearer access to unlimited rides. It was one of the few perks for having endured a metal mouth for a couple of years.

Maxie popped out a clear bottom-teeth retainer with her tongue before pushing it back in. "Please, why do you think I wear this thing? It keeps me on his patient list. Totally worth it."

Quinn sat down on the parking space's concrete bumper. Maxie had been the one to ask her to meet in the small lot behind the coffeehouse, where hardly anyone ever went, but Quinn noticed her friend was still scanning the perimeter, just to make sure they were alone.

Interesting.

Quinn decided to get right to it. "So, thanks for meeting me."

Maxie hunched her shoulders. "Yeah, well, I might not have liked Tricia—like, at all—but it sucks she's dead. I don't know how you think I can help, though."

"You never know. Something you heard or saw that appeared inconsequential at the time may mean more now."

They were sitting side by side, legs straight out. Maxie was jiggling her feet, knocking her shoes together. The sound was, frankly, annoying, but Quinn thought better than to bring it up. She knew Maxie didn't want to talk about Tricia, so if she needed to release some nerves, then so be it.

"Their office is right down the street, and I know Trina and Tricia live on coffee and not much else. You saw them here often?"

Maxie stopped knocking her Doc Martens together. "All the time. They treated this place like it was their second office. They met their clients here, they hung out with each other here, on and on, yada yada . . . They were always together, until Scott came into the picture."

Quinn tucked her legs under her. "They've both had boyfriends before. What made him different?"

"Well, for one thing, Scott stood up to Trina, especially if he thought she was pushing Tricia around, which she did. Not all the time, but enough. Trina did *not* like that."

"Do you think they had a falling out?"

Maxie scoffed. "I don't think. I *know* so. I'm surprised you didn't hear about it."

"Hear about what?"

Maxie smacked her purple-glossed lips together. "Well, about a month ago the sisters came in as usual, talking between themselves, and the next thing I know, Trina starts yelling at her sister, and is this close"—she held up her thumb and forefinger an inch apart—"to flipping a table or something. I mean she got *loud*, saying Tricia would never make it through law school, which I was like, whoa, Tricia is going to law school? And that she was barely smart enough to carry her end of their real estate business . . . blah, blah, blah . . . yada yada yada."

Quinn couldn't believe her ears. "Wow, that sounds . . ." She couldn't even finish her sentence.

"Yeah, it was *bad*. I never saw them in the coffeehouse at the same time after that fight. And then Tricia died."

Quinn nodded, staring off into nothing. *Well, that answers your question about why Trina wasted no time getting new real estate posters made.*

She opened her bag and retrieved the list of 2013 Nissan Altimas and Honda Accord sedans. "Last thing, Max . . . can you take a quick look through these and see if any of these names rings a bell, at least in terms of being connected to Tricia's or Scott's families?"

"Sure," she said, taking the list from her. Quinn knew it was another long shot, but she was willing to try almost anything at this point.

Maxie was only on the second page when she stopped. "Do you mean anyone connected to the families, even if they didn't know Tricia?"

"I guess so, sure."

"Then here you go." The tip of her finger pointed to a name: Lorenzo Diamond.

Quinn had never heard of him. "Who is that?"

"We're friends. He was in band with me back in school. People call him 'Ren' for short. Playing the drums—that's his true passion. Although he hasn't gotten around to playing as much. He used to have regular gigs at Jammin' Java. He's, like, totally gorgeous, by the way. Unfortunately, I'm in the 'friend zone.'"

"Yeah, been there. Sucks."

If 'Ren' Diamond played at Jammin' Java, that meant he must've been really good. It was a local music club with a national reputation. Vienna might be the quintessential suburban town, and yet in its midst was a rock 'n' roll institution. Of course, its name was the ultimate irony because, in spite of being named after the beany brew, the coffee there was awful.

Quinn was lost. "I'm not getting the connection."

"Oh, right. Well, even though Ren's a musician like me, he's got bills to pay, just like the rest of us. I mean, I like coffee just fine, but would I work here if I could make a living off playing my sax? Uh, that's a big nada. No way. Anyway, Ren pays *his* bills by working for his family's landscaping business. I guess he must've met Scott Hauser's parents on the job. They hit it off well enough for Mr. Hauser to offer to rent out the guest cottage on the back of their property. I've been over there a couple of times for jam sessions. Let me tell you, that place is sweet."

Quinn let what she had said sink in. "C'mon, Max, everyone knows Dr. Hauser is a sweetheart, but I'm having a hard time imagining Milly Hauser agreeing to such an arrangement, let alone getting along with some twenty-something-year-old drummer-slash-landscaper."

That made Maxie chuckle. "Totally. Nah, I think he and Dr. Hauser were the ones who got along. Ren said Scott's dad played the guitar a little. He was taking lessons over at the School of Rock, but supposedly Mrs. Hauser was less than thrilled over his new hobby, saying a surgeon should be more careful with his hands, which I was like, *dude*, it's not like he's taking up ax throwing or something. Yeesh, controlling much?"

Maxie checked the time on her phone. "Oh shoot! I've got to go." She slapped her thighs, then bounced up. "I hope I helped. Even just a little."

"You really did. Thanks, Max."

Quinn was about to follow her in and grab herself a muffin, but her phone rang. It was her mom.

"Hey, Mama, I'm on my way back. Do you want me to pick you up anyth—"

Her mother was panicked. "Something's wrong with RBG! You have to come now! I don't know what's happening . . ."

Quinn froze. "What are you talking about? What's wrong with RBG?"

"I don't know! She's throwing up, convulsing, out of nowhere!"

Oh God, please don't let this be happening. "Okay, okay. I'm leaving now."

"Everything okay?" Maxie asked.

"I don't know." Quinn hung up, shoving her phone in her back pocket and bolting out of the lot, down the street, and back to the store. Thank the Lord it wasn't far, because Quinn was already out of breath by the time she arrived. Her parents were sitting on the pavement next to her dog baby, who had vomited—a lot. She was whining too, the most heart-wrenching sound Quinn had ever heard.

"Oh, thank goodness you got here so quickly."

Quinn crouched near her RBG, the dog's chocolate-brown–eyed gaze locking with hers. RBG's eyes were pleading for help. She was in pain, trying to tuck her usually wet nose under Quinn's armpit.

"Her nose is dry. That can't be good," she mumbled to herself.

"I said the same thing to your mother. Something's really wrong. Totally out of the blue."

Stay calm. You can't help her if you're a wreck.

RBG started heaving again, her body retching something awful.

"I have never felt so helpless in all my life."

Adele nodded. "Welcome to motherhood."

Her dog baby vomited again, and as disgusting as it was, Quinn got a closer look at the mess. One glance at the contents of RBG's stomach sent off alerts in her brain.

"Wait a second, I didn't feed her anything that looks like this. Did y'all give her a treat or people food?"

They shook their heads. Quinn darted over to the water bowl, smelling it. It was fine. But that's when she spotted something. "What's this?"

Tucked behind one of the potted plants, there was an open plastic bag filled with dog treats. "Is this ours? When did we start providing doggie biscuits?"

"Since never," her mama said. "That's not ours."

"Maybe a customer forgot it after bringing it along for their dog?"

Maybe. Maybe not.

Quinn sniffed the treats, but they didn't really smell like anything. They were definitely not the kind one could buy in a grocery store. They appeared homemade. It seemed gross, but Quinn picked them up and licked them too, to determine their content. They smelled and tasted like regular dog biscuits to her.

She opened her messenger satchel and dug up a couple of clean doggy bags, the kind she used to pick up her dog's messes during their walks. She shoved the treats in one bag, and with the other, she picked up a sample of the vomit.

"Dear sweet Jesus, what on earth are you doing, Quinn?"

"Mom, she may be allergic to something in these biscuits, or she could've gotten into something else left out here. I'm bringing samples in case the vet asks."

She thrust both bags inside her messenger bag.

"That's actually a really good idea. I would've never thought of that."

She adored her mama, but she didn't have time for this. "Dad, I need you to lift RBG and bring her to the car. We've got to get her to the emergency vet."

Without hesitation, Finn lifted RBG and jogged her over to the family's station wagon, with Adele hitting the unlock button. Quinn held out her hand.

"Keys."

"I can drive, honey. You stay in the back with RBG."

"Mom, you're slow on a good day. I'm driving."

Thank Jesus, Moses, and Buddha that she didn't argue, handing Quinn the car keys before climbing in the back with her dad and the dog. Quinn climbed inside the driver's side and turned on the ignition, but not before catching a glimpse in her rearview mirror.

RBG was still whining, panting, and starting to convulse again. Quinn closed her eyes for a second, willing herself to keep it together, before she put the car in drive and hauled tail to the animal emergency room.

She prayed the good veterinarians could save RBG in time.

Chapter Twenty

"I wanted to tell her that I was getting better, because that was
supposed to be the narrative of illness:
It was a hurdle you jumped over, or a battle you won.
Illness is a story told in the past tense."
—John Green, *Turtles All the Way Down*

They had already waited for what seemed like forever, but
no one on staff could give them an update on how RBG
was holding up.

After speeding to the other side of town, the three Caines
had run into the vet emergency room, describing RBG's symptoms and handing over the biscuits and the other "goody"
bag. The nurses had taken one look at RBG in mid-convulsion
and escorted her right in. Quinn and her parents had
followed.

In no time, Dr. Eric Cryan had come in the room, all business, examining RBG's eyes and inside her mouth, and listening for her heartbeat. "Gail, bring those samples to Nruti in the
lab. Maybe they're the key to figuring out what's causing this
reaction. Good call on bringing those in, Quinn."

She took little comfort in his praise; she just hoped they'd help provide answers for the vet staff. "How long until we know what's wrong with her?"

Dr. Cryan offered a gentle smile. "I promise to send someone to talk to you as soon as we know something. Are you waiting here, or do you want us to call you at home?"

Quinn didn't hesitate. "Yeah, we're not going anywhere."

That conversation had been over three hours ago.

Since then, her parents had taken over making calls to everyone. Her mom was able to have Sarah cover the store, and Bash promised to come over after his shift at the firehouse. Fortunately, he was at the tail end of his seventy-two hours. He'd be exhausted, but he'd be there. Her dad contacted her cousin, along with Aunt Johanna and Uncle Jerry. They were picking Daria up from the abbey and heading over too.

She was grateful they were contacting everybody, because all Quinn could do was stare at the television in the waiting room. And for the life of her, if someone had asked what she was watching, she wouldn't have been able to say. It was just white noise. Something to look at without really seeing.

After searching through her messenger bag, she realized she had left her AirPods on her nightstand at home, which was a shame because music would have been the perfect distraction, although . . . what's the perfect playlist for when your dog baby is fighting for her life? She just wished she could go to bed. Draw the covers over her head and never come out. All she wanted was for the pain to stop. She didn't even have one of her funny enamel pins on to make her smile.

She felt a warm hand on top of her head. "Quinn . . . Quinn?"

The warm hand left, replaced with two fingers caressing her cheek.

"You're starting to worry me, duck. Do I need to get a doctor for you too?"

It was hearing the nickname "duck" that snapped Quinn out of her stupor-a name he hadn't used since she refused to get out of the pool during Vienna Woods' mandatory pool break.

It was Aiden. She craned her neck. He was a mountain of a man when she was standing. He was even more massive when she was the one sitting down.

Never had she seen him gaze at her the way he was now. In those gray eyes, she bore witness to his concern, his warmth, and a gentleness that shattered something deep inside. He was letting her know it was okay to fall apart because he was going to be the one to hold her pain. He knew she was strong, capable; it wasn't about her being weak. It was about her allowing herself to show what made her vulnerable.

And that's what broke her wide open. Quinn let out a sound between a wail and a moan, hot tears running down her cheeks. He immediately bent to his knees and enveloped her in his arms.

"Shh, it'll be okay. I've got you."

He was warmer than home, stroking her hair as he soothed her.

"She's young and strong, Quinn," he said to her, a low, gravelly voice near her ear. She had the other one pressed against his chest, the sound of his heartbeat keeping her grounded.

She wiped her tears with the back of her sleeve, making her feel like she was seven years old again. "It's been over three hours already. And not a word."

"No news can be good news," he told her. "If she was taking a turn for the worse, they'd bring you back to say goodbye.

That's not happening, which tells me she's fighting hard in there."

Daria came over with a cup of coffee for her.

"Thanks. When did you get here?"

Her cousin shared a look with Aiden. "I've been here for over an hour. I came over and said 'hi,' but you barely looked away from the TV."

"I'm sorry. I didn't mean to be rude. I—I didn't hear you."

"I know," she said. "Don't worry about me. Is there anything else I can get for you? Are you hungry?"

Quinn made a sour face. "Ugh, the idea of eating . . . no thanks. But coffee's always appreciated."

"I know—I'm not new here."

"Quinn Caine?" a voice called.

Hope jolted through her. "That's me."

Dr. Cryan walked over, his face haggard. Quinn stood, along with Aiden.

"Well, let me start off with the good news: RBG will pull through unless something out of the ordinary occurs. I'll admit, it was touch-and-go for a little while there, but she's stabilized now and resting."

She felt bathed in gratitude. "Oh, thank God."

Her parents hugged each other and, together with Daria, breathed out a collective sigh of relief.

Aiden was impassive—his cop eyes were back. "Any idea what caused the illness?"

The vet's face sobered. "Yeah, that's the bad news I have to share. I'm sorry to tell you, but someone poisoned your dog."

A sharp buzz pained her left ear, which she ignored. Aiden didn't even blink.

Her dad's jaw hardened. "Who would ever want to hurt a dog? That's unconscionable!"

"I—I can't believe that," her mother said, her hand covering her mouth. "Are you absolutely sure?"

The vet removed the surgical hair covering he was wearing and scratched the top of his shaved head. "Unfortunately, yes. It's a real good thing you brought her in right away, because if you'd waited, she'd be dead. No question."

Aiden took a small notepad and pen out of his back pocket. He flipped through until he arrived at a clean page. "This is now an investigation. Talk to us, Doc. What do you know so far?"

Dr. Cryan sighed, hands on his hips. "RBG presented with an elevated heartbeat, dehydration due to vomiting, fever, diarrhea, and stiffness in the neck and face. By the time you brought her in, her arms and legs were in spasm. If you had waited—I'm talking a couple of hours, not days—she would have died from asphyxiation or sheer exhaustion from the convulsions."

Quinn's throat went dry and tight. "And you're sure it was poison?"

She knew she'd asked the same thing just seconds before, but it wasn't sinking in.

Aiden rubbed his hand over his face. "Sounds like strychnine, Dr. Cryan."

The vet nodded. "Yep, spot on. You know your poisons, Detective."

"Occupational hazard. Although it's been a long time since I've seen someone intentionally poisoning someone else's dog."

For Quinn, the facts weren't adding up. Everyone loved her dog. "Is it possible RBG could've gotten into some rat poison placed around someone else's house? I mean, I don't let her wander off-leash, but there's a doggie door in my farmhouse. The yard is fenced, but maybe there was an opening and she got out when I wasn't home and—"

Dr. Cryan shook his head, gently interrupting. "Quinn, we found enough strychnine in those dog biscuits to kill five grown adults."

And that's when the ground beneath her feet crumbled into a million little pieces. She was still standing. She was taking in what the good doctor told her, but gravity had lost its pull. She was weightless, with lead feet. Blood surged through her ears, deafening her to everything except her own heartbeat.

Aiden was holding her up.

The vet continued explaining. "Treatment for strychnine poisoning consists of removing the drug from the body. We ended up having to go in so we could perform a surgical wash of her colon and digestive tract. And now we are giving her round-the-clock intravenous fluids as well as medications for the convulsions and spasms, as well as administering cooling measures for her high temperature. If all goes well, she'll be back home by the end of the week."

Finn Caine shook his hand. "Thank you, Dr. Cryan, for everything you and your staff have done. We are eternally grateful."

Quinn could barely hear over the whoosh in her ears. "Can I see her?"

Dr. Cryan shook his head. "Come back tomorrow. She's heavily sedated from surgery. The next twenty-four hours are critical." He gave her a once-over. "Did you, by chance, touch those biscuits with your bare hands? Did they get on your clothes?"

Her mind was blank, but Adele Caine gasped. "You did. I saw you touch them. Do I remember right? Did you *lick* them too?"

The doctor's face grew more determined. "As a precaution, I'd highly recommend you take a thorough Silkwood shower, wash your clothes, maybe go over to either urgent care or the hospital for a round or two of IV fluids.

"A Silkwood shower?" She had never heard of such a thing.

Aunt Johanna cleared her throat. "It's from the movie *Silkwood* about a whistle-blowing nuclear power plant worker. When she was exposed to radiation, they had to strip her down and scrub her skin raw. That's what the doc is talking about—it was God-awful."

"*Sounds* awful," Daria mumbled.

"Again, probably more than you need to do, but you're a young woman, and I'd rather you be safe than sorry." The vet took a pad and pen out of his coat. "Unfortunately, I can't write you a prescription, but I can write you a note, explaining the situation. That should be enough. They can give me a call on my direct line if they have any questions." He scribbled his directives, then peeled the paper off the pad, handing it to her.

"Okay, I'll drive over right away."

Aiden let out a low grunt. "Oh no. I'm going to drive you. After I get you home to shower, I'll take you over to urgent care myself."

Daria cleared her throat. "That's sweet, Aiden, but you've got a potential dog assassin to find, along with Tricia's killer. We'll take her."

Aiden didn't even blink. "Oh, I'll catch them—and I'm going to apprehend Tricia's killer too. I won't rest until I do. But first, I'm taking Quinn to urgent care. You're her family, so I'm sure she'll want you there. Right?"

Quinn was struck dumb and nodded.

"Good, then it's settled."

Daria started saying something, but Aiden interrupted.

"I know I'm being pushy, but I'd be lying if I said I cared. Because you need to know there's nothing you're going to be able to say to change my mind. I'm not letting Quinn out of my sight until I know she's safe. Nothing hurts her. Not on my watch. Until then, Caine crew, get used to having me around."

Chapter Twenty-One

"Most everything you think you know about me is nothing
more than memories."
—Haruki Murakami, *A Wild Sheep Chase*

Daria fanned herself with a thousand-year-old *People* magazine from the urgent care waiting room. "I'm sorry, but I
can't help it. It has to be said."

Quinn opened her eyes. She was in a faux-leather chair with
a needle in her left arm, an IV bag hanging from a pole next to
her. "What needs to be said?"

Daria looked around before saying, "Awful strychnine poisoning aside, that whole speech Aiden gave back at the vet clinic
was *hawt*." She deepened her voice to sound like him, "'I'm not
letting Quinn out of my sight until I know she's safe. Nothing
hurts her. Not on my watch. Until then, Caine crew, get used to
having me around.' He's not even my type, and I was almost
ready to throw my wimple in the recycling bin after that speech."

"Cute."

Daria smacked Quinn's needle-free arm with the back of her hand. "Don't you get it? He *likes* you. And before you say, 'Oh sure, like a little sister' or 'No, Daria, just as a friend,' trust me when I say that man *likes* you likes you."

"See? This is the problem when your best friend joins a convent. Your finely honed man mind-reading skills have gone soft. Way soft. I'm almost embarrassed for you. If wanting to make sure I'm okay after potentially being *poisoned* is your notion of someone being into me, well then, you must think the guy who helps carry my groceries to my truck is gearing up for a proposal any day."

She rolled her eyes. "Fine, Quinn. Don't listen to me. Maybe I should ask Aunt Adele what she thinks of my little theory."

Quinn coughed into her free hand. "You are evil, you know that? You'd think you'd be nicer to me after I was accidentally *poisoned*."

"You can play that card for the next forty-eight hours. After that, time's up."

Even though they were separated from the others in the urgent care bay by a curtain, they heard someone say, "Knock-knock."

"Come in."

The curtain pulled back. It was Bash, still in his firefighter gear, soot smeared across his face.

"Well, no need to ask where you've been."

Right behind him was one of the male nurses. "If he's here with you, that means your friend needs to wait with the others in the lobby. Only one person back here at a time."

Daria's back straightened, chin up. "I'm here providing spiritual counseling after a trying ordeal. I'm with Guinefort House. Surely both myself and one of Fairfax County Fire's finest can stay with her."

The nurse grimaced before glancing over his shoulder. "All right, *fine*, but keep the curtain drawn and the talking on the quiet setting. Otherwise, I'm going to get chewed up and spit out by the doctor on call."

Bash patted him on the back. "We've got you covered. Thanks, man."

"No problem, but FYI," he said, looking sternly at Daria, "the giggling from all your 'spiritual counseling' got loud." And with that, the nurse pulled the curtain for privacy as Bash grabbed a chair, positioning himself next to Daria.

Bash's expression was contrite. "Sorry I couldn't get here until now."

"Well, you were busy saving lives. That's a very good excuse." Quinn took in her brother's gear. "Are you okay?"

"Please, for me it's just a regular Tuesday. I'm actually off-duty now, but I wanted to see you before going back and getting into my civilian clothes." He peeked on the other side of the curtain before pulling it back in place. "You and RBG are the ones everyone is freaking out about. I've never seen Aiden so worked up."

Daria's eyes blazed with mischief. "Oh *really*?"

Quinn glared at her cousin.

If Bash noticed, he didn't let on. "Yeah, Aiden's been on the phone, barking orders, having half the squad interview everyone on Church Street to see if anyone got eyes on who planted those dog biscuits. The urgent care staff made him go outside, he was so riled up."

The curtain drew back. It was one of the doctors.

"Let's see how our patient is doing." She checked Quinn's chart, making a mental note of the almost-empty IV bag. "Hello, I'm Doctor Coffy. How are you feeling?"

"I'm good. Really. Ready to go home."

The doctor smiled. "Understood." Then she caught sight of Bash and did a double take. "Oh, um, I didn't know we'd have a visit from a bona fide firefighter."

He gave a polite nod. "Just here to make sure my sister's all right. She gave us a real scare today."

The doctor jotted down some notes. "Well, everything looks good. We'll get the results of your blood work in a few days. Until then, I'm going to need you to stay with a friend or family member. You need to be on the lookout for muscle spasms, especially in the neck and back, as well as seizures, abnormal pupil dilation, convulsions." She pointed to her clipboard. "Don't worry about remembering everything. I have all the instructions here for you."

Quinn swallowed. Hearing everything that could go wrong made the reality of what had happened hit home even more.

Dr. Coffey paused. "Do you have any questions?"

She shook her head.

The doctor handed her a small stack of papers. "These are for you. If you experience any of these symptoms, I want you to go straight to the hospital. I have my phone number on here as well," she said, sneaking a blushing glance over at Bash. "Feel free to call me if you think of something later."

Great, I might've been poisoned, and Doctor McFlirty Pants wants my brother to text her for a date.

Daria stood up. "Thanks, Doc, we'll take it from here."

Once they got to the waiting room, Quinn expected to find her family. What she didn't expect was to also find Sarah from the store, Amy Lyon from Maple Ave Restaurant nor Eun and Greg Hutton from Church Street Eats. Also there were the sisters from Guinefort House, the Clink-n-Drink ladies, along with Pastor Johnny. Maxie was there too, as well as Michael from Caffe Amour.

There were so many people, they were spilling out the doors and onto the sidewalk.

Quinn turned to her brother. "What's going on?"

He draped his arm around her shoulder. "Everyone heard what happened. They stopped by to see how you're doing."

"Really?"

"Heck yeah," Sister Daria said. "This town loves you."

Her parents walked up. "Yes, that's true, but we need to get you home."

As she walked out, Quinn hugged and thanked everyone for coming over to check on her. It took awhile because there were so many of them. Just as they got to the car, she heard her name.

"Quinn!"

She turned around. Rachel Slingbaum was running in their direction.

"Quinn! Quinn! Wait up!"

She turned to her family. "Hold up. Rach is coming."

Barely out of breath, she caught up. "I just got Bash's message and came right over. Oh my God, are you okay?" She didn't wait for a response, throwing her arms around her. Quinn smiled to herself because she had forgotten that about her: Rachel was a world-class Olympic hugger.

"I can't believe someone would want to hurt Ruff Barker G." She spoke into Quinn's hair, swaying back and forth. "If something had happened to you . . ."

"I'm okay. Promise," Quinn told her. "But I need to get home. It's been a day."

Rachel released her, still holding Quinn by her shoulders. "Of course. Sorry. Can I come by tomorrow, to check on you?"

Quinn smiled, placing one of her hands on top of one of Rachel's. "You never have to ask permission to spend time with family."

Rachel's eyes teared up. "I've missed you," she said to Quinn before locking eyes with Bash.

Please, please give him another chance. Open your heart just one more time.

"Yes, what Quinnie said. Come by anytime, Rachel." Her father opened the car door, but Quinn spun her head around. "Wait, where's Aiden?"

A shadow crossed Bash's face. "He got a call a little while ago. They found the 2013 Nissan Altima at the Hauser property. The tires are an exact match to the markings left on Nutley Street. And by the way, I don't know if you know him, but the car belongs to Lorenzo 'Ren' Diamond. They've brought him in for questioning."

Chapter
Twenty-Two

"Parents are like God because you wanna know they're out there, and you want them to think well of you, but you really only call when you need something."
—Chuck Palahniuk, *Invisible Monsters*

Aiden glanced down at her feet. "I heard Ruff Barker Ginsberg has been glued to your side since she was released from the vet. Now, I see the proof here for myself."

Quinn scratched her girl behind her left ear, her favorite spot. "Yeah, it's weird. She was the one in danger, but she insists on protecting me. The last couple of times I tried to leave the house, she had the equivalent of a doggie meltdown."

Quinn could tell Aiden was trying to keep a straight face.

"And how does a 'doggie meltdown' present itself?"

Quinn's eye narrowed. "It's not funny, Aiden. She whines and barks. She tore into one of my couches. I even caught her chewing on the corner of a wall—saw it on the house cam. She's never done that before."

He frowned. "I didn't know it was that bad. But at least the security cameras help you see what's going on. Besides keeping you safe, that is."

After she had been released from urgent care, Quinn had stayed with her parents for a few days. At first, her time at home felt like nostalgic decadence, staying in her old room—kept exactly as she had left it—with her mom and dad fussing over her. Surrounded by her pale sage walls, white Formica furniture, and shelves teeming with her old school art projects, she slept late, binge-watched Netflix series, and received visitors checking on her.

But savoring special treatment had turned into being suffocated. Seemingly overnight, Finn and Adele Caine had become helicopter parents, making sure one of them was in the same room with her at all times. Even taking her vitals every few hours. They took turns waking her up from a dead sleep, just to check for symptoms. Once she received the "all clear" from the doctors and RBG was released, Quinn couldn't get back to her own bed fast enough.

Little did she know that privacy, as she had once experienced it, was gone forever. Aiden and Bash took it upon themselves to install high-tech security cameras all over her property. They even convinced her auntie and uncle to alarm their house and get a monitoring system for their fencing.

It was total overkill. Quinn thought everyone sweet, but illogical. And for the Caine family to lose its reasoning, one of their most precious assets, worried her.

"The thing is, Aid, I always felt secure in my home. Someone tried to kill my dog at the bookstore, not here. It doesn't make any sense to have all this"—she waved her arms around—"this *stuff* around. What if some creeper hacks into the spy cam feed thingy and tries to watch me taking a shower? I'm telling you right here, right now, Detective Harrington, I will be none too pleased if I end up naked on the internet." She shuddered. "Trust me, I am not the kind of girl who could shake that off."

Aiden's brows shot up before he barked out a laugh. "Okay, first of all, there are no cameras in your bathroom. There aren't any in your bedroom either. So, you can let that go." The humor melted away. "And second, did you even consider the fact that if someone's bold enough to come after your dog in a public place, then it's not much of a stretch to target you at home?"

Quinn looked aghast because she hadn't even considered the idea that what had happened with the poisoned dog treats would be anything more than a one-time incident.

It was early morning, and Aiden was keeping Quinn company while she walked RBG—something that was becoming a regular occurrence for them. So were Quinn-and-Aiden evening walks. Truth was, he was in her atmosphere any spare moment he had. Not that she was complaining. The first morning had been a surprise. He hadn't informed her he was stopping by, and once he realized Quinn wasn't a morning person, he'd brought her a medium, iced, white chocolate mocha latte to quell her "mood beast"—his term, not Quinn's—when he showed up the following morning. As she had enjoyed her chilled latte, she'd snuck peeks of Aiden as he drank his hot, black coffee, marveling how he didn't break a sweat, even with it being over eighty degrees outside.

As much as her schoolgirl heart wanted to believe his attention was their beginning as "Q & A," her grown-up-woman brain understood that his frequent check-ins were more about being vigilant for a family friend's safety than about him developing any romantic notions. But as one day turned into two, and two turned into four, and then a week, a tiny flicker of hope returned. Only the size of a grain of sand, her wish was surprisingly tenacious and strong. She hammered reason and logic at it: *Don't forget our failed history,* she reminded herself; add on his limiting

259

perception of her as the extra cherry on top. Nevertheless, the dream of Quinn and Aiden didn't have the good manners to die a quick and painless death.

There was only one way to kill a stubborn wish on life support—she'd have to pull the plug. She hated to do it because her current drug of choice was his company, but Quinn had enough self-respect not to allow herself to be led on, even if he didn't have a clue that was exactly what he was doing.

"You don't have to keep coming around, Aid. I know you've got your own life."

He eyed her for a second, taking another sip of his coffee, but not responding.

Okay, that's annoying. "Aren't you going to say anything? I'm letting you off the hook here. Acknowledgment would be appreciated."

He chuckled. "Well, it's either I keep my mouth shut and we continue to have a good morning, or I answer that nonsense with what I'm thinking, and we have a fight."

"It's *not* nonsense. In case you've forgotten, I've traveled all over the world by myself. I don't need a knight in shining armor for protection."

His eyes sparkled with amusement. "Are you saying I *am* your knight in shining armor?"

Wait a sec. Is he flirting with me?

"You know what I mean, Aiden."

"I do." He smiled, warm and gentle, only adding to those hopeful grains of sand. "But humor me and let me look after you."

They were halfway down Church Street when Quinn spotted Purple Maxie coming out of a consignment shop with 'Ren' Diamond. They were laughing, with him sneaking a kiss on her cheek before they clasped hands and headed toward the coffeehouse.

Quinn stopped walking. "Well, *that's* new."

Aiden nodded. "Yep, I noticed that too. She's the one who picked him up after questioning."

"I thought they were just friends."

He shrugged. "One of the many things I've learned being a cop: Nothing's better than a crisis to help people figure out how they feel about each other."

Hold the phone, is he talking about Ren and Max—or us?

Well, there was no way she'd ever have enough courage to ask, so she went for the redirect.

"Wait a second. I thought his car tires were a match with the ones left at the scene."

"Oh, they're a perfect match. Your field trip to Lucas's garage aside—"

She interrupted. "Wait—how do you know about that?"

He gave her his "you must be joking" face.

Bash. Traitor.

It was as if Aiden could read her mind. "And before you get tied up in knots, no, your brother did not betray your trust. He mentioned it in passing because he assumed I already knew. Because, of course, you'd go to the cops with any information— right, Quinn?"

She stopped in her tracks. "Excuse me, but I *did* reach out. And you never called me back!"

"I was tied up on another case, and, by the way, I did text you back."

Quinn started walking again, picking up the pace, which was ridiculous because his legs were a block long. There was no way she was going to outwalk him.

"Oh right, I got a whole four words," she huffed. "If you had bothered to respond in any real way, you would have heard my plan to talk to Lucas."

"Well, if you'd texted *that* to me, I would have gotten in contact with you sooner, to let you know it was a waste of your time. We were handling it."

She was already over this conversation. "Whatever, Aid."

He grabbed her elbow and stopped walking again. "Quinn, you need to get something straight: I don't work a typical nine-to-five. My hours are all over the place, and when a case heats up, I sometimes go off the grid. Not for long and not often, but it happens—something I was planning on discussing with you, by the way, but didn't get a chance to before you decided to be a human guinea pig and sniff out RBG's strychnine snacks for yourself."

She met his gaze but didn't know what to say.

After waiting a beat or two, he added, "I thought we had a deal, Quinn. And I have to admit, I'm disappointed you didn't at least give me the benefit of the doubt."

Ah craptastic. He has a point. They may not have made a pinkie promise or sworn with one hand on the Bible, but she had agreed. Something her dad said a long while ago echoed back: *"Everything can be taken away from you except two things: your knowledge and your integrity. The rest turns to dust sooner or later."*

Both Adele and Finn had also taught her that if she made a mistake, she should own it. Take your medicine. Because trying to squirm out of responsibility was a worse violation than the original offense. She only hoped Aiden felt the same way.

"You know what? You're absolutely right, and I'm sorry. I promise, from now on I will assume the best—not the worst."

"I need you safe, Quinn." He threaded his hand through his dark, thick hair. "Is there anything else I need to know?"

"Nothing I can think of."

That was the truth, at least.

He studied her expression, his eyes scouring hers, and must have decided he believed her, which was good because she'd meant what she said.

"All right, let's move on." He started walking and so did she. "As a gesture of good faith, I'll give you the following nugget of information. It won't be released to the public until later today: Ren Diamond has a rock-solid alibi, so while his car may have been at the scene—he sure wasn't."

"Wow, so someone else used his car?"

"That's what we're thinking. Whoever stole it made sure to bring it back to the exact spot where the car had been left. They were also careful not to leave any of their DNA or fingerprints inside the vehicle. And before you go off on your Scott Hauser theory—who, by the way, is a person of interest, but not, I repeat, *not* a suspect—it could've been anyone because Ren's a popular guy who had a lot of visitors. He also had a habit of leaving his car unlocked with the keys tucked under the visor."

She sighed. "He's not the only one. Half my family does the same thing. Vienna's safe, but it's not like people have to go through a magical wardrobe or something in order to get in." Dread washed over her. "That must mean the murder was planned?"

He hedged. "Maybe, maybe not. It's possible Tricia's death was accidental, but the assailant took his or her time figuring out how they were going to dump the body without leaving any evidence. They certainly didn't bother to give her any medical care. What we do know so far is that Tricia Pemberley did not die at that park. The autopsy report indicated that organ failure occurred over an eight- to twelve-hour period."

Quinn bit the inside of her cheek. "What exactly does that mean?"

"It means she had a long and painful death, the kind you wouldn't wish on your worst enemy, even Tricia Pemberley."

Chapter
Twenty-Three

"There are crimes of passion and crimes of logic. The
boundary between them is not clearly defined."
—Albert Camus, French philosopher and author

So much of what Aiden had said was on a repetitive loop:
Quinn kept mulling over and over again what she knew so
far. She was grateful for the slow day at the store. It gave her
time to think while working on Rachel's family journal.

She popped in one of her older mixtapes, one she had made
back in college that had withstood the test of time and personal
taste. Anyone could throw together a collection of songs and
call it a mix, but they would be wrong. That was amateur hour.
Going to college at a Catholic-affiliated university wasn't easy
for a left-leaning, Anglican-raised feminist. But then again, she
hadn't fit in at her Young Life group during high school either.
It's not that she hadn't had friends there. And Quinn appreciated both institutions' call to serving a higher purpose. She
respected the earnestness of her peers. But none of them wanted

to discuss the themes of intersectional inclusivity in works by Audre Lorde and Kimberlé Crenshaw or analyze history through a Foucault-inspired, postmodernist lens of history.

But there was one thing they all had in common: music. Every Thursday, from seven to ten at night, Quinn would DJ at her college's radio station and spin vinyl of songs that spoke to her. And that's how she had found her people. Music, like love, was transcendent and universal.

Each playlist she curated had to have a theme and a purpose. For example, the mixtape she had on now, *The Revolution Will Be Memorized*, was one she had made to help her concentrate while studying, by female artists who kicked butt in a male-dominated industry. It was pure old school, with artists such as Joni Mitchell, Stevie Nicks, PJ Harvey, and Kate Bush, to name a handful. They serenaded her as they always did, mournful and strong, hopeful and true.

It was years later, and she still loved that mixtape, listening while she worked. She kept trying to sort through the pieces of the investigation in her mind, to reveal what she couldn't yet see. By the time Daria came by, suggesting they grab lunch, she was beyond frustrated and ready to admit: she was stuck.

Tiny little bells greeted them as they walked into Church Street Eats. Like her store, the eatery was surprisingly quiet for midday. Greg gave a chin lift from the grill while Ms. Eun pointed to two seats at the counter. "Be right with you!"

They settled onto their stools, not even bothering to glance at the menus.

"Here's your usual," Ms. Eun said as she plopped down one glass of seltzer and another glass of ginger ale. "Should I even bother to ask what you two want?"

Quinn spoke up. "I'll have Bash's burger."

"I'll have my usual," Daria said.

Ms. Eun smirked. "Good choices. Be right up."

Quinn glanced over. "Are you going to get in trouble with the Reverend Mother, being over here with me?"

"No, she's encouraging me to take some time with you and the family while she works through a reassignment for me."

Quinn's face paled. "Are you leaving Guinefort House?"

"What? No. It's a reassignment in the house."

All right, glad that's not going to be an issue.

Daria stared. "Okay, I know that look on your face."

"What look?"

She chuckled. "The one you get when you're ready to pull your hair out."

Quinn sighed. "I don't know if I should find it a comfort or an annoyance, you knowing me so well."

"Chose the former because the latter will just tick you off more."

"Fair enough." Quinn did a quick glance around the place to make sure no one they knew was around to listen. Well, anyone besides Ms. Eun and Greg, but the lunch rush would start any minute, which she hoped would keep both of them into their customers and out of her business.

Daria smirked. "Coast clear, Madam Detective?"

"Ha-ha."

Daria wiped her mouth with a napkin. "All right, let's review: you've been talking with Aiden several times a day. That has to be helpful, right?"

Quinn took a long draw from her seltzer. "Yes and no." She wasn't in the mood to share the personal torture it was to spend so much time with someone she would never have for her own. "Let's go over what we know. Wyatt Reynolds, now off the force, remains a person of interest. He was on-duty the night someone dumped Tricia's body in the park, so that's a seemingly solid alibi, on the surface. But Aiden told me the autopsy report indicated she died beforehand, hours before, actually—at least eight to twelve hours. So maybe Wyatt slipped her a little something-something not detected in an autopsy. Although anyone could've done that."

Two sandwiches with fries and pickles slid in front of them. "Chow's ready."

"Thanks, Ms. Eun." Quinn grabbed the ketchup, unscrewing the top. She was about to pour, until she noticed Ms. Eun wasn't walking away.

She had her hand on her hip, an impish smile on her face. "Can I help you?"

Ms. Eun tilted her head. "What are you two talking about?"

Quinn glanced over at her cousin. "What *were* we talking about? It flew right out of my head."

Daria took a bite, pointed to her sandwich. "Can't talk wif mouf full."

Ms. Eun's eyes darted back and forth. "Uh-huh."

Greg hit a bell with the end of his spatula. "Hey, orders backing up!"

She twisted in his direction. "Imaginary friends don't count, Greg. There's only one other customer in here."

"Well, then, his order is up, bride of mine!"

As soon as she was out of range, Quinn leaned close to Daria's ear. "We may need to find a new lunch spot."

She swallowed, wiping her mouth. "You think?"

Quinn scanned over her shoulder, noting Ms. Eun was on the other side of the eatery, serving the only other customer. "Okay, so Wyatt is still, technically, a suspect. What else do we know?"

Her cousin popped a pickle slice in her mouth. "You tell me. You've been on the case much more than me these days."

Quinn pounded the back of the ketchup bottle, releasing the sweet tomato spread onto her plate. "All right, well, I also found out Ren's vehicle is a match for the car that left the scene."

Daria's eyes widened. "Wow, okay. Is he a suspect?"

Quinn shook her head. "Not anymore. He was taken in for questioning and had an alibi. He also said that while Scott's a person of interest, he is not a suspect. Aiden did tell me that the autopsy results not only proved Tricia died hours before I found her, but she died in another location. Also, the degree and depth of damage to her internal organs showed it took a long time for her to die."

"Ugh, that's awful."

Quinn glanced down at her plate of food. She suddenly wasn't that hungry anymore.

Daria was almost finished with her lunch, and Quinn shook her head to herself: *Well, at least some things stay the same. Nothing ever killed her appetite.*

"So, we need to find out how—and with whom—Tricia spent her last day on Earth," her cousin said, pushing her plate away. "Agreed?" Daria held out her fist.

Quinn reciprocated the gesture, giving her cousin a bump before making exploding sounds and jazz hands.

Ms. Eun refilled their drinks. "Every time I see you two do that fist thingy, I'm just waiting for the sound of sirens to follow."

"Now that's not fair. We were only picked up twice. And that was years ago."

Daria cackled. "Speak for yourself. The siren call came for me many times."

She's regained her sense of humor about her prodigal past. That's a good sign.

"Yeah, you were more interesting back then," Greg said. "I miss hell-raising Daria. No offense."

"Ignore him." Ms. Eun rested one palm on the counter; the other held her pencil and pad hoisted on her hip, elbow out. Her head twisted toward her husband. "You are not as charming as you think you are, my 'king.'"

He returned a wolfish grin. "Well, *I* know that Eun, but I can't help it if *you* don't." He glanced at Daria and Quinn, giving them a friendly wink. "The woman can't get enough of me. What can I do?"

Daria snorted. "Yeah, yeah, it's the curse you live with. Such a trooper."

Quinn wasn't getting involved. She had too much on her mind with the investigation. As soon as Ms. Eun walked away, Daria continued where they left off.

"Okay, so someone 'borrowed' Ren's car to move the body. What else do we know?" she asked.

Quinn folded the paper from her straw into sections, keeping her hands busy, unable to eat just yet. "Well, the problem is, Ren made a habit of leaving his car unlocked with the keys inside."

"Wow, are there people really that trusting out there?"

Quinn shrugged, taking a small bite. "Apparently so, which means anyone could've taken it. But I don't think just 'anyone' did. He rents the Hausers' cottage on the back of their property. I've never been there, but I hear it's a massive house on several acres of land. It's also kind of in the middle of nowhere, for Vienna that is, so I don't think some random person took that car."

Daria finished her sandwich. "Well, it couldn't have been the Hausers. My parents said Milly was genuinely devastated over losing Tricia."

Quinn made a "so-so" motion with her hand. "I don't know about that. Scott told me at the funeral that his mother seems to like Tricia a lot better in death than she ever did when she was alive."

"Yeah, but it's a big jump from typical mother–daughter-in-law rivalry to having the girl murdered and dumping her body."

Quinn considered her cousin's point. "That's fair. But truth is, we can't rule anyone out unless the police have already. We need to learn everything that Tricia did the last two days and who she was with."

Daria rolled her eyes. "Well, Trina said she hadn't seen her sister in days."

"We need to find out if she's telling the truth. We should also talk to her parents, then Scott and his parents. And any friends she had."

Daria gave some side-eye. "Okay, you take on Scott and Trina, and I'll handle the rest."

"This isn't like calling shotgun so you can sit in the front seat. Let's talk to whoever will talk to us. Together." Having a plan of action made her feel better. Quinn attacked her sandwich.

Ms. Eun came over and placed the check on the counter. "Trina didn't have friends. She had colleagues. So you can take that off your list."

The cousins shared a glance.

Ms. Eun had more to share. "But I'm telling you—and I don't wish to speak ill of anyone—but Trina was only happy if she was leading someone by the nose. My theory? Tricia marrying Scott, wanting out of their real estate business, was something her twin wasn't going to tolerate. Everyone knows what a scene Trina made over at Caffe Amour. I'm not saying she killed her sister, but it wouldn't surprise me either."

Quinn's phone rang: the caller ID said "Vienna PD." "I need to take this."

Ms. Eun nodded. "There's only one other customer in here right now, honey. You don't need to go outside."

"Thanks." She slid the bar on her phone. "Hello?"

"Hey, it's Aiden. Are you busy right now?"

It turned out, Detective Harrington didn't just have cop eyes, he had a cop voice too, one that went an octave deeper when he was at work.

"We're just finishing lunch. What's up?"

"I need you to come down to the station and take a look at something."

He did not sound pleased.

"Sure, but can you give me a heads-up what it is I'm going to see?"

He paused. She could almost hear the wheels turning in his head.

"Security camera footage."

She drew a blank. "I don't understand."

"We finally got hold of something useful. It's video footage of the person who tried to poison RBG."

Chapter Twenty-Four

"It is a capital mistake to theorise before one has data."
—Sir Arthur Conan Doyle, *The Adventures of Sherlock Holmes*

Aiden was waiting for them at the lobby of the police station.

"Thanks for coming right away." He didn't seem surprised that Daria was with her. He gave her a chin lift as a greeting. "How are you holding up?"

Daria shrugged. "I'm all good. What about you?"

He stopped cold. "Really? You're good? Even after being held against your will with a gun to your head?"

Daria sucked in air.

His reaction knocked the sass right out of her.

He went on. "You find you're not 'all good,'" he said, using his fingers as air quotes, "you let me know, right away. I'll connect you to Victim's Services, make sure you see a counselor who knows what they're doing. In fact, consider it done. I'll call the Reverend Mother and let her know."

Quinn noticed the veins in Daria's neck thrumming hard. Aiden was right to call her out on her frivolous attitude. That's something *she* should have done. Had Daria been covering this whole time, acting as if she were right as rain while personally struggling with what had happened to her at Guinefort House?

"Thanks, Aiden, but I swear I'm okay."

"Then seeing a trauma-informed social worker will be a quick visit for you."

Quinn watched them both, wondering what would happen next.

Daria's face muscles tightened, and her cousin couldn't tell if her reaction was due to being annoyed or actually afraid. "Fine," she said. "I'll go. Satisfied?"

Those gray cop eyes of his assessed her cousin. Quinn guessed he was mollified with what he saw because the hardness melted away as he nodded. "All right, follow me. You can come in together."

They walked through the station, just like she had weeks before. Quinn was glad to see Officers Carter and Johnson laughing over something. They stopped when they saw her walk by, and each gave her a nod.

Aiden led them to a part of the building she'd never been in. Judging from the slew of computers and tech equipment, she assumed they were in Vienna PD's IT division. He opened a door at the end of the hall. There was already someone sitting inside, facing a huge screen, his fingers moving at lightning speed across the keyboard.

"Quinn, Daria, this is Gavin. He's going to run through the footage we found. Have a seat."

There were two chairs, one on either side of Gavin, who offered a perfunctory head nod while his eyes remained glued to the screen.

Positioning himself by the large screen, Aiden got started. "As you may or may not be aware, we have police cameras positioned on Maple Avenue and Lawyer's Road, since those are the main arteries running through town. We have only one on Church Street, and that's on the Glyndon cross street, which, as you know, is too far down to have captured anything. But we still caught a break. Okay, go ahead and roll the footage, Gav."

He hit "Play." Aiden turned off the lights in the room before returning to the screen. "This camera belongs to that new restaurant across the street from Prose & Scones. It took us longer than we'd like to get hold of the footage, and unfortunately it's not great quality, but something is better than nothing.

"Their camera doesn't run twenty-four hours, but they do have it recording from dusk until dawn, give or take an hour or so on either end. The time stamp here"—he pointed to the screen—"indicates it was 5:38 AM. The suspect must have parked out of frame from this camera, but, okay, here you see them walking toward the store."

Quinn watched the assailant move at a fast clip, but then the feed popped and zapped, distorting the image. The picture zapped back, and the suspect entered the patio. The person's back was to the camera, wearing a hoodie about three sizes too big. Just as the person took something out of his or her pocket, the feed cut out again for several seconds.

Aiden let out a frustrated breath. "Yeah, as you can see, the quality stinks, but based on what we have ascertained, the suspect is about five eight, with a slender build in spite of the baggy clothes."

Daria leaned back in her chair. "No offense, Aiden, but that describes most of Vienna already."

"No offense taken. You're right. But keep watching. See if there's anything about them you recognize."

They kept watching the video feed as it cut back in. Quinn's heart was beating fast. Just watching someone planning to hurt her dog made her want to jump out of her skin. If there was a way to run away and clobber someone at the same time, she would have done it.

"Unfortunately, once they enter the courtyard, it's too dark for us to see them laying down the tainted biscuits. Whoever it was, they were in there for no more than ten seconds."

Quinn watched the jerk face walking away from the patio. Aiden asked Gavin to zoom in some. "Of course, we can't be a hundred percent sure, but from their gait, we're thinking the suspect's male. Quinn, I want you to watch him move. Is this person familiar in any way?"

Quinn watched. "Can you replay that part again?"

Gavin nodded. "Sure thing."

She wanted to be sure. The tape played, and Quinn studied it as if everything depended on it. Because it did.

Quinn peered at the screen. "I just wish I could see his face."

Aiden glanced over at her, wearing a pained expression. "Yeah, whoever this is, he wasn't taking any chances." He motioned to his colleague. "Gavin, pause the video for a sec. Thanks. As you can see, he pulled the strings of the hood tight. I don't even know how he was able to see where he was going."

Daria peered closer. "All I can see is a nose sticking out."

Gavin tsked. "Due to the low resolution of the footage, we can't get a real description. We can't even be sure if it's a male or female."

Daria piped in. "Could be someone non-binary, you know."

"True," Aiden said. "We have just enough here to make assumptions, which is a dangerous thing."

Quinn let out a sardonic laugh, which was something, considering none of this was funny.

Gavin went on. "We were able to determine one small identifying marker—the crisscrossed fish logo from the hoodie brand he was wearing. It's one I've never heard of, but maybe you two have. It's called Hering."

Quinn drew a blank. Daria seemed just as clueless.

Aiden leaned against Gavin's desk. "I did a little research. They're a huge Latin American textile and retail company, with clothing stores in Brazil, Chile, Paraguay, Uruguay, Bolivia, and Venezuela. It's an unusual brand for someone to wear in the States. Maybe this guy does business down there. We're checking it out. You can stop the feed. Thanks, Gav."

"No problem, boss."

Aiden kept his eye on the screen. "Do you know someone who wears that clothing line?"

She hunched her shoulders up. "A Latin American brand? I don't think so."

"So, when you and Scott were, um . . . dating, he didn't wear anything like that?"

"No, he only wears either Vineyard Vines or Ralph Lauren. It's his thing—something about him wanting to buy American or something like that."

Aiden pushed himself off the desk and turned on the lights. "I figured as much, but we had to try." He gestured out of the room. "C'mon—I'll walk you two out."

They followed, neither cousin feeling much like chitchatting. Once they returned to the lobby, Aiden placed a gentle hand on Quinn's shoulder. "Can I talk to you for a second?" He glanced over at Daria. "She won't be long."

Awareness colored her gaze. "Take all the time you want. I'll wait outside."

He must have given some sort of unspoken signal to the other staff working the front desk, because they took off too. Once they were alone, he dropped his hand.

"We're going to catch the guy, Quinn. I won't rest until I do."

She realized he thought she was disappointed in him. "Aiden, I have faith in you. That's not why I'm feeling . . . actually I can't quite put into words what I'm feeling. I'm all over the place."

"That's to be expected."

"I just don't get it. Why would someone want to hurt my dog?"

Those cop eyes steeled. "It was a message to stop doing your own investigation. You must have someone tweaked."

She stared off, remembering the other day. "Did Bash tell you how we bumped into Mrs. Hauser at Lucas's place? She overheard a bit of what we were talking about, about the tire treads left at the scene. Then Lucas pulled a bunch of pine tree twigs out of her wheel well, ones that looked identical to the stuff stuck in the treads of the getaway car. Obviously, her car wasn't the getaway car, but it was the lead that got me thinking—"

"And onto someone's radar," he interrupted. "Yeah, Quinn, I know all about it."

She could tell he was annoyed. "Aiden, that wasn't Mrs. Hauser in that video footage. It wasn't any Hauser, including Scott."

"No, but it could've been someone she hired. It could be someone else not even on our radar yet. Everything is still speculative, but we *will* figure it out. And the next time, *you* could be the target—or someone else you love."

She hadn't thought of that. The idea of someone in her family being hurt. Poisoned. Run over by a car. Strangled. The rabbit hole, endless. She shuddered.

"Maybe you're right. I wouldn't be able to live with myself if something happened."

He let out an audible sigh. "Good."

"You know, I have to admit . . . after living just a brief time in your shoes, I don't know how you do it."

He scratched the side of his face. "You've got to follow the evidence where it leads. It's okay to have a working theory as long as you don't try to shape the facts to fit whatever theory you have. It's not easy, but it can be done. In time, and with practice, which you'll no longer be trying for, right?"

She crossed her arms in front of her chest. "Is there something you want to say?"

"I don't know, Quinn. Are you a woman who keeps her promises?"

Ouch, that stung. But he was right. She had broken her word, and they both knew she was taught better than that.

"I will keep my promises to you, Aiden."

He grunted in response. She guessed that was a "yes" or an "all is forgiven" in hot-guy detective code.

There was still a problem: it had become too dangerous to go in search of answers. But there were too many questions left dangling, and it was going to drive her crazy.

"Do you think the person who poisoned RBG is the same one who killed Tricia?"

"I think someone wanted to send you one hell of a message, and they wouldn't do that unless they're either the culprit or trying to protect someone else who is." He took a step closer, taking a deep breath. "In the meantime, I hope you know I've got your back. Can you let that be enough for a while?"

She thought she'd never deny Aiden Harrington anything. She sure didn't want anyone she loved getting hurt, especially because of her actions. But there was a killer still out there. How could she sleep at night, knowing she or he was free to hurt more people?

By the time she rejoined Daria outside, Quinn didn't know what she was going to do or where she was headed. She was lost, right in the heart of her hometown.

Chapter Twenty-Five

"Now I know what a ghost is. Unfinished business,
that's what."
—Salman Rushdie, *The Satanic Verses*

M ay mornings in Vienna, Virginia, usually dropped hints of
the insufferable summer to come. Swells of spindly, black
mosquitoes hanging low and heavy in the swamp air, just waiting
to latch onto oncoming ankles. People moved slowly, dragging
themselves down the street as if sloshing through viscous mud.
Since it was the first Friday of the month, Quinn was driving
down Church Street, as per her usual. In front of the storefronts,
on the corners of childhood haunts, bulky bags of dog food
waited for her, slumped forward and misshapen, like tired old
men on porches with nothing better to do than sit and watch
other people living life.

Even with the windows down and RBG sticking her head
out, her long tongue dangling out the side of her mouth like a
scarf in the wind, Quinn didn't have her heart in it. She wasn't

able to soak in her town's usually delightful mix of Southern charm and Northern cleverness.

On the surface, nothing had changed. People still waved. She got her fill of "Good morning" and "Say hi to your mama." None of it touched her. And being from there, Quinn knew, down to the marrow of her bones, that her neighbors weren't feeling it either. They were all going through the motions, every one of them holding their breath without even realizing they were doing it.

Tricia may have been in the ground, but her soul wasn't at peace. And Quinn knew that because she was everywhere. She smelled her perfume while getting coffee. Out of the corner of her eye, Quinn could've sworn she saw her as she was leaving the abbey after the donation drop-off. She wanted to ask Daria if she was experiencing the same phenomenon, but her cousin was tied up with novitiate duties and couldn't meet her at the truck or come for brunch afterward. Quinn opted for takeout and headed to see another friendly face, turning right on Lawyers Road, then making a left on West Street.

"Sounds like she's haunting you."

Quinn gave her brother a pointed look. "Don't tell me you still believe in ghosts."

"Oh, they're real. Trust me on that one. I've been through enough abandoned buildings and old houses to know the dead walk among us."

She stopped what she was doing, staring at her brother. "Are you telling me, Sebastian Monroe Caine, that you've actually seen a ghost?"

He placed the journal down, his expression losing any trace of humor. "No, I haven't seen *a* ghost: I've seen two."

Quinn was visiting her brother at the carriage house, the one on the back of their parents' property. He had turned down the loft listing the Pemberley twins had shown him and was now debating whether to stay put or rent something for a little while.

They both knew, without verbalizing it, that he was waiting for Rachel. In that spirit, he had asked his sister to come over—and bring Granny Nora's journal.

It took Quinn staying up into the wee hours of the morning, but she had managed to finally finish repairing the diary. The results went beyond expectations, if she did say so herself, but in order to complete the project overnight, she'd had to forego reading the rest of Nora's story. Bash had asked her to bring it over so he could read it for himself.

"Let's see, the first ghost I ever witnessed—and met—was Merle. There was an uncontrolled blaze on twenty acres in the middle of the Adirondack Mountains. He must've lived out there for, I don't know, thirty years, in a cabin maybe ten people knew about. It was a freak accident—unbeknownst to him, one of his propane tanks had sprung a leak, and it exploded when he lit a fire for himself that night. Why he had the tanks anywhere near the vicinity of his firepit was beyond any of us, but anyway . . . by the time we put the fire out and secured the perimeter, the only light around was from the stars and our headlamps. Merle came walking up to me, looking almost as solid as you sitting there, and apologized for causing so much trouble."

"Tell me you're kidding. Because you know I'll believe you. I'm completely gullible."

Her brother cracked a sly grin. "Oh, don't I know it, but I swear to you, that's a true story."

She sat down, crisscross applesauce. "What did he say next?"

He shrugged. "Nothing. Just walked into the woods and disappeared, like Shoeless Joe did into the corn in *Field of Dreams*."

Quinn's eyes must have been as wide as saucers. "Whoa . . . freaky. Tell me more."

His brows went up as he leaned back in his chair. "Let's see . . . then I met another one while at a national FEMA conference held at the Houston Public Library. It was the end of the second day, and I went wandering off by myself. I could've sworn I heard someone playing violin, and sure enough, I happened upon Julius Frank Cramer. Now he had more of a ghostly appearance . . . you know, floating around, see-through body. He must've been able to read my thoughts because he said it's because he'd been dead since 1936."

"Why was he there?"

"He used to be the janitor," Bash answered, balancing on the back legs of his chair. "A janitor who enjoyed playing his violin after work hours. He said the acoustics were much better in that section than in his basement apartment. He played me a decent rendition of 'Aura Lee' and Mozart's Concerto Number Five in A Major."

"Well, at least they were friendly ghosts."

Bash agreed, but his mind was now clearly somewhere else, staring out the window.

Quinn waited before waving her hand in front of his face. "Hello? You in there?"

He did a quick headshake, like a wet dog. "Yeah. I was just thinking of a dream I had last night."

"You should tell it to Mom. She loves that stuff."

This was true. Ever since they were little, they'd come to their mother with their dreams, and she'd tell them what they meant—the advantages of having a mom who considered herself a "kitchen witch" of sorts.

"Well, this one was pretty straightforward. The ghost of Rachel's great-grandmother visited, telling me not to give up on her and that you were going to help me win her back."

Quinn's jaw dropped. Bash sat, straight-faced, staring at her.

"Oh my gosh, really? That's so cool! It's a sign!"

He gave her a look. "I was kidding, Quinnie."

She blinked. "What? So, wait—Granny Nora didn't visit you?"

The smart-ass started cackling.

She bolted out of her chair, grabbed a pillow off his bed, and proceeded to wallop him like a whack-a-mole. "You are really and truly evil and terrible! And awful. The family stories are true—you *were* dropped as a baby! No wonder you're not right in the head!"

He laughed, then grabbed the weaponized pillow with one hand, easily able to rip it away from her. "All right, all right—let's call a truce."

Red-faced, her auburn hair tussled, Quinn asked, "Were the other two ghost stories true?"

He crossed his heart with his finger while raising the other hand. "They were. I swear. True stories."

She grumbled "Fine" under her breath and plopped into the seat next to him, by his breakfast table. "If only Nora were to come back from the other side to give you a hint of what to do."

Last time they had spoken, Bash had informed her that Rachel had asked for some space. As much as he wanted to orchestrate a grand gesture, he wasn't going to cross her boundaries to execute it.

"I did hear some good news, though," he said. "Supposedly, she broke up with Lyle."

"Oh yeah? When?"

"Shortly after Tricia's funeral."

Quinn nodded, thinking. "Wait, if you're giving her space, how do you know this delicious piece of information?"

He answered with a wicked smile. "I have my ways."

She flicked the side of his ear.

He jerked his head back. "Ow! That hurt!"

"Good! Because that answer was more creepy than informative."

"Fine. Her brother Stuart told me. Satisfied?"

Rachel was the youngest of three, with two older brothers, Zach and Stuart, two years apart from each other, with Stuart being the middle child. According to Bash, both were certifiable man-babies, wanting—and expecting—everything to be done for them except going to work every day. But they were good guys who loved their sister and liked the idea of Bash and Rachel together—certainly more than the idea of her with Lyle.

"Stuart said he and Zach couldn't stand the guy. No sense of humor. He thinks Rachel only kept him around for as long as she did because Oliver and Sylvia were really pushing it."

Oliver and Sylvia were Rachel's parents.

"Why would they do that? They adore Rachel and want her to be happy."

Bash's mouth got tight. "The Slingbaums are good friends with Lyle's folks. They attend the same synagogue, and the dads shared a bunk or something at some Jewish sleep-away camp. In short, they go way back."

He opened the journal again and started reading. She reached across the table, placing her hand on his forearm. He glanced up.

"Listen, I don't want to sound like a Debbie Downer or something, but when I suggested you read Granny Nora's journal and make the big gesture, it was when you two were still talking to each other."

His eyes searched hers, confused. "Right. What's your point?"

How could she say what she needed to say?

"Do you really see the point in continuing reading if she won't even see you?"

He righted the chair legs, back on the floor. "I hear you, but I also heard you a few weeks ago. In fact, I haven't been able to think of anything else."

Her face went blank as she searched her memory.

He grimaced. "When you and Daria concurred that I've had it too easy when it comes to women?"

Oh . . . that.

"Rachel may or may not decide to have anything to do with me again. If I love her the way I say I do, that means doing whatever it takes to get to know her now and honor what makes her happy."

Quinn sat there, stunned.

He pointed his finger down. "This journal was important enough for her to want you to restore it. It means something to her, which means I want to read it. You were right, Quinn: every woman is a rare first edition, and it's my job to do my homework. So that's what I'm going to do."

Then he went back to reading as if he hadn't just blown his sister's mind with his maturity and insight.

"All right then, what happens next?"

He turned the page, reading a bit further. "Well, I was able to catch up to as far as you got and then some," he said with a wink, his not-so-subtle brag that he was a wicked-quick reader. "She's still fighting with her parents about David. Granny Nora was convinced that if she couldn't marry David, she didn't want to marry anyone."

Quinn balked. "What was she, nineteen, when she wrote that?"

"It was different back then."

Bash's cell phone rang.

"Don't answer it! I need to know what happens next."

He peeked at the screen. "It's Rachel's brother. I've got to take it."

She blew out a frustrated sigh. "Fine, go ahead."

"Hey, Stuart, how's it going?"

Quinn doesn't know what's worse—not knowing if Nora and David's story ended for good or wondering what Stuart wanted with her brother.

"Uh-huh . . . uh-huh . . . I don't know, man . . . Well, sure I want to go, but that's not the point . . . uh-huh . . . uh-huh . . . Oh, my parents are invited? They didn't say anything. All right . . . Yeah, let me think on this—I'll call you back."

He hung up.

"Talk to me."

Bash blew out a frustrated breath. "He invited me to his parents' anniversary party."

"That's perfect! Rachel will be there. I'll help you pick out a killer outfit for the party."

"Thanks, 'Mom', but I've been dressing myself since kindergarten." He shut the journal. "But it doesn't matter anyway because I'm not going."

"What do you mean you're not going? He just invited you!"

Bash got up from the table, nervous energy making him pace. "Rachel said she needed space, and I'm thinking me showing up at her parents' anniversary party violates the spirit of that request."

He had her there.

Quinn eyed Nora's diary. "Well, at least let's see what happened with her grandmother. You can't leave me hanging."

He scoffed, his hands fisting his hair. "We will. I can't right this minute." Bash grabbed his keys. "I need to get out of here, clear my head."

She got the hint. "I understand." He'd always been like this, not running away from his emotions, but needing to move, be physical, in order to sort through them. She lifted the strap of her messenger bag over her head. "I need to walk RBG anyway. Come by if you want company."

He nodded, but his eyes told her he was already somewhere else. As Quinn walked out of the carriage house with Bash, she glanced over her shoulder with the smallest smile.

And it was because Rachel's great-grandmother's journal was on his table, something he'd never have bothered to read through mere months ago. Whoever said people never changed never met a Caine.

Chapter
Twenty-Six

"Love meant jumping off a cliff and trusting that a certain person would be there to catch you at the bottom."
—Jodi Picoult, *Second Glance*

As always, her dog baby gave Quinn an ecstatic homecoming—a series of short "ruffs" at mid-range pitch. Her happy bark. The lower registers meant she was displeased at best, or at worst, ready to throw down if she sensed danger. Of course, danger to a dog from the suburbs usually meant a squirrel was getting too close to her dance space, but whatever. As soon as she got to the door, her girl had the odd habit of licking Quinn's calves and ankles—her toes too if she was wearing flip-flops. Since RBG was Quinn's first dog, she didn't know if that was typical canine behavior or a Ruff Barker Ginsburg eccentricity. Not that it mattered. They shared unconditional love.

Before hooking her to the leash, she stood outside, door opened, shuffling through her mail. Bills. Coupon pack. Advertisement for a new mattress store—the last thing the town needed.

There were already four of them. Quinn's theory was some foreign drug cartel used these inexpensive franchises to launder their dirty money, picking one of the most desirable places to live for their nefarious deeds. Hiding in plain sight. Years ago, she had shared her hypothesis with Aiden and Bash. Her longtime crush had barked out a laugh, and her brother had told her she'd been watching too many episodes of *Ozark* on Netflix.

Sandwiched in between all the junk were two hidden gems. The first was the invitation to Hammock's art show, benefitting The Women's Center, the Sunday of Memorial Day weekend. Ms. Withers had even written a little note in the corner:

I know I already gave you a flyer,

but I wanted to make sure you were on our list!

Great seeing you and Sister D—hope to see you on the 26th ☺

"Aw, that was sweet of her, wasn't it, RBG?"

The dog wagged her tail and "woofed." Quinn took that as a yes.

The next lovely piece of mail came in a thick, embossed envelope, a celadon-green melted wax seal on the back, with the initial "S" indented. Quinn opened the ivory flap, admiring the gold lining inside. Swirls of gold and silver skipped and danced around the calligraphed insert, and—surprise, surprise—it was an invitation to the Slingbaums' anniversary party. A handwritten note was attached with an adorable butterfly paperclip:

You have to come, Quinn!
It's all my parents' friends.
Promise it'll be fun.
Bring a date if you're seeing someone.
Miss you. ☺
Love, Rachel

The Slingbaum party was on the twenty-fifth, the day before The Women's Center fundraiser. "Looks like our Memorial Day's all booked up."

"Well, at least tell me we're doing something fun."

She didn't need to look up because she'd know that voice anywhere.

Aiden.

Quinn was surprised to see him. He had missed walking with her and RBG for several days, and she had assumed his vigilant watch had ended. No calls or texts letting them know he couldn't come. Just . . . nothing.

"*We* are not doing anything," she said, willing herself to keep her tone light and breezy. Why couldn't she be like the charming creatures of whimsy in her books, the ones who had men falling all over themselves in love? A dandelion spirit with pieces of herself floating on a breeze. Tiny seed hearts only landing where they might grow, fertile and wild.

Because you're a human being. Not a weed. Not some literary manic-pixie-dream-girl device to further some Peter Pan's individuation process. Give yourself a break.

Without her leash, as soon as she spotted Aiden, RBG bolted straight for him, barking happily, like a girl seeing her Army beau finally home from the war. Standing on hind legs, she rested both paws on his hips as he beamed down and gave her a proper scratch.

Way to be cool, girl.

Quinn wasn't going to give him the human equivalent. "What are you doing here?"

He glanced up before stroking RBG's head, telling the dog in a butter-smooth voice to calm down, which of course she did right away. Aiden walked up the gravel path, RBG trotting alongside as if she was born to be there.

Great. Now I'm jealous of my own dog.

"I'm sorry I haven't come by recently. The case picked up."

"It's fine," Quinn said too fast, stuffing her mail back into the box by her front door. "As I said from the start, I don't need you to keep me safe. I have RBG." She let out a whistle, bending from the waist while patting her thigh with one hand and jiggling the leash with the other. "C'mon, girl. Let's go for our walk."

RBG tilted her head but didn't move.

Of course her dog was confused. Quinn wasn't the only female who had gotten used to their routine of walking with Aiden. She recalled reading a bunch of articles about forming new behaviors, saying it took an average of sixty-six days for a habit to become part of an individual's routine for the long term. She gave herself a mental reminder to write those scientists scalding notes later, informing them their research was one big bucket of bull poop, and she had the proof, because it only took her and her dog baby a little over a week—twice a day—to become accustomed to Aiden's presence in their lives. The positive reinforcements of coffee in the morning for her and the liverwurst treat for her dog certainly seemed to have sealed the deal for her impressionable basal ganglia.

He held his hand out. "Give me the leash. I'll hook her up, and then we can get going."

Quinn made her way over to RBG. "I've got it. Don't worry yourself." Keeping her eyes averted, Quinn clipped the leash to the dog's collar. "I'd love to catch up, but I really need to walk her so I can get going." She gave a short tug and shimmied around him, forcing a smile. Small miracles, her girl followed, falling into step with her.

Unfortunately, Aiden was undeterred, jogging up next to them, RBG in between. "I should have called to let you know I wasn't going to be able to join you, once things got crazy."

"Not at all," Quinn said, straightening her spine and quickening her pace. Chin up. Gaze straight ahead. They were off the gravel path and onto Windover Avenue. No sidewalks, but plenty of mature-growth trees lining the street. One of the store's regular customers drove by, and she waved. Quinn eyed Aiden with an expression she hoped said, "Oh, you're still here? Cool. Whatever."

But who am I kidding? She'd never been, nor would she ever be, the cool girl.

"I'm disappointed in you, Quinn."

That made her stop. "Excuse me?"

He halted, both forefingers hooked through his belt loops. "I always thought you were the kind of person who always shot straight, who didn't play games."

How did she respond to *that*?

"If you're upset with me—which you have every right to be, by the way—just tell me. Lay me out. That's how the adults do it."

"Are you seriously mansplaining how I should be angry with you right now?"

If she could have killed him and gotten away with it, Quinn would've done it. She already had a calligraphed list forming in her head.

"No, I'm just calling you on your crap."

Sitting between them, RBG whined.

Quinn sighed, gazing down. "It's okay, girl. Mommy and daddy aren't fighting."

Aiden chuckled. "Even when you're acting all pissy, you're still the funniest girl I know."

"What?"

He folded his arms across his chest. Lopsided smile and gray eyes dancing. "It's true, Quinn. When you're relaxed and being yourself, you're totally unfiltered and make me laugh long after I've hung out with you. You're also one of the smartest people I know—so whip-smart, it's scary sometimes—and that's not even close to the best part of you."

"I just read a lot," she said, wondering if the blood rushing to her face was making her blush.

He wasn't done. "You were the kind of kid who volunteered on weekends not because you were looking for something to pad your college application, but because you are invested in this town, which is pure Adele and Finn Caine. I knew that to be true then, but you proved it with your work over the last three years and with the donation stuff you coordinated for the abbey as soon as you got back."

"You're making me out to be some kind of saint, Aid, and I'm far from one, I promise you. Yes, I taught English because I wanted to help the kids, but what I really wanted was to experience the world outside this little bubble for myself. And I coordinate the dog food pickups because I'm trying to build a life here as an adult—beyond being Adele and Finn Caine's daughter." She sighed, brushing the hair away from her forehead, which was sweaty from her standing on the asphalt in the sun. "Also, since you value honesty, I help the sisters because it gets me and my head out of a book once in a while."

He took a step closer, his gray eyes locked on hers. "I am sorry—really sorry—I didn't call or text, letting you know I got busy with the case. It was thoughtless. You promised to stop sniffing around and stirring things up, and I promised to keep you safe and find the person who poisoned your dog and murdered Tricia. You've held up your end of the deal, and I didn't hold up all of mine. There's no excuse, so I won't disrespect you further by trying to sell you one. Bottom line: I'm hoping I can earn your trust again, over time."

"I appreciate that," she said, "but there's nothing to 'earn,' Aid. You apologized. I accepted. Clean slate." She averted her gaze, her mind still working. "Now, if it kept happening, that's a different story. I'm forgiving, but I'm not a schmuck."

"Good." He took the leash out of her hand. "Let's get a move on. Our dog baby has been patient while 'Mom and Dad' work things out."

She emitted a pretend groan, rolling her eyes. "That was a joke, to cut the tension."

He shrugged, walking as if he had all the time in the world. "I don't know about that, Quinn. You know what Shakespeare said: 'Many a true word hath been spoken in jest . . . just sayin'."

They made a left. "Everyone knows that one," she said.

"True . . . What about 'Humor is the good-sided nature of a truth'?"

Her mind went blank. "Who said that?"

"Mark Twain."

She was impressed. "I'll have to remember that."

"Mm-hmm."

They fell into a comfortable silence. Rays of light filtered through the tree canopy. A favorite of hers. It was still hot—she'd guess high eighties—even though it was close to six o'clock in the evening. But that wasn't what was really on her mind. Any thoughts with even a hint of a possible "Q&A" happy ending she pushed away and shut in a mental box. What she did allow was the nugget he had dropped at the beginning of their talk.

"So, you've made headway in the case?"

"Yep."

That's all she got.

"Care to elaborate?"

He kept his focus straight ahead. "Nope."

"Oh, c'mon! I've proven I can be trusted."

"You absolutely can be trusted."

Well, at least that's something.

"Still not going to tell you anything," he said.

Ugh! I take it back. Bumping him off is so totally worth going to prison.

His phone rang in his back pocket. He reached for it, saw the number, grimaced, and answered. "Harrington speaking."

No *uh-huh*'s or *mm-hmm*'s uttered. He just listened to the person on the other end. After several minutes, he eyed Quinn, handing her the leash. RBG wasn't bothered by the change in command; she was sniffing near an azalea bush on someone's lawn.

"Yeah, I got that. I'm about eight minutes out. Right."

He hung up. "I've got to go. Let's get you back home."

They had walked in a wide semicircle, not too far from her parents' place. "No need. I'll just hang out at Caine central for a while. I'm supposed to have dinner there anyway."

"Really?"

She shooed him. "Go. I'm fine."

"Okay, good plan. You know you can always talk to me, Quinn. No matter what?"

"Sure. Yes, of course."

He nodded, then jogged off back toward Walnut Lane, where he had left his SUV. She understood he couldn't share police business, but she was dying to know if he had to leave because of a crack in the Pemberley case. Or if they'd found that monster who poisoned RBG.

Glancing over at her dog—with those warm chocolate eyes—she wished RBG could sniff out the killer. Lead a path right to that person. Give her answers. Something. Anything.

And with that, her dog baby squatted and deposited a big pile of dog poop for her to clean up. *Such a giver.* She pulled one of the biodegradable bags out of the dangling holder attached to the leash, slipped her hand inside, and bent down to pick up the mess and tie the bag tight.

While bent down, she heard voices coming from the other side of the bushes.

"Milly, honey, are you sure you're feeling okay? I don't feel right, letting you drive home by yourself."

While still crouched down, Quinn peaked through the hedges. RBG took the cue and laid down on the grass beside her, content to take a breather. Milly Hauser was leaving the house next door, saying goodbye on the porch to someone Quinn didn't know. *I guess it's possible I don't actually know everyone on this side of town.*

However, instead of wearing one of her usual dressed-to-the-nines, well-heeled designer outfits, Mrs. Hauser was in a pink tracksuit and sneakers, her ebony hair in a tight ponytail, and she didn't have on a stitch of makeup. Her coloring was off, like the other day at the garage, but even worse.

"I can't seem to shake this bug. I've been to the doctor, but he says it's probably viral, so there's nothing he can do. Something must be going around."

"Let me call Carlson to come and get you, or leave your car here and I'll drive it out your way as soon as Henry comes home."

She shook her head. "Absolutely not. He's in surgery all day, with real medical emergencies. And you shouldn't be bothering Henry with such nonsense."

"Well, at least will you let me bring over some chicken soup tomorrow?"

Milly shook off the offer before pressing her hand to her lips, as if she were holding back from getting sick right there. "I can barely eat a thing."

Her friend gave her a look. "You *never* eat, Milly."

"Well, it's even less now, so don't bother. You're a dear, though."

Her friend wrung her hands, a pained expression on her face. Mrs. Hauser scoffed. "What now?"

"I don't know, Milly. Maybe you should forget it and—"

"Don't back out now." She grabbed her friend's wrist. "Please, Ophy . . . I need this. Otherwise, Trina says the deal is off."

"Haven't you done enough for that girl? She should be bending over backward for *you*—not the other way. With Tricia dead—"

Milly held onto her friend. "I need to know we still have a deal."

The other woman patted Milly's hand. "Fine. *Yes*—happy now?"

Her shoulders dropped, and Quinn witnessed a first: Milly Hauser smiling, looking happy. "You are aces! And I promise, you won't be sorry."

"I'm quoting you on that." Her friend sighed, waving as Milly got herself into her Lexus, driving down the road.

If Quinn could've run all the way to Guinefort House, she would've, but she couldn't, which made her consider joining the new gym because—whoa—her legs ached and her lungs burned like the devil, and she had only jogged five blocks. She dropped off her girl at home, who actually seemed relieved for the break as she crawled straight for her doggie bed. Quinn hopped in her truck and proceeded to violate at least three rules of the road on her way to her cousin and best friend—the only person who could help her figure out how to catch Tricia's killer—her would-have-been future mother-in-law, Milly Hauser—and the one behind it all, Tricia's own sister, Trina Pemberley.

Chapter
Twenty-Seven

"Plans are of little importance, but planning is essential."
—Winston Churchill, British politician and author.

"A re you sure you heard right?"

Quinn got lucky that Daria was available when she arrived, because lately she'd been swamped with her duties at the abbey.

"What do you mean 'if I heard right'? Of course I did! They were on the steps of the house next door! No cars driving by. No lawn mowers roaring. I had my head inside a hedge of azalea bushes when Milly Hauser practically admitted to killing her future daughter-in-law for Trina."

"Shh!" Daria said, her forefinger to her lips as she closed the door to her room. "I don't want anyone to hear you. Technically, you're not even supposed to be up here."

"Wait—why can't I be up here? It's not like I'm some boy you're trying to sneak into an all-girls dorm or something."

"Because this *isn't* a dorm, Quinn. This is the home of my order, and we don't have outsiders traipsing around up here. Also, Sister Ceci is my roommate and as annoyingly eager beaver and chipper as she is, I can't imagine she'd maintain that perky disposition if she found you in her personal space."

She made a fair point. This order was her new-ish life, and Quinn needed to respect Daria's choice. "I just didn't know who else to turn to. I promised Aiden I wouldn't interfere in the case anymore, but it's not like I can help what I overheard."

Daria leaned her weight against the closed door. Quinn could tell from the look on her face that her cousin was in strategic thinking mode. "No, you can't help what you heard. That's for sure. But if you were a killer, would you talk so casually about what you did? Outside, for anyone to see and hear you?"

"No, I'd sneak into the upper-floor residence of my nun cuz."

"Ha! You probably would," she said. "Who was this woman again that Milly was talking to anyway, and what does she have that Milly needed so desperately for Trina?"

"I don't know—a new kidney? The contract for her soul from the devil?"

Daria's mouth quirked. "Well, it has to be something just as significant; otherwise, you know Milly Hauser wouldn't be on that lady's turf, begging for anyone to see."

"True, true." Quinn tried to concentrate, jog something familiar, but her mind palace felt closed for summer refurbishing. "I thought I knew everyone in the northwest section of town, but I don't remember ever seeing this woman."

Daria eyed Quinn's messenger bag. "Did you bring your laptop?"

"Yeah . . . ooh! That's a good idea! Why didn't I think of that? Hold on." She sat on Daria's twin bed, undid the flap of her bag, and retrieved her computer. Firing it up, she was relieved it was fully charged, giving her the illusion of actually having it together for a change.

Daria sat next to her, both peering at the screen.

"It's cool y'all have Wi-Fi. What's your password?"

"JesusBeMyFireWall."

Quinn snorted. "That's hilarious. I'm assuming you came up with that one?"

Daria gave her a playful shoulder bump. "Of course I did. They didn't even have a website before I came along."

Quinn looked up from the screen. "They're lucky to have you . . . and so am I."

"Ditto, but don't get cheesy on me now."

"Fine, have it your way . . . All right, let's see what we can find." Quinn typed the address into Google Search. There were a bevy of results. "Well, the owners of that house are Henry and Ophelia Patron. They've lived there for six years."

"See if you can find her on Facebook. Maybe her social ties will tell us more."

Quinn banged away on the keyboard. "See? This is why I need you—that's good."

Ophelia Patron was easy enough to find, especially since she didn't have any of the privacy settings on for her page. *Rookie move.* Quinn scrolled through her time line. Lots of cats. A couple of memes about getting older. A few humble brags about her daughter.

Daria shrugged. "Standard suburban mom stuff, if you ask me."

Quinn clicked on her albums. Profile pics. Time-line photos. Mobile uploads. "Ah, let's see here . . . 'Good Old Days'?" She perused those. "Bingo—look! Ophelia and Milly were in the same sorority."

Daria sat back on her bed, leaning against her headboard. "All right, so they have history. Again, none of this proves anything."

"We have to get closer."

Daria made a face. "But you promised Aiden you wouldn't put yourself in danger again."

Crap. That was true. She couldn't break her word, especially after he had come over with that heartfelt speech and apologized. "What am I supposed to do? Just let Milly Hauser loose in town? She's probably the one who stole Ren's car to dump Tricia's body, framing him for a life sentence. She had easy access. And now she's dragging this Ophelia Patron into this."

"I know! Ugh, I really hope this is all a big misunderstanding. It's one thing for Milly Hauser to be a ladder-climbing elitist; it's another to be a cold-blooded killer."

"And what about Trina? Arranging to have your own twin murdered? And what does she have over Milly to make her do such a thing?"

Daria shuddered, rubbing her hands up and down her arms. "Trina Pemberley has always given me the creeps, like there's nothing behind her eyes."

"Oh, there's something there alright—it's called pure evil. She also had a tight hold on her sister, but would she really have her murdered just because Tricia wanted to get married and go to law school?"

"She didn't see it that simply. For Trina, it was the ultimate betrayal. Ending their real estate partnership must have been like breaking the bonds of sisterhood, at least in her eyes. And if what Maxie said to you was true, about Trina being threatened by Scott . . ." Daria let out a heavy sigh. "It's beyond awful, but it adds up."

Quinn closed down her computer, slipping it back into her bag. "I don't know. Aiden said to me the other day that it's important for the evidence to speak for itself; that it was cool to have a working theory as long as the investigator doesn't try to shape the evidence to the theory."

Daria gnawed on her bottom lip. "Maybe Milly didn't need convincing or to be blackmailed."

Quinn's brows furrowed. "What do you mean?"

"I mean, Scott told you his mother couldn't stand Tricia when she was alive. She about said as much to your face at Church Street Eats when you were there with Bash. It's gross to even think about, but that woman has always had an unhealthy attachment to her son, like he's the husband instead of, well, her *actual* husband."

Quinn curled her knees to her chest, like a human shield from the truth. "Whoa, so you're thinking Milly Hauser didn't need any convincing to off Tricia, that she was fueled by control and jealousy?"

"Yes. Trina may be a lousy human being, but she's not stupid. She knows how to read people. As Scott and Tricia became serious about each other, I'm sure the families socialized together. Trina read the situation and made Milly an offer she couldn't refuse."

Quinn mulled that one over. "Or didn't even want to refuse. Nice *Godfather* reference. Two points for Slytherin."

All humor left Daria's face. "You know, you might have promised Aiden to keep out of it. But I didn't."

"Uh, no. No way. It's too dangerous."

"Oh, so it would be okay for you, but not for me?" She tsked, shaking her head. "I'm the one with the mad skills, remember?"

"This isn't jump-starting a car for a joy ride. This is putting yourself in the path of a possible murderer."

"Please, I can take Milly Hauser. What is she—five foot nothing and ninety-five pounds soaking wet?"

It was tempting. Her cousin had been a badass back in the day. "It's just . . . if anything happened to you." Quinn's throat got tight. "For the rest of my life, I'll never get that picture out of my head, of Wyatt pointing a gun at you."

Daria nodded, grasping Quinn's hand. "I get it. But this is important. I'm not talking about confronting Milly head on. I'm just suggesting we poke around her stuff, see what we can find."

Just then, they both heard the sound of a car pulling up. Daria peaked out her window. "It's the Reverend Mother and Sister Lucy. They must be back from their appointment. You've gotta go."

Quinn nodded, grabbing her bag as her cousin followed her down the stairs. Just before she left, Daria cleared her throat. Quinn turned, her hand on the knob of the front door.

"Two words I want you to ponder," she said.

"And they are?"

Daria gave a mischievous smile. "Clandestine methodology."

Chapter Twenty-Eight

"I only fear danger where I want to fear it."
—Franz Kafka, *The Metamorphosis*

Next to the smell of books, the scent Quinn couldn't get enough of was leather. She had Rachel's journal parked under her nose, eyes closed.

"Should I leave the two of you alone?" Bash asked.

She peeked. "Just tell me you read it before I proceed to wrap it up."

Her mama walked in. "Well, get to it then! We're leaving in five minutes."

Her brother whistled. "Wow, the Caine women clean up good."

Adele Caine giggled, doing a twirl in the family kitchen. Both clapped, as did their dad, who walked in wearing a sharp suit and tie. "There's my girlfriend." He kissed Adele's cheek.

"Make a note, Quinn," her mama said. "You want a man who still looks at you like he did on your wedding day."

They were a stunning couple. She was wearing a tea-length, taffeta, A-line cocktail dress in a rich aubergine shade that made her pale blue-gray eyes pop; a pair of kitten heels and a matching silk purse complemented the outfit. For a finishing touch, she was wearing a porcelain brooch depicting Cupid in flight. Whimsical, sentimental, bordering on *schmaltzy*: perfect for an anniversary celebration.

"Man, I should've worn one of my enamel pins."

Her mother pooh-poohed her. "You are perfect exactly the way you are. And I adore your dress. Is it new?"

"Actually, it belonged to Daria before she took her first vows. If only all nuns were as stylish in their former lives."

Bash gave a warm smile. "It suits you."

Adele made a motion toward the journal. "Now hurry up and wrap that thing already. I don't want to be late."

Quinn already had everything on the kitchen table. Once Bash had returned the diary (reading the whole thing without telling her how it ended), she'd called Rachel to inform her it was done. Rachel asked her to gift-wrap it and bring it to the party tonight. She made another request as well.

"By the way, tell your brother he can come too. If he wants. Otherwise, it's weird if all the Caines are present and not him."

Bash was so stoked, he went out and bought himself a new suit for the occasion.

Quinn perused his designer duds. "You look sharp, brother of mine."

He grinned. "Why, thank you."

"Ever find out why Rachel really changed her mind?"

He adjusted the knot on his tie. "Isn't it obvious?"

"Seriously?" She threw a gift-wrap bow at his head, which he caught with one hand and tossed back.

Bash shrugged. "Actually, after you told me Rachel said I could join the party, I called Stuart."

She cut the gift wrap from the roll. "And? What did he say?"

"Well, being Rachel, of course she found out her brothers had told me to crash the party."

"Of course. She finds out everything."

Her brother handed her the tape. "First, she let them have it over inviting me behind her back. But then Stuart informed her how I passed on their offer in order to respect her wishes. That took her off guard."

Quinn peeled the paper off the back of the bow and stuck it in the center of the present. "I don't understand."

He blew out air. "The Bash she knew would've crashed the party."

"Ah."

"Proof I'm growing up all up in here," he said, pointing to his head.

She rolled her eyes.

Her father cleared his throat. "Okay, time to go, you two."

*   *   *

"Wow, the Slingbaums really know how to throw a shindig."

Those were her father's words—borrowed straight out of 1955—and he was right.

They had rented one of those glorious white tents pitched high in their backyard, but this was no run-of-the-mill house party. They'd had a wooden dance floor installed. There were two bars stocked with premium liquor. They even had crystal chandeliers hanging from inside the tent. And the food smelled divine. No surprise. When Rachel wasn't fighting for social justice as an attorney, she was a fully committed foodie who adored entertaining.

And the minute Bash spotted Rachel from across the room, Quinn got to witness two people falling in love all over again. Rachel was exquisite. Tendrils of loose, dark curls framed her pixie features, especially those huge blue eyes. Her dress hugged her curves, a shimmery gold and silver frock made for dancing, with sparkly fringes that hit the knee.

Bash made a beeline her way, and the room held a collective breath as he took her hand and led her to the dance floor. Everyone around fluttered, all caught up in young love and whispering to one another. Quinn even noticed Zach and Stuart giving each other a high five.

She heard her mother let out a happy sigh. "Maybe someday they'll dance like that at their wedding."

"Let's not get ahead of ourselves, honey," her dad said. "This here is just a small opening she's given him. It's not a victory dance."

"*Yet*. But it will be. My brother, as he so eloquently said, is 'growing up all up in here.'"

Finn Caine turned to Adele, offering his hand with a slight bow. "Let us ignore our children's abhorrent vernacular, my lovely. May I have the honor of this dance?"

She blushed, placing her hand in his. "I thought you would never ask."

Adorable.

As Quinn glanced around, she realized Rachel was right: there really weren't very many young people at the party. It made sense. This was a thirty-sixth wedding anniversary celebration—as their invitation stated, a double chai. The number eighteen was considered lucky in Jewish tradition, represented by the Hebrew word *chai*, "to life." Quinn thought them honoring a double chai anniversary was both charming and unique. But now, with Bash back in Rachel's orbit, she felt rather out of place at the party.

She really wasn't that hungry, but she decided to peruse the buffet anyway. Maybe nibble a little. Anything to stop watching other people dancing. Even Rachel's two doofus brothers were pulling their wives close on the dance floor.

With care, Quinn placed the wrapped journal on the gift table and walked over to the buffet, trying to remember the last time she'd had a date. A real one. That's when it hit her: the walks with Aiden and RBG were the closest thing she'd had to a date in a long time, and those weren't even dates. They were escorted safety patrols.

I am sooo not living my best life.

Without RBG or her cousin around as a distraction, Quinn felt something she hadn't been able to fully identify until that night: loneliness. Rachel had encouraged her to invite a plus one, and her first instinct—hand to God—had been to take her dog or to ask Daria if she were free.

Ironically, she was not. Her cousin, who had sworn off men for the rest of her life, was spending this particular Friday night at a church function.

Wow. The nun has a better social life than I do.

Quinn grabbed one of the patterned china plates and began to pick and choose items from the buffet. Southern fried chicken legs. Truffle mac and cheese. Latkes with sour cream and caviar. Dressed-up comfort food.

Even though there was plenty of seating—Rachel had opted for plush sofas and chairs instead of the typical ten-rounds with folding chairs—Quinn chose to eat standing near the bar. If she didn't have anyone to talk to, at least she could listen to the conversations of others with fully actualized lives.

Two women about her parents' age approached the bar. "I'll have a Dubonnet with a twist." One woman turned to the other. "Did you see the framed family photos by the sign-in book?"

"I did!" She smiled and said to the bartender, "I'll have the signature cocktail."

I need to get one of those: vodka and champagne with ginger and mint. Hello yummy.

Baby-boomer lady number one wasn't done with the appreciative sharing. "And did you taste the latkes? The ones with the sour cream topped with caviar? They are divine!"

"I heard Rachel made those from her late uncle's recipe, the one who died several months ago. It's her way of honoring his memory. The rest of the food is catered."

Quinn took a bite and OMG, where had these fried potato pillows of heaven been all her life? These ladies knew what they were talking about—they *were* divine.

The other woman gasped, her hand to her cheek. "That is the loveliest tribute! He would have loved everything about this party."

"He really would have. He adored this family, especially his sister. Can you imagine, a surgeon of his caliber moving here and starting over?"

"Well, his wife cleaned him out in the divorce."

"I never did like that woman. So cold!"

"And a *schnorrer* to boot. Not once did she host Break Fast or Passover."

"Awful. Just awful," the other woman said, shaking her head before both she and her companion accepted their drinks and walked away. The people waiting behind them gave one another knowing looks.

The wife requested a Jack and Coke, then turned to her husband. "Those two ladies must be talking about Doctor Chaim Levine."

The husband told the bartender he'd have the same.

"Oh, I know they were. Because two weeks after Dr. Levine died, Milly was bragging how her husband's referrals went up by fifteen percent."

Quinn pretended to be occupied with the food on her plate so they wouldn't notice her eavesdropping. All the while, she was quietly freaking out. Both Tricia and Dr. Levine had died of mysterious causes with similar symptomology. Was it possible Milly Hauser had knocked off Dr. Levine because he was competition for her husband?

A melodic voice came from behind. "Having fun?"

Quinn nearly jumped out of her skin before whirling around. It was Rachel.

"Hi!" Quinn gave Rachel a one-armed hug, holding her plate with the other hand. "Wow, you look amazing!"

She beamed. "Oh please, *you* do. I love, love, *love* your dress. Emerald-green is definitely one of your colors."

"Thanks, Rach. It's a great party, by the way."

She gave a pained smile. "I've been a lousy friend tonight. I take one look at your brother, and I totally bail on us hanging out. You came here to keep me company, and I repay you by—"

Quinn cut her off. "Stop it. We're fine. You know I'm thrilled you're giving him another chance."

"We'll see," Rachel said with a sigh. "Tonight doesn't mean we're back together. It just means I'm thinking about it. I'd be lying if I said I wasn't scared out of my mind."

"You set the pace, okay? My brother will do whatever you want."

She nodded. "It's really good to see you. I've missed you over the years. A lot."

"Me too," Quinn told her. "Hey, can I ask you something?"

"Of course! Anything."

"I know you said it was okay if I read Granny Nora's journal, but I didn't get a chance to read the whole thing. What happened between Nora and David? I'm dying to know!"

Rachel opened her mouth to respond.

"Don't you dare answer her." It was her brother, wreaking havoc as usual. "For the first time since Quinnie was born, I've got something over her. Besides fighting fires. And I plan on milking the suspense for as long as possible."

Quinn pretended to glare at him. "Rach, remind me to taunt and torture this one later."

He gave his most naughty cackle. "Less talking. More dancing." He winked at Quinn, then took Rachel's hand, staring the whole time. "C'mon, one more dance. Then I'm going to wolf down the rest of those latkes. I've been craving them for years."

"Do you mind?" Rachel asked Quinn, her bottom lip between her teeth, eyes wide.

She shooed them away. "Go forth. Prosper. Have fun. I'm going to cut out early."

"Are you sure?"

"Positive. Have fun. We'll catch up."

They took off, and Quinn stayed just long enough to sign the guest book and say goodbye to her parents, who said they'd get a ride from someone and gave her the car keys.

Good thing, because Rachel's parents' house was on the other side of town, and there was no way Quinn would have been able to walk the whole way home. She took off her heels, holding them by the straps in one hand while retrieving her phone with the other. It was a longer walk to the car than she had expected, because her dad had dropped her and her mom off at the front. The Slingbaums had their fair share of friends, and they had invited family from all over as well—which made for quite a schlep to where her dad had parked the car. Looking at the street names, she realized she was fairly close to the Hausers' home. The thought made her shiver.

Scrolling through her contacts, she found the number she was looking for.

"Hi, Aiden, it's Quinn."

"I know who it is. Are you okay?"

She let out a nervous laugh. "I'm fine. Listen, sorry to call you so late, but I overheard something at the party tonight—and the other day while walking my girl. I promise I haven't been investigating, but you said if I heard something . . ."

She then proceeded to share with Aiden everything else she'd heard regarding Tricia and Trina—from Milly Hauser herself, at the Patron residence. She recapped the conversation about Dr. Hauser's uptick in referrals. She even offered her theories on the case. By the time she got to the car, she had told Detective Aiden Harrington everything. She felt good too. Clean. Like she could sleep in peace for the first time in a long while.

What she didn't realize was, the whole time she was talking, someone else was listening, taking an evening stroll and keeping just close enough to hear everything she said.

Chapter
Twenty-Nine

The truth does not change according to our ability to stomach it.
—Flannery O'Connor, American novelist

All through the night, and into the following morning, her favorite detective/rock star's words echoed on a loop in her brain.

"I don't want you to worry about a thing. My team and I are on top of it. Let me bring in Tricia's killer. You go to the fundraiser, take Daria to Viva Vienna, and have some fun for once. The Vienna PD's got this."

And so that's exactly what she was doing. She picked up her cousin and walked into The Women Center's art fundraiser. Her family was probably already there.

"Wow, I had no idea the place would be this packed."

Quinn had to agree. "It's probably because they're featuring Mrs. Hammock's art. She's a big deal. I know my mother couldn't stop talking about it."

"Daria! Quinn! Over here!"

It was her mom, standing with her dad. She made eye contact and waved, then shimmied through the crowd in order to get to where they were standing.

Quinn tried to be heard over the crowd. "Why are you all the way up here?"

Her mother's face was scarlet, rivulets of sweat dripping down her temples. "Because the auction is going to start any minute, and I'm not missing a chance to own an original piece of art from Withers' mom!"

Her father blanched. "It's a bunch of urns and teapots, Adele. You can get the same thing at the Bowman House art show for a fraction of the cost."

Her mother rolled her eyes and shook her head. "It's a good thing he's handsome . . ."

Ms. Withers walked up to the podium and, gavel in hand, started banging on the wood block to get everyone's attention. "We are going to begin the auction in five minutes. Remember, one hundred percent of what we raise tonight will go toward The Women's Center. Since 1974, The Women's Center has provided affordable mental health care, support, and education to Northern Virginia and D.C."

Finn Caine started patting up and down his person, spelunking into his pants and jacket pockets. "Oh, for Christ's sake, don't tell me I—"

"What's wrong, Dad?"

He let out a frustrated groan. "I left my checkbook and wallet on the desk in my home office." He turned to her mother. "Del, did you bring your wallet?"

She held up a clutch the size of a credit card. "I brought my lipstick and my driver's license. That's all."

"Really? You don't have anything on you? What would you do if you needed money for a cab?"

She looked at him as if he'd lost his mind. "Why would I need money for a cab? I could walk home from here. Besides, I'm here with you. Are you planning on leaving me here?"

This argument was going nowhere. "Guys, guys! I'll run home and get Dad's wallet and the checkbook. You stay here and enjoy the auction."

"I'll come with you," Daria volunteered.

"Nah, don't bother. I'll be in and out in a jiff. Besides, I know you. You've been dying to see her work for a long time. You love art more than I do. Stay and have fun."

Daria gave her a grateful smile. "Well, that's very nice of you. Hurry back, though."

"You bet." She turned around and made her way out of the party room, secretly grateful she had an excuse to get away from the crowd and have a bit of air.

She hopped in her truck and made it to her parents' place in no time. Quinn unlocked the front door and walked into her father's study.

Wow, what a mess.

For someone so fastidious about his books and files, his desk was like the floor of a crime scene. She searched through his papers: bills, invitations to speak at law conferences, a list of books he planned to review for the store's newsletter, junk mail.

Geez, Dad, remind me to introduce you to a fabulous utilitarian device called a trash can someday.

Then there was also a small booklet—hand-printed by The Vienna Mycological Society. She smiled, thumbing through it, remembering her outing with them not too long ago. The publication was a combination field guide/brag book/membership directory. It seemed all the members had their own page to write about whatever they wanted—mushroom related, that is. She skimmed through her dad's page—full of puns, arcane 'shroom trivia. Typical Finn Caine. Ned Carter wrote about his affection for any time he was able to spend in nature—'in the green,' as he called it—and Barbara Franklin was a hoot, saying how her professional mission as an allergist was to learn about everything and anything in nature that might set off a reaction.

Then there was a page she didn't expect—one member who hadn't been present that day she had gone foraging with the group. Someone whom no one had ever mentioned, including her father.

It was Dr. Carlson Hauser, M.D.

On his page he wrote about how he initially got interested in foraging because of his wife, Milly, a vegetarian, who enjoyed the different ways he used mushrooms in his cooking. But then his interest grew as he became fascinated by claims of their medicinal properties.

> Twice a year, I travel to South America with the medical philanthropic organization Surgeons without Border Walls to donate my time and skills to those less fortunate. Through the years, many of my patients have sworn by the medicinal benefits of certain fungi. I began to study them, curious whether their belief was evidence-based or simply folklore. In the process, I've become an avid mycologist. While I have yet to find a mushroom to cure heart disease, I have found plenty that could kill you. I offer my expertise to the group, to identify those that are medicinal and those that are poisonous for human consumption.

And holy Jesus, Mary, and Joseph—in the photo he was wearing a hoodie—with a crossed fish logo. Just like in the video footage.

Quinn's hands started to shake. *I can't believe it . . . he's the one who killed Doctor Levine and Tricia Pemberley!*

A wooden floorboard squeaked behind her.

Her heart pounded into her throat, the blood rushing fast and fierce through her ear canals. Quinn found it hard to breathe.

She turned around. Slowly. Carefully. As if one wrong move would shatter the floor beneath her feet.

And there was Dr. Hauser, standing less than six feet from her.

"Imagine my surprise, after following you from the fundraiser, to find you here. You left your front door wide open, Ms. Caine. Didn't your parents ever teach you to lock the door to keep out danger?"

It was a rhetorical question.

"It's almost going to be too easy."

His pupils were almost fully dilated. And he had a wet cloth in his hand.

"Too easy for what?" she asked.

His head cocked. "Why, to kill you, of course."

She stopped breathing. "But I thought you were supposed to be the nice Hauser."

He offered a slow, creeping smile. "Brilliant, no? I fooled everyone."

Quinn eyed the front door, open wide. His cheek ticked as he shook his head. "Oh no, dear, it's too late for that." Before she had a chance, he lunged forward, smothering her face with the cloth, a sickly sweet smell invading her nostrils, smothering her lungs.

And then everything went black.

Chapter Thirty

"I love stories where women save themselves."
—Neil Gaiman, British author

She had no idea how long she'd been unconscious, but by the time Quinn came to, her mouth was as dry as a desert, and her limbs were heavy like concrete. She felt like she'd been run over by a bus. With effort, she opened her eyes, hoping to find herself in her own bed, with the memory of what happened being just a bad dream.

Instead, she was on a concrete floor, her back against something made with aluminum siding. No windows. No air-conditioning either. It felt like she was in a steam room without any way to breathe.

"Oh, thank God, you're finally up. Please tell me someone is coming to rescue us?"

She knew that voice. Cracks of light peaked through the bottom of the door in front of her. It was just enough illumination to make out the form next to her.

"Mrs. Hauser?"

"Yes, it's me. He's gone crazy. Please tell me someone knows you're here. I don't have much time!"

Images rushed back. The auction. Her father's desk. The mushroom directory. She tried wetting her lips, but it was like all the saliva had been vacuumed out of her mouth.

"What do you mean, you don't have much time?"

She groaned. "My own husband! I can't believe it. I think he's been poisoning me."

"But why would he hurt you? I don't understand."

She started crying. "Neither do I! I thought we were fine. Is anyone coming? Did someone see him take you?"

"I don't know. I was at my parents' house. He used something to knock me out. They were at the auction."

She got quiet. "Then we're going to die in this shed, behind my very own house."

The door to the shed lurched open. It was Dr. Hauser. Quinn's instinct told her to try to make a run for it, but then she saw the gun.

"Don't even bother screaming, because no one will hear you."

With the light pouring in now, Quinn could see Mrs. Hauser more clearly—her complexion was the color of ash. If she looked off the other day, Milly Hauser was gravely ill now. Still, she tried smoothing down her hair, feigning a smile for her husband.

"Please, honey, let's talk this out. Just give me the antidote, and I promise I won't press charges. I'll do whatever you want."

He shook his head, a look of disgust on his face. "It was *you* who was supposed to die, not Tricia. I put enough poisoned mushrooms in that quiche to kill an elephant."

He waved the gun back and forth between them, sweat dripping down his face. "Can you believe it, Quinn? The one time she decided to act like a human being and offer that girl a touch of kindness. She invited Tricia over for dinner so Scott could quietly prepare his proposal in the backyard. She offers her a big

319

slice of my quiche; which Tricia ate because she wanted to please my witch of a wife." He turned his attention to Milly, who was still on the floor. "You took a photo of my boy on one knee, the happiest day of his life, something you didn't deserve by the way. All the while, Tricia's got the poison meant for *you*." His maniacal gaze locked back on Quinn. "This one over there," he said pointing the gun at Milly, "only eats a few bites herself in order to watch her figure. I got home later that night and saw a chunk of it gone, and I thought, 'Finally, I'm free. Now I just have to wait.' You can't imagine my reaction when she told me how Tricia scarfed down the quiche and wanted the recipe so she could make it for Scott. I wished I could've warned her, but that would've given me up and, well, my boy will find someone else. My only consolation is, I finally convinced Milly to eat more than her usual two measly bites. She'll be dead by nightfall."

Quinn's head was spinning, and it wasn't from the effects of the chloroform.

"I thought Mrs. Hauser was the one who killed Tricia. I heard you say to Mrs. Patron how you had to finish what you started for Trina."

Milly's lids were heavy, her lips cracked and bloody. She looked like she hadn't had water in days. "What? Oh, you mean . . . I wanted to work for Trina's group—as a *realtor*. Ophy is an old friend. She was going to let her house be my first listing. That's what you heard. I would never—"

How could I have been so wrong?

"Cut the sorority chitchat." He reached for Quinn, grabbing her by the arm—hard. "I only came back here for you to tell me whatever else you know. I heard most of it last night while you were on the phone with that detective, but I need to know the rest."

He jammed the gun into her stomach, hard. She sucked in a sharp breath. "Like what?"

He was right in her face. "Right now, they all think Milly did it, don't they?"

"Don't tell him anything, Quinn! He's going to kill you as soon as he doesn't need you anymore!"

He squeezed his eyes shut, pressing the barrel of the gun to his wife's temple. *"Will you stop talking for one second of your life! Your voice is like nails down a chalkboard! I can't think* with that voice in my head!"

Milly Hauser used whatever life force she had left to straighten up. "I'll stop talking as soon as you let her go. Then I promise I'll never say anything again. Quinn is innocent in all this. If you let her go, I'll give you all the money you want. You can run off and never come back. Just don't hurt her. She's young. She has her whole life ahead of her."

He started laughing, high pitched and crass, jamming the gun back into Quinn's ribs. "Oh, so now you've finally grown a heart? Maybe I should've poisoned you *years* ago. Maybe those death caps somehow killed the nasty in you. But you've got the right idea . . . a new start. Marry myself someone young and sweet, and forget I ever laid eyes on you."

He was so caught up in his rant that he moved the gun away from Quinn's middle, using it to gesture around the tiny shed, but he still had a vise grip on her arm.

Then the sound of sirens stopped him cold.

Milly's head lolled to the side, her breathing shallow, but she still had some vinegar left. "They're coming for you, Carlson. I may die in this shed, but it'll be worth it just to see them take you away in handcuffs. You were always weak. If you didn't have that gun, you'd be nothing."

He was ignoring his wife, panic written on his face. "Crap, I've got to get you out of here!" He pulled Quinn's arm hard enough that she heard it pop. There was a flash of pain, but she couldn't focus on it. He was dragging her out of the shed. The light blinded them both.

On the other side of the door someone yelled. "Now!"

Dr. Hauser grumbled. "What the heck?"

That's as far as he got. It was so bright, he didn't see the real threat barreling down the grass, straight for him.

Quinn was having a rough time focusing too, but her hearing was unaffected. And that's when she heard it—two growls, one from a Rottweiler and the other from a German shepherd. Both were headed dead center for their target, the rottie for the throat and the shepherd for the leg.

"Ahhhh! Get them off me! Get these mongrels off me now!

Then Quinn heard the sound of a low groan behind her.

Omigod . . . Ms. Milly!

Her left arm was useless, hanging loose down her side, like a sausage roll from a hook, but Quinn spun around and ran back into the shed.

"Quinn!"

She heard Aiden calling for her, but she didn't respond. There was no time left. Milly Hauser had shown signs of being ill weeks ago at Frankie's Garage. Then again at the Patron house mere days ago. Her husband must have been poisoning her, little by little at first, before realizing that approach wasn't working. That's when he had insisted she eat one big piece of quiche—a substantial dose. Death by mushroom quiche. Had Dr. Hauser used the same method to off Dr. Levine, his professional competition?

She had a lot of questions, but none of that mattered. Mrs. Hauser was dying. She had to save her.

Quinn scanned the inside of the shed, noting that Ms. Milly had somehow crawled into the corner and curled into a fetal position. Eyes closed. A low, whimpering moan the only sound she was making. Quinn ran to her.

Shoving her shoulder under Mrs. Hauser's armpit with her good arm, Quinn said a silent prayer, then hoisted her up.

"Noooo, I can't. Just leave me . . ."

Quinn scoffed. "No way, Mrs. Hauser. We're getting out of this shed together. Hold onto me as tight as you can!"

She started making a deep sound, like a wounded animal. "I deserve to die. You go. Tell my boy I'm sorry . . ."

Quinn wasn't having it. "No! You hold on, you hear me?" With a strength she didn't know she had, Quinn pulled the woman up and toward the doorway. Mrs. Hauser's feet couldn't hold her weight and she stumbled into Quinn, whose body slammed against the doorjamb on her useless shoulder. She didn't know pain like that even existed. The pain went from white to yellow, searing the retinas of her eyes. As much as she wanted to, Quinn knew she couldn't hold on. Still grasping Mrs. Hauser, she felt her body fall forward.

She braced herself to hit the concrete. Every muscle tensed, even as the yellow around her turned black, closing in. The last thing she remembered was falling into someone, not something. Strong arms surrounded her, and Milly's weight vanished.

"I've got you, Quinn. You're both safe now. You did it—you got 'em."

She knew she must have been dreaming because Quinn was floating on air, with Aiden flying next to her, telling her everything was going to be okay.

Chapter Thirty-One

"A warrior is defined by his scars, not his medals."
—Matshona Dhliwayo, Canadian philosopher and author

"It's always the nice quiet ones that end up being all the trouble."

Quinn knew her cousin was attempting to find the funny, but it had only been a couple of weeks since she had been rescued by Aiden and the Vienna PD from the Hausers' backyard. Her left arm was in a cast, broken in two places and with a dislocated shoulder. She was recovering from a concussion as well.

When Dr. Hauser had dosed her with chloroform in her father's office, he'd carried her out and into his waiting car in the back, knocking her head against almost every desk corner and wall surface of the Caine house on the way out. For over a week, Quinn hadn't been able to see straight, taking even reading and watching TV out of the rotation of leisure activities.

Today was the first day she hadn't felt like hurling her cookies all over herself.

"I still think it's too soon for you to be going out."

Almost everyone in her family was standing over her. Hovering. She knew they meant well, but Quinn was desperate to get out of the house. And she had a feeling RBG felt the same way because she trotted right to the front door as soon as Quinn rolled herself off her parents' couch.

"I know it's a little soon, but I promised." Quinn tried reaching for her purse, but it was just out of reach. Daria, her mom, and her dad all lunged for it at the same time. Quinn thought it a miracle they all didn't crash headfirst into one another.

Her mother won that particular race, handing her the clutch. "You know, there's no shame in canceling. Everyone would understand."

"No way. I can't," Quinn insisted, leaning on her father's arm. "Listen, we'll go there and right back. No lingering afterward. No stopping off for a bite to eat." She could tell from their expressions that she wasn't doing a good job of convincing them.

"Listen, I don't expect y'all to understand. But I have to be there, especially since . . ." Quinn took a shoring breath. "Especially since she can't be."

They all shared a look.

"No, we understand. You're right." Daria interwove her fingers with those on Quinn's free hand. "Let's get you there on time then."

The four of them piled into the Caine station wagon—her mom and dad, Daria, and of course RBG. Her parents had found someone to watch the store for a while. Her brother was picking up Rachel and meeting them there.

Quinn was expecting a small crowd. It was midweek, in the middle of a workday, so most people in town would be working, which was fine because she wasn't interested in a big fuss. However, she knew something was up when they pulled into the Vienna Community Center parking lot only to find it jam-packed.

"What the heck is going on?" Quinn asked, craning her head around. "Are they giving away free memberships or something in there?"

Her father scanned the lot. "Let me drop you all off in the front, and I'll find a space."

Quinn smiled, grateful for the suggestion. She didn't want to say anything, but the idea of walking a distance in upper-nineties heat, while still trying to find her land legs, was enough to make her swoon, and not in the romantic, happy-ending way.

Taking her time, Quinn made her way inside, flanked on either side by her family. She was there to receive a special citizen's commendation from the Vienna Police Department, for her role in trying to catch a killer. Frankly, Quinn thought, if anyone should receive an award, it should've been her cousin. She had been the first to notice Quinn was missing and, after alerting the police, had retrieved both dogs to assist in the search and rescue. But Sister Daria had refused any recognition, so-once again-Quinn was the consolation prize.

As soon as she walked into the assigned room, realization dawned on Quinn: it was standing room only in the auditorium, and everyone was there for her.

She swallowed a lump in her throat. "Oh noooo," Quinn dragged out. "There must be some kind of mistake."

A voice off to the side piped up. "No mistake. This is all for you."

It was Aiden, in his dress blues, looking like the Vienna PD version of Richard Gere in *An Officer and a Gentleman*. She half-expected him to swoop her up in his arms and carry her away into endless summer.

Hey, she knew it was probably never going to happen between them, the beginning of Q&A, Quinn and Aiden. But in the first split second she caught sight of him, she imagined there was an "us," that impossible girlhood wishes had become a grown-up reality. Those brief seconds? She granted herself that small indulgence.

He placed his hand on her good shoulder. "Hey, I know crowds make you nervous, but I'm going to be with you the whole time."

The warmth from his touch spread across her skin, soothing her. "Okay, good."

She trusted Aiden, without question. Ever since Dr. Hauser's arrest, Aiden had come by every day-and if he was running late, he made sure to text her right away. That was more of a challenge than ever before since the case-and Aiden-had received national attention. It made sense. He had been the one to find the opened Mycological membership book on Finn Caine's floor, putting two and two together. But Aiden blew off any attempts at praise, saying, "Quinn had already dragged herself and Milly halfway out of that shed. She had already saved herself."

"Hey, did I miss anything?"

Her dad was back from parking the car.

Aiden offered his hand. "Good to see you, Finn."

Her dad beamed. "Always good to see family."

Another police officer approached Aiden. "It's time, sir."

"Right." He offered his arm to Quinn. "Let's do this thing."

The crowd took their seats as Aiden led her down the aisle. Quinn scanned the faces in the audience as they worked their way up to the front of the room. The Huttons were there, holding hands and smiling her way. The sisters of Guinefort House almost had a full row to themselves, with Daria sitting right in the middle, looking relaxed and happy. They all brightened when they spotted her, even Sister Theresa. The staff of Prose & Scones—Sarah and their new hires, Leah and Melanie, waved. She was glad her parents had closed the store for the hour so they could all be here.

Getting closer to the front rows, Quinn was pleased to see Maxie in all her glory, her hair in rainbow-colored braids this time, and next to her was her old friend and new boyfriend, Ren. After being cleared of all charges, Quinn had heard through the grapevine he had sold that car as soon as it was released from the police impound. No one could blame him. The idea of Dr. Hauser—a man sworn by the Hippocratic oath to save lives—transporting Tricia's body in his car in order to dump it was too much for Ren to bear. He was living back home with his parents, but with the way Ren and Maxie were gazing at each other, Quinn wouldn't be surprised if she heard they were moving in together sooner versus later.

"Can you make it up? The steps?"

She nodded. "Just don't let go, okay?"

Aiden stilled, his eyes darkening. "Never, Quinn."

She was just about to work up the courage to tell him something, when someone tapped on the live microphone. Someone was giving introductions, informing everyone of what Quinn did to try to find Vienna's killer.

"Why don't we all give a round of applause to our woman of the hour, the recipient of Vienna's Special Commendation Award, Ms. Quinn Caine!

The mayor started clapping, and the whole auditorium followed, a roar of applause and whistles. She even heard a "Go, Quinn!" from her brother in the audience. With Aiden's help, she walked up the stairs to the podium.

Mayor Laurie DeBlasio stopped clapping as she handed Quinn an engraved plaque. "Quinn Caine, on behalf of our town, we want to commend you with our highest honor. Because of your quick thinking—twice—our residents can rest in safety, knowing that justice has prevailed."

Quinn took the award and thanked the mayor. She really hoped they didn't expect her to give a speech, because her mind was blank, and her spirit was still heavy.

The mayor leaned towards the microphone. "The town of Vienna and our esteemed police department aren't the only ones who want to thank Ms. Caine for her heroic efforts. We have someone else here to see you, someone who's gone through much to get here today."

Quinn couldn't imagine who it could be. She looked back on the people seated. Rachel was sitting next to her brother, giving her a thumbs-up. Bash didn't know it, but during one of Rach's visits earlier in the week, she had let Quinn in on what had happened between Granny Nora and her beloved David. Short version, he was her great-grandpa—but they had gone through hell and back before they earned their happily-ever-after. Quinn hoped Rachel and Bash fared better. She scanned the rest of the people and couldn't figure out who was missing.

And that's when, coming from behind the stage-right curtain, Scott rolled Milly Hauser out in her wheelchair.

She handed Aiden the award, unable to take her eyes off her. "I can't believe you're—" She didn't even finish her sentence before bolting across the stage and throwing her arm around her.

Mrs. Hauser's arms wrapped around her shoulder as she pulled Quinn down. No one could tell if the women were laughing or crying. Maybe a little bit of both.

Quinn broke her embrace to gaze at Milly. "How is it you're here? The last time I saw you, you were in a medically induced coma!"

"I know! I was there! Well, sort of," she teased.

It was like seeing a ghost in plain sight. She might have even squeezed Milly's hands several times just to make sure.

"The doctors—they didn't think you'd live to the end of the week."

Milly threw back her head and laughed. "Well, that was your first mistake. Doctors don't know *everything*, you know." And then, Milly Hauser winked.

The mayor motioned the three of them to the front of the stage. "Why don't we get some photos of all of you together. Give this horrible story a hopeful ending."

They did as they were asked, Quinn's right hand holding Milly's left, with Scott behind her and Aiden on her other side. Flashbulbs went off in staccato succession, making her blink black and yellow spots.

Trying to whisper, Quinn leaned toward Scott to ask, "So, how is she doing for real?"

He shrugged. "She's a fighter, what can I say? We almost lost her a couple of times, as you know, but she bounced back. It's kind of a miracle."

He was right. While Quinn was in the hospital, she had visited Milly in her room, even if the woman didn't always know she was there. Turned out her husband had been poisoning her for months—or at least trying to. As he had stated in the shed, because his wife ate like a bird, his earlier attempts had failed until he increased the dosage.

With everything that had occurred, Aiden was able to convince the Slingbaum family, without having to resort to a court order, to allow an autopsy of Dr. Chaim Levine. Now that the medical examiner's office knew to look for traces of *amanita phalloides*, otherwise known as death cap mushrooms, they were able to test his remains for that substance. It's a poison not part of a typical toxicology report—something Carlson Hauser knew as a physician.

And sure enough, they determined that Rachel's uncle had received a lethal dose. Only that time, Dr. Hauser hadn't put them in a quiche: he'd dried and ground the mushrooms into a powder, which he added to a medicinal herbal tea mix he'd heard Dr. Levine drank, one that tasted awful anyway, so the added mushroom powder wasn't detected by taste or scent.

Some "welcome to the medical neighborhood gift" that turned out to be.

The Vienna PD found what was left of the tea in the doctor's home. "Thank Christ he didn't share it," Aiden had said during one of his many visits to Quinn while she recovered, keeping her updated. "Otherwise, we'd have a mass homicide on our hands. Two were bad enough."

One thing Dr. Hauser hadn't been lying about: Tricia had been an unfortunate accident, an unexpected casualty. Milly had invited her over for dinner, a diversion for Scott to set up a dream-come-true proposal scenario in the backyard of his family's estate. Ironic, considering Tricia and Scott were both trying to get away from their families' suffocating influences, but as Scott had shared with the police, the ring was a family heirloom, so he felt compelled to have the proposal on their property.

Milly had served the mushroom quiche her husband had intended only for her. By the time Dr. Hauser got home later that night, Tricia was already too ill to drive and was going to have Scott take her home. But Dr. Hauser insisted she stay at the Hausers' so he could "keep an eye on his future daughter-in-law." That part had also been true. He wasn't sure if she'd had enough to cause her death. With that particular kind of poisonous mushroom, victims initially feel awful, but then seemingly recover from all symptoms over several hours. "That's actually when they're in the most danger," one of Quinn's doctors had informed her while she was still in the hospital. "The patient thinks the worst is over and returns to normal activities. Meanwhile, the internal organs are starting to shut down. By the time the paralysis hits, it's too late." The same had happened to Tricia: in a few hours, she felt like herself, so Scott drove her home.

Milly Hauser may have been in good spirits at the award ceremony, but Quinn could tell something still weighed heavily on Scott. Of course, he was still grieving over the loss of his fiancée, but Quinn sensed there was something more. She waited for the photographers to get all their shots and for people to file out of the auditorium.

"Scott, are you okay? I mean, all things considered."

He was not able to meet her eye. "No, I'm not okay. I'm never going to be okay."

The mayor's face reddened. "I'll leave y'all to talk." She offered an awkward half grin before walking away.

Scott's mother turned her wheelchair to face her son. "It's going to take time, honey. This has been a loss on many levels."

The pain in his eyes was palpable. "I left Tricia's place that morning, convinced whatever had made her sick had passed, and didn't think twice about it. I didn't even call later in the day to check in with her, just to make sure."

Aiden took a step closer. "Man, this is not on you. Do you understand me? There was no way for you to know she'd be dead by that afternoon. You know who did know what was coming?"

Scott's head dropped. "My dad."

"Yeah, that's right. Him, not you."

Scott met Aiden's steely gaze. "I know, but—"

"But nothing," Aiden insisted. "Your father admitted to trailing Tricia that day, pretending to bump into her near one of her listings, then convinced her to come back to his house so they could discuss wedding plans. He could've gotten her help at any point, and he didn't because he knew it would be traced back to him. Your father let her die and then used Diamond's car to dump her body."

Milly grabbed her son's hand. "Listen to him! This was a tragedy, but none of it is your fault. Please don't take that on, son."

Aiden removed a business card from his coat pocket, handing it over to Scott.

"I already have your number," Scott said.

"Yeah, I know. This is the number for Victim's Services."

Scott reluctantly took the card.

"I have it on good authority you haven't used that number yet—not a good idea considering all that's happened."

"I'm fine."

"Don't do that. Don't pretend." His mother sucked in a lungful of air. "Don't let pride get in the way, like I used to."

Something changed in her son's expression, a softening. He put the card inside his wallet. "Okay, okay. I'll call them. As soon as we leave here."

Quinn let out a quiet sigh of relief.

Aiden seemed pleased. "Good. And call me if you need to talk."

Scott nodded. "I will."

Quinn gazed down at his mom, still surprised to see her all pink-cheeked and healthy. "Mrs. Hauser, I can't begin to tell you how much it meant to me that you came."

She held up her plaque. "Nonsense! I'd never miss an opportunity to add to my trophy collection."

"What other trophies have you won?" Quinn asked.

"Oh, for golf. Some for tennis. I was quite the athlete back in high school and college."

"I'm not surprised," Scott added. "You succeed in everything you try."

Milly's eye teared. "That's one of the nicest things you've ever said to me."

"Just the truth." He glanced at the time on his phone. "We better get you back home. If you expect to start in a couple of weeks, you need all the rest you can muster between now and then."

Quinn gave a small smile. "Oh, that's right. I had heard you were joining Trina's realty team. Are you excited?"

Personally, Quinn thought it wasn't the greatest idea, having Milly a member of the Pemberley Group. She still didn't trust Trina, but there was no way she was going to dampen Mrs. Hauser's excitement.

Milly beamed. "You know what? I am soooo motivated! And don't tell her I said this, but Trina is a powerhouse. I'm going to learn a lot from her."

As far as Quinn could tell, she had learned a lot already. A brush with death because her husband had wanted her dead seemed to have given Milly Hauser a change of heart . . . and attitude.

Aiden cleared his throat. "So, um, I hate to bring this up, but Scott, did you get word on your father's prison assignment?"

Scott grimaced. "Yeah, he got his wish to stay close to home, although I don't know why. I don't want to see him. It was bad enough what he did to my mom and Tricia, but killing off a colleague just to eliminate the competition? I never want to see that psychopath again."

"Well, he received two life sentences without a chance for parole, so you'll never have to see him again if you don't want to."

Just then, Quinn's parents approached the stage. That's when she noticed her mother wearing a phoenix pin. She smiled to herself, appreciating the symbolism of the mythological bird rising from the ashes. Quinn's pin for the day was more direct—an homage from one of her favorite movies, *Beetlejuice*. It simply said, "Never trust the living."

Adele Caine cleared her throat. "Honey, I know it's been important for you to catch up"—she beamed at Mrs. Hauser—"and, Milly, it is so good to see you up and around, but—"

Milly interrupted. "Not a problem. I'm feeling worn out too. We're going. I'll check on y'all in another week or so?"

Finn Caine nodded, placing his arm around his wife. "That would be nice. We'd love to have you and Scott over for dinner."

They finished their goodbyes, and Scott wheeled his mother off the stage. Quinn scanned the audience, expecting Daria to have stuck around.

"Your cousin told us to tell you she'd talk to you later. She needed to get back to the abbey. She has a lot on her plate."

"Oh, of course," Quinn said, trying to hide her disappointment. Ever since she'd checked out of the hospital, she had seen Sister Daria, but not quite as much as before. Her cousin had explained that now that the community crisis had passed and Quinn was recovering, it was time for her to become more fully immersed in her life at Guinefort House. It made sense, but Quinn would be lying to herself if she didn't admit to missing her.

"Ready to go, kiddo?" her father asked.

"Actually, Finn, Adele, can I have Quinn meet you outside? I'll walk her out. I just need to talk to her for a sec."

Her parents shared a glance. "Sure thing. Honey?" Her father directed her way. "We'll be waiting outside in the car. We'll drive it up front."

Before Quinn even had a chance to reply, they spun around and took off.

Weird.

She returned her focus to the detective. "Everything okay?"

He took in a deep breath, shoving his hands inside his pockets. "Yeah, yeah . . . everything's fine."

Both her brows shot north. "You wanted to ask me something? Is it about the case?"

He rocked back and forth on his heels; his shoulders hunched up to his ears. "No, nothing to do with the case . . ."

She waited, not knowing what to think.

Aiden sucked in some more air before letting it out in a gust. "Oh heck—listen, I know you're still recovering and all, but can we meet for lunch tomorrow?"

"Lunch?"

He hedged. "Or coffee, if lunch out is too taxing right now."

"Well, you know I never say no to coffee," she teased.

His shoulders relaxed, a warm smile returning to his face.

She still wasn't getting it. "What do you want to talk about?" Quinn couldn't imagine what else he needed. The case was closed.

"With you? I want to talk about everything and nothing, for as long as you'll let me."

Her face was still blank.

Aiden let out a soft laugh as he took a couple steps toward her, his gaze lingering on her lips before meeting her questioning eyes. "Let me put it another way . . . Duck, I'm trying to ask you out."

Did he just say what I thought he said?

"Can you say that again?" Quinn knew she must seem as dense as a thicket, but she didn't care. She needed to be sure.

He was right in her space. Breathing the same air. "Quinn Victoria Caine, may I have the pleasure of your company tomorrow morning for coffee? Lunch, if you're feeling better. We'll work our way up to dinner . . . in time."

And that was all it took. Three sentences were just enough to make what once was dormant, presumed dead, illuminate again.

"Yes, Aiden. I'll have coffee with you. On one condition."

Steely determination set in. "Name it."

She smiled. "That we can bring RBG along. My girl and I, we're a package deal. I suggest you bring her one of those liverwurst cupcakes. It'll be important to stay in her good graces."

He let out a deep belly laugh, with the biggest grin she'd ever seen on him.

"I wouldn't have it any other way."

Vienna's Secret Recipe Trove

My mama would tan my hide if she knew I was sharing her most sacred, secret recipes with you. The Huttons from Church Street Eats would also be none too pleased with me. But y'all deserve a treat for helping me find the killer who brought such havoc to my peaceful hometown of Vienna, Virginia. Now, everything can get back to normal—right?

Mama Caine's Magical Garden Ginger-Mint Iced Tea

5 cups filtered water

3.5 ounces peeled and sliced ginger root

½ cup fresh mint leaves, finely chopped

5 tea bags (pick whatever flavor you want)

1 cup wildflower honey

In a large saucepan, put ginger into five cups of filtered water and bring to a boil. Remove from heat. Add tea bags and mint. Cover with a lid and allow to steep for a minimum of 20 minutes. Strain liquid into your favorite, fancy-pants crystal pitcher, the one your great-aunt bought off your wedding registry. Fill three-quarters full, and add ice.

Tastes best when served during the Town of Vienna's Walk on the Hill!

Greg's Gooey Grilled Cheese Sandwich

2 slices fresh sourdough bread

6 slices fresh mozzarella cheese

2 tablespoons mayonaise

2 tablespoons unsalted butter

One shake of fresh ground pepper

1 grill press

Spread mayonnaise on top side of each piece of bread. Heat a nonstick skillet over medium heat. Put 1 tablespoon of unsalted butter into the skillet and let melt. Then place 1 slice of bread, mayonnaise side down, into hot skillet; layer the cheese slices onto the bread. Then season with pepper. Top with second slice of bread, mayonnaise side up. Heat for 3–5 minutes, until the bottom piece of bread is golden brown. Take off heat and add the remaining butter. Let it melt, and return sandwich to the skillet, untoasted side of the bread down. Put grill press on top. Leave for five minutes, to melt mozzarella cheese. You may need to reduce the heat some and leave on longer because fresh mozzarella will take longer to melt than other cheeses. Once golden brown, serve immediately!

Bash's Burger

1/2-pound fresh ground chuck (80/20 the perfect fat-to-meat ratio)

1 egg

1.5 tablespoons Costco Steak seasoning

1 brioche bun

Condiments of your choice

Mix egg and seasoning thoroughly into your ground chuck. Then form meat patty. Do not overmix. You want to be able to still see the strands of meat in your patty. Place burger on either a hot grill or in a hot pan. Let it cook until the fat puddles on top of burger patty. DO NOT PRESS DOWN ON THE BURGER. Greg says all you're doing is draining the meat of its juiciness. Flip burger once. Place your brioche bun into toaster on a light setting (or on grill, if you have space. Keep out of direct flame). Once burger is done, put right onto bun. Add whatever condiments you like and serve hot.

Simon & Garfunkel-Inspired Roast Chicken

6 chicken quarters (legs & thighs attached, skin on)

2 tablespoons fresh parsley

2 tablespoons dried sage powder

2 tablespoons fresh ground rosemary

2 tablespoons dried thyme

Olive oil spray

Salt and pepper to taste

6 pats of unsalted butter

Heat oven to 375 degrees. Cover a flat cooking sheet with aluminum foil, and coat with non-stick olive oil aerosol spray. Pat down chicken until dry, and place on cooking sheet. Take each pat of butter and divide into pieces with your fingers. Rub into the skin of each chicken piece (each one gets its own pat of butter). Most fresh rosemary will come in sprigs. I suggest you grind the leaves in a coffee grinder until they become finely ground. Mix the freshly ground rosemary with your thyme, sage, salt, and pepper. Finely dice the parsley, and add to mixture. Sprinkle generously all over the chickens. Place in oven until the skin turns golden brown and bubbly, and the juices run clear when poked with a fork.

Shredded Herb Chick Omelet

3 ounces of pulled herb chicken, room temperature (use leftovers from Simon & Garfunkel Roast Chicken recipe, or use a rotisserie chicken)

2 eggs

1 ounce sharp cheddar cheese

1 ounce Colby Jack cheese

1 dollop half and half

1.5 tablespoons salted butter

Salt & pepper to taste

Heat pan on medium heat. Place butter in pan until melted. While it is melting, scramble eggs and pour half and half into the same bowl. Pour mixture into pan, making sure to use a spatula to lift edges of egg mixture as it cooks. Add cheeses and chicken evenly in pan. Sprinkle with salt and pepper. When cheese is almost melted, fold half of egg mixture over to form a half moon in pan. When golden in color—not brown—slide out of pan onto plate and serve.

Acknowledgments

This book would have never been possible without the many characters that live and work in the Town of Vienna, Virginia. Don't be fooled by all the Eddie Bauer and LL Bean-gear. Under the yuppie-wear resides much delightful weirdness. Thank you for making this outsider feel like a native.

Thank you to the Vienna Police Department, particularly to MPO Juan Vazquez, for answering all of my questions and for being a beacon of positivity. Thank you to our mayor, Laurie DiRocco for your enthusiasm and support as well. Your efforts-and that of the Town Council- help make Vienna an enviable place to live.

A special acknowledgement needs to go out to the Bards Alley staff, past and present. Thank you for being the inspiration for this series, especially to Pauline Murphy, Lynne Kohls, Sarah Katz, Cory Hill, Melanie Kosar, Leah Grover, Amy Lane, Will Ryan, and Jen Morrow.

Thank you to Christ Church Vienna for your love, support, and answering all my questions regarding the Anglican church.

As always, thank you to my literary agent, Jill Marsal, who helped me brainstorm the idea for this book years ago-who heard my pitch for a small-town Southern mystery series with a feminist heroine, a dog named after Ruth Bader Ginsberg and a superfluity of nuns and thought 'well, it's a lot on the page, but somehow, it works'.

Thank you to Faith Black Ross, my editor at Crooked Lane, for your candor, humor and lightning-fast turnaround. Every author has a dream editor in mind and you are that wish actualized.

Thank you to the editorial and marketing team at Crooked Lane: Matt Martz, Ashley Di Dio, Melissa Rechter, and Jenny Chen. You are tireless champions-and I sincerely appreciate every one of you.

Thank you to my fellow cozy mystery authors, whom have made me feel truly welcome, especially those at Crooked Lane.

A most grateful thank you to Misty Simon, Queen of the Cozy. If it wasn't for your friendship, encouragement and late-night phone calls, I wouldn't have had the nerve to enter the cozy mystery genre. I adore you beyond reason.

And lastly, but never least, to my family: David, Hunter, and Samara. You are my roots and wings and are proof of God's love for me.